ROCKSTAR

USA Today and International bestselling author

Lauren Rowe

Rock on!

Lauren Rowe

BOOKS BY LAUREN ROWE

Standalone Novels

Smitten

Hate Love Duet

Falling Out Of Hate With You

Falling Into Love With You

The Reed Rivers Trilogy (to be read in order)

Bad Liar

Beautiful Liar

Beloved Liar

The Club Trilogy (to be read in order)

The Club: Obsession

The Club: Reclamation

The Club: Redemption

The Club: Culmination (A Full-Length Epilogue Book)

The Josh and Kat Trilogy (to be read in order)

Infatuation

Revelation

Consummation

The Morgan Brothers (a series of related standalones):

Hero

Captain

Ball Peen Hammer

Mister Bodyguard

ROCKSTAR

The Misadventures Series (a series of unrelated standalones):

Misadventures on the Night Shift

Misadventures of a College Girl

Misadventures on the Rebound

Standalone Psychological Thriller/Dark Comedy

Countdown to Killing Kurtis

Short Stories

The Secret Note

To Cuz and Baby Cuz. The rockstars in my life, literally and figuratively. I love you both more than paltry words could possibly say.

PART ONE
THE BEFORE

ONE

DAX

Y ou want to engage in the best people-watching of your life? Then attend a party at Reed Rivers' sprawling bachelor pad in the Hollywood Hills celebrating the kickoff of Aloha Carmichael's world tour. Dude, this place is lit. Filled to bursting with celebrities and wannabe celebrities from both the music and entertainment industries. Which makes sense, given that Aloha Carmichael is a former child star turned pop queen and Reed Rivers is the current prom king of LA. Not only is Reed the owner of the world's hottest independent record label, he's also a baller in the movie industry, thanks to an indie flick he bankrolled last year that wound up crushing it at the box office.

At the moment, I'm standing in line for drinks with my two bandmates in 22 Goats, Colin and Fish. As we inch toward the bartender, Colin is flirting like a boss with one of Aloha's backup dancers, Fish is flirting like a minimum-wage worker with a woman with resting bitch face in front of us, and I'm staring off into space, thinking about what Reed said to me earlier in his kitchen.

"Don't expect 'People Like Us' to take off immediately," Reed said, referring to my band's first single that's dropping in three days. "It always takes a minute for a new band's debut to gain traction. But once the world sees you in that scorching-hot music video on Sunday, the song is going to start rocketing up the charts. And once *that* happens, hold onto your nuts, Golden Boy. You three goats—but especially *you*—won't be able to walk down the street in any city of the tour without getting mobbed."

I knew Reed said all that stuff to pump me up about what's to come. And, for the most part, it worked. I'm super stoked. But some of what Reed said also made me want to get on my motorcycle and disappear. Why would I want to get *mobbed* walking down the street? If Reed thinks that sounds appealing to an artist like me, not to mention an introvert, he doesn't know me at all. I'm all about the music, man. Not fame or fortune or easy women. And certainly not about getting *mobbed.*

And another thing. Did Reed really have to set the bar so damned high? If "People Like Us" doesn't "rocket" up the charts like he's predicting, but, instead, slowly *creeps* up them—or maybe doesn't chart at all—will Reed yank 22 Goats from the Red Card Riot world tour? Or maybe even drop us from his label altogether? I shudder at the thought.

"What's your favorite thing about modeling?" Fish asks the bitchy-looking woman standing in front of us, drawing me out of my thoughts.

Blah, blah, blah, she replies, revealing herself to be as vapid and boring as she is physically gorgeous. "Plus, I love getting to hang out with interesting people," she says, shooting me a suggestive smile.

What the fuck? Why is she flirting with *me,* when I haven't said a word? The fact that she's treating Fish, the only guy who's said a word to her, like he's invisible only confirms my bad impression of her. Look, I get that Fish doesn't look like an action hero. But so what? He's the coolest, sweetest dude I know. Why don't girls like this model ever look past Fish's shaggy, lanky exterior and give him a shot?

Thankfully, before the model says another word, we reach the bartender and order our drinks. A few minutes later, Colin, Fish, and

I are ambling into the heart of the party, our drinks in hand... and, goddammit, that model on my tip.

When the three of us goats, plus the model, come to a stop in the thick of the party, she leans into my shoulder and compliments my hair. "I've always had a thing for guys with long hair," she says.

Rather than reply, I take a long sip of my vodka and pretend I didn't hear her above the blaring music. *God, I hate star-fuckers.*

She taps my shoulder. "So, why are you guys here? I was in 2Real's music video last year, but even then, I had to *beg* to get onto that list at the door."

I gesture to Fish, like, *Take it away.* My assumption is that Fish will tell the model the unsexy truth: our good buddy, Zander, Aloha Carmichael's new bodyguard, put us on the list. But, nope. Fish says the thing that's most likely to get him laid. Or, so he hopes.

"We're in a band that's signed to River Records," he says. "It's the same label as Aloha."

Oh, for the love of fuck. I realize Fish hasn't had much luck with the ladies since the three of us moved to LA to write and record our debut album. Not the way Colin and I have. But come on. If a guy feels like he needs to brag to get laid, then he should seriously reconsider the kinds of girls he's hitting on.

I glance at Colin and he rolls his eyes, telling me he's as annoyed as I am. Although Fish's comment to the model was technically true —22 Goats is, indeed, signed to River Records—that's not what got us through the door tonight and Fish knows it. Indeed, when Reed first saw us walking into his house tonight, he bellowed, "I didn't know my favorite goats were coming to the party!"

The model asks Fish, "Does your band have any songs I might know?"

"Not yet," Fish replies... and then he proceeds to babble about our forthcoming album and single and the fact that we're about to open for Red Card Riot on a world tour.

Of course, at Fish's mention of Red Card Riot, the woman loses her shit. Unfortunately for Fish, however, the woman loses it all over *me.*

As the model grabs my arm and freaks out, my immediate reaction is to glare at Fish for bringing this plague of locusts upon my house. But when I see the look of abject humiliation on Fish's face, my irritation with him evaporates. Why does he *always* swing for this particular kind of fence? If he finally got a taste of this kind of creature, I'm confident he'd be instantly sated for life, the way I am. Like I keep telling Fish, these days, I'd rather go home to my guitar and Netflix than hook up with a girl like this one. But I guess there's only one way for Fish to reach a similar state of disinterest in star-fuckers and clout-chasers—and it ain't me *telling* him to reach it.

"Hey, sorry, I can't get too flirty with you," I say, peeling the model's grip off my arm. "My girlfriend is around here somewhere, and she's the jealous type."

It's my usual lie—the one I always pull out when I'm not feeling it, but don't want to flat-out reject someone—and it works on the model like a charm. She releases me and turns toward Colin. But before she's said a word, Colin—a dude who suffers fools even less gladly than I do—cuts her off. "I've actually got a boyfriend around here somewhere," he says. "And he's the jealous type, too."

Well, that's a new one. I look down to hide my smile.

Colin says, "But, hey, Fish Taco here is straight and single and, so I've heard, hung like a horse. Plus, he's best friends with all the RCR guys, so he's the one to ask all your RCR questions."

I can't keep from chuckling at Colin's pack of lies. It's all ridiculous, other than Fish being straight and single.

But Fish isn't chuckling with me. He looks irritated. "Don't lie to the girl," he says, his voice edged with annoyance. He turns to the model. "Sorry. Colin's yanking your chain. The jealous boyfriend he's referring to is *me*. Sometimes, my boyfriend and I like to flirt with women at parties in front of each other, just to make each other jealous. Sorry if we wasted your time." With that, my awesome best friend strides away with his head held high and a little extra swagger in his fish tail—making me love the dude all the more, which is something I didn't know was possible.

"Don't give that model a second thought," Colin says to Fish once we've caught up to him. "She's nothing but a clout chaser, man."

"Fuck it, shit happens," Fish says.

It's what Matthew "Fish" Fishberger always says at times like this —when a woman he's flirted with has stiff-armed him. It's the catch-phrase Fish coined in middle school, when even teachers had stopped calling him Matthew, that turned his nickname into an acronym and his troubles into a self-deprecating joke.

Fish stops walking at the edge of the dance floor, so Colin and I follow suit.

Colin says, "Look, Fish Head, I know you're jonesing to have your first Star-Fucker Experience. But this party isn't the time or place. There are too many dudes here with actual fame to even try to attract a fame vampire tonight."

Fish looks unconvinced.

I say, "If you're bound and determined to get laid by a star-fucker, then at least be efficient about it and wait for the tour. When groupies see you sharing a stage with Red Card Riot, you'll have your pick— and you won't have to brag like a douchebag to get their attention."

Fish rolls his eyes.

"Either way," I say, "just do me a favor and don't brag to anyone else here, okay? Every woman here had to be on that list at the door, which means there's a fifty-fifty chance anyone you hit on will have some connection to Reed—personal, professional, or both. A woman you hit on could turn out to be someone Reed's fucked or wants to fuck. He's got our dreams in the palm of his hand, man. Let's not do anything to unwittingly piss him off tonight. Not when we're mere days away from everything finally happening."

Colin laughs. "Okay, Rock Star. I was with you until that last part. Are you saying *every* woman at this party is off-limits, simply because she *might* be on Reed's past, present, or *future* To Do List? Because I'ma tell you right now, if I get a shot at that backup dancer from the bar line, I'ma take my shot."

"The dancer would be fine because she's *vetted*. We know for a fact she's here because she's on Aloha Carmichael's tour, and not because Reed's trying to get into her pants. But some bitchy model with zero personality who got cast in 2Real's music video? Um, not vetted, son. We need more information."

Fish pulls a snarky face. "And how do you propose we 'vet' someone? When we're leaning in for that first kiss, should we stop and say, 'Hang on, baby. Have you ever fucked Reed Rivers?'"

Colin chuckles, but before he's said a word in reply to Fish, his hot backup dancer from earlier in the drink line emerges from the packed dance floor right in front of us.

The dancer's face aglow, she smiles pointedly at Colin. "I've been looking for you."

Colin doesn't miss a beat. "And I've been looking for you. Are you down to find a quiet spot to talk?"

"You've read my mind."

And off they go.

"Casanova strikes again," Fish says. We watch the pair depart for a beat, but when they're just out of earshot, Fish puts his hand to the side of his mouth and calls out—his voice swallowed by the thumping music in the room, "Don't forget to ask her if she's ever fucked Reed Rivers!"

TWO

DAX

Fish and I plop ourselves down on either side of Zander on a large leather couch and immediately begin telling him about the bitchy model. But midway through my story, it's obvious Zander's not paying attention—that, in fact, something on the dance floor has attracted his full attention. Or, rather, *someone*. Because when I follow Zander's intense gaze, I discover the source of his distraction: Aloha Carmichael grinding with one of her male backup dancers.

I lean into Zander's broad shoulder. "Just concede defeat on the bet now, Z. You're never gonna make it three months on tour without making a move on her."

"Stay in your lane, Rock Star," Zander says, his eyes still trained on Aloha. "I'm gathering intel about The Package. I'm her bodyguard, remember? And that means... Ho! The Package is on the move, baby doll. I gotta dip. Make good choices!" And off Zander goes without looking back.

Laughing, Fish puts his hand to the side of his mouth and calls out, "Make sure to ask her if she's ever fucked Reed Rivers!" But, again, thank God, Fish's voice gets swallowed by the loud music in the room.

I lean back into the couch. "And then there were two, Fish Taco."

"The best two," Fish replies. "The fish taco and the rock star."

"Dude, you gotta stop calling me Rock Star. Anyone who hears you these days won't know my family's been calling me that since age two. They'll think I'm some douchebag who snagged an opening slot with Red Card Riot and instantly decided he was the main event."

"Dax, I've been calling you Rock Star since grade school. Lifetime habits are hard to break."

"Try harder."

"Luckily, I'll only have to remember not to call you that for about a month. After that, 'People Like Us' will be such a megatron smash hit, the whole world will be calling you Rock Star. Not just your family and friends."

"Can we please lower our expectations about the single blowing up? I feel like all the hype is setting us up for failure if the single does anything but hit number one."

Fish launches into a pep talk about "People Like Us" being a "shoo-in" for global smashdom... but I tune him out when a striking young woman across the party catches my eye. *Who is that?* She's in her early twenties, I'd guess. Same as me. And a head turner. But there are lots of head turners at this party, and not one of them has caught my eye like this. Even the woman standing next to her, a leggy strawberry blonde who checks all conventional boxes, is practically invisible to me right now.

My girl is something much hotter than hot. She's *intriguing.* A study in contrasts. Lights and darks swirled together. Lines and curves living in harmony. She's elegant yet accessible. Sexy but quirky. In short, she's got my skin tingling.

Her dark hair is styled into a sharp, chin-length bob with box-bangs—the kind of chic hairstyle assassins wear in movies. And yet, the hair frames a Kewpie doll's face: big eyes, small nose, lush lips. Actually, she'd make a perfect hitwoman because nobody would ever see her coming.

Her outfit is definitely not one a shrinking violet would choose. Hip-hugging white pants and a white, sleeveless suit-vest that's giving me an eyeful of toned arms, smooth shoulders, and mouthwatering cleavage nestled between extra-wide lapels. Speaking of those extra-wide lapels, they're covered in sparkles—a perfect disco complement to the wide flares at the bottoms of her hip-hugging pants. If it weren't for those lapels and flares, I'd say this girl was trying to come off as a sexy *femme fatale*. But it's awfully hard to ignore the disco energy those bling-y accents add to her otherwise elegant outfit. As it is, I don't know if she came here tonight to commit murder-for-hire or break into singing "Dancing Queen." Or maybe "Jailhouse Rock"?

Lyrics.

They're suddenly flooding me.

My heart leaping, I pull out my phone and start furiously writing them down:

She's no wallflower
No shrinking violet
She's not a passenger
The engine, the pilot
Do as she says, son
And no one gets hurt
Unless you're on the kill list:
Dead as dirt

I add some notes about a possible chord progression and an idea for a bridge, feeling electrified. But when I look up from my screen, I'm jolted to find a code-red situation in progress. *Some GQ motherfucker in a designer suit is hitting on my hitwoman dancing queen!*

Whoa. This dude's got some serious big-dick energy. And so does his friend, who's currently hitting on the blonde. Damn. That's the bad news. The good news, however, is that, based on my girl's body language, I'd bet anything the guy's a "telemarketer." That's what my brother, Keane, calls a dude who's making a "cold call": hitting on a girl he doesn't know.

Oh, shit. Mr. GQ is gesturing toward the dance floor now. Well, he's got me beat there. That's something I'd never do. I don't dance, disco momma. Not unless I'm onstage with my guitar or shitfaced at a family wedding. I mean, come on, what sober person without a guitar in his hands would stand in a crowd, shaking his ass, when he could be sitting in a quiet corner, people-watching or talking to a small group of friends?

Thankfully, my hitwoman dancing queen shakes her head in response to Mr. GQ's invitation to dance. They talk for another couple minutes until, finally, the guy saunters away, his head held high, like getting stiff-armed by the most striking girl at the party was his plan all along.

Lyrics.

They're flooding me again. I pull out my phone, my heart racing, and jot them down:

She might kiss you
And she might kill you
And then throw on her blue suede shoes
I don't dance, disco momma pretty baby
But I'd sure as hell dance with you

My blood is coursing with adrenaline. Excitement. But, shit, when I look up from my phone, my muse is being hit on by yet *another* tele-marketer. Jesus! This one with as much swagger as the first guy.

This second guy is wearing the "L.A. uniform," not a designer suit like the last guy: dark jeans and a $200 T-shirt. Like Mr. GQ who came before him, however, Mr. L.A. motions to the dance floor after chatting up my muse. But rather than turn down her suitor immediately, like she did with the first guy, this time, my muse bites her lip suggestively, turns her head... *and looks straight at me for a long count of three...* before returning to Mr. L.A., smiling sweetly, and shaking her head.

And just that fast, I'm a goner. Putty in her hands. That look was the sexiest thing I've ever seen. *She's no wallflower or shrinking violet, indeed.*

When Mr. L.A. saunters away, my girl finds me across the room again. Our eyes lock. Only this time, she doesn't look away after three seconds. No, she *scowls* after three seconds, as if to say, *Why the hell are you taking so long to come over here?*

I laugh, simply because she's so cute. Sexy. Magnetic. Quirky. And my laughter transforms her comical scowl into a beautiful, beaming smile that's so radiant, so lovely, it leaves a little mark in the shape of a lipstick kiss on my very soul.

My heart exploding in my chest, I mouth the word, *Hello.*

Her lips part, like she's going to reply in kind, but before she does, her blonde friend grabs her arm and pulls her attention away from me.

Lyrics. Again. Oh my fucking God. I pull out my phone, yet again, and furiously write them down:

You kissed my soul
Disco momma pretty baby
Kissed me, and left me to bleed
You've got me craving, wanting
Needing a taste
Am I just another fatality?

When I peek up from my phone this time, my muse is still chatting with her blonde friend, so I call to Fish on the other end of the couch and point her out.

"Yeah, she's definitely a stand-out," Fish agrees. "She's Uma Thurman from *Pulp Fiction* at an Elvis convention."

"Ha! Now I know exactly how to describe the girl of my dreams. Seriously, though, am I wearing the world's most powerful weed-and-whiskey goggles, or is this girl intriguing as hell?"

As Fish knows, "intriguing" is some next-level shit for me—my highest compliment when talking about a beautiful woman. A way bigger deal than me calling a woman "hot."

"She's definitely intriguing," Fish replies.

"She's already inspiring lyrics, man."

Fish looks at me, shocked. *"Lyrics at first sight?* When was the last time a girl did that to you?"

"Never. Since we moved to L.A., no girl has inspired lyrics, at all. And back in Seattle, nobody ever inspired lyrics quite like this. So fast and furious. They're crashing into me like a tsunami."

"This sounds serious, son."

"Meh. I've got no time for serious. In three days, I'll be sitting on a plane headed for London. The only thing I've got time for tonight is a drive-by dabble, followed by a heartbreaking 'we'll always have L.A.!' goodbye."

"Just as long as you *vet* her properly." Fish pulls a snarky face, letting me know he still thinks my "vetting" comment from earlier was just plain stupid.

Rolling my eyes at Fish's dry facial expression, I return my attention to my muse, just in time to see Reed Rivers, accompanied by a buddy, both of them dressed in designer suits, approaching my girl's blonde friend.

I sit forward on the couch, staring as Reed gives the blonde a polite hug. When he disengages from her, I hold my breath, waiting for the other shoe to drop. But to my relief, Reed doesn't hug my girl. He only smiles briefly at her.

I'm surmising introductions are being made, although in what combination I'm not sure. If I had to guess, Reed is introducing the blonde to his buddy. The blonde is introducing Reed to her friend. After brief conversation between the foursome, Reed's buddy and the blonde take off for the dance floor, leaving my muse standing alone at the edge of the dance floor... with Reed fucking Rivers.

Shit.

My heart rate instantly spikes. This feels like a catastrophe waiting to happen. Did I sit here on this couch, getting a psychic hand job from those goddamned lyrics, one minute too long?

Reed says something to my muse that makes her smile. She says something that makes him chuckle. But, thank God, after not too long, Reed motions over his shoulder like, *Sorry, I've gotta go,* and she motions like, *Yeah, no problem.* And off Reed goes, causing every cell in my body to shudder and buck with relief.

The minute Reed disappears into the crowd, my girl jolts me by turning her head and looking straight at me again. She flashes me a pointed look—a come-hither glare filled with such heat—such *impatience*—my dick begins thickening in response. Holy shit! She's looking at me like it's already a given that she's mine and I'm hers and I've let this ridiculousness go on long enough. Ha! I think I'm in love. *No shrinking violet, indeed.*

I flash her a look that says, *Okay, okay, I'm on my way, honey.* And she replies with an adorable expression that says, *Well, it's about fucking time.*

"Hey, Daxy!" Fish shouts behind me as I stride away. "Don't forget to ask her if she's fucked Reed Rivers!"

THREE

DAX

As I zero in on my Hitwoman Elvis Disco Momma, I'm able to gather some new intel about her, stuff I couldn't make out from across the room.

Grayish blue. That's the color of her stunning eyes. They're the color of a stormy ocean—the kind that makes sailors disappear without a trace.

Cleavage. The gloriousness peeking out from her lapels is even more mouthwatering than I'd realized. And that's saying a lot, seeing as how I was practically drooling onto the couch cushions over there.

Dragonfly. That's what's inked on her upper arm, just below her toned right shoulder. A small, elegant, sexy dragonfly. And I'm diggin' it.

Stud. Besides being one, she's also got a tiny stud pierced into her nose, right above her right nostril. It's barely there. Nothing flashy. But the fact that it's there at all makes my pulse quicken. I've always had a thing for girls with extra piercings. Not to mention a well-placed tattoo. See above.

I come to a stop in front of her, butterflies whooshing into my stomach. "Hi," I say lamely, suddenly feeling overwhelmed by the electricity coursing across my skin.

"Hi."

I extend my hand. "Sorry I took so long. I'm Dax."

She laughs. "Hi, Dax. I'm Violet. I forgive you."

Holy fuck. I'm shook. *She's no shrinking violet...* I just now thought those exact lyrics... and it turns out her name is *Violet?*

"Is something wrong?" she says. She looks down at her white vest. "Did I spill margarita all over myself?"

"No, no. You're spotless."

Perfect. Flawless.
One look at you
And I'm wild, lawless.
No vetting gonna happen
No, not tonight
Now I've seen you close up
I'd sell my soul to get inside you.

She's staring at me, waiting for me to say something. I'm the one who walked over here, after all, and now I'm standing here, thunderstruck. "Sorry," I say. "This is gonna sound like a cheesy line, but it's the truth. The minute I saw you, I started writing a song about you. One of the lyrics was 'She's no wallflower, no shrinking violet...' So, to find out your name is Violet is kind of blowing me away."

"You've been sitting over there writing a song about *me?*"

My gaze flickers to her breasts—damn, those are nice—and quickly returns to her stunning eyes. "I have."

She smirks like she doesn't believe me.

"I know it sounds like a line. But it's the truth."

She cocks an eyebrow. "What are the rest of the lyrics?"

"Just a bunch of stuff about you being a killer, basically."

"A *killer?*"

I laugh. "It's hard to explain."

"What kind of song is this?"

My eyes drift over her dragonfly tattoo before landing on her eyes again. "An alt rock song with a sort of retro, disco groove, I'd say."

"Sounds awesome."

"We'll see."

"Is it a love song?"

Those tits. Jesus. "More of a sex song."

She laughs. "Well, thanks for your honesty."

"I'm nothing if not honest, especially when it comes to my songs."

She pauses, like she's holding her breath. And then, "So, I've gotta ask. Are you some famous rock star and everyone at this party knows exactly who you are but me? Because, if so, forgive me. I live in my own little bubble."

"Nope. The only people who know about my band at the moment are either super into indie bands or from Seattle."

"What's your band called?"

Her lips. They're gorgeous. That little piercing in her nose. Holy hell. Everything about her is perfection. Like kryptonite to me. With great effort, I force my eyes to return to hers, even though I want to drink her in, from head to toe, on a running loop. I clear my throat. "My band is called 22 Goats."

She stares blankly, and I'm in heaven. If things go the way Reed's predicting, this might be the last time in a long while—maybe even forever—an intriguing woman at a party has no idea who I am. And, honestly, I'm savoring the moment.

"You've never heard of us," I say. It's a statement, not a question.

"Sorry, no. My friend said you look familiar, though. And she's really into all kinds of music. Maybe she's heard of you."

"Is your friend from Seattle?"

"No, San Diego, same as me. But she lives in L.A. now. Do you guys ever play in L.A.?"

I'd sell my soul to kiss those lips. Not to mention those beautiful tits. "Yeah, but in small clubs. We only moved down here recently. Our biggest following is still in Seattle and the Pacific Northwest."

"That's cool. Good luck growing your following."

I've got to see those tits, wild and free. "Thanks. We're working on it."

"So, if you don't mind me asking, if you're truly not some under-cover rock star, how'd you get past those two dudes checking names at the door?"

"My buddy is Aloha Carmichael's new bodyguard."

Her shoulders relax, like she's deeply relieved I'm some nobody aspiring musician, rather than the mega rock star she was assuming. She says, "Is your bodyguard friend that African-American guy who was sitting next to you on the couch earlier?"

"That's the dude."

"That's so funny. I noticed him staring at Aloha on the dance floor earlier, but I just thought he was really into her."

"Oh, I'm sure he is. *And* he's her bodyguard."

She laughs, and butterflies release into my stomach at the glorious sound. Oh, God, that laugh. It's guttural. Sexy and raw. The kind of laugh that instantly makes me wonder what kinds of beautiful noises she makes during sex.

"Well, it looks like Aloha's in good hands," she says.

"I'm surprised you noticed me when my friend was still sitting there. I thought you only noticed me a few minutes ago."

"Honey, I noticed you the minute you walked through the front door."

My dick tingles at her admission.

She adds, "But then you got accosted by a gorgeous girl in the drink line, so I figured that was that."

"That girl in the bar line was a nonstarter."

"Why?"

"She was boring. Self-involved. Vapid." *And a clout-chaser.* "Plus, my friend was interested, and I'm a big believer in the 'bro code.'"

"She was pretty, though. And obviously into you."

My fingertips feel alive with the desire to touch Violet's smooth skin—to run my fingers across that dragonfly tattoo. And especially those breasts. "Pretty girls are a dime a dozen," I say. "But a girl who lights up a room? A girl with charisma—whose personality shines from across the room? Now, that's a girl I'm interested in getting to know."

The radiant smile that splits Violet's beautiful face simultaneously snatches the air out of my lungs and sends a rocket of desire straight to my dick. But since I'm the asshole who made a big thing about the need for Colin, Fish, and me to "vet" women tonight, I force myself to investigate a bit before going in for the kill. "So, what brings you to this party tonight, Violet? My guess is you're the next Lady Gaga. Or maybe you're a famous actress, and I'm just too clueless to recognize you."

Violet chuckles. "I'm just a student. Not famous in the slightest and don't want to be."

I exhale with relief from the bottoms of my feet. "Do you go to school in San Diego?"

"No, that's where I'm from, but I go to art school in Rhode Island. I'm just here in L.A. for the weekend. It's my best friend Miranda's twenty-first birthday."

"Are you twenty-one, too?"

She nods. "You?"

"Twenty-two." I can't help noticing Violet didn't answer my question about how she got into the party. Is she purposefully evading my question? I decide to ask it again. "How'd you girls get past the dudes at the door?"

She waves vaguely at the air. "Miranda's got a connection."

Relief washes over me. From the brief interaction I witnessed earlier between Violet's blonde friend and Reed, I'm guessing her "connection" is Reed Rivers himself. But I don't blame Violet for not name-dropping. In fact, I respect her for it. Why would she want to give me, some nobody, aspiring musician that information? What if I'm the kind of dude who'd flirt with Violet, solely to get myself an introduction to Reed? All that matters is that it's now obvious it's Violet's *friend,* not Violet, who's got the juice to get them through Reed's door. Which means Violet is now officially vetted, every bit as much as Colin's hot backup dancer. And that's a very good thing, since I can honestly say I've never felt this kind of instant chemistry in my life.

I indicate Violet's empty tumbler. "You want to get refills and head out to the patio to chat without that Top 40 shit blaring in our ears?"

Her smile sends a flock of butterflies into my belly. "Let's go."

FOUR

DAX

As soon as Violet and I settle onto a loveseat in the far corner of the patio, our knees touching and heat wafting between us, I take a page out of my older brother Ryan's playbook: I ask her a question designed to elicit info about her hobbies, hopes, and dreams. Or, as my brother Keane has coined 'em, "the ol' H, H & Ds."

I ask, "What are you studying at art college?"

"Fashion design."

I chuckle. "And just like that, your mack-daddy outfit makes so much sense. Is that Gucci or Armani or something like that?"

Violet's gorgeous chest expands with pride. "Nope. It's a Violet original."

"*You* designed that outfit?"

"I sure did. For a school assignment. We were told to 'reimagine an icon.' So, I reimagined Elvis."

I palm my forehead. "That song I started writing about you is called, 'Hitwoman *Elvis* Disco Momma!'"

"Liar."

"Swear to God! 'She might kiss you, and she might kill you, and then throw on her blue suede shoes. I don't dance, disco momma pretty baby, but I'd sure as hell dance with you.'"

"I love it." She bites her lip. "Why am I a hitwoman?"

"Because you look lethal." I gesture. "That hair. Your cheekbones. Those incredible lips." I pause and then decide, fuck it. "Your insane cleavage."

She doesn't look the least bit offended by that last compliment. Only turned on. "I've got *lethal* cleavage?" she says. "Wow."

"Hell yeah, you do, disco momma."

She giggles adorably, and, just that fast, I know she's not the assassin I'd imagined her to be. She's something far sweeter and gentler than that. But that doesn't make her any less attractive to me. Indeed, the sweetness wafting off her, intermingled with that incredible sensuality, is actually making her even more appealing to me.

"Why don't you dance?" she asks.

I shrug. "I just feel stupid when I dance. Self-conscious. I dance onstage with my guitar, when the music consumes me and I can let go completely. And I'll sometimes dance at family weddings, but only when I'm shitfaced."

"I *love* to dance. No guitar or alcohol required."

I'd definitely like to see that, I think. But since it will likely come off as smarmy to say it, I move on. "Why'd you pick Elvis to 'reimagine' for your outfit? You could have picked any icon, right? Why him?"

"My stepfather used to play Elvis songs all the time, so I've got a special place in my heart for him. I almost picked Amelia Earhart, but then I realized Elvis would be a much weirder choice. And I like weird."

I can't help smiling at that. This girl just gets better and better. "You want to be a fashion designer?"

"I thought I did when I started college. But by the end of my first year, I realized I was most interested in designing two things: wedding gowns and costumes."

"Costumes, as in Halloween...?"

"No, like for the entertainment industry—for stage, film, music.

Also, superhero costumes for kids. I started this club at school called The Superhero Project. We create customized superhero costumes for kids with cancer. Not known superheroes like Superman or Batman. We turn each kid into their own original superhero."

I'm blown away. Drowning in attraction for her. Tingling. Electrified. *Getting hard.* "That sounds amazing. You personally started this club?"

"Yeah, I got the idea my freshman year three years ago. And then my friends started wanting to help out, and now we're an official, chartered club."

Yeah, I've clearly misread this girl. She's no hitwoman. She's something even more intriguing to me. She's genuinely *good.* "That's so cool, Violet."

"Believe me, I get more out of the whole thing than the kids do. They're so inspiring to me." She flashes me a lovely smile. "So, tell me about you. What makes you tick, Dax?"

"Music. It's everything to me. When I'm writing a song and it's flowing, that's like a hand job for my soul. When it's finished and I get to play it for the first time from beginning to end, that's the blow job. When I play it for someone else for the first time, that's fucking. And when I perform it for a whole club full of people..." I shudder. "Oh, baby, that's the orgasm."

She looks equal parts amused and aroused. Her cheeks are flushed. Her chest is heaving. "That's literally the sexiest thing I've ever heard in my life," she says. She pats the loveseat next to her. "Scoot closer and tell me more, sexy boy. This is getting good."

My dick throbbing, I scoot closer to her on the loveseat and, instantly, when our thighs touch and our bodies meld, I feel a current of electricity course between us. I grab her hand and she makes it clear she's glad I did.

"What do you want to know?" I ask softly, my eyes locked with hers.

She rubs the top of my hand, sending a current of arousal into my dick. "Tell me more about songwriting. Tell me how it makes you *feel.*"

I can't remember the last time I felt this drawn to someone. I'm having a chemical reaction to this girl. Like she just slipped me some molly or something—like every cell of my body is suddenly wracked with energy and light and yearning. "Songwriting is my art," I say. "It's what I was born to do. It makes me feel alive. It makes me feel like a *superhero.*"

She smiles at that. "I feel the same way about my designs. If I'm feeling down or blue, I pull out my sketch pad and let my imagination run wild, and I'm instantly feeling good. It's like a drug."

"*Exactly.*"

Our conversation flows easily. We ask each other questions and laugh and nod profusely with understanding. It turns out, we're two of a kind, Violet and me. Kindred spirits. And it feels amazing. Like walking through the front door of my childhood house and smelling my mom's home cooking in the air. Maybe my brother's dog, Ralph, greeting me at the door. It's a feeling of rightness. Of being seen. It's a feeling I never get with new people. Ever. But, holy fuck, I'm getting it with Violet, in addition to wanting to fuck the living hell out of her.

The conversation twists and turns, and, soon, I'm telling Violet about how I regularly lose track of time for hours on end while writing or playing. And Violet laughs and hoots and says the exact same thing happens to her.

She says, "I just go and go for hours, without stopping to eat or drink or even pee! When I get really, really passionately focused on something, eight hours can pass in the blink of an eye."

"Oh, God, *exactly,* Violet."

One of Violet's legs is slung over my lap at this point. My arm is resting comfortably around her shoulders. And by the look on her face, I know her heart is beating as wildly as mine.

"God, losing track of time like that is *bliss,* isn't it?" Violet says. "I live for it."

I nod enthusiastically. "Did you know there's a name for that psychological phenomenon? When the ego falls away, and you lose track of time completely, and every action flows into the next without conscious thought?"

She shakes her head. She looks like she's hanging on my every word.

I touch her dragonfly tattoo, wishing I could touch a whole lot more of her than that. "*Flow*. That's the technical name for it—what psychologists call it."

"*Flow*," she whispers reverently. And, holy hell, the way her lips form the shape of a perfect "O" when she says the word makes my cock strain against my jeans.

"I think people like us," she says, "the ones who experience *flow*, are the lucky ones."

People like us. I can't believe Violet's sexy mouth just uttered those particular words, unprovoked. That's the name of the best song I've ever written in my life—the song that's about to be released as my band's first single on Sunday. When I wrote it, I had a fantasy girl in mind. Nobody in particular. But now that those words just came out of Violet's sensual mouth, I'm suddenly bone-certain I wrote every word of "People Like Us" about her.

"Flow is the best feeling in the world," Violet says, apparently unaware I'm sitting here, rocked to my core and hard as a rock. She adds, "Flow is even better than sex, don't you think?"

I pause, trying to determine if she's joking. And when it's clear she's serious, I say, "Uh, no. Flow is fucking awesome. And it's definitely way better than *mediocre* sex. But there's no way in hell it's better than *fantastic* sex, because that's the kind of sex that itself generates flow. The sickest kind of flow imaginable, actually. Way better than any drug."

Oh, I've definitely got Violet's attention now. To put it bluntly, she suddenly looks like she wants to suck my dick. "You've experienced flow... during *sex*?"

I grab her thighs and pull them unequivocally over my lap. "Not every time. Rarely, to be honest. But, yeah. Now and again. Just like I experience genuine flow only rarely when I write songs. It's always the goal. The brass ring. The pinnacle. But flow is lightning in a bottle, in any context, right? The exception, not the rule."

She slides her arm around my neck as she nods her agreement.

My lips are mere inches from hers. "But when flow *does* arrive... especially during sex... oh, God, Violet. Talk about bliss. It's ecstasy like nothing you've experienced before."

She looks like she's about to have an orgasm, right here and now. I take her hand and swirl the pad of my thumb around and around the top of it, the same way I'd swirl it over her clit if she were naked in my bed right now.

I whisper, "You've never experienced flow during sex, Violet?"

She shakes her head and levels me with her stormy eyes. "I'd very much like to, though."

That's all the invitation I need. I lean in and press my lips against hers... and when she immediately opens her lips and invites me inside, I slide my tongue into her mouth and devour her lips with mine.

Fireworks.

As my tongue dances with Violet's, as my lips assault hers, it's the Fourth of July inside my body. I put my palm on Violet's face as our kiss deepens and intensifies, every fiber of my body hungry for her. I feel compelled to get inside this incredible girl, to touch the farthest reaches of her, the places nobody else has touched, and Violet kisses me back with the same frenzied need, like her next breath depends on this electrifying kiss.

After several minutes of passionate kissing, we break apart, both of us panting and glowing with our mutual desire. She looks around the patio, like she's only just now remembering where we are. Or, maybe, she's feeling embarrassed she just swallowed my face in public. Either way, she's adorably self-conscious. Bashful, even.

I trace her lower lip with the pad of my thumb. "You wanna get out of here?"

Her chest heaves. Her stormy eyes ignite. "Do you live nearby? I'm staying with Miranda this weekend, so..."

"Yeah, I live nearby, but my roommate texted me fifteen minutes ago to call dibs on our apartment tonight. I'm down to get us a hotel room, if you're up for that. I mean, no pressure. We can just kiss and talk, if that's all you want to do. I just want to be alone with you, Violet. Lie down with you... Get naked, if you're willing."

She smiles. "Seeing as how merely kissing you sent me into a state of *flow,* and since I'm only here for the weekend, I most definitely think we should have sex."

A huge smile spreads across my face. "Sounds good to me."

Violet bites her sexy lip. "If sex with you feels even half as good as kissing you, then I'm gonna be 'flowing' with you all night long."

FIVE

VIOLET

Our clothes are strewn on the floor. My panties are flung across the hotel room. And my thighs are spread wide—as wide as they'll go—as Dax eats me with the passion of a starving man. Oh, God, this boy is good. Passionate and talented beyond anything I've experienced before. Not only is he voraciously licking and fucking me with his tongue and lips and mouth, he's doing insane things with his hands, too. Stretching my folds wide with one hand while stroking a precise spot deep inside me with his other. It's not my G-spot he's manipulating so deliciously. *Relentlessly*. Like a convict tunneling himself out of prison with a plastic spoon. It's a location on my body I didn't even know existed. A spot that's giving me such outrageous pleasure, I've already had two orgasms from his manipulations... and I'm just about to have my third.

I grip the top of Dax's long, blonde mane as my pleasure rises higher and higher. Holy hell, my eyes are rolling back into my head. I'm making crazy noises. Losing my mind. Finally, the pleasure that's been mounting inside me releases ferociously into the most intense orgasm of my life.

When I come down from my body-quaking climax, Dax is sitting up, looking feral. His long hair is wild and looks like it was spun from pure gold. His lips and chin are smeared with evidence of my arousal.

"I gotta get inside you," he growls.

"Do it," I whisper, drifting my fingertips across my breast.

He grabs a condom off the nightstand, lies on his back, and guides me onto his hard-on with a fierceness that snatches my breath from my lungs. I moan loudly at the invasion of his body inside mine and he replies with a guttural moan.

"Violet," Dax blurts, his fingers gripping my hips, his cock impaling me. "What are you doing to me?" As I ride him, he sits up and begins furiously devouring my breasts. With a low moan, he sucks on my left nipple so hard, I think I'm going to pass out—and, a moment later, an orgasm of such indescribable intensity slams into me, I literally scream with pleasure.

Dax comes inside me, gritting out my name, and I throw my arms around his neck and collapse into a sweaty heap.

Good lord.

That wasn't just sex to me. It was a spiritual experience. An awakening. My body did things it's never done before. I felt pleasure I didn't know was possible. I just had multiple orgasms? *Come on.* And the way our bodies fused together... the way we *fit.* God help me, I felt like our *souls* fused when we were at the peak of pleasure together. I'm sure I'll never forget it as long as I live.

Dax nuzzles my nose. "That was incredible."

"Magic," I whisper.

"You're magic."

"So are you."

"Please say you're not in any rush to get out of here. That you can stay the whole night with me and let me fuck you, over and over again, Lionel Richie Style?"

I tilt my head. "*Lionel Richie Style?*"

He grins. "'All Night Long.'"

I giggle. "Yeah, I've got all night. If I didn't, sweetheart, trust me, I'd cancel all my silly plans."

SIX

VIOLET

"Okay, ask me another one," Dax says with a seductive smile.

We're leaning back on opposite sides of a large, luxurious bathtub, our legs intertwined, and we're playing a game of Ask Me Anything. Dax's long, blonde hair is tied loosely behind his head. My naked breasts are pink and flushed from the hot bath water—or, maybe, my constant state of arousal in Dax's presence. I've never felt so comfortable this fast with anyone. So safe. So free. *So incessantly turned-on*. If I had a genie in a bottle, I'd wish for this amazing night to never end.

"What's your lucky number?" I ask.

Dax doesn't hesitate. "Five. I'm the fifth of five kids—I've got three older brothers and a sister. So I've always believed good things come in fives."

"Aren't good things supposed to come in threes?"

"Three as a lucky number is for underachievers."

I laugh.

"What's *your* lucky number?" he asks.

"Three."

We both laugh.

"I'm not joking, actually," I say, giggling. "Three's always been my lucky number."

"Aim higher, dude."

I splash him playfully and he laughs.

"Ask me another one, disco momma," he says. "You ask the best questions."

"Okay." I bite my lip. And then, "What's something sneaky you did as a kid?"

"Something *sneaky*?" Dax chuckles. "Hmm. So much to choose from. Well, the first thing that comes to mind is the time I was goofing off in my family's dining room—a room I wasn't supposed to play in— and accidentally broke my mother's prized crystal vase."

"Uh oh. How old were you?"

"Eight or nine. And rather than tell my mother what happened, I went straight to my oldest brother, Colby, for help. He's ten years older than me, so I legit thought he had magical powers. Colby was like, 'Okay, little dude. Calm down. I'll help you Superglue it back together because, one, I'm betting Mom won't even notice, and, two, I've always hated that stupid vase. But if Mom *does* notice, you've got to promise you'll come clean, right away, and without mentioning my name.' So, of course, I said, 'Deal.' So, we Superglued the stupid thing back together—horribly, I might add—and slipped it right back on its shelf in the dining room."

I giggle. "And did your Mom notice?"

"Yeah. *Five years later.*" He chuckles. "One day, out of nowhere, she was suddenly like, 'What are all these lines and cracks on my vase? *Which of you hooligans did this despicable thing?*'"

I laugh and laugh. "Did you come clean?"

He nods. "A promise is a promise. But, come on. Five *years*? I said, 'Look, Motherboard, if it took you five *years* to notice my busted-ass glue job, then this vase clearly wasn't as 'precious' to you as you've been claiming. I think we can both agree the window for punishment of this crime has long since closed.'" Dax laughs heartily, and so do I. "She was pissed at me for, like, five seconds, but then she couldn't help laughing her ass off. I mean, come on. Not noticing that dumbass glue job for five freaking years was a bigger crime than the original one."

I can't stop giggling. "I love that your mom laughed about it. I don't think mine would."

"That's my mom. She runs a tight ship in some ways. But she's also a huge believer in choosing joy. She always says, 'Forgive, forget, and laugh, whenever you can.' They're not just words to her. She absolutely lives them."

Out of nowhere, I feel like I've been zapped by a Taser—like the glorious, beaming smile on Dax's face has *literally* stunned me. I take a deep, steadying breath. "Did you ever tell your mom about Colby's involvement?"

"Hell no. Colby did, though. At Thanksgiving dinner that year. Mom mentioned the vase and Colby was like, 'Oh, yeah, about that...'" Dax shakes his head, chuckling. "Oh, man, Mom was *shocked* to find out Colby had helped me. She'd thought Colby was incapable of deception, just because he's this real-life Superman kind of dude. Not to mention, he's horrible at lying, just like me. But what my mother didn't fully appreciate about Colby is that, yes, he's Superman—but I'm his kryptonite. For some reason, Colby's always had this fatal soft spot for me. Whenever I've gotten into a jam in my life, Colby's been right there to help me out. Now that I'm older, I've realized I have to be extra careful not to take advantage of him, just because Colby will not only give me the shirt off his back, he'll give me every shirt in his closet, too. Plus, his pants and shoes and underwear."

My heart physically hurts at the beautiful expression on Dax's face. Holy hell. What is this creature in this bathtub with me? It was one thing for him to light up like a beacon when talking about his mother, but about his brother, too?

Dax grabs my leg underneath the water. "What about you? Have you ever done the equivalent of breaking your mother's prized crystal vase and secretly Supergluing it back together?"

"Not really. I mean, I've been sneaky, of course. In high school, I used to sneak out my bedroom window to meet up with my boyfriend. But that's pretty much it. Nothing as scandalous as Super-gluing a prized vase back together."

Dax chuckles. "Yeah, a high school girl sneaking out at night is definitely a misdemeanor in my book. A kid methodically Super-gluing a vase back together? Now, that's a first-class felony."

We both giggle.

"You got another question for me, disco momma?" he asks, his blue eyes blazing. "I'm digging this game."

"Heck yeah, sexy boy. I've got endless questions for you." I twist my mouth for a moment. "Tell me about your hair."

"My *hair*?"

"Yeah." I stroke his calf muscle underneath the water. "Something tells me it's a window into your soul. Did you consciously decide to grow it long—or did it just sort of happen by default because you forgot to go to the barber for a few years? Is it a message to the universe that you're not willing to play by The Rules? Basically, I'm wondering if your hair is somehow tied to your sense of self-identity, or if it's just... hair?"

"Wow, fantastic questions. Really insightful." He pauses for a long moment, considering his answer. "I think my hair is an easy shorthand for me. Without me needing to open my mouth, it tells people I'm not willing to drown in a sea of conformity and sameness. Being the fifth of five kids, I've always felt the need to distinguish myself. To not blend into the pack. When I was really little, my mom let me grow my hair out pretty long, because, she said, I was a little shit about haircuts. But then, for kindergarten, she took me to get my first professional haircut. As the story goes, I saw myself in the mirror with really short hair for the first time and bawled my eyes out. According to my mom, I turned to her and said, 'Now how will you know which boy is me?'" Dax laughs, sending a flock of butterflies whooshing into my stomach for the tenth time since we crawled into this bathtub together.

"I love your laugh," I say. "It gives me butterflies, every time."

Dax shoots me a look that hardens my nipples. "I don't get butterflies when you laugh." He touches my thigh. "I get *fireflies*. I feel lit up from deep inside."

His words have sent an electric current straight into my heart. But since I have no desire to fall in insta-love with a one-night stand, I tell myself this sexy boy has probably said those exact words to countless girls before me. Maybe even some of them while sitting naked in a bathtub, just like this. I smile flirtatiously. "Aw, I bet you say that to all the girls."

Dax suddenly looks earnest. Not playful at all. "I've never said that to anyone in my life. Because these fireflies I'm feeling are a first."

I open and close my mouth, searching for a witty retort, but I can't speak. My heart is thumping. My chest feels tight.

Dax's blue eyes are smoldering. "I've never met anyone like you, Violet."

My heart is beating out of my chest. "I've never met anyone like you. I've got fireflies, too. And they're most definitely a first for me."

I'm telling the truth. I've been in love. Once. But I've never felt this kind of instant connection. I've never felt so completely *seen*. Not like this.

Dax trails his fingertips up and down my inner thigh. "Did you know those guys who hit on you at the party?"

"No."

"Why'd you turn them down? They had swagger."

I run my toe across the ridges of his abs. "Because there was a beautiful boy with long blonde hair across the room I kept hoping would come say hello to me."

Dax bites his lower lip. "It was sexy as hell the way you scolded me from across the room, when I didn't come over fast enough to your liking."

I giggle. "I was just being silly."

"You were just being sexy."

Heat passes between us.

"Ready for another question?" I ask.

"Go for it," he says, still running his fingers up and down my inner thigh.

"Have you ever had your heart broken?"

"Oh, boy. The hitwoman is getting down to business now, folks." He flashes me a smile that melts my ovaries. "Yes, I've had my heart broken. Once. At fourteen, I went to a month-long, sleep-away music camp. I know it sounds dorky, but it was really cool. And she was there. Julia Fortunato. She'd just turned sixteen and she was 'experienced,' unlike me. Not only that, she had the voice of an angel and curves that made me pop a boner every time I looked at her. She had her pick of guys at camp. But she made it clear she wanted *me*."

"An older woman," I say. "Impressive."

"We did a whole lot of making out throughout the summer. And then, the night before camp ended, Julia said she wanted to give me a lifelong memory. She wanted to be my first. So we went to this shed where they stored kayaks and stuff and we lay down on a blanket and she rocked my world." He shakes his head and chuckles. "I told her I loved her that very night. And I honestly believed it."

"And you said you've never felt fireflies before me."

"I haven't. I didn't say I've never fallen in love. I have. More than once. But, honestly, before tonight, I've never met someone who's made me feel the way you do. Especially not this fast. One thing you need to understand about me, Violet, is I'm not a bullshitter. I say what I mean and I mean what I say. I figured out a while ago that being honest—with myself and others—is the only way I can write songs. Well, good songs, anyway. Not to mention not have a constant stomach ache. So I made a pact with myself not to say shit just to say it. If I say something, I'm saying it because I mean it."

Holy hell, sex appeal wafts off this boy like a physical thing. My clit is throbbing like crazy. "I'm a people pleaser by nature," I admit. "I sometimes say things to avoid confrontation or make someone else happy. With you, though, I feel like there's no choice but to tell the truth."

"Good."

"I feel like I've known you for months. With you, it's crazy just how..." I pause, searching for the right word.

"*Right* this feels?" he supplies.

I nod. "Exactly."

"Yeah, I know."

My heart flutters. "So this Julia girl from camp wound up breaking your heart?"

"She smashed it. Camp was over the morning after Julia rocked my world in that shed. We said our goodbyes and promised to keep in touch across the miles. I went back to Seattle. She went back to wherever she was from. Somewhere with cornfields. And then I proceeded to text her, just like I promised I would... *waaaaaay too often.*" He grimaces. "Did I mention I was fourteen? Oh, God, I handed that girl my entire heart with both hands. Poems, songs. Little texts to say hi. Memes to make her laugh." He rolls his eyes. "That first taste of pussy, man. It was powerful stuff." He shakes his head. "Julia answered me for about a week, and then... *poof.* She was a ghost."

"She *ghosted* you?"

"She did. No goodbye. No 'this isn't working for me.' She just disappeared and never said another word to me."

"Maybe something happened to her?"

"Nope. A friend from camp stalked her for me and found out she'd just gotten herself an older boyfriend back home—a college guy who could do a whole lot more for her than write sappy love songs from a thousand miles away."

"Aw, poor Dax."

"It's okay. Thanks to Julia Fortunato, I learned a much-needed lesson in texting etiquette." He chuckles. "Plus, I found out I *love* writing love songs. Sex songs. I'm-gonna-die-if-I-don't-get-inside-you songs. Even if what I'm feeling is one-sided or a figment of my imagination, I learned getting my heart smashed into bits is good for my creativity. To be honest, ever since Julia Fortunato, a twisted, fucked-up part of me kind of craves getting my heart shattered again, just to see what kinds of epic songs might come of it."

"Sick bastard."

He grins.

"What would you say to Julia if you ran into her now?"

"*Say* to her? No, sweetheart. This fantasy doesn't involve me *saying* a word. It involves me fucking the living hell out of her, rocking her world like it's never been rocked before, telling her we should keep in touch, and then ghosting the fuck out of her."

We both burst out laughing. And, once again, a flock of butterflies —no, *fireflies*—whooshes into my belly.

"Okay, your turn, disco momma," he says. "Ever had your heart broken?"

"Just once. Same as you. When I was seventeen. He was my first boyfriend and I loved him with all my heart and soul. Oh, God, how I loved him, Dax. He was a bit older than me, and he had to move away for a job, and everything turned to shit. Just like you with Julia Fortunato, I learned long-distance romances are a pipe dream."

"Yeah, no doubt about that."

"If only I was a songwriter, right? I could have used the heartbreak to make art. As it was, I didn't have much use for the pain."

"Aw, Violet. Beautiful girl." He pulls me to him, making me bend my knees on either side of his hips and smash my center into his penis under the warm water. He kisses me and runs his hands down my wet back and, soon, I feel his erection hardening against me.

"I'm sorry you got your heart smashed," he whispers into my lips.

"It was for the best," I say. "Soon after that, I went off to college and started a new life. But for a little while, I was positive my poor, broken heart would never mend."

"Aw, baby." He nuzzles his nose into mine. "It was his loss."

My nipples are hard. My clit is throbbing against his hard tip. I whisper, "I wouldn't change a thing. Especially right this very minute."

He kisses me. I wrap my arms around his neck. He cradles my back. And I'm instantly lost in him again.

"'People Like Us,'" he whispers. "You said that at the party."

I look at him quizzically.

"That's the title of my favorite song I've ever written. Now that you're here, I feel like I wrote it about you."

"Who'd you actually write it about?"

"You."

"For real, though."

"Nobody. The woman in the song didn't exist when I wrote it. She was a *wish*." He smiles. "And now, here you are. My wish fulfilled."

That's it. I'm a goner. Aching with lust and yearning. "Do condoms work underwater?" I whisper.

"No, unfortunately. Come on. If I don't get inside you right now, I'm gonna die."

He pulls me up, and we barrel, dripping wet, into the bedroom. And that's where Dax grabs a condom from the stash he bought in the hotel lobby, gets himself covered in record time, plunges himself inside me... and fucks me to heaven, once again.

SEVEN

VIOLET

"Okay, your turn," Dax says.

We're playing another round of Ask Me Anything. This time, while sitting at a little table in the corner of our hotel room, eating breakfast from room service. I'm wearing one of the fluffy white robes that came with the room. Dax is wearing nothing but white briefs and a smile. The sun rising through a window behind Dax is creating a glowing, halo effect around his blonde head. And I feel physically drunk on this beautiful boy.

I purse my lips for a moment. "Have you ever cheated?"

"Yes," he says without hesitation. "Regretfully. But only once. And it was for a good reason."

I press my lips together disdainfully. There's never a good reason for cheating, as far as I'm concerned. *Ever.* But I keep my mouth shut and wait for his explanation.

Dax says, "My niece, Izzy, was taking for-fucking-ever in a game of checkers, and I just wanted it to be over. So, regretfully, I cheated to let her win."

I throw my napkin at him. "You know what I meant. *Have you ever cheated on a girlfriend?*"

"*Oh.*" He grins adorably. "No. I'm a Morgan. If I've promised fidelity to a girl, then I'm true blue. By the same token, if I'm not feeling it anymore, I tell her the truth and move on. Better for everyone that way, even if the truth hurts at first."

I make a face like, *I sure would have appreciated that kind of honesty.*

"You've been cheated on?" Dax says.

"I have. And it's not fun."

"By that long-distance boyfriend?"

"That's the one. Thanks to him, I'll take the pain of brutal honesty over the pain of dishonesty any day."

Dax pulls a face. "Shit. In light of that, I feel like I should come clean about something." He pauses, clearly about to drop a huge bomb. "I haven't *cheated*, per se. But I have been in a polyamorous relationship."

My jaw drops. "With how many women?"

"Three." He winks. "Your lucky number."

My jaw drops even farther. "And all three women were on board with that arrangement?"

He nods. "I was up front about it from the beginning. In fact, I gathered them all together and sat them down to clearly explain the deal."

My stomach hurts. "Wow..."

"Now, granted," Dax says, "I was in kindergarten. But, still. I think it's only fair you should know."

I throw a packet of sugar at him. "You dork."

Dax laughs with glee. "You should have seen your face. Priceless."

I throw a strawberry at him and he laughs even harder.

"Hey, don't initiate a food fight unless you're willing to fight to the death," he warns. "I'm the youngest of five, remember? I'm a scrappy motherfucker."

Laughing, I pick up my coffee cup. "Tell me how this harem of yours came about."

"There were three little girls who wanted to sit next to me at story time, play with me on the playground, play house and doctor with me at playtime. It was exhausting. And then, fuck my five-year-old life, Valentine's Day came around and all three wanted to be my *only* valentine. They demanded I *choose*."

"How stressful."

"It was! So I thought about it and quickly realized there was only one logical solution. They needed to do what my parents and teacher had always taught me to do with the best toys: *share*."

I burst out laughing and Dax does, too.

"So, I sat the girls down and laid down the law and they agreed. And then I went home, proud of myself for brokering world peace, and told my mom how brilliantly I'd handled the tricky situation. And, to my shock, my mother wasn't nearly as impressed by my problem-solving skills as I was."

"You mean your mom didn't encourage you to maintain a harem?"

"Nope. Weird, huh? She did laugh her ass off when I first told her the story. It's one of my earliest memories of my mom, actually—watching her cry with laughter that day, and not understanding why. But then she sat me down and explained that sharing a person is different than sharing a toy."

"So, what you're actually telling me is girls have been throwing themselves at you your entire life."

He blushes. "Women have historically been pretty assertive with me," he admits. "Which is fine with me. But what I hate is women assuming I'm all about getting laid. Maybe I'm supposed to be, but I've always wanted more. A soul connection. And that's hard to find. Nearly impossible, I'd even say."

My heart is thumping almost painfully. Did he just tell me he feels a soul connection with me? I think he did! Which is good, because I feel one with him, too.

Excitement passes between us. A bit of shyness, too, about the soul connection we've both nonverbally admitted we're feeling.

Dax's cheeks turn bright red, and he looks down and busies himself with his breakfast for a long moment. When he looks up, he's still blushing. "My turn to ask a question?"

"Go for it."

His sweet smile from a moment ago turns wicked in a heartbeat. "Have you ever faked an orgasm?"

"Here we go, folks. The sexy boy goes in for the kill." I shrug. "Yeah, lots of times. But not with you."

"Why do girls feel the need to do that?"

"Because boys watch porn and girls want to fulfill their fantasies. Because when young, inexperienced girls have sex with young, inexperienced boys, not a whole lot of whiz bang boom is typically going to happen. And if girls don't get off the way a boy does, the way porn stars do, then girls assume there's something wrong with *them*. And, God forbid, they don't want to seem like anything but a freak in the sheets, so they play the part. But like I said, I didn't fake it with you."

"Yeah, no shit, you didn't fake it with me. I could feel your muscles rippling, multiple times."

"You're amazingly talented at getting the job done. I'm deeply impressed."

"I've got older brothers, remember? My Master Yodas. Right out of the gate—well, right *after* Julia Fortunato, unfortunately for her— they schooled me about what to do to get the job done."

"Thank them for me. I'm grateful for their tutelage."

He chuckles. "Your turn."

I gesture to a small tattoo on the inside of Dax's right forearm. "What's the story behind those three smiling... what are those things? Dogs? Cows? Haystacks with legs?"

Dax grins. "They're goats. That's my band. The three *goats* of 22 Goats."

I can't stop laughing. "When you told me your band is called 22 Goats, I pictured 'goats' in all caps, as in 'Greatest of All Time.'"

"Everyone thinks that. They're always trying to figure out who the twenty-two GOATs are that we're tipping our caps to. But, nope. We're named after farm animals." He looks down at his tattoo, chuckling. "The three of us got the same matching tattoos on Colin's twenty-first birthday. Unfortunately, the guy who tattooed us was even more stoned and drunk then we were at the time. Also, he wasn't a tattoo artist, he was just this random dude at a party who said he'd recently bought a tattoo gun and wanted to practice."

"Dax!"

He laughs and laughs. "In our defense, he said he'd tattoo all three of us for free, and we were dirt poor."

"Well, you got what you paid for, didn't you?"

"We sure did."

He laughs with glee... and, yet again, I'm flooded with flapping wings and lights.

"When we woke up the next day, we were like, 'What the fuck are these smiling blobs on our arms?' Colin was like, 'Dudes, we gotta get this shit covered up, right away.' But Fish and I were like, 'Hell no. This shit is so horrible, it's awesome. It stays.'"

"Why are they smiling like that? Are they *demonic* goats?"

Again, he laughs. "It goes back to how we named our band." He tells me the story, which, in summary, is that Colin, Fish, and Dax were partying with some girls, one of whom grew up on a farm. The farm girl told the guys several factoids about various farm animals, including the fact that goats smile. "We thought she was messing with us. So, she pulled up this *BuzzFeed* article to prove it. Hang on. I'll show you." He taps something onto his phone and hands it to me. "See?"

I look at his screen. It's displaying an article entitled "22 Goats Smiling at You."

"Those smiles aren't photoshopped," Dax says. "Goats actually smile."

I scroll through photo after photo of smiling goats on Dax's phone, variously shaking my head and giggling. "This is the cutest thing I've ever seen. And the weirdest."

"You wouldn't believe how much effort fans put into trying to figure out the deep meaning behind our band name. Why did we pick *twenty-two* GOATs—all-caps? Did we pick one GOAT from every sport? And if so, did we pick LeBron or Michael Jordan?" He takes his phone back from me and lays it on the table. "We don't tell anyone the real story, just because the theories are way cooler than the lame reality."

"Ah, but that's so much of life, isn't it? Knowing when to keep your mouth shut so people think you're way cooler than you actually are? Like, I don't know, letting them think you're some cool hitwoman, for instance?"

"You're still a hitwoman to me," he says. "You're killing me, baby."

"Oh, that was smooth. Bravo."

He winks.

I point at a tattoo on Dax's left bicep—a galaxy of stars and hearts and planets. "What's the story behind that one?"

Dax looks down at his arm, like he's only now discovering he's got a tattoo there. "That's my family. The ones I love the most." He raises his arm and points. "This is my mom here." He points to the sun. "Because we all revolve around her. And that's my dad because he's the largest planet. The largest planets have the strongest gravity. And these here are my three brothers and sister and me." He looks up. "That's how this particular tattoo started. With my core family members. But then my two oldest brothers and sister got married. And then they all had kids. So I added stars and hearts for all of our new family members. And that made me realize I should add my honorary brothers—my bodyguard friend from the party, Zander, *here,* and my two bandmates, Colin and Fish—*here* and *here.*" He looks up and flashes me a smile that sends warmth pooling between my legs. "I'll be adding another heart really soon for my oldest brother Colby's baby girl. She'll be arriving in a few weeks."

Oh, my heart. I've never met someone like Dax before. Someone who'd tattoo his entire family onto his arm. That's not normal. At least, not to me. "It's amazing you're so close to your family."

"You're not?"

I pause. I don't normally tell new people my family history. But Dax makes me want to tell him everything there is to know about me, even the parts I usually keep hidden. "I've got two family members, and I'm close with both of them. Just one at a time. I've got a mother and a brother, but I never see them at the same time because my brother hates my mother with the fiery passion of a thousand suns."

Dax looks floored. "Why?"

"My brother is my half-brother. We share a father. Well, we *shared* a father. My father passed away. And my brother blames my mother for breaking up his parents' marriage. Which she did."

He processes all that for a moment. "I'm sorry about your father. When did he die?"

"When I was nine. But don't feel sorry for me about that. I hadn't met him when he died, though I knew exactly who he was."

"Did he know about you?"

"Yes."

"And he never wanted to meet you?"

"I don't know. He went to prison when I was three, and I never visited him in prison."

Dax looks tentative, like he's considering what to say next, so, I answer the question he's surely wondering.

"Securities fraud," I say. "My father bilked a shitload of people out of their life savings. He wound up hanging himself in prison. But, hey, at least my father wasn't a serial killer, right?"

"Sounds like you had a rough childhood."

I shrug. "Not having a father was all I knew, so I thought it was normal. And my mom and I were super close. My mom was only nineteen when she had me. She was working part-time at my father's company to pay her way through college. He was the big boss, twenty years her senior, married with a son. She wound up having a whirl-wind affair with the big boss that ended when she found out she was pregnant with his child. When she told him about the baby, he demanded she abort me and she refused. So, he bought her a small condo by the beach in San Diego as a pay-off, and off she went to have her baby on her own and start a new life. Unfortunately for my father, his wife somehow found out about the condo—which led to her finding out about my mother and me. Not to mention some other women my father was screwing on the side. My father was, appar-ently, so scorched-earth in the divorce and custody dispute that followed, the wife wound up having some sort of a nervous breakdown and the son was therefore passed from relative to relative when our father went to prison. Or so my brother later told me."

"Did you and your brother connect when your father died?"

"No. It was later. My mom married this nice guy named Steve when I was ten. A year after that, they had a baby boy—the best thing that's ever happened to me. The great love of my life." I pause, my heart suddenly feeling like it's bleeding. "He died of leukemia at age three, unfortunately, right before I turned fifteen."

Dax looks deeply anguished. "Oh, God, Violet. I'm so sorry."

I take a deep breath and pull down my bathrobe to reveal the dragonfly on my upper arm. "This is for him. At the park one day, a dragonfly started buzzing around my baby brother and he got scared and ran to me. I told him, 'It's okay, buddy. Dragonflies are the nice bugs. They protect us.' And that's all it took for that dragonfly to become his best friend." I smile at the memory. "He spent the rest of the afternoon, running around the park, yelling for that dragonfly to come back and play with him again." I replace my robe onto my shoulder and sigh. "On the day of my baby brother's funeral, I was standing over his casket, crying my eyes out, and a dragonfly started buzzing around my head. I knew it was my brother, telling me he was safe and happy and chasing dragonflies in heaven."

Wordlessly, Dax gets up from his chair. He lifts me out of my chair, and wraps his arms around me. "I'm so sorry."

I rest my cheek on Dax's shoulder and let him hold me. "Losing my baby brother was the worst thing that's ever happened to me. I've got a Jackson-sized hole in my heart now, and always will."

"His name was Jackson?"

"Mmm hmm."

Dax kisses the side of my head. "Jackson is my middle name."

I lift my head from Dax's chest, my eyes wide and my heart in my mouth. Holy crap. Call me crazy, but that sure feels like another dragonfly buzzing around my head. I twist my mouth. "Wait. Your name is *Dax Jackson*? Did your parents want you to become an action star when you grew up?"

Dax chuckles, leads me to his chair, and guides me to sit on his lap. "My given name is *David* Jackson, but my family started calling me Dax the day my parents brought me home from the hospital. My family is fanatical about nicknames. It's our *thing*. So, my two oldest brothers renamed me Dax that first day and my mom went with it."

"How'd your dad feel about that?"

"Meh. I'm the fifth kid. Dad didn't give a shit what I was called."

I chuckle through my emotion.

"Aw, baby," he says. He grabs my hand. "My heart aches about Jackson."

"Thank you. I miss him every day. I can't begin to express how much happiness he brought me."

"That's why you make superhero costumes for kids with cancer."

I nod. "I've got to do something. It's not much. But it's what I can do. Those smiles I get from those kids remind me of him so much."

He looks at me like he pities me.

"This is why I never talk about my family," I say, wiping my eyes. "I know my life story makes me sound like a train wreck. Especially to someone like you, with a normal, happy family."

"Violet, if there's one thing I've learned over the years, it's that *nobody* has a normal family. In fact, my family is the most *ab*normal of anyone's I know. All my friends' parents are divorced, and the ones whose parents are still married, they're not happy. If anyone's family isn't *normal*, it's mine." He kisses my cheek. "So, you were going to tell me how you hooked up with your brother...?"

"Oh, yeah. He contacted me when Jackson died, out of the blue, to offer his condolences. I already knew he existed at that point, but we'd never interacted. And I just needed a shoulder to cry on so badly in that moment, I pounced on him, poor guy. My mother was distraught over Jackson's death and incapable of consoling me. My stepfather had his hands full with my mother and his own grief. I felt like I needed someone from the outside. Someone who hadn't lost Jackson. So I asked him if we could meet in person. And he said yes, he'd like that." I smile at the memory. "He came to San Diego to meet me and I proceeded to cry on this poor stranger's shoulder for six hours straight. And that's how I lost a brother and gained a brother, all in one week. Shortly after that, my mother cheated on my stepfather and their marriage collapsed, and I leaned on him even more."

Dax makes a sympathetic sound.

"Unfortunately, since my new brother hated my mother's guts, I couldn't very well invite him to Christmases and birthdays. But he was really sweet about keeping in touch with me. He was a life saver."

Dax looks distressed. "I feel so sorry for your stepfather. Losing a kid and then being cheated on? Brutal."

"Yeah, I know. And he's such a sweet guy. I think my mom just didn't know how to handle her grief. She cheated with this guy from her support group. They didn't last."

"Have you stayed close with your stepfather?"

Emotion rises inside me. I swallow it down and take a deep breath. "No. Steve wound up remarrying a woman with three kids and moving to Seattle. We don't keep in touch. I wanted to stay close with him, but I think it was just too painful for him, after everything that happened." My heart pangs sharply. "I was sad about it, but not shocked. Steve never officially adopted me or gave me his name, even though Mom and Jackson both had his name. So a piece of me always knew he wasn't making any long-term promises to me."

Dax looks absolutely heartbroken. "Oh, Violet."

"It's okay. I grew up without a father. It was nice to have one for a few years. I really enjoyed it. But, like I said, a piece of me never expected it to last."

"What's your last name?"

"Rhodes. It's my mother's name."

He smiles. "*Violet Rhodes* from Rhode Island." He nuzzles his nose into my hair, and inhales deeply. "Violet Rhodes, thank you for telling me all that."

I close my eyes and enjoy his closeness. "I don't normally tell people the whole story. I know it's a lot."

"I'm glad you told me."

"It doesn't make you want to run out of this hotel room and never look back?"

"It makes me want to kiss your blues away."

"Who says I'm blue?"

"Your eyes. They give you away. They're filled with sadness."

"But I'm happy, despite it all. I truly am."

He studies my face for a long moment. "Maybe that's why I'm so attracted to you. You've got every reason in the world to be blue, and yet you're happy. I've got every reason in the world to be happy, and yet, I sometimes feel like I was born with the weight of the world on my shoulders. That's why I make music. To get that weight off me."

My chest heaves.

Longing. Need. Yearning. Lust. Understanding. It all passes between us palpably.

"I'm drowning in your stormy eyes, Violet Rhodes," Dax whispers softly. "I'm drowning and I don't want anyone to throw me a lifeline."

With that, he rises from his chair, scooping me up as he goes, and brings me to the bed... and that's where Dax proceeds to strip off my bathrobe and peel off his briefs, kiss my naked body, and make love to me tenderly... making me forget, at least for a little while, all the things that have smashed my heart to pieces... until, soon, he's got me focusing on nothing and no one but the unparalleled pleasure, the safety, the *rightness* I'm feeling right here and now with this beautiful boy.

EIGHT

DAX

I open my eyes and blink in the California sunlight streaming through the window.

I'm lying in bed naked with Violet, her cheek pressed against my chest and her warm thigh draped over mine. It feels like the most natural thing in the world, having my body intertwined with hers. Indeed, this whole night with Violet has felt like I'm reliving a distant memory with her. Acting out a hazy dream.

I glance at the clock on the nightstand. 11:06. Shit. I'm pretty sure the hotel clerk at the front desk last night said checkout this morning was at eleven. But I don't care. I'd rather have to pay for a second night I can't use than wake up Violet right now. If my family weren't flying into L.A. today to throw me a going-away dinner party tonight, I'd already have booked this room for a second night.

Taking care not to wake Violet, I grab my phone off the night-stand and swipe into my family's group chat, intending to find my mom's text from a few days ago about my family's travel plans today. But when I look at my screen, it's lit up with texts about some video on *TMZ* that posted early this morning. Apparently, it features none other than Zander and the woman he's being paid to guard, Aloha Carmichael.

Watch with sound on, my brother Ryan texted to everyone, attaching the video link.

Ryan: Looks like Z already lost the bet on night one. Either that, or he's damned close to losing it.

I turn my sound on, set to low, click on the link, and promptly lose my shit. Oh, Zander. He's so predictable. After the way he drooled over Aloha last night at the party, I knew he wouldn't resist her charms for long. But I never thought he'd succumb to them on night *one* of Aloha's tour.

I tap out a text, joining my family's raucous back-and-forth about the video. And the minute my text posts in the group chat, my mother pounces on me for not answering her flurry of texts from last night about the family's travel plans today. She tells me everyone is on their way to the airport in Seattle right now. She asks me to confirm I'll be at their hotel in L.A. when they arrive and that I'll be staying the next two nights at their hotel, just to make things easy for our trip with the little ones to Disneyland tomorrow. In all caps, she ends her text with "ANSWER ME, DAXY, SO I KNOW YOU'RE ALIVE!"

Dutifully, I tap out a reply to my mother, fully intending to tell her yes, yes, yes, to all of it. But, suddenly, I pull back before pressing send. Yeah, I'll meet my family at their hotel this afternoon... and, yes, I'll eat dinner with them for my going-away party tonight. But will I be staying the next two nights at my family's hotel? Suddenly, I'm not sure I want to confirm that. I've got two nights before I leave for London, after all, and Violet's here in L.A. until Sunday, too. What if Violet is game to spend tonight or tomorrow night, or *both*, right here with me? If she is, I gotta admit, I'd ditch sleeping at my family's hotel in a heartbeat.

I delete my text and start again, and finally press send on a message that says simply, "I'll see you at your hotel when you get here! Can't wait!"

Without waiting for my mother's reply, I return my phone to the nightstand because a) I'm well aware I didn't answer her questions about sleeping arrangements, and b) texting with my mom is the last thing I wanna do while I've got a naked girl lying next to me. I pull Violet's sleeping body close, inhale the intoxicating, flowery scent of her hair, and let my mind wander. I've got a thousand things to do before my flight the day after tomorrow—a bunch of errands to run, especially since I'm going to Disneyland with everyone tomorrow. But I can't seem to motivate myself to leave this bed and get moving. I mean, fuck it, there are jackets and toiletries in London, right? I don't *have* to do all my errands here in LA.

A sharp knock at the door jolts me. "Housekeeping!" a female voice calls out, prompting Violet to stir against my chest.

"Not yet!" I shout toward the door. "Come back later!"

Purring with sexual satisfaction, Violet sits up. Her dark hair is a sexy, rumpled mess. Her face looks groggy but gorgeous. She's a woman who was fucked well last night, and it shows.

She rubs her eyes and looks at the clock. When she sees it's almost noon, she grimaces. "I didn't mean to sleep so long." She reaches for her phone. "I'm sure Miranda's been texting me all morning." She looks at her screen. "Oh boy. She's using all caps."

Violet sits up to tap out a message, and the sheet covering her torso slides down to reveal her breasts. And just like that, my cock begins hardening.

"Hey, Violet," I say as she continues typing. "What's your schedule like for the rest of the weekend?"

She looks up. "Hmm?"

"What are your plans before you head back to Rhode Island on Sunday?"

She lowers her phone. "It's Miranda's birthday weekend. We're going to the spa this afternoon. And then my brother is taking us out to dinner tonight." Her face lights up. "Oh! You should come to dinner tonight!" She pulls back. "I mean, no pressure, of course. I just—"

"I'd love to come," I say. "But my family is flying in from Seattle today and I'm doing dinner with them tonight. How about we get together tomorrow night?"

Violet looks disappointed. "Miranda and I will be in San Diego tomorrow night visiting our mothers. We're driving there tomorrow afternoon and staying overnight. Miranda's going to drive me to LAX on Sunday morning, straight from San Diego."

My shoulders droop.

"How about brunch tomorrow before I leave for San Diego?" Violet says. "We're not leaving L.A. until around one."

I exhale with resignation. "I'm going to Disneyland all day tomorrow with my family. We're taking all my nieces and nephews. I can't miss it."

Violet looks exactly the way I feel: *deeply disappointed*. But she manages to smile and say, "Disneyland will be a blast with little kids."

But I simply won't accept defeat. "How about tonight, after our dinners? I'll book this same room for another night. I don't need to sleep to be able to walk around Disneyland with my family tomorrow. And you could sleep on the drive to San Diego, right?"

Violet throws her arms around my neck and kisses me like she's just won the lottery. My heart soaring, I wrap my arms around her and return her passionate kiss.

"Where there's a will, there's a way," I say, inhaling the scent of her hair.

"I'm so excited." She pulls back from my lips, smiling broadly. "I'll pay for the room tonight, okay? You paid for last night."

"I've got it."

"But this hotel is expensive, Dax."

"I've got it."

"At least let me pay half."

"Violet, listen to me. I'd sell a kidney to get one more night with you. Fuck it, I'd pay *you* to get one more night with you."

She giggles again and kisses me. And, soon, fuck the maid, I'm covered and she's fucking me and I'm kissing her and smelling her hair and thinking crazy thoughts like, "Maybe long- distance relationships *can* work with the right person."

I reach between us and massage her clit as she rides me and, quickly, she goes off like the Fourth of July—which, of course, makes me go off, too. As we come down, we kiss for a while, until, finally, Violet pulls away and kisses my cheek.

"I gotta get showered, sexy boy," she says. "Miranda is picking me up at the front of the hotel in thirty minutes. If I make her late for her birthday massage, she'll never forgive me."

"Yeah, I've gotta get out of here, too. I'm meeting my family at their hotel. And right after that, we're having our big going-away dinner, so I've got to squeeze in some errands real quick before they arrive."

"Ah, the outside world," Violet says, rolling her eyes. "It's such a bitch." With that, she rolls out of bed, grabs her clothes and undies off the floor, and saunters naked into the bathroom, swaying her hips as she goes like she knows full well I'm watching her every mesmerizing move.

NINE

DAX

When the bathroom door clicks shut behind my beautiful muse, I pull on my T-shirt and jeans, grab my phone, and sit on the edge of the bed, furiously jotting down the latest torrent of lyrics throttling me:

> *You caught me violet-handed, baby*
> *And now I'm drowning in blue*
> *Not seeing red flags anymore,*
> *Cuz all I see is you*

> *No green thumb on my hand,*
> *Or red tape to cut through*
> *Can't eat no brown sugar or black-eyed peas*
> *Girl, all I want is you*
> *You caught me Violet-handed, baby*
> *And now I got them Violet blues*

. . .

Just as I'm tapping out my last line, Violet emerges from the bathroom, looking like my Hitwoman Elvis Disco Momma, yet again. She grabs her strappy heels off the floor and sits on the edge of the bed next to me. "So, who's going away?" she asks, bending over to secure a buckle on her shoe.

"Huh?"

She sits upright and smiles. "You said something about a going-away dinner with your family. Who's going away?"

Oh.

I hadn't realized I'd mentioned that.

Last night, when there was no doubt Violet and I were having nothing but an amazing one-night stand, I didn't feel the impulse to tell her about my record deal and imminent tour. In fact, I *liked* Violet not knowing about that stuff. But now that we've made plans to meet up again later tonight... and I know for sure Violet likes me for *me*... I see no reason *not* to tell her about the amazing stuff on the horizon.

In fact, I'm excited to tell her—to share my good news, and my anxieties, too. I suddenly want to tell Violet everything there is to know about me, the same way she's done with me. Because, just this fast, I feel like, if there's one person in the world who could calm me down and pump me up about what's to come, it's my Hitwoman Elvis Disco Momma. Obviously, I'll have to wait until tonight to tell Violet the details about the tour, just because we're short on time, but there's no reason I can't tell her the gist now.

"The going-away dinner is for me," I say. "Although, to be fair, I'm not entirely convinced my family didn't use me as an excuse to take my nieces and nephews to D-Land."

She looks at me quizzically.

"I didn't tell you before now because I didn't want it to hijack all our conversations, but, actually, on Sunday, my band is headed out on our first tour."

"*Shut the front door!*" Violet shrieks. In one fell swoop, she pounces on me on the bed, straddles my lap, and hugs me enthusiastically. "Congratulations!"

I laugh underneath her and grab her hips. "Why, thank you."

She bats my shoulder. "I can't believe you didn't tell me! I would have ordered champagne and toasted you all night long!"

"That's why I didn't tell you. I didn't want my band and the tour to consume our every conversation."

"But this is huge, Dax. A massive milestone. You must be *ecstatic.*"

"I am. But as pumped as I am, I'm also a bit stressed, too. I'm the guy who stands front and center during every show. The one who writes our songs. If we crash and burn, that's gonna be on me."

"Crash and burn?" She whacks my shoulder again. "Are you insane? You're not gonna crash and burn. You're gonna smash and *slaaaay,* baby!"

I laugh. She's giving me fireflies again. "You've never even heard my band play. For all you know, we suck."

"Do you?"

"No. We're awesome."

"See? I knew that. The minute I saw you at the party, I thought to myself, 'Now, that's a guy who's either a big star or he's gonna be a big star one day.' A person simply can't have the kind of charisma and confidence you do without having a whole lot to back it up." Squealing, she peppers my entire face with kisses, making me laugh like a hyena, until, finally, she pulls back, smiling brightly. "How long is the tour? Is it just a West Coast thing, or will you be coming to any cities along the East Coast? Maybe even... *Providence,* by any chance?"

"Yeah, we're gonna play a whole bunch of East Coast cities. I don't think Providence, though. I'll have to check the schedule."

Violet leans over me and nuzzles her nose into mine, purring with excitement. And, once again, I find myself inhaling her hair and feeling euphoric.

"Wherever you're playing on the East Coast, I'll be there," she says, skimming my lips with hers. "I'll drive or hop a quick flight. No problem." She pauses. Pulls back. "I mean, if that's okay with you."

I put my palms on her cheeks. "*Of course.* Violet, baby, I'll be counting the days until I see you again."

She squeals and kisses me and, suddenly, I feel a whole lot more than lit up. I feel *in love*. I mean, intellectually, I know I'm not. But it's how I *feel* in this moment. Like she's the great love of my life and I'm her man forever and we're meant to be and that's that. And it feels fucking amazing.

"I can't wait to see you perform," she says.

My smile is hurting my face. I sit up, taking her with me, and she wraps her legs around my waist on the bed.

"I'll get you backstage passes for any shows you want," I say excitedly, my heart pounding in my ears. "For you and however many of your friends. And then we'll spend the night together in my hotel room, every time."

"You mean we're gonna *flooooow* again?" she says flirtatiously.

"Hell yeah," I say. "You and me, baby. We're all about the *flooooow*."

Laughing, she slides her arms around my neck and kisses me enthusiastically again... and I feel pure, uncomplicated happiness. Even when I found out my band got signed by River Records, my happiness didn't feel like this. Because, as happy as I was in that moment, I also sensed the enormity of the situation. The pressure. The chance to fail. But this moment? This is nothing but pure euphoria. Unadulterated glee. *Joy*.

"I've got some big projects for school coming up this month," she says. "And my classes have a strict attendance policy. We should probably look at the East Coast dates together so I can get them down on my calendar and figure out which ones are going to work for me."

My stomach sinks into my toes. She's assuming I'll be on the East Coast within the next *month*? Obviously, she's thinking I'm going on a normal kind of first tour—the kind where a nobody band like mine drives themselves from city to city in a beat-up van. Oh, man. She's gonna keel over when she finds out the truth.

"Is your schedule online?" Violet says, sliding off my lap and reaching for her phone.

I put my hand on her arm, stopping her from grabbing her phone. I don't want her to search "tour" and "22 Goats" and unwittingly stumble across those three little words—Red Card Riot—that are going to shock the hell out of her. I want Violet to find out the jaw-dropping truth about my band's first tour from me.

"Violet, hang on," I say, my heart thumping. "The tour is eight months long."

Her jaw drops.

"On Sunday, we're heading to London for two weeks of promo and rehearsals before kicking off the international leg with two shows in London. After four months overseas, the domestic leg will start on the East Coast and wind up in L.A. in July."

Violet looks utterly flabbergasted. Like she's about to tip over. "You said... you're not a rock star. You said nobody at the party had any idea who you are."

"That was true. We're a nobody band at the moment."

"Nobody bands don't get booked for eight-month *world* tours."

"22 Goats is the opening band. Our debut single and music video are dropping on Sunday. But even then, I've been warned it'll take a while for the world to care, if they ever do. Trust me, nobody on this tour is coming to see 22 Goats."

She looks like she's holding her breath. "Who are they coming to see?"

I pause.

"Who's the headliner, Dax?"

I know the minute I say a certain three little words, Violet's going to freak out. Maybe even feel like I've been less than forthcoming with her while she's poured her heart out to me. But it can't be avoided. "Red Card Riot."

Predictably, Violet's jaw clanks to the ground.

I can't help chuckling at her adorable expression. It's almost cartoonish. "It's crazy, right? We're signed to the same label as RCR, and, for some reason, the guy who owns the label decided to give my band—a nobody band from Seattle—the shot of a lifetime. But none of this is why we were at the party last night. I told you the truth about that. My friends and I were at Aloha's party because of Zander.

The guy who owns the label didn't even know we were coming to the party. He was surprised to see us there."

She's frozen. Speechless. Looking like her brain is melting.

"*Surprise*," I say with weak jazz hands.

I know Violet's got to be stunned. But what she does next surprises me. Unsettles me. *Worries me.* She bows her head for a long beat and exhales like my news has taken the wind out of her sails.

But then, thank God, she takes a deep breath, lifts her head, and hugs me fervently. "I'm so happy for you," she chokes out, her voice awash in emotion. "*Congratulations.*"

There's no doubt in my mind she's sincerely happy for me. But I also know she's processing the fact that we won't have a chance to see each other again for a full four months. And that, when we do, I'll most likely be in a very different place in my life than I am now, having toured the world for months with the hottest band in the universe. What will my life look like by then? *Who will I be?*

Her nose in my hair, Violet whispers, "I know all your dreams are going to come true. The whole world is going to fall desperately in love with you, Dax. There's not a doubt in my mind."

My heart pangs. I clutch her to me. *Why did that sound like goodbye?* "Violet, I can tell this is freaking you out. And I don't blame you. It's freaking me out, too. But this doesn't change anything between us. You already thought we'd be living three thousand miles away from each other. So, no matter what, we weren't going to be able to commit to anything, right here and now. We were always going to have to keep in touch and see what happens." My heart is racing. If I were being completely honest, I'd admit I've been thinking crazy thoughts all morning long—thoughts about us calling this thing between us "exclusive." Thoughts of us carrying on a committed relationship over FaceTime for the next however long. But I'm not too far gone to know the very idea is insane—the ramblings of a madman. Not to mention, a tall order for me to deliver on, considering the great unknown that lies ahead of me.

My heart aching, I kiss her cheek, her hair, her ear. "Violet, I know four months feels like a long time to wait to see each other again, but time will fly. If we can maybe just keep in touch until we see each other again..." I trail off, suddenly realizing my words are having the exact opposite effect I'm hoping. They're obviously not reassuring Violet. They're making her stiffen and pull away. I can see it. I touch her cheek, my breathing shallow. "Sweetheart, I know you got your heart broken when you tried a long-distance relationship in the past. I know your first love really hurt you. But it won't be like that with us. We'll both be free and single, so there won't be any expectations. I wish I could make promises to you, right here and now. It's what my heart wants to do. But my brain knows I can't. I have no idea what my life will be like on tour. And I don't want to make any kind of promises to you I can't..." I trail off again. I'm most definitely not helping my cause here. Something's changed for Violet in the blink of an eye. She's closed up shop. She's done.

Violet smiles thinly. She releases her grip on me and lets her arms fall to her sides. "I think we got ahead of ourselves for a minute there. Or, at least, I did. Your whole life is about to change in ways you can't fathom. The last thing you need is for some girl in Rhode Island to be sitting around waiting for your next text. And the last thing I need is to be that girl. I've been the girl who sits by the phone in the past. And I swore to myself I'd never be her again."

I feel like I've been punched in the stomach. *Fuck*.

"You like complete honesty, right?" she says.

I nod, even though I'm not sure I'm going to like whatever completely honest thing Violet is about to say to me.

"I'm already starting to have intense feelings for you. And I don't think keeping things 'casual' with you for months and months—while you travel the world, living the rock 'n' roll lifestyle—will be easy for me. Actually, no. If I'm being honest, it's going to be impossible for me. Confession? Last night was my first one-night stand. I saw you and instantly decided I wanted you, no matter what. But it was a first for me. I know your perception of me is I'm some kind of *femme fatale,* but I'm not. I'm not a huge partier. I don't have casual sex. My idea of a fun night is getting in my jammies, eating popcorn, and playing board games. And, most of all, I don't willingly put myself in situations where it's crystal clear I'm going to wind up getting my heart broken."

My heart is beating like a steel drum. I know this is the moment where I should tell her I won't break her heart. That I'd be a fantastic long-distance boyfriend. Faithful and true. But the words won't form. How can I reassure her of anything when I've got no idea what's in store for me on the other side of that plane ride to London?

Violet sighs. "I think, for my own sake—and, frankly, yours—we should quit while we're ahead. Say our goodbyes now and leave this amazing night, burned into our memories, untouched and perfect."

My heart feels like it's physically cracking. "So, tonight is off?"

Violet nods. "Believe me, I'm doing you a favor. Helping you dodge a bullet. Who the hell feels the way I'm feeling about you *this* fast? It's ludicrous." She sighs. "Dax, I'm worried if I spend tonight with you, knowing what lies ahead, my feelings are only going to grow and become... unmanageable for me. And then this amazing thing we've got is only going to become a source of pain. And neither of us wants that, especially me. You might crave getting your heart broken, just to see what awesome songs come out of it, but I sure as hell don't."

I swallow hard, my heart feeling like it's bleeding. "Will I see you at my shows on the East Coast?"

She pauses, like she's considering it. But, ultimately, she shakes her head. "Let's make a clean break. I've told you about my life. I've got baggage. I've worked on myself, really hard, but if you're looking for a cool, carefree girl with no issues or hang-ups, who's gonna video chat with you on occasion and then show up to fuck you in New York and then disappear again with a happy wave goodbye, then I'm not that girl. I'm scared to death of abandonment and this entire situation is going to fuck with my head. I know I seem like a hitwoman to you, but, trust me, I'm not." She wipes her eyes. "Just go and have fun, Dax. I want that for you, sincerely. Make your dreams come true. Do whatever—and whoever—you want, without being tied down in any way to some chick in Rhode Island who's sitting by the phone. Have the time of your life." She kisses my cheek and shocks me by heading quickly toward the door.

"Violet," I blurt, panic flooding me. "*Wait.*"

She turns around, her hand on the doorknob.

My eyes and nose are stinging. I swallow hard. "Can I come see you after the tour? I'll come to Rhode Island."

As she considers my suggestion, her face contorts like she's hosting a tug of war inside her brain. She exhales. "If you're still thinking about me when the tour finishes up in L.A., call River Records and ask for Miranda. She's interned there for the past two summers and she's planning to work there full time after she graduates in May. If the planets are aligned by then—if we're both single and still thinking about each other—then, yeah, maybe we'll reconnect then."

My bleeding heart fills with hope. "I'll see you then."

Violet doesn't look convinced. "A lot can happen in eight months, Dax—especially to a guy going on a world tour with Red Card Riot." She smiles mournfully. "Enjoy the ride, David Jackson. I swear, I'll be cheering you on, every step of the way. No matter what happens, even if our paths never cross again, please know I'll never, ever forget you or this magical night."

With that, she blows me a kiss and slips out the door, taking a piece of my heart with her.

As the door closes, I get up from the bed and stride to it, intending to chase her down. To beg her to meet me tonight. Or to at least give me her phone number.

But I don't open the door. Instead, I lean my forehead against it and sigh.

Getting Violet's number would only create the expectation that I'll use it. And regularly, at that. And that's not something I can promise to do. Reed warned us tours are grueling and exhausting and that even the most well-intentioned guys lose their grip on the outside world while they're in the eye of the storm. As addicted to Violet as I'm feeling in this moment, as certain as I am that I want to stay in close contact with her—shit, if I'm being honest, I feel psychotically certain I could pledge myself to Violet forever, right here and now—a piece of me knows I can't rationally deliver on what I'm feeling. And the last thing I want to do is break a promise. Or a heart. Least of all, my own.

Fuck.

As much as it pains me to admit, I think Violet was right. She just did me a huge favor. She set me free to fully experience whatever's coming my way, without guilt or trepidation. She gave me the gift of complete freedom, coupled with hope that, one day, when and if the timing is right for us, we'll reconnect.

My heart aching, I shuffle to the bed and sit. Why did I have to meet Violet mere hours before heading off on the greatest adventure of my life? Why couldn't I have met her—

There's a sharp knock on the door. "Housekeeping!"

"Just a fucking second!" I shout, and then immediately regret my asshole tone. "Sorry! Just gimme a minute, okay?"

Sighing, I grab the pillow Violet slept on last night, bury my face in it, and inhale her flowery scent. My heart aching, I strip the pillow-case off the pillow, deciding I need a memento of the best night of my life—and then I shove the pillowcase underneath my arm and drag my sorry ass to the door.

TEN

VIOLET

When Miranda pulls up in front of the hotel, I swing open the passenger door, tumble into her car, and burst into tears. "He's in a band called 22 Goats that's opening for Red Card Riot on their world tour."

Miranda gasps.

"I only found out this morning—about twenty minutes ago—*after* I'd already fucked him a hundred million times and fallen head over heels for him."

Miranda palms her forehead. "I knew he looked familiar. *Damn.* How the hell did all that not come up *before* you left the party with him?"

"It's not my fault. I asked him how he got into the party and he said his buddy is Aloha's bodyguard. He said nothing about being signed to River Records." I cover my face with my hands. "I asked all the right questions, Miranda. I swear."

Miranda sighs. "Okay, calm down, Vi. It's not the end of the world."

I come out from behind my hands and look at her incredulously. "It's pretty damned close."

"Would you have done anything differently last night, if you'd known?"

"*Of course.* I would have run the other direction."

Miranda laughs. "You're such a liar. The minute you saw that boy, you were a goner. Wild horses couldn't have kept you from doing exactly what you did with him last night, complications or consequences be damned."

"No."

"*Yes.* Violet, I've never seen you so instantly attracted to anyone in your life."

She's right about that. The lightning bolt I felt when I saw Dax was all-consuming—and definitely a first. "At least, I would have told him the trouble he was getting into if he messed with me," I say, rubbing my forehead. "Drive, Miranda. God forbid Dax comes out here and sees me and I lose my willpower and agree to come back here tonight, like he wanted me to."

Miranda pulls out from the hotel. "He said he wants to see you again tonight?"

"And I said no. Well, I said yes, at first, before I found out about the tour. And *then* I said no, even though it physically *pained* me to do it." I groan. "Oh, God, I already feel addicted to him, Miranda. He's not like anybody I've met before. He's *magic.*" I gasp. "What if he says something about me to someone on tour?"

Miranda chuckles. "Not trying to be harsh, but even if it was the best sex of his life, he's almost certainly not going to mention a one-night stand to anyone. At least, not in detail."

"But what if he does? It could be catastrophic for him if he says the wrong thing to the wrong person. His band could get bounced off the tour."

"Okay, let's say he mentions you—this random girl he fucked one night in L.A. What are the odds he'd mention you by name? When was the last time I mentioned a one-night stand by name to you? I always say 'that hot cop,' or 'the guy with the Porsche.'"

My shoulders relax slightly. She's got a point there.

"He'd never say, 'I fucked this girl in L.A. named Violet Rhodes.'

If he says anything at all, he'd say, 'This one time, I fucked this amazing girl in L.A. and she was a freak in the sheets.'"

I let out a long, slow exhale. I think Miranda's right about that. "Just to be safe, though," I say, "do you think I should call him and warn him? You could get his number, right? Did I blow it by not getting his number?"

"Don't contact him, Vi. The best thing you could do at this point is leave him alone and let him do his thing. You know how musicians are—they have the attention span of a gnat. A week from now, he won't even remember his own name, let alone yours."

I look down, feeling like Miranda just punched me in the stomach.

"Oh, sweetie. I was just trying to be reassuring. I'm so sorry, love."

"It's fine. I know what you meant."

We come to a red light and Miranda turns to look at me sympathetically. "You really like him, huh?"

I don't know how to adequately describe the otherworldly connection I felt with Dax. So, I decide to use Dax's stunning words to explain it. "I told Dax he gave me butterflies, and he replied that I gave him more than butterflies. I gave him *fireflies*. Because, he said, I made him feel lit up from deep inside."

Miranda exhales. "Wow."

"And I swear on all things holy, it wasn't a line. Our connection was just that amazing. It was like nothing I've felt before."

The light turns green and Miranda drives her car through the intersection. "*Never?*"

"Never."

She pauses, letting that shocking statement sink in for a moment. "What did you say to him when you left?"

"The truth. Just not the whole truth. I told him I can't sit by the phone and do something 'casual' with him when I'm feeling such intense feelings for him. It was all true. I just didn't tell him the rest. The stuff he doesn't need to know."

"I think you did the right thing," she says. "Why stress him out when he's about to have the adventure of a lifetime?"

"Exactly. I didn't want to put that on his shoulders." I look out the passenger window. "It was for his own good, as much as mine. If he got kicked off the tour, I'd never forgive myself."

"Absolutely. You did good, honey." She glances from the front windshield to scrutinize me. "You didn't give him your number?"

"No."

She returns to the road ahead of her. "Good girl. If it were me and I had that kind of connection with a guy, I probably wouldn't have been as strong as you. I would have broken down and given him my number. I'm proud of you."

We drive in silence for a moment, until I feel the need to confess my sins.

"Okay, I wasn't quite as strong as I'm pretending. I told him you'll be working for River Records by the end of the tour and that, if he's still thinking about me by then, he can track me down through you."

"*Violet.*"

"I know, I know. I just couldn't resist. I figured... or, rather, *hoped*... he might be bulletproof by then—so successful, no one could fuck with him or his band, even if we gave it a whirl."

Miranda looks at me like I'm a puppy that just took a gigantic crap on the carpet.

"You think I'm wishing for rainbows and unicorns," I say.

"I think if you let yourself sit around, wishing and hoping for him to be bulletproof enough to date you, you'll just be setting yourself up for disappointment."

I look out the passenger window again. "It's probably a moot point, anyway. The odds are slim he'll track me down after the tour. We had an amazing night—but, still, I have to remind myself it was just one night, even though it felt like so much more. I'm the one going back to my quiet life at school. He's the one whose entire life is about to be turned upside down. I'm sure last night will stick with me a whole lot longer than with him."

Miranda says nothing. But she looks extremely sympathetic.

"Plus, why would he want to mess with me when he gets back, a girl with so much baggage, when there are infinite girls out there who wouldn't screw things up for him in the slightest?"

Miranda looks pained. "I'm so sorry, Vi."

I force a smile. "It's fine." I look out the passenger window again. "Just do me a favor. Don't bring him up again, okay? From here on out, just for my own sanity, I'm going to try to pretend last night with Dax never happened."

ELEVEN

DAX

Everyone relaxes with their newly filled glasses and dessert plates as my sister, Kat, stands at the front of the room trying to figure out a glitch with the restaurant-supplied projector, aided by our family's fixer—our big brother, Ryan. My entire family is here in this private dining room. Colin and Fish were here throughout dinner, but once dessert was served, they left to meet up with a bunch of Colin's cousins.

Finally, the screen behind Kat fills with bright light from the projector and my family cheers. As Ryan resumes his seat next to his wife and baby boy, Kat turns to the room, a huge smile on her face.

"Family Morgannn," Kat booms like an announcer at a prizefight. "I giiiive youuuu... my co-Wonder Twinnnnnnn... the boy I'd be if I were a boooooy... the boy we've called Rock Star since age twooooooo... our beloved Baby Brother... the one, the only... the man, the myth, the legennnnnd... *Daxyyyy Morgannnnnn!*"

As the crowd cheers, Kat brings up her first slide—the most "rock star" image of me ever captured—and the crowd's cheers turn to enthusiastic hoots.

The shot on the screen was taken by Kat last year during a 22

Goats show at a small club in Seattle, and it just so happened to capture clichéd rock-star perfection. In the photo, my hair is wild and tinged electric blue from the overhead stage lights. My muscles are taut and flexing and glistening with sweat as I play my electric guitar and sing my heart out. And best of all, the thing that's making everyone howl and scream the most: I'm making my patented "guitar face" in the shot—the expression that consumes my features whenever I've reached maximum musical ecstasy. I'm assuming it's the same face I make when I have an orgasm. And in the instant caught in this photo, it's clear my soul is splooging to high heaven.

"The dude in this photo is now a *bona fide* rock star," Kat says, pointing at the screen. "But the question is: how did he get here?" She addresses me, a huge smile on her face. "Daxy Morgan, *this is your life!*"

She brings up a new photo, and, again, the room erupts. It's a Morgan family classic—our mother's all-time favorite shot of her five kids. In this one, I'm a newborn in diapers, held by a smiling, ten-year-old Colby. Eight-year-old Ryan is standing at Colby's shoulder, holding our sister, a towheaded preschooler, and the two of them—Ryan and Kat—are laughing hysterically as they perfectly mimic Colby and me. And what's Keane, our family's designated neon sheep, doing in the shot? Well, a handstand, of course. As one does.

Her face aglow, Kat returns to the crowd. "From the day Mom and Dad brought 'David Jackson' home, we knew he was special."

"*Dackson!*" Ryan bellows... because that's what Ryan is legally required to bellow whenever someone utters my given name. It's a contraction of "David Jackson." The nickname Ryan coined the minute he saw me for the first time.

"Hey, that's Dax, son, to you!" Colby shouts in reply to Ryan, right on cue... because that's what Colby is legally required to say whenever Ryan bellows "Dackson!" It's the same thing Colby said twenty-two years ago when he heard Ryan's off-the-cuff nickname for me.

According to Morgan family lore, it was thanks to this exchange between Ryan and Colby twenty-two years ago, on the day I was brought home, that I became Dax forevermore, rather than David. Apparently, right after Ryan and Colby had their aforementioned exchange, they told our mother they preferred the name Dax to my actual name. And much to their surprise, our mother agreed with them. She liked Dax, better, too. And since our father didn't give a shit what his fifth kid was called, and Kat and Keane were too little to get a vote in the matter, I became Dax from that moment forward.

The sound of my parents' laughter to my right draws my gaze to them. They're sitting together, their hands clasped, staring at Kat's presentation. They look happy together. Proud of their family. The sight of them fills me with warmth.

Kat's voice draws me back to her at the front of the room. She says, "Daxy, from day one, you melted our hearts with your sweetness, amazed us with your intelligence and talent, and, of course, entertained us all by constantly letting us paint your little toenails, style your hair, and practice makeup techniques on your cute little face."

"Pretty sure all that last stuff was just you, Kitty Kat," I say.

"And you loved every minute of it," she replies brightly.

She's right. I did. But only because it was Kat who was administering the happy torture. Growing up, as long as Kat was paying attention to me, for good or evil, I was thrilled.

Kat brings up her next photo—another Morgan family classic. In the shot, I'm a towheaded toddler in diapers, enthusiastically playing air guitar in front of the TV while Kat cheers me on. From what my mother has always said about this shot, some famous guitarist was shredding on TV and two-year-old me leaped up and passionately started mimicking his actions, thereby earning myself a lifelong family nickname on the spot: *Rock Star*.

"This was the moment we all knew you'd grow up to play arenas," Kat says. "Or, at least, *I* did."

Ryan snorts. "Kat, you were *six* in this photo. You didn't know what an arena was, let alone that Dax would grow up to play in one."

"Oh, let the girl be hyperbolic," our mother says. "We all know Kitty's full of it sometimes, but it's part of her charm."

And so it goes. Kat brings up photo after photo, each one eliciting laughter and snarky commentary from my family. We see my first haircut—a shot in which, predictably, I'm bawling my eyes out. There's a photo of Keane and me, dressed in our dinosaur jammies, jumping on our respective twin beds in the room we shared until Keane turned ten. There's a shot of Ryan wheeling me around in a wheelbarrow as my mom gardens in the background. One of four-teen-year-old Colby teaching four-year-old me to throw a football. There's ten-year-old Kat painting my six-year-old toenails blue, and a later shot of Kat and me, ages sixteen and twelve, dressed as the Wonder Twins for Halloween.

Photo after photo lights up the screen, and with each passing slide, an overwhelming serenity—a lightness of being—washes over me and fills my crevices to bursting. A feeling of rightness I only ever feel with these specific people—plus Zander, Fish, and Colin, too, of course. A feeling that...

Violet.

Out of nowhere, she hijacks my thoughts. Suddenly, I'm right back in that warm bath with her—staring at her lips and eyes and gorgeous tits—touching her bare thigh underneath the water—and feeling this same kind of serenity I'm feeling now. I know Violet said she did me a big favor by sending me off without any ties, and my brain believes her. But my heart can't help feeling rejected. Kind of stomped on, to be honest. If only she would have given me her number, I'm sure I'd be texting her right now. Telling her I can't stop thinking about her... probably shamelessly begging her to meet me tonight, no matter what she said earlier.

Everyone around me hoots and catcalls, distracting me from my aching heart. The photo on the screen this time is one of Fish, Colin, and me, as young teens. We're playing in my parents' garage while Ryan, Keane, Zander, and Kat look on. The three dudes watching us in the shot are visibly unimpressed by whatever they're hearing. But

Kat? She's enthralled. Cheering wildly with her hands in the air. I smile to myself: *some things never change.*

A few more photos and we're looking at Colin, Fish, and me on the night we got signed by River Records. That life-changing night happened during Kat and Josh's destination wedding week in Maui, after Kat had cleverly arranged for 22 Goats to play a concert for all her wedding guests early in the week—a guest list my sister knew included a certain friend of Josh's with a record label.

"And the rest, as they say, is history!" Kat says with a flourish. She grabs her glass of wine, raises it to me, and wishes me success and happiness and *fun.*

Everyone claps and cheers and raises their glasses to me. My niece, Isabella, presents me with an adorable drawing of my band that makes me bizarrely emotional. My niece, Beatrice, not to be outdone, pops up and gives a speech that turns into a pronouncement of her own personal intention to become a rock star one day, too. "But not like Uncle Daxy," she explains. "Like Aloha Carmichael. Because she's pwetty."

When everyone's speeches and presentations and announce-ments of future career goals are finished, I stand and say a few heart-felt thank yous. To Colby for always letting me borrow his truck for gigs when Fish's van broke down, which happened often. To my parents for always letting my band rehearse in our garage. And to Kat, my beloved Wonder Twin, and to her husband, Josh, too, for letting my band play that fateful show in Maui. My voice breaking, I promise to video chat with my entire family once a week, and to regu-larly call my nephew, Theo, to help him with his songwriting. I make a bunch of other promises and say a few more thank yous, but it all becomes one big emotional, rambling blur after a while.

When I'm finally done babbling, drinks are refilled and normal conversation resumes. After a while, I find myself sitting with my three brothers at the end of a long table, telling them about my conversation with Reed last night—the one where Reed said I should expect to get "mobbed" walking down the street in a month's time.

Ryan says, "If you didn't wanna get mobbed, then it's a damned good thing you made a porno disguised as a music video. Good thinking, Daxy. That ought to keep people from coming at your introverted ass."

"It's not a porno," I grumble. "It's artistically done. Like a European movie."

"When the hell are you gonna show us this European-style porno?" Keane says. "I'm dying to see it."

"You can see it with the rest of the world when it gets posted on Sunday—when I'm safely on an airplane headed to another continent and won't have to listen to you guys mercilessly razzing me about it."

"Oh, we'll mercilessly razz you," Keane says. "Just by text."

"Have you told Mom about the porno yet?" Colby asks.

"No, and it's not a porno, guys. The way it's shot, it feels artistic. Like a cool sex dream, you know?"

"Oh, well, we stand corrected," Ryan says dryly. "Mom will totally get the distinction between a porno and a cool, artistic sex dream."

"Filmed in Europe," Keane adds.

"Maybe she won't see the porno," I say.

"Dude, she's gonna see it," Ryan says.

"Not if we trick her," I say. "How about this?" I look at Keane. "Peenie, ask Maddy to slap 'People Like Us' over some *Outlander* footage and send it to Mom. We'll tell Mom it's the official music video for my song and she'll be so mesmerized by that Jamie guy she loves so much, she'll never even think to question it."

"Genius," Colby says, laughing.

"Meh, don't worry about Mom," Keane says. "Surely, I broke her and Dad in for you when I was a stripper. Other than maybe a full-frontal shot, you couldn't possibly shock them more than 'Ball Peen Hammer.'" He smirks. "You don't happen to show your peen in the porno, do you? Because that would be hella European."

I laugh. "No. Pretty much everything else, though. There's a nice, clear shot of my ass. Plus, I do a whole lot of simulated fucking in this porno."

"Oh, Dax," Ryan says, mimicking our mother perfectly, and we all laugh our asses off.

"Hey, don't stress it, little brother," Keane says. "If all goes according to plan, I'll be distracting Mom from your porno soon. I just found out I'm gonna be auditioning for a part on a huge show that'll require me to do a couple graphic sex scenes. My agent warned it's possible they might even want to include a glimpse of my peen, just for shock factor."

Ryan chuckles. "Peenie is gonna show his peen? Wow, how meta."

"Meh, it's just skin," Keane says.

"Yeah, *fore*skin," Ryan says, and everyone laughs.

"Do me a favor and show your balls, too," I say to Keane. "You do that, and Mom would *thank* me for only showing my bare ass and simulating graphic fucking on a beach."

"I'll tell my agent to put it in my contract," Keane says. "Just for you."

"Thanks."

"Why'd you agree to do such a racy music video if you're so embarrassed for anyone to see it?" Colby asks.

"I'm not embarrassed for 'anyone' to see it. Just my family. There's no scenario in which I'm dying to have my brothers, sister, and parents watch me roll around naked with a beautiful woman on a beach and pretend to fuck her." I shrug. "Otherwise, I'm fine with it. I mean, it's not my preference to sell my music with my face and ass—I'd have a bag over my head in the video, if I could. Or, hell, there'd be no video at all. But Reed was super pumped on the video concept. He said it's gonna launch us into the stratosphere. So, why wouldn't I give it a shot, if he's that sure? What do I know about music market-ing? Plus, I was a bit of an artistic asshole during the recording process—not willing to pander—and Reed backed me up each and every time there was a difference of artistic opinion with my producer. So, I figured, hey, since the music itself turned out exactly the way I wanted it, I might as well step aside and let Reed do his job on the marketing side of things. If he thinks a scorching hot,

'European-style' music video sex dream porno is gonna sell the shit out of the album—the album I poured my heart and soul into—then I'm gonna trust him and find out if he's right. In a perfect world, there wouldn't even be such a thing as music videos. But that's not the world we live in."

"We live in a visual world," Ryan says. "I think it's good you're letting Reed do what he needs to do."

I shrug. To be honest, I'm not completely sure I made the right call regarding that video. But it's too late to worry about it now. In mere hours, it'll be out in the world, no turning back.

"Hey, look at it this way," Keane says. "If the album bombs, you can always go into porn."

We all laugh, including me.

Ryan lifts his drink. "To Reed selling the shit out of your awesome record, Baby Brother. It's the best thing I've ever heard, and it deserves to conquer the world. If you gotta sell your face—and your ass—to get that record heard, then so be it. Good for you."

"Amen," Colby says. "Get that music out there, Daxy."

"To you, Rock Star," Ryan says. "May you take over the world."

"Yee-boy!" Keane says.

The four of us Morgan boys clink and drink. And, again, I feel light and *right*.

"So, hey, Daxy," Keane says. "I saw you macking down on some chick at Reed's party last night. Did you leave with her?"

"Yeah. Colin put the proverbial sock on the doorknob at our apartment last night, so I took her to a hotel."

"You like her?"

My entire body floods with tingles at the mere thought of Violet... followed immediately by a sensation of longing and loss that physically squeezes my heart. "Yeah," I manage to say. "I like her a lot."

"Who'd Colin leave with?" Keane asks.

"One of Aloha's backup dancers."

"Oh, snap! I saw him with her on the dance floor. She was a cutie."

"Yeah, he was losing his mind about her today. We were both

pretty bummed about the timing of it all." I sigh. "Although, even if I weren't leaving on tour, my girl goes to fashion school in Rhode Island, so I guess it would have been tough, regardless." Oh, my heart. It's aching with yearning for Violet. I can't shake the feeling that she rejected me, even though my brain keeps telling me she did the right thing for both of us. I clear my throat. "It just wasn't good timing. My brain knows that."

Colby looks sympathetic. "And your heart?"

"Not so much."

Ryan groans. "Dude, come on. Now isn't the time for you to be moping about some girl in Rhode Island! Get your head in the game. You're about to have the time of your life."

"Says the guy who pined for his future wife for months after he met her in a bar," Colby says.

"I wasn't twenty-two and about to go on tour with Red Card Riot," Ryan snaps. "At Daxy's age, I was on a tear. And rightfully so, because it's what got me ready to meet my awesome wife years later— and to then be able to know she was The One when I did. I shudder to think how badly I would have fucked things up with Tessa if I'd met her too young, before I understood who I was and what I truly wanted in a woman." He looks at me. "Everything happens when it's supposed to, Dax. Trust me on that. Yeah, I flipped out over Tessa and wanted her on *my* timetable. And look what happened. I tried and tried to connect with her, to no avail, only to find out the universe had other plans."

I really don't want to hear this "everything happens for a reason" pep talk from Ryan right now. I'm aching to see Violet again too damned much for this little speech to do anything but make me want to punch Ryan's face. But, of course, since I'm a non-violent sort of dude, rather than punch my brother, I take a long swig of my vodka and nod weakly.

Ryan lays his tattooed forearms on the table. "Daxy, listen to me. Your Master Yoda. If you're meant to reconnect with this girl from last night, then you will. But only when the *universe* decides it's time. Until then, if you don't go on this tour and have the time of your life and embrace every aspect of this amazing ride—including getting mobbed on the street, if that's what's destined to happen—then I'm gonna track you down in London or Paris or Berlin or wherever the fuck you're moping, and I'm gonna pummel your moody fucking face. Now, get your head in the game and get ready to have the time of your life."

TWELVE
DAX

Ultra Violet Radiation
Burning up my cheeks, lips, heart
Ultra Violet radiation
It's tearing me apart
If I could split myself in two
I'd give half to the world
And the rest to you
Would give anything
For another night with you
Cuz I got a feeling
A girl like you
Comes along once...
Only once
Once in a violet moon

"Hey."

Startled, I close my notebook and look up... and promptly lose my shit. It's *Caleb Baumgarten*. Or C-Bomb, as the world knows him. The tatted, bearded, badass, ripped, sick-as-fuck drummer of Red Card Riot. And he looks even more badass in person than he does onstage and in music videos and on awards shows and in interviews—all of which I've seen, and devoured, like the fanboy I am.

Today, C-Bomb's reddish-blonde hair—which he wears in all sorts of different styles—spikey, Mohawk, shaggy—is shaved down to the nub, like he's a Marine in boot camp. It's a look that's making his prominent beard, and him, look especially badass. Seriously, the dude looks like a stone-cold killer standing before me.

When Fish, Colin, and I boarded this private plane a half hour ago, C-Bomb and the other three guys from Red Card Riot—Dean, Clay, and Emmitt—were engaged in some sort of intense conversation with Reed and a couple other suits at the front of the plane. So, of course, not wanting to bother anyone, we three goats headed to the far back of the plane, got ourselves situated with some whiskey, water, soft blankets, and pillows, and then quietly geeked out among ourselves as the plane taxied down the runway. Five minutes ago, once we reached our cruising altitude, Colin, Fish, and I debated whether we should head to the front of the airplane to introduce ourselves to our idols, or wait a bit longer so we didn't seem overeager and lame. Ultimately, we decided to wait exactly fifteen minutes before heading up front... but, now, a mere *eight* minutes into my timer, Caleb Baumgarten is standing here, greeting us like it's the most natural thing in the world for him to do.

Somehow, Colin, Fish, and I manage to say hello to C-Bomb, the sickest drummer in the universe, without screaming or shedding tears. In fact, I think we're coming across pretty chill.

After I introduce myself, Caleb shakes my hand. "You're the singer, right?"

I nod. "And guitarist."

Fish shakes C-Bomb's hand. "Hi Caleb. I'm Fish. I play bass. But, just between you and me, I think these guys have kept me around more for my sparkling personality than my musicianship."

"Not true," I say. But it's kinda true. Fish is actually a sick-ass bass player. But he's also been my best friend since second grade, and that's far more important to me than his musical contributions. "He's definitely a team player, though," I say. "He originally wanted to play guitar in our band, but he agreed to pick up bass when it became clear that's what we needed."

"Isn't that always the case?" C-Bomb says. "What kid dreams of playing bass in a band? It's either guitar or drums. Speaking of which..." He turns to Colin. "You must be the drummer?"

"Yeah. Colin. Great to meet you, Caleb."

Wow. I gotta say, I'm thoroughly impressed with Colin right now. It's not every day a dude meets his musical idol, and Colin just handled it with big baller energy.

C-Bomb asks us a few questions about our band, and we answer them. I tell him the story of how Reed signed us in Maui, and he says, "Right on. Reed came to one of our shows when we were puppies and signed us on the spot, too. Great feeling, huh?"

Out of nowhere, Colin exhales a loud puff of air, like he's been holding his breath underwater, and blurts, "Caleb, I gotta tell you: you're the sickest drummer out there, man. I can't tell you how many times I've blasted you in my headphones and pounded along with you for hours, determined to one day be able to keep pace with you without missing a single hit."

Fish and I laugh. So much for Colin's big baller energy.

"I appreciate that." C-Bomb grins. "Can you?"

"Huh?"

"Keep up with me?"

Colin chuckles. "Hell no. You're the best. Nobody can keep up with you."

"Colin's actually obsessed with you, C-Bomb," Fish says.

"True," Colin says, apparently not the least bit upset at Fish for outing him.

Fish adds, "At one point early on, he demanded we call him a 'C dash' nickname, in tribute to you."

"Well, *Colin* called it a tribute," I say. "We called it stupid."

Colin laughs. "Yeah, it didn't work out so well. My last name is Beretta, and I was like, 'Call me *C-Ber!*' And they were like, 'Hey, dumbfuck, it works for C-Bomb because his last name is Baumgarten. With your name, it sounds like you're saying *cyber*. Do you want people to think you're a hacker?' And I was like, 'Fuck you, C-Ber is dope!' So then I went to a party and introduced myself as C-Ber to this hot chick and she was like, 'Huh? Are you a hacker?'"

Everyone laughs.

"And I was like, 'No, no, *C-Ber*. Like C-Bomb of Red Card Riot?' And that was it. All she wanted to talk about after that was how hot C-Bomb is and how much she wanted to fuck C-Bomb—which, of course, by implication meant she didn't want to fuck *me*. I was so pissed at you, man. I was like, 'Thanks a lot, C-Bomb, you fucking cockblocker!'"

C-Bomb howls with laughter. I mean the dude really and truly belly laughs. And, just that fast, I know we're gonna get along with this beast of a drummer just fine.

"Believe it or not, 'C-Bomb' started out as a joke," C-Bomb says. "The guys started calling me that in high school to make fun of me for being such a fanboy over the drummer of Rx Bandits. This guy called—"

"C-Gak," the three of us goats say in unison, right along with C-Bomb.

"Oh, you guys know Rx Bandits?"

"Yeah, we love 'em," Colin says. "They're a huge musical influence for us."

"For us, too," C-Bomb says.

"Along with you guys, of course," I add.

"Ever seen Rx live?" C-Bomb asks. "They're one of the best live bands you'll ever see."

"Yeah, we've seen 'em a couple times and they're incredible," I agree. "They're right up there with you guys as far as live performance goes."

"Oh, you've seen RCR live, have you?"

"Twice," Colin, Fish, and I say at the same time.

"In Seattle," I add. "That's where we're from."

"Oh, I love Seattle," C-Bomb says. "Great town."

The conversation continues. We three goats ask questions about RCR's prior tours and albums and hang on C-Bomb's every word.

"What's going on over here?" a new voice asks.

I turn my head and nearly shit my pants. It's Dean Masterson standing before me, the lead singer and guitarist of Red Card Riot, accompanied by Reed Rivers. Holy shit. I've idolized Dean Masterson since age sixteen, since RCR first burst onto the worldwide scene with their smash hit "Shaynee" and instantly made me realize the pop-punk thrashers I'd been writing weren't coming from an honest place. That they were, in fact, a brazen attempt at *portraying* coolness and angst, as opposed to revealing the truth.

I remember the electricity I felt the first time I heard "Shaynee." When I first heard the sound of Dean's wailing, plaintive, *honest* voice on that song, and the tormented weeping of his guitar, I beelined to my bedroom, my guitar in hand, determined to learn it. I sat on my bed until I learned every note and lick of that amazing song, and then proceeded to play the damned thing so many times on a running loop, my parents finally threatened to kick me out of their house if I didn't switch to a different song. So, what did I do? I learned the rest of RCR's debut album and played those songs into the ground, as well.

In retrospect, I wasn't playing RCR's songs to mimic them. I was learning about myself as an artist. Shedding layers of bullshit and self-consciousness. I was transforming.

When I emerged from my one-week obsession with "Shaynee" and RCR's debut, I was a new man. A fearless one who understood who he wanted to be as an artist.

Right after that, I broke the news to Colin and Fish that I wanted our band to go in a new direction. And, to their credit, my two best friends said, "Whatever, Rock Star. Just tell us what you want to play and we're down." A month later, we were no longer Dax Attack, thank God—the stupidest band name in the history of time. We were 22 Goats Smiling at You. A close second for that title. A month later, we'd shortened our name to 22 Goats because Ryan said it sounded like we were a band of pedophiles who played children's parties to scout their next victims, and we never looked back. We started playing garage parties and all-ages clubs and getting a decent following. Bar gigs and festivals followed. A small mini-tour of the Pacific Northwest. And through it all, we were slowly but surely becoming who we were meant to be.

And now, here we are, six years since I first heard "Shaynee," sitting on a private plane with Dean Masterson and Red Card Riot, heading to London to kick off an eight-month world tour with them. And it's all thanks to me hearing Dean's honest voice and guitar on a song that showed me what a "love song" could be in the right hands.

"I've just been sitting here, getting to know our support band a bit," C-Bomb says to Dean. "They're hilarious, man. You're gonna love 'em."

Reed introduces the three of us goats to Dean. We find out Emmitt and Clay are both asleep at the front of the plane, and that they'll surely come back to say hi whenever they wake up.

"Hey, no rush," I say. "We're gonna be together, day in and day out, for months. There'll be plenty of time to get to know each other."

I clamp my mouth shut, realizing I just now sounded like a serial killer grooming his next victim. Fuck! I've got a thousand things I want to blurt to Dean. Questions I want to ask him about his songwriting process. But now isn't the time. Slow and steady, Dax. There's no need to bombard the poor guy on day one and come off like a stalker.

"Hey, did you guys have fun at my party the other night?" Reed asks.

"We had a blast," Colin says. "I wound up hooking up with one of Aloha's backup dancers, and Dax hooked up with an 'intriguing' party crasher."

"And I got stiff-armed by a bitchy model," Fish says brightly, making everyone laugh. "Good times."

Colin addresses C-Bomb and Dean. "Have you guys ever met a particularly amazing girl, right when you had to leave?"

"Of course," C-Bomb says. "That's touring for you. A way of life."

"But have you ever tried to keep it going with someone like that?" Colin asks.

Violet. Her beautiful face just flashed across my mind. Those eyes. That smile. The way she purred when she came.

"Speaking for myself, it's impossible," Dean says. "If you want it to work out with a girl, then you've pretty much gotta bring her on the road with you. At least, for an extended tour. Having a girl waiting for you back home during a world tour never works out, even if she's the best girl in the world."

I can't help thinking, *But what if she incites fireflies in a way nobody else has ever done?*

"I had the best girl in the world when we left on our first tour," Dean continues. "An amazing girl. And I just couldn't keep my head on straight. And I wasn't the only one. When we headed out on our first tour, three of the four of us had serious girlfriends. By the end of the tour, all four of us were single."

But what if the girl isn't just amazing, she's one in a million? Once in a violet moon?

C-Bomb says, "Touring at this level is like nothing you've experienced before, guys. There's no way to explain the craziness. It fucks with your head. Makes you do things you never thought you would. Especially that first tour."

Dean says, "Jesus, that first taste of fame fucks with you. Even the best guys become flaming asshole sex addicts during their first tour."

C-Bomb laughs. "Even Emmitt went off the deep end for a while. Remember that?"

Dean chuckles. "That's right. And so did I. God, during our first tour, I lost my mind. People treat you like a god, day in and out. Nobody calls you on your shit. Everybody wants a piece of you.

People come out of the woodwork. You lose the ability to *connect* with people in a real way for a while." Dean looks at me. "My money's on you to go completely off the rails. At least, at first."

"Me?" I choke out, shocked at being singled out. "Hell no. It won't be me. Put your money on Fish. He's the one chomping at the bit to experience the rock 'n' roll lifestyle. Not me."

"Yeah, but he's not the one baring his ass and simulating fucking in a music video. For the love of fuck, man. Women are gonna lose their minds when they see that thing."

Everyone laughs but me.

"You've already seen the video?" I say.

"I sent it to them a few weeks ago," Reed says, smirking. "Oh, don't turn shy on me now, Golden Boy. It's a little late for that. The video posted to the River Records YouTube channel three hours ago. There's no turning back now. Your ass is hanging out there, literally, for the entire world to see."

C-Bomb says, "It's an amazing video. Brilliant, actually. It's gonna be huge."

Dean says, "Honestly, when Reed said he'd plucked some band called 22 Goats from obscurity to open for us for the whole tour, all four of us were like, 'Who? Huh? *Why?*' This was before you'd shot the video, so Reed sent us a rough cut of the song. What's it called again?"

"'People Like Us,'" Reed replies.

"That's right. So, Reed sent us the song and he was like, 'Guys, trust me. You're gonna wanna be a part of this band's origin story.' So I listened and immediately knew he was right. I mean, wow, that song is *really* good, man. So I was like, 'Okay, maybe this nobody band really *is* gonna take the world by storm, just like Reed keeps saying.'"

I'm dying inside. Did Dean Masterson just say a song *I* wrote is "really good"?

C-Bomb says, "And then Reed sent us a rough cut of the video and we were all like, 'Oh, for the love of fuck. They're not just gonna have a *hit*. These fuckers are gonna have a monster-smash-world-wide-number-*one* hit.'"

Dean says, "So, that's when we were like, 'Yeah, okay. We don't want to look like the pricks who were too stupid or vain to give the boys an opening slot. Count us in.'"

"Hey, however we got here, we're grateful," I say, my heart pounding like crazy.

"Reed mentioned it was you who wrote that song?"

"Yeah," I say.

Dean nods his approval. His blue eyes are blazing. "Much respect. I heard it and instantly wished I'd written it. That hardly ever happens to me. It's my highest compliment."

Holy fucking shit. For a moment, I feel light-headed. But I breathe through it and, finally, choke out, "That means a lot, coming from you. You're a huge inspiration for me, Dean. I admire your artistry so much."

"Thanks," Dean says. He grins. "Well, I'm gonna watch a movie now. Maybe get some sleep. I just wanted to say hi and welcome you to the tour."

We thank him and say our goodbyes, and then Dean and Reed head to the front of the plane. But, to my surprise, C-Bomb hangs back to talk shop with Colin, his counterpart in our band, for a while.

"Dude," Fish whispers to me, settling into his seat next to mine. "What just happened?"

"I don't know," I whisper back. "I'm reeling. How is this is our *life*?"

"I expected them to be dicks to us," Fish whispers. "I've heard horror stories about headliners being total pricks to opening bands, just for the sport of it."

"I've heard the same. But they treated us like bros." I shake my head in awe. "I can't wait to tell Kat. She partied with RCR a couple years ago in Vegas."

"Oh, yeah. I forgot that story. You should tell C-Bomb about that."

"Yeah?"

"Totally."

I wait for C-Bomb and Colin's conversation to reach a lull, and then insert myself. "Hey, Caleb. Fun fact: a few years ago you partied with my big sister, Kat, in Vegas."

"Uh oh. Our friendship is over this fast? Sorry."

"Huh?"

"I slept with her?"

I laugh. "No, no. Our friendship is intact. You just partied with her. Her then-boyfriend, now-husband, is good friends with Reed, so Reed took them to a party he was throwing for you guys in his hotel suite. Apparently, your tour had come through Vegas that night?"

C-Bomb shrugs.

"My sister looks exactly like me, only the very hot female version of me. She said she stomped through Reed's hotel suite, dripping wet in nothing but her bra and underwear?"

C-Bomb laughs, but the look on his face tells me he doesn't remember the party at all, let alone my half-naked sister. "Sorry, doesn't ring a bell," he says. "Which is probably for the best. I wouldn't want to have to worry about you putting arsenic into my vodka during the tour."

"Even if you'd slept with my sister, you wouldn't have to worry about that. There's not enough arsenic in the world for me to poison every guy Kat's slept with."

"Jesus," C-Bomb says, bursting into laughter.

"I'd make that joke if Kat were sitting right here, by the way. In fact, if she were here, she'd make that joke about herself. She's happily married now, but back in the day, my sister made no apologies about her sex life. If she wanted to hook up with someone, she did, the same as any dude. No apologies. No hang-ups. My sister was always really selective, actually. And she could be, because everyone who met her wanted her. But if she wanted to get with a guy, then she did it, without worrying what anyone thought. I've always admired that about her."

"*Admired* her?" C-Bomb says. "That's interesting. I've got a little sister and I'm not nearly as chill as you are about that stuff. Just the thought of some fuckboy getting his hands on her makes me wanna commit murder. In fact, I almost killed a guy once when he grabbed my sister's ass in a bar."

"Oh, well, I'd be right there with you, on the cusp of murder, if some asshole did that to Kat. And so would my three older brothers. But that's different than my sister having sex because she wants to have sex. If she's doing what she wants, then I say, 'Go forth and conquer, sister. Hell yeah.'"

"I'm just *super* protective of my little sister. Like, crazy-protective. No fuckboys allowed. No liars, cheaters, or douches, either. Nobody touches my little sister unless he's gonna treat her right and commit to her. Plus, she's not like your sister. She doesn't sleep around."

Ooph. I hate the subtext of that comment. *She doesn't sleep around.* I can't help feeling like that comment is a slur against not only my sister, but against Violet, too, and any woman who has sex the same way most guys do. The way C-Bomb surely does. As far as I'm concerned, when it comes to sex, what's good for the gander is always good for the goose. But, whatever, I force myself not to defend Kat's honor—and the honor of Violet and all womankind—against this kind of lowkey slut-shaming.

"Is Kat younger or older?" C-Bomb asks.

"She's four years older than me. There's a brother in the middle of us."

"Ah, well, maybe that's the difference," C-Bomb says. "My sister is younger than me. And, not only that, it's just me and her. Our dad was a total prick. So I can't help feeling like it's my job to protect her and take care of her like a father would."

I nod. "Yeah, I respect that. I'm the baby in my family—I've got three older brothers besides Kat. And our dad and mom are still happily married, so I've never felt like I had to step into the shoes of a father figure in that way. I'm protective of my sister, but having three older brothers, two of whom are older than Kat, has probably made me feel less like her protector and more like her confidante."

"Well, there you go. My sister tells me absolutely nothing."

We both laugh.

C-Bomb says, "I'm sure if you asked your two oldest brothers, they'd say they feel similar to the way I do—like they want to pummel any guy who gets near your sister."

"Yeah, I'm sure you're right about that."

He's *not* right about that. When it comes to Kat, Colby and Ryan might be a bit more like C-Bomb than me, especially Ryan, but neither of them is a full-blown caveman like C-Bomb. But whatever. Now isn't the time to call C-Bomb out on his brand of brotherly protectiveness, for obvious reasons.

"Refills, gentlemen?" a flight attendant asks, and everyone in the group answers with some variation of "Hell yes."

Booze gets poured. Snacks get passed out. A few extra pillows and blankets are distributed.

Finally, when everyone is situated, I lift my refilled glass to C-Bomb. "Thanks for being so welcoming to us. We've heard stories of headliners being dicks to openers, so we were ready for anything."

C-Bomb clinks everyone's glasses. "I've been known to be a bit of a dick to newbies on occasion, but only when they cop an attitude. But you guys are humble. I can already tell. And that's particularly cool, given how good you are."

My heart skips a beat. "Thank you."

C-Bomb takes a long slug of his drink. "I'm stoked to have a front row seat to whatever's about to happen to you guys over the next few months. I mean that sincerely." He leans back in his bucket seat and closes his eyes. "Just do me a favor. When you guys get to the top, which I predict you will, don't turn into a bunch of fucking dicks."

THIRTEEN

VIOLET

Right after my plane touches down in Providence, as it's taxiing to the gate, I turn on my phone to see what I've missed during my five-hour flight.

First up, I've got a text from Miranda, attaching a YouTube link with the following message.

> *Miranda: If you're in public, watch this with earbuds and where nobody can peek over your shoulder. NSFW! I know you want to pretend Dax doesn't exist, but something tells me you're going to run across this video, with or without my help, so I wanted to be the one to give you the heads up.*

Of course, I'm dying to watch whatever video Miranda's sending me, especially if it's "not safe for work." But since I'm sitting on a crowded plane and my earbuds are stuffed into my bag, I scroll to the next text. It's from my mom, saying she already misses me. Dutifully, I shoot off a sweet reply and scroll again. The next text in line is from my brother, wishing me safe travels. I tap out a reply to him, wishing him safe travels, too, even though I doubt he'll get it until after he arrives in London.

I scroll again and come upon a text from an unknown number... and when I click on the message, I gasp. It's from that baller dude from the party! *Holy shit.* When Miranda pointed him out and told me who he was, I never thought in a million years I'd get to talk to him that night, let alone that he'd text me three days later. My heart thumping in my ears, I read the guy's text for a second time:

I'd be happy to put you in touch with some people I know in the industry who might assist your efforts to break into costume design after graduation. That's an unconditional offer. Apart from that, though, I'd also love to take you out on a date. I'm in NYC on business frequently. How about I swing by Providence the next time I'm on the East Coast to take you to dinner? Or, if you're willing, I'll fly you to NYC to meet me. Don't feel obligated to say yes to a date to get those professional introductions out of me. One doesn't have anything to do with the other. Say yes to a date only if that's what you sincerely want to do. Cheers.

Whoa. This dude is smooth as silk, which I already knew, based on his reputation. Plus, he's confident and sexy in a way men my own age typically aren't. He certainly filled out his designer suit nicely at the party. We didn't talk long that night—hardly at all—but it was quickly obvious he's charming as hell, in addition to being gorgeous and wildly successful. And he certainly made it plenty clear he's physically attracted to me. His eyes turned into a five-alarm fire when he looked down at my boobs—which he did several times during our brief conversation.

Dax.

Out of nowhere, his beautiful, smiling face sitting across from me in that bathtub leaps into my mind. In particular, the way his gorgeous eyes caught fire whenever they drifted down to my naked boobs at the water line.

I close my eyes and chastise myself. *Stop it, Violet.* Throughout the entire weekend, and then all day during my flight today, I've been consumed with endless thoughts of Dax. His blue eyes blazing at me. The way his hair felt when it brushed against my breasts or thighs. The way his laughter made my entire body vibrate with arousal, yearning... *joy.* The way he made love to my body, so tenderly, with so much care and attentiveness, after I told him my life story. Oh, God, we were magic together! Being with Dax felt like clicking a last jigsaw puzzle piece into place.

But I've got to stop obsessing about him now. He's going to be on tour for the next eight months, during which time he's undoubtedly going to become a *mega* rock star. There's no other possible outcome when a guy who looks like Dax embarks on an eight-month world tour with freaking Red Card Riot. Surely, Dax, as I know him, won't even exist by the time he gets back to L.A. Indeed, the odds are high, like Miranda said, he won't even remember my name.

Passengers around me begin standing and opening overhead bins. I peek out the window of the plane and realize we're parked at our gate.

With a lump in my throat, and without replying to Mr. Big Shot's text, I stuff my phone into my purse and begin pulling my stuff together. Frankly, I'm not sure what I want from that baller dude who invited me on a date, if anything. All I know in this moment is three things: one, Mr. Big Shot is undeniably charismatic and sexy, two, I'm hella flattered he's pursuing me when he could have anyone, literally, and, three, if I don't stop thinking about Dax on a running loop, I'm going to lose my freaking mind... and, almost certainly, wind up with a broken heart.

FOURTEEN

VIOLET

I wheel my carry-on suitcase into my tiny apartment and find my favorite roommate, Trevor, splayed out on the couch, watching a cooking show. I live with three roommates in this loft apartment near campus—two guys and a girl. The girl being the only one of us who doesn't have sex with dudes.

"Hey, baby," Trevor says from the couch. "Welcome home. Come tell me all the things."

I plop myself next to him and tell him about my trip. I begin with a description of the Aloha Carmichael concert and then move on to the raging after-party where I met Dax... which, of course, leads to me to telling Trevor about my big news: *This weekend, I had my first-ever one-night stand.*

"*What?*" Trevor shouts, sitting up. "Our sweet little Violet is finally a trollop like the rest of us?"

"I am. And it was the best night of my life."

Trevor high-fives me and we laugh together.

"Unfortunately, the story ends with a shocking twist," I say. "On Friday morning, I found out Dax's band was leaving today on an eight-month world tour. They're the opener for guess what band?"

Trevor shrugs.

"Trevor. *Guess.*"

Trevor gasps. "No."

"Yes."

"Holy shit! Did you tell Dax?"

"No." I tell Trevor what I told Dax before leaving our hotel room, and he agrees I handled the situation the right way, for Dax's sake and mine. I begin to tell Trevor about the rest of the weekend, not that any of it compares to my amazing night with Dax, but my story is interrupted by a text from Miranda.

Miranda: Have you watched the video yet? CALL ME AFTER YOU WATCH IT.

"Oh, crap," I say to Trevor. "Miranda sent me a video while I was on the plane. I think Dax is in it. She said it's 'not safe for work.'"

"Sounds like my kind of video," Trevor says. "Cue it up."

With Trevor looking on, I click onto Miranda's link... and instantly freak out as the music video for 22 Goats' debut single, "People Like Us," unfolds before my wide eyes:

As the first guitar riff of the song rings out, we're on an airplane packed with bored passengers. As Dax's vocals begin, we see Dax, followed by his two bandmates—all three of them decked out in patterned, tailored, hipster suits—boarding the airplane in slow motion like models walking down a runway in Milan. Dax, in particular, looks scrumptious in the slow-motion shot. His long hair is tied back, showcasing his chiseled features, which are perfectly lit. The cut of his suit shows off his taut, lean frame. His eyes are crazy-blue. In short, he looks like a hundred billion bucks.

Dax takes an aisle seat, and his bandmates take the aisle seats immediately behind him. Across the aisle from Dax, a sexy, buttoned-up young woman in a tight suit and glasses, her hair in a bun, is clacking away on a laptop.

As Dax gets settled, she glances up from her work... and does a double take worthy of a Bugs Bunny cartoon. She reaches across the aisle and touches Dax's arm. He looks at her, smirks, and winks.

And... cut to the cramped bathroom of the airplane, where Dax is fucking the living hell out of the woman as his voice serenades the action with the same raw intensity he's displaying in the scene. Holy hell. Maybe I should feel jealous to see Dax kissing and screwing this woman—whoever she is. But I don't. I'm nothing but turned on. He's absolutely glorious on that screen. Pure sex. Passion. *Need.* The same way he was with me when it was for real. Oh, God, my ovaries hurt.

We see a brief glimpse of a flight attendant bent over one of Dax's bandmates. She's offering him a drink with a sexy wink, while a third bandmate, the lanky guy with shaggy hair and a beard I noticed sitting next to Dax at the party, flirts with a blonde bombshell sitting next to him. The shaggy guy looks out the window and we see an endless aquamarine ocean below.

Suddenly, we're back to Dax and his woman, settling into their seats. Dax's tie is untied. His shirt half unbuttoned. His hair is coming loose. His gorgeous fuck buddy looks even more disheveled— and extremely satisfied. But just as the pair buckles their seatbelts, the plane jolts and the oxygen masks come down...

In a flash, we jump-cut to 22 Goats rocking out, performing their song on a stage with an aquamarine ocean behind them. The guys aren't dressed in suits in this scene, but, rather, in dark, ripped jeans and T-shirts. Dax, in particular, looks like a rock god. He sings, "People like us. We hurt and need and bleed. People like us. Got more than mouths—our souls—to feed."

We cut away from the performance to find Dax and his woman safely lounging on a yellow life raft, just the two of them. They're drifting away from an armada of yellow life rafts in the distance carrying the rest of the plane's passengers. We get a quick glimpse of Dax's two bandmates on their respective rafts, and see them cuddling with the women they flirted with on the plane.

And now we're back to Dax and the boys, clad in jeans and T-shirts, performing their song. Dax sings, "All my life, been looking low and high. Aching to find the ones to call my tribe. But now I know, people like us, baby, there's no group. People like us. There's only two. We're a tribe of two, baby. It's just me and you."

Cut to the beach of a deserted island. Dax and his fuck buddy have landed ashore and crawled out of their life raft, and now they're taking in the jungle paradise before them. They turn to each other and smile, clearly excited they've landed here together.

Without hesitation, the pair starts peeling off their wet clothes, and the next thing you know, they're having sex on the beach. Like, oh my God, that's some sexy fucking. You can't really see anything too clearly... except, wait, scratch that. That was definitely Dax's ass. Holy hell. That's a fine ass. But, otherwise, the scene is a blur of skin and limbs. Lips. Eyes. Sand. Water. Sun. Dax's long, golden hair is free and glorious now. His blue eyes are smoldering. His cheekbones are unreal. And the way he's touching this woman, kissing her, grinding with her... I'm losing my freaking mind.

"This is literally the hottest thing I've ever seen in my life," Trevor declares next to me. "It's better than porn. And just to be clear, by that I mean 'it's better than *gay* porn.' My highest compliment." He chuckles. "Was this what it was like to be with him for real?"

"Better than this. It was like being in a movie, only I could *feel* him."

"Oh, for the love of fuck."

"Hush now," I say, my eyes riveted to the screen. "Please. I want to pretend you're not here, T. No offense."

There's another quick flash of the band's performance. And then Dax and his woman are shown in a montage. They're sleeping together in a makeshift hut, their limbs intertwined. They feed each other fruit in the jungle. They kiss in a waterfall. And through it all, Dax is the star of this thing, not the woman. She's absolutely stunning. Brown skin. Long, black hair. Full, pouty lips. She's utterly spectacular, actually. But she's clearly a prop designed to show off Dax's muscles, tattoos, skin, eyes, lips, and hair. My God, I've got to hand it to this woman. She's doing her job fabulously well, because Dax Morgan looks *literally* like a golden god.

After another performance scene, Dax and his woman are sitting on a beach. He's singing the song to his woman while caressing her face lovingly—the same way he caressed my face lovingly when he made love to me. He's singing to her that she's his tribe of two... just as a ship comes into view in the distance. A close-up of the ship deck reveals a bunch of people partying. Closer still, and we see it's all the people from the airplane, including Dax's two bandmates and their women. But, of course, Dax and his woman look at each other and exchange a look that conveys they're not tempted to signal to the ship. Indeed, they're blissfully happy right where they are.

We head briefly back to Dax and the band, rocking out, and then return to the island story. As the song reaches its last chords, we see Dax opening his woman's legs and kissing her thighs, clearly heading straight for her bull's-eye... *The End.*

"Holy fuck," Trevor says. He looks at me. "I can't believe you fucked him."

I don't reply. I'm too overwhelmed by memories of what Dax said to me about this song to speak. When we were sitting in that bathtub together, Dax stroked my inner thigh under the warm water and said he felt like he wrote his favorite song—"People Like Us"—about *me.* And now that I've heard the song, I know what he meant. He felt like we were a tribe of two, exactly the way I did. I stand up. "I'm gonna head to my room for a bit. I was up early to catch my flight."

"Yeah, I think I'm gonna head to my room, too," Trevor says. "To watch that video on a running loop."

When I get to my room, I do exactly what I'm sure Trevor is doing in his room: I watch Dax and touch myself. It doesn't take long to reach orgasm. When I'm done, I take a hot shower and masturbate again, which isn't at all normal for me.

After I'm done giving myself an orgasm in the shower, I press my forehead against the tile wall and stuff down tears. *You can't have him, Violet. He's off-limits. Forget him.*

Resolve washing over me, I get out of the shower, wrap myself in a towel, and head to my phone. My hair still dripping and my heart pounding, I call Miranda.

"I watched the video."

"And?"

"I'm never going to watch it again, or else I'm going to have a nervous breakdown."

"I get it. I haven't even fucked Dax and I can barely watch that thing without falling in love with him."

My heart squeezes. "Tell me again I did the right thing by sending him off without giving him my number."

"You did the right thing. You really did. At least for now, it's best to leave him alone."

I sigh. "I've got to go. It's been a really long travel day."

"Love you, Vi. Thanks for a great weekend."

"It was the best weekend of my life."

I'm telling the truth. Although, truth be told, my statement has a whole lot more to do with Dax than Miranda.

After Miranda and I say our goodbyes and end our call, I stare at the text from Mr. Big Shot for a long time, and finally tap out a reply.

> **Great to hear from you. I'd love to have dinner with you. I'm game for Providence or NYC. But if you decide to bring me to NYC for our date, please know I'll need a separate hotel room, if I stay overnight. Looking forward to it.**

I stare at my screen for a moment, trying to decide if I should press send. He'll probably think I'm playing coy regarding that separate hotel room thing, but I'm not. Just because I had my first one-night stand with Dax doesn't mean I'm planning to do it again any time soon. Especially not with this guy, whose reputation as a fuck machine precedes him. Yeah, dude, I know about you. Miranda told me the gossip she's heard.

My heart thudding in my chest, I finally press send on my text. And then, just because I'm weak and prone to self-flagellation, I watch Dax's music video again, despite what I said to Miranda about never watching it again. And that makes me touch myself *again*, which is so unlike me, I'm beginning to think maybe I should worry.

Finally, I close my eyes and pull my covers over me and try my best to stop obsessing about Dax—the boy my brain knows I can't have, but my heart wants desperately, in a way it's never wanted anyone before.

FIFTEEN

DAX

It's the goats' first day off in London after four straight days of hard-core rehearsals and all kinds of promo and interviews. Fish and Colin are too hung over from last night's pub-crawl to leave their rooms this morning, so I head down to breakfast in the hotel restaurant.

As I walk through the main doors, I notice C-Bomb sitting in a corner, eating breakfast at a small table by himself. He sees me and motions for me to sit. We talk easily. Make each other laugh. I tell him about Fish and Colin being in the fetal position upstairs and he tells me some wicked fetal-position stories about his own band.

"So, what are you gonna do with your free day?" he asks.

"I've got no concrete plans. I was just gonna wander around London."

"You like the Beatles?"

"'Eleanor Rigby' is one of the greatest songs ever written. Period."

"Come with me, Daxy boy."

An hour later, I'm standing in front of a display case at the British Museum filled with the most amazing thing I've ever seen in my life: an array of handwritten Beatles lyrics, including the sacred words of

"Eleanor Rigby" on a sheet of lined paper. Of course, I freak the fuck out. I mean, Jesus Christ. I feel like I'm seeing the Holy Grail.

C-Bomb laughs at my exuberant reaction. He says, "I remember Dean losing his mind the exact same way the first time he saw this. Somehow, I knew you'd react just like him. You remind me of him. You've got that same 'disdain for fame' vibe going on. I can tell you're all about the music, same as him."

"You're not?"

"I'm here for the music, first and foremost, absolutely. But the rest of it, the perks... hey, those can be lots of fun, too, if you embrace them and don't think too much."

I make a face that says, *Easier said than done.*

"Yeah, I figured 'not thinking too much' would be a tall order for you. Same as Dean. That dude never stops thinking deep thoughts. It's his greatest strength and biggest weakness, all in one."

"Yeah, that about sums it up."

C-Bomb claps my shoulder. "Here's the deal, man. You can't have massive success in this business without massive fame, unless you just wanna be a songwriter behind the scenes. But if you wanna be onstage playing music you created, if you want maximum ears to hear that music, then you're gonna get batshit famous. It's as simple as that. And if you're batshit famous, people are gonna wanna suck your soul *and* your dick. It's just the way it is. So you might as well embrace the good stuff and have fun with it while it lasts. Do that, and you'll save yourself a whole lot of pain."

I don't know how to reply to that, so I don't.

"Come on," he says. "The rest of this place is pretty cool, too."

We wander around the sprawling museum together for the next few hours, interrupted only now and again by RCR fans who recognize C-Bomb, despite his low-slung baseball cap and sunglasses and the jacket covering his iconic tattoos. As we wander, we talk about music, fame, and the music industry. We talk about our musical influences. He tells me a few stories that make it clear he's partied pretty hard at times—which isn't something I've ever done. I'm strictly a booze and weed kind of guy, acid and molly on rare occasions—and I've got no desire to expand my repertoire.

C-Bomb tells me a couple stories that make it seem like he's a bit of a dickhead at times. Like, stupid shit easily pisses him off. Or, maybe, he just gets bored and likes to fight to amuse himself. Who knows? He also tells me some shit that makes it clear he views sex with groupies with indifference. Sometimes, he's in the mood for a little groupie bang, and he goes for it. Sometimes, he's not interested at all, and he heads to his room by himself. To him, it's all about his mood. Same as picking toppings for a pizza.

"The bottom line is you're not gonna fall in love on tour," he says. "The schedule is too grueling, and people don't connect with you like a real person. So you've either gotta bring your girlfriend with you on tour, or you're gonna wind up having sex with fans, at least now and again." He gestures to the next room of the museum. "Are you dying to go in there, or are you good?"

"I'm good," I say. "Thanks for taking me here. It's been cool."

"I love museums," C-Bomb says. "I never went to college. My band got signed when I was eighteen. Our first world tour happened when I was nineteen. So I'm always trying to learn when I can."

He pulls his baseball cap down even lower and we exit the museum. After a few blocks, we're stopped by a group of men and women who recognize Caleb. He does the selfie thing with them and then shocks me by telling them they should get a selfie with me, even though they have no idea who I am. He says to them, "In about a month, you'll be glad you have a photo with this dude. Trust me on that."

After our fan encounter, we walk a few blocks and duck into a nearby pub for some pints. Beer ordered, we sit at a table in the back and continue talking.

"I'm surprised how infrequently you've been bothered by fans today," I say. "I could see people recognizing you all around me, but they pretty much left you alone."

"Yeah, when I wear a hat and sunglasses, people get the message. Plus, I'm just the drummer. I'm not Dean. I swear, that dude can't go anywhere without getting stopped every five seconds."

"But you're the best drummer out there. And you're a hard guy to miss."

C-Bomb puts down his pint. "Yeah, but your average person, someone who's not a diehard fan, needs to see my hair and tattoos to recognize me. Or they need to see me in context, with one of the other guys. I mean, if you were Clay, there'd probably be people at our table right now. And if you were Dean, forget about it. They'd have to shut this pub down. Dean couldn't be here, just hanging out, without a couple bodyguards. But I can walk around, especially with some random guy nobody recognizes, as long as I cover my hair and tatts. If I took off this hat and strutted around like 'Yo, I'm C-Bomb, motherfuckers!' I guarantee there'd be people buying us beers and asking for selfies in three seconds flat."

"Show me," I say.

"Show you what?"

"Take off your hat and jacket and strut around. I wanna see how fast you get recognized. I'll time you."

He rolls his eyes. "Fine. But only because you're the little brother I've never had. Just let me finish my beer first, because the minute I turn into 'C-Bomb,' someone is gonna buy me a drink and I wanna be ready for it when it comes."

He finishes his beer and stands. Takes off his hat and sunglasses and puts them on the table. Finally, he removes his jacket, displaying his most famous tattoo—the letter "C" inside a round, gray, cartoonish bomb with a fuse—and then he winks at me, turns, and struts across the small pub toward the bathrooms.

Three steps. That's how far C-Bomb makes it before a woman pops up from the bar and approaches him. She asks him if he's "that drummer" from Red Card Riot. He says he is. She asks for a selfie and gets it and, soon, he's *swarmed* by people, men and women, all of them wanting selfies.

As all this is going on, the bartender catches my eye and shoots me a look like, *Must be nice to be him.*

I nod, even though I'm honestly thinking, *I wouldn't want to be him.*

I realize I'm in the minority in this world—in our celebrity-obsessed culture—but the whole idea of fame is baffling to me. The idea that some "chosen" people get exalted to godlike status, not out of respect and admiration for their character or good works or talent, but because their faces have become a brand, drives me fucking insane.

Finally, when C-Bomb returns to our table, he's got a new drink for me, as well as for himself, both supplied by a fan, plus four pretty girls in tow. C-Bomb and the women sit down at our table and we begin to chat. An hour later, when C-Bomb and I get up to go, two women rise and flank him—and it's clear they're planning to join C-Bomb back at our nearby hotel. A third woman in the group hugs me goodbye, theoretically, but, as she does, she whispers in my ear that she'd love to come to my room.

"I've got a girlfriend," I say, even though I don't. But the thing is, I'm not all that attracted to her. Plus, I'm pretty drunk, so, even if I were attracted to her, I'm not sure I could get it up right now. More-over, I promised to video chat with my family tonight on this app where we all talk at once like we're *The Brady Bunch.* Also, Violet. I've been thinking about her all day. So much so, the idea of drunk-dialing my family appeals to me more in this moment than hooking up with anyone who isn't my Hitwoman Elvis Disco Momma.

"Okay, well, good luck on your tour," the woman says. "Your girlfriend is a lucky girl."

"Thanks," I say. "Great to meet you, British Girl."

I follow C-Bomb and his new friends to the hotel and into the elevator. I say goodbye to them when I get off on my floor, which is several floors below C-Bomb's gigantic suite on the top floor. And then I stagger drunkenly down the hallway to my tiny room and call my family. I tell them about the past few days of rehearsals. The museum with C-Bomb today. I tell them about the interviews we're going to be doing on BBC radio tomorrow, which, apparently, is a super big deal. And, finally, I tell them I'm tired and gotta go.

"Tired or drunk?" my father says.

"*Yes.*"

Finally, blessedly, I strip off my clothes and sniff my Violet-scented pillowcase and work on a song about Violet called "In This Bathtub." And then, I jerk off, naked, to fantasies of Violet—hey, I guess I *can* get it up!—and, finally, roll over, smash my face into my Violet-scented pillowcase, and pass the fuck out.

SIXTEEN

VIOLET

"Huh?" I say. "I'm sorry, Ashley. I was daydreaming."

"It's okay. I daydream all the time, too," Ashley says.

"What do you daydream about?" I ask.

She looks out the window of her hospital room. "That I'm outside, playing like a normal kid."

I slide my hand in Ashley's. "Aw, honey. You'll be out there in no time, running around and feeling great."

Ashley sighs and absently touches the knit cap covering her bald little head.

Oh, my heart. Every time I do this, it breaks for what these poor kids have to go through, every bit as much as my spirit soars when I get to deliver costumes. It's a constant push and pull of emotions, this thing I do. Honestly, some days, I want to quit, just so I don't have to subject myself to the pain of seeing kids like Ashley, ravaged from cancer. But the desire to quit doesn't last long. If I push through, that feeling is always supplanted, sooner or later, by a thumping need to provide hope and joy, any way I can.

My sketchbook in hand, I ask, "If you were outside right now, what would you do?"

Ashley shrugs her scrawny shoulders. "I'd play with a puppy."

Oh, God. She's so beautiful and innocent. So hopeful. She's been in here for two months straight, her parents said. And she'll likely be in here for a solid month more, due to complications from her treatments. But by the way she's smiling at me right now, just thinking about a puppy, you'd think Ashley's life was all rainbows and unicorns.

Ashley says, "When I get out of here, my mom and dad said they'll get me a puppy. Any one I want."

Emotion rises inside me, but I push it down. I glance at Ashley's parents in the corner of the room. They look emotional. "How wonderful." My eyes are stinging, aching to well up with tears, so I do what I always do in times of stress: I begin drawing on my sketch pad. As I sketch, I ask, "What kind of puppy will you get?"

"Any kind. Just as long as it likes to run and play."

My throat feels like it's closing up, so I take a deep, steadying breath. "What's your favorite color, Ashley?"

"Pink."

I pull out a pink colored pencil and run it lightly over my sketch. "What color should your puppy be?"

"Brown."

"Aw, a brown puppy. Cute." I pull out my brown colored pencil and fill in the puppy shape. "Okay, honey. Now, this is just a rough sketch, just to give you an idea what your superhero hospital gown might look like." I turn my sketch pad around and Ashley "oohs" and "aaahs" and tells me my design is wonderful. I turn my pad toward Ashley's parents in the corner and they gasp.

"So adorable," Ashley's mom says. But it's clear the poor woman is going to cry if she says more, and that Ashley's father is in the same boat, so I turn away from them and focus on Ashley again.

"Can I have it?" Ashley says, gesturing to my drawing.

"Of course. Let me take a quick photo of it so I'll have it as a guide when I make your hospital gown." I take the photo. "What should we call you when you're a superhero?"

"Ashley."

I giggle. "Right. But you know how there's Wonder Woman and Superman? If you were a superhero, what would you be called?"

"Puppy Girl!"

"Perfect." I write the phrase at the top of the drawing and hand it to her. "Okay, Puppy Girl, it's time for me to go, honey. Thanks for hanging out with me for a bit. I'll bring your superhero costume as soon as possible."

Ashley beams a darling smile at me. "Thank you for coming. I had fun."

"Me, too. So much fun."

My heart clanging, I kiss my fingertips and then press them against Ashley's little arm. And then, after hugging Ashley's parents, I briskly exit the room.

In the hallway, I stand in place for a moment, catching my breath. And then I shuffle toward the nurse's desk to turn in my visitor's badge. When I arrive at my destination, I find three nurses huddled together, their backs to me, looking at something on one of their phones.

My breathing hitches. Dax's unmistakable voice is wafting at low volume from the nurses' huddle. I peek over a nurse's shoulder and there's Dax's stunning face as he walks in slow-motion in a hipster suit and tie down an airplane aisle. Dax is singing:

All my life, been looking low and high
Aching to find the ones to call my tribe
But now I know
We're not many, not few
People like us,
Baby, there's only two
It's us against the world, baby
Me and you

"He's so gorgeous," one of the nurses whispers.

"His voice!" the other one says. "It's like he's singing straight to my soul."

"I'm obsessed," the third one says. "I swear I've watched this twenty times."

"Fifty for me," the other one says.

"Can you imagine being that woman?" the first one says.

I clear my throat and the women lurch apart.

"I'm heading out," I say. I slide my visitor's badge onto the counter. "I'll be back next Wednesday. Same as always."

"Thank you so much," one of the nurses says. "The kids always love it when you come."

"I love coming. It makes me feel like I'm helping in a tiny way."

"Oh, you are. You always make everyone smile."

I smile weakly and say goodbye. And then I turn and head down the hall to the elevator.

Oh, God, those lyrics. That face. That *voice*. I miss him. I want him. I can't stop thinking about him, no matter how hard I try. When will this acute ache I feel for Dax ever go away? Or am I going to spend the next eight freaking months feeling like my heart is cracked?

Holding back tears, I ride the elevator down. My chest tight, I stand in the lobby and get bundled up for the chilly weather. My gloves on and neck wrapped in a scarf, I head out and walk the few blocks to the bus stop... And by the time I sit on the bus stop bench, I've got tears streaming down my face. I want Dax so badly... and with each passing day... and each time I'm reminded he's every woman's fantasy, I become more and more wrecked by the growing certainty I'll most likely never get to see him again.

SEVENTEEN

DAX

"Yeah, we've done basically the same stuff as last week," I say. "Rehearsals and promo appearances by day. A little bit of sightseeing when we can squeeze it in. Pubs at night. We don't wanna get over-rehearsed, so we're taking these last couple days off before the first show to relax."

I'm video-chatting with my entire family again. It's the fourth time in twelve days. Yet again, thanks to that nifty app, we're video-chatting, all of us at once, like we're on the opening credits of *The Brady Bunch*.

"Actually, the reason I called is I have some amazing news," I say. I pause for effect, a wide smile splitting my face. "I just found out 'People Like Us' cracked Billboard's Hot 100! We're number ninety-two, baby!"

Predictably, my entire family goes ballistic.

"But the tour hasn't even started yet!" my mom shrieks, clutching her cheeks. "I thought Reed said it would take at least a month!"

"Things are happening way faster than Reed predicted, thanks to that music video going batshit viral."

Oh, God, that video. It's exploded beyond our wildest expectations—which, in turn, meant radio stations started playing the single on heavy rotation, and downloads and streams went through the roof, and promo requests started flooding in. *And then Billboard put us on their chart.*

"I watched the video, even though you told me not to," Mom says.

"*Mom.*"

"I know. I couldn't help it. Even Aunt Jeanie had seen it. I wanted to see what all the fuss was about."

"And?"

She makes an adorable face. "I'm scarred for life."

Everyone laughs, including me.

"It was pretty racy, honey. I mean, you did a great job in it. You're very, very handsome in it. I can see why it put you on the map."

"That was Reed's master plan."

"Yeah, well, it's clear to me Reed Rivers knows exactly what he's doing," Mom says. She smirks. "And so do you, apparently. Good lord, Daxy."

Everyone hoots with laughter.

"Don't worry, Mom," I say. "Reed just scheduled a shoot for the second video during the tour, and I'm definitely keeping my clothes on next time."

"What a novel idea," she says.

"Just forget you ever saw the video, okay, Mom?"

"I already have."

"Ditto," Dad says, and then he makes a face of pure torture that makes everyone laugh.

"Has anyone recognized you yet, Daxy?" Kat asks.

"Yeah, actually. A woman recognized Fish, Colin, and me in a pub the other day. She was about our age, maybe a little older. She came over to where we were sitting and she goes, 'Hey, you're the bloke from that music video!'"

Everyone marvels.

"She did not say 'bloke,'" Ryan says. "That's blatant poetic license."

"Swear to God, she said 'bloke.'"

"So rad," Keane says.

"You're the *bloke*?" Colby says. "Not *blokes*? What about Fish and Colin? Weren't they there, too?"

"Yeah, but she didn't recognize them at first. Just me. But when I told her who they were, she asked for selfies and autographs from them, too. We invited her and her friend to sit down and have a beer with us."

"Wow, that's so rockstar!" Kat says. "Our Rock Star is *actually* a rockstar!"

"Yeah, except for the part where the three of us kept saying, 'Wow! You're the first person to recognize us from the music video! Can we have *your* autograph?'"

Everyone laughs.

"She was really sweet," I say. "We had a great time talking and laughing with her and her friend, comparing our accents and talking about slang and stuff."

"Oh, that sounds fun," Mom says.

"It was."

I'm telling the truth. It was lots of fun. Of course, I'm telling my family the G-rated version of this story. In truth, after the first woman and her friend sat down at our table and chatted us up, we were having so much fun, comparing words and accents and slang, those two wound up calling a couple more friends who came down to the pub, too. And before we knew it, we were having ourselves a genuine party. So much so, I drunkenly texted C-Bomb to get his "arse" down to the pub and he shocked us all by actually showing up twenty minutes later. And not alone, either, but with Clay and Emmitt and four bodyguards. Which, of course, blew the roof off the tiny pub and made us look like such ballers, we couldn't believe it.

At that point, the bartender started blaring Red Card Riot songs —and then "People Like Us"! And then C-Bomb bought drinks for everyone in the entire place, and the place went nuts, like England had just won the World Cup.

A little while after that, we all wound up moving our drunken party to C-Bomb's huge suite at our hotel. And then Fish disappeared with one of the girls from the pub for the rest of the night, which made me so fucking happy, I couldn't stop smiling about it.

We partied like it was 1999 that entire night until the sun came up. Which was a very bad idea, actually, since Fish, Colin, and I had rehearsal that whole next day. But, fuck it. It was worth it. It was our first rockstar moment followed by our first night of genuine rockstar debauchery. I was on such a high by the time the sun came up, just from laughing and having so much fun, I wound up taking this one girl back to my room and fucking her.

It was the first time I'd had sex since Violet. The first girl I'd kissed since Violet. And, goddammit, all it did was make me yearn for Violet all the more. Truth be told, while I fucked that British girl, I felt horribly guilty about it, like I was betraying Violet. And, frankly, that pissed me off. I'm a single dude! And not only that, I'm the one who wanted to keep in touch with Violet! I'm the one who wanted her number! In fact, if I'd had Violet's number that morning, there's no doubt in my mind I would have said goodbye to that British girl, headed to my room, and had drunken FaceTime sex with Violet. I truly believe I would have done that. But the thing is I *didn't* have Violet's number because she refused to give it to me. A fact that's made me crazier and crazier with each passing day.

All I can think is that Violet must not have felt the same fireflies I did, no matter what she said. Or, at least, she didn't feel them as intensely as I did. Because if she had, she never would have been able to say goodbye to me, no matter what. Man, it hurts to admit that to myself—that Violet probably didn't feel the same thing I did. It hurts far more than Julia Fortunato from summer camp ghosting me ever did. But what can I do about it? *Nothing.* So, fuck it, Violet doesn't want me the way I want her? Okay, then, I fucked a British girl. And then proceeded to feel guilty as hell about it, even though there was zero reason for me to feel that way, since I'm a single dude.

And the worst part of all is I felt guilt and remorse for what turned out to be highly mediocre sex! I mean, come on. At least if I was gonna feel like I was doing something against my moral code, let the sex be smoking hot. Let me feel flow. But, nope. It was nothing like sex with Violet. Not even close. With Violet, I reached flow every time we fucked. *Every. Single. Time.* But with that British girl, every minute ticked by in exactly sixty seconds. Sometimes, ninety. There was no magic with her. I felt no butterflies, let alone fireflies. Which is why I came away from the experience feeling almost desperate for Violet. Which, obviously, was the exact opposite result I was going for.

In the big picture, it was a good experience, though. Because it made me realize I'll never be able to recreate that night with Violet—that *feeling*—with someone else, so I shouldn't even try. This is gonna be a long eight months if I keep feeling guilty for doing things a single guy has every right to do. Especially since Violet was the one who rejected me. If I don't figure out a way to move on from Violet, then I'm just gonna be miserable and lonely throughout this entire tour. Maybe even for my whole life. And I don't want to be miserable or lonely. I want to be happy. *I want to have fun.*

And that's why I've officially decided to unplug my body and mind from each other for a while. When I get back to L.A. in eight months, if I'm still thinking about Violet by then, I'll contact her through her friend. Even if she's gonna wind up rejecting me again, I need to find out if she felt fireflies, the same way I did. I just have to know.

But, until then, I'm putting Violet out of my mind, and that's that. I mean, of course, I'm still going to sniff that pillowcase now and again, simply because it gets me off. And, obviously, I'll continue writing songs about Violet, if they come to me, simply because I'd never turn away the muse. And it goes without saying I'll think about Violet every time I jack off, just because she's literally the sexiest creature I can imagine. But, otherwise, I'm going to put Violet out of my mind and stop looking for anyone to touch my soul when they touch my dick. For the next eight months, my soul and dick are gonna be two totally separate things.

"Have you done any more sightseeing?" Mom asks, drawing me out of my thoughts.

"Yeah, a bit." I tell them about a recent trip I made with Fish, Colin, and C-Bomb to Westminster Abbey and Buckingham Palace, and they ooh and aah. Mom asks me if I've seen Harry and Meghan and I tell her the royal family doesn't actually hang out in front of palaces, greeting tourists. For a split-second, I have a fleeting impulse to tell my mom about the Harry and Meghan Christmas ornament I put in the mail to her yesterday—a little something for the Christmas tree I won't be seeing this year. But I bite my tongue. Better to surprise my mother with that little token. Same thing with the "Mind the Gap" T-shirts and onesies I sent along for all my nieces and nephews.

"And how's it going with the guys from Red Card Riot?" Kat asks. "Sounds like you've bonded with C-Bomb. How about the others?"

"They're all great. C-Bomb's the one who hangs out with us the most, though. He's already become a surrogate big brother to me. But last night, I finally got the chance to hang out with Dean Masterson. We talked about music and songwriting, and I somehow kept my cool, at first. But then, unfortunately, when I got a few too many whiskeys in me, I couldn't stop telling him how much he inspires me."

"I'm sure Dean thinks you're adorable," Mom says. She pauses. "Sounds like you've been drinking a lot, honey. Do you think maybe you're overdoing it?"

"Don't worry, Mom. It's just how it is on tour." I'm about to shout "Sex, drugs, and rock 'n' roll, baby!" But I stop myself. *Know your audience, dude.*

"Just watch yourself," Dad says. "You've got a job to do, son."

"I'm well aware," I say. "I promise, I'll keep my head on straight."

"Good boy," Mom says. "We know you will."

"Well, I gotta go, fam. Time for my one-on-one call with Theo before I hit the sack."

I tell everyone they're the ones I love the most, and we say our goodbyes. I call my nephew, Theo, and listen to his latest song. And then, since the guys have been razzing me lately for acting like a hermit-introvert and being a buzzkill, I head downstairs to meet C-Bomb, Clay, Fish, and Colin in the lobby of our hotel, and we five head out into the wet London night to party like rockstars till the break of dawn.

EIGHTEEN

DAX

"You boys ready?" the stage manager says to Colin, Fish, and me from the doorway of the green room, and we nod like it ain't no thang, even though we're all shitting bricks.

After two weeks in London, and a lifetime of dreaming, we're about to walk onstage in the first arena of the tour to play our set for whatever RCR fans happened to have arrived early enough to catch the opening band.

"Ready," the three of us goats reply in unison.

The stage manager smiles. "Follow me."

Before we follow her, Colin, Fish, and I quickly huddle up. We make little goat sounds and put our hands in the middle. "One, two, three, *goats!*" Finally, we follow the woman through the expansive backstage area.

"How full is the arena?" Colin asks the woman as we walk.

"About a quarter full. But don't worry. As the tour progresses, you'll get bigger audiences."

"No need to apologize," Fish says. "Even at a quarter full, this will be the biggest audience we've ever played."

"By far," Colin says.

Colin and Fish chuckle, but I can barely breathe, let alone laugh.

This is it. My lifelong dream—the thing I've wanted since I was two years old—is about to come true. God, I wish my family were here to see me do this.

Violet.

Out of nowhere, she flickers across my brain. What I wouldn't give to have her sitting in the front row tonight, looking up at me as I sing "People Like Us."

We reach the wings of the stage and I peek out. Wow. It looks pretty empty out there. But I don't give a shit. There are humans out there, somewhere. Real people with ears and hearts and souls. They came out tonight to hear Red Card Riot, but they're about to find out 22 Goats isn't the booby prize they're assuming.

The stage manager tells us it's time, and Colin, Fish, and I spontaneously put our hands into the middle again—our way of saying, *All for one, and one for all.*

The lights in the arena dim.

The crowd titters and cheers in anticipation...

I hit my glowing mark on the darkened stage. A roadie hands me my guitar. Colin settles behind the drum kit. Fish gets handed his bass.

I hear the stage manager's voice in my ear monitors. Colin counts us off, exactly as we've rehearsed... Right on cue, the lights above me flash to life and blaze like the sun in my eyes.

I come down hard on the strings of my electric guitar, and, like a match scraping against flint, my soul ignites. I lean into my microphone and begin to sing, and, holy shit, it's *my* voice filling this huge arena. The sick sounds of *my* guitar. Every cell in my body is vibrating like a tuning fork, telling me I'm doing what I was put on this earth to do. I'm channeling the gods right now. *I'm no longer mortal.* I happen to catch sight of some random dude's face in the front row, and by the awed look on it, I can suddenly see my future as well as the microphone in front of my face. *My band is going straight to the top—and I'm never going back to my old life again.*

PART TWO
THE AFTER

NINETEEN

DAX

The room is spinning like that tilt-a-whirl ride at the fair—the one that always made me barf as a kid. I'm sweating profusely. Shaking. If I could, if I had arms, I'd grip the mattress beneath me, just to keep myself from hurtling into the walls and ceiling as the room spins out of control, as the empty booze bottles and glasses and cups strewn everywhere in my hotel suite swirl and crash around me in a violent tornado.

"My arms," I grit out frantically. "Where are my fucking arms?"

"Dax," a voice next to me says urgently. "You've got arms, man. Enough with that 'no arms' shit, okay?"

I turn my head and discover Fish, looking rumpled, lying next to me on top of the bedspread. His shaggy hair is a riot. His eyes are bloodshot. And he's looking at me like I've shredded his last nerve.

Fish says, "You can still play guitar. You're okay. *You have arms.*"

He waggles something in the air in front of me, and when I look down to see what it is, it's attached to my shoulder. An arm. *Attached to me.* I grip my hands and forearms for a long moment, shuddering with relief that they've somehow gotten reattached—until the sudden tilting of the room makes me grip the bedspread so I don't whip off the bed and crash into a wall.

A loud knock in the other room sends shooting pain flashing through my head like a fiery spear. I sit up, shouting that I'll get the door, but Fish hurls himself across my torso, pins me down, and says I'm not going anywhere.

I hear Colin's voice in the other room, urgently greeting someone. I hear the words "birthday party" and "won't stop freaking out." But before I can make out more, a sensation of acute seasickness overtakes me. I feel like I'm on the *Titanic* and it just tilted ninety degrees before going down. I push Fish's lanky body off me without much difficulty and leap out of bed and stagger to the bathroom, inadvertently kicking empty Solo cups and a booze bottle as I go.

When I get to the toilet, I drop to my knees and pray to the porcelain gods. As I hurl, I hear a voice in the bathroom doorway behind me—a voice I know as well as my own. It's my oldest brother, Colby. My Master Yoda. He's saying my name like he's deeply concerned.

Another voice. This one belonging to my second oldest brother, Ryan. He says, "Happy birthday, dumbshit. Mom would be so proud."

I turn around to greet my brothers—to tell them the great news that I have arms again!—and immediately discover my head-swivel was far too ambitious a maneuver for my revolting stomach to bear. With a loud heave, I whirl back around and barf again.

"His *hair*," Ryan says. "Oh, God, pull it back, Bee."

As I groan in agony, I feel Colby's hands pulling my hair away from my mouth and rubbing my back. He whispers, "You're okay, Baby Brother. You've got arms and you're safe. We've got you."

Relief registers throughout my entire body, even as I continue hurling. *Colby.* Now that he's here, I'm gonna be okay. I feel like I'm dying at the moment, true, but I know he'll take care of me, like he always does. And not just because he's a first responder—a firefighter-paramedic in Seattle—but because he's my Colby. The one I love the most.

Colby slides his fingers to my neck and holds them there. "Your heart is racing, Dax. What'd you take?"

But I can only hang my head and barf.

I hear Ryan in the other room, barking orders. He's telling people to clear the fuck out. He's shouting that the birthday party is over. Yelling at Colin to get "this fucking place cleaned up." He's in full-on Ryan the Fixer mode. And, clearly, he's pissed as hell.

"Daxy, answer me," Colby says, his fingers checking my pulse again. "What did you take and when did you take it?"

"She said it was molly, Bee. But molly's never made my arms melt off before."

"Who was she?"

"I don't know. She had the same hair as Violet, and I just wanted it to be her. Why didn't she give me her number, Colby? Why didn't she want me?" I groan loudly. "I just want to feel fireflies again! That's all I want. So, I kissed the girl with the hair and knew right away, she wasn't Violet. Same as the others. Because nobody's ever Violet, not even when they have the hair!" I choke down emotion. "I would have called her every night of the tour, if only she'd given me her fucking number. I would have FaceTimed her, rather than fuck anybody else. It killed me not to track her down. I almost tried on the East Coast. But then I remembered she didn't feel fireflies the way I did." I shudder violently and bow my head. "So I took the pill from the girl with the hair, and then the room started spinning, and my arms melted off, and there were these weird goblins crawling on the ceiling—"

"Tell me what it looked like."

"Dark with bangs. Like Uma Thurman."

"Not the girl's *hair*. What did the *pill* look like?"

"White, like her pantsuit. She was 'Elvis reimagined' and so hot. No, she was *intriguing*."

Colby sighs. "Jesus, Dax. I thought you were smarter than this. Do you have any idea how many times I've had to scrape dead people off the ground after they'd taken a little white pill?"

"She said it was molly."

"Goddammit, Dax. A bunch of kids just dropped dead in New York after taking what they thought was molly."

"I don't need your 'disappointed dad' energy right now, fucker. I think I'm dying and I need to feel happy so my arms stay attached."

Colby sighs. "I'll hold onto your arms so they stay attached, okay? All you need to do is sleep. Ryan? Help me get Daxy into bed."

Ryan mutters something about wanting to pummel me, but he complies. While Colby takes one of my arms—my beautiful arms!—Ryan takes the other and they physically drag me like a paraplegic to the bed, my chin hanging against my chest.

"Are you in L.A. for my birthday?" I mumble.

"The whole family is here for the weekend, remember?" Ryan says. "We're taking you to dinner tonight for your birthday, going to your show tomorrow night, and then attending the wedding on Sunday night."

I can't process any of that. Dinner? Wedding? Huh?

"We'd just landed when Fish called," Colby says. "So Ryan and I ditched the rest of the family at the airport and raced straight here."

I curl into the fetal position on the bed and close my eyes, aching to slip away, but a second later—or has it been an hour?—a female voice jerks me to consciousness. When I open my eyes, I see a middle-aged Asian woman. Very pretty. She introduces herself as a doctor. She takes my vital signs, and asks me a bunch of questions. Finally, she says to Colby, "He's going to be okay. He just needs fluids and sleep."

I close my eyes, intending to fade to black, but a sudden panic wrenches my eyes back open. "Colby?"

He's in the doorway, escorting the doctor out. He turns around. "I'm just going to call Lydia to tell her I'm staying here with you all day."

"Don't leave me."

"Don't worry, Daxy. I'm not going anywhere."

"I'm not going anywhere, either," Ryan says dryly from an armchair in the corner. "Just in case you were wondering."

Panic floods me. "I can't do a family birthday party tonight."

"I've already handled it," Ryan says. "I called Kat and told her the situation. She's telling Mom and Dad you're hung over from too many tequila shots for your birthday."

"Just sleep," Colby says. "Ryan and I will both be here when you wake up. And so will your arms."

I sigh with relief and close my eyes. "Thanks for coming, Master Yodas. I love you the most."

"We love you the most, Daxy," Colby whispers. "Sleep."

I close my eyes. "Will you call Violet's friend with the blonde hair and get Violet's number? I'm finally in L.A. That was our deal. I just had to make it to L.A. She might not want me, but I have to know..." I trail off midsentence as the world fades to black.

TWENTY

DAX

When I wake up, it's the dark of night outside my hotel window. The sheet underneath me is covered in sweat, but, thank God, the room isn't spinning anymore. Oh, and I've most definitely got arms.

Colby is asleep next to me, fully dressed on top of the covers. Ryan's passed out in a chair, his laptop open on his lap. The glowing numbers of the clock on the nightstand tell me it's just after eleven. Which means I've slept literally all day.

I get up and take a piss, gulp down water straight from the faucet, and look at myself in the mirror. I look like roadkill.

When I crawl back into bed, Colby and Ryan are both awake. They ask me how I'm feeling. I tell them I'm feeling human again. Shitty, but human. And hungry as hell.

"You got arms?" Ryan asks.

"Yep." I pat my biceps. "Welcome to the gun show, fuckers."

"Don't get too cocky with those things," Ryan says. "Or I might rip them off your body and use them to beat the living hell out of you for scaring us."

I smile.

He winks.

"I'll order room service," Colby says, picking up the hotel phone.

"Good," Ryan says. "Let Daxy dazzle us with how brilliantly he uses his fancy new arms to shovel food into his mouth." Ryan gets up and drags his chair next to my bed. When he sits again, he leans forward and levels me with an intense blue gaze. "So, here's the deal, Rock Star. The walking-cliché rock-star thing you've been doing for the past several months? It stops now. You wanna drink a bit too much booze and smoke some weed with your buddies, now and again? Godspeed. You're twenty-three, rich as fuck, and everybody's celebrity crush. We get it. But everything else—the kind of shit that makes you think your arms have melted off?—that's firmly off the table from now on."

I roll my eyes. "I don't party nearly as hard as you think. I was celebrating my birthday and the end of the tour last night. It was a special occasion."

Our food order placed, Colby sits on the edge of my bed. "Quit the bullshit, Dax. Are you in trouble or not? If you are, we'll get you help."

"Trouble?"

"Are you addicted to something? Booze? Coke? Something even harder?"

"I'm not addicted to anything. Yeah, I've been partying too much lately. But that's only because there's nothing else to do on tour. And no downtime." I suddenly realize I'm dying to tell my brothers about my insane life. "I've got to be 'on' all the time. Everywhere I go, I'm bombarded with requests for selfies and offers of blowjobs. Fans grab at me—and not just my arms and back—they grab my ass and dick, too, if there's a crowd." I gulp at the air. "And you wouldn't believe how fucked up my body clock is these days. I can't get into any kind of rhythm or sleep pattern, because travel is constant and time zones are fucked up and the hours we keep are crazy. There's never time to recharge. Never time to write. And if there is a moment of peace and quiet, I can't use it to write because I've got horrible writer's block. It's like I need Viagra for my soul. I know Reed wants the second album recorded as soon as possible, but I'm not even close to done with the songs for it yet. But how could I be? It's always people, people, people—"

"Okay, calm down, Daxy," Colby puts his hand on my shoulder. "It's okay."

"I'm just trying to explain why I'm losing my mind lately. It's not because I'm addicted to anything. Nobody could live like this and *not* party. But don't worry. C-Bomb said it happens to everyone at first. He called it 'tour madness.' He said when I get back to real life and a normal schedule, when I'm finally able to shut myself in a quiet room for a week with my guitar, I'll be okay and the writer's block will be cured."

Colby scoffs. "Sorry, but C-Bomb's 'cure' for what ails you ain't gonna cut it. Your Instagram account looks like one nonstop party, and for the past month and a half, you've blown all of us off, even Kat."

I rub my face. "I'm sorry. I've just been overwhelmed."

"You haven't called Theo in weeks, Dax. Do you have any idea how rejected he feels?"

Oh, God. *Theo.* "I'll call him tomorrow."

Colby pauses. He looks like he's gathering himself. Trying to calm his anger. "I made you an appointment with a psychologist for this coming Wednesday—for therapy. It was the first appointment I could get."

"What? No, that's stupid."

"It's not negotiable. Lydia asked around and got a referral to a therapist in L.A. who specializes in celebrities. He told Lydia there are unique pressures related to fame, especially fame that happens quickly. He said he's excited to help you deal with your astronomical success so you can enjoy it without falling apart."

"It's just the wacked-out situation that's been getting to me lately, the fact that I never get any downtime. But I can handle it on my own. Like C-Bomb said, I just need to—"

"Fuck C-Bomb!" Colby bellows, shocking me. "He's in the bubble with you, Dax! He doesn't even know what's fucked up anymore. And he doesn't know you like we do. He doesn't know what you look like when you're actually *happy*. Whether this is 'tour madness' or not, whether C-Bomb says it's normal or not, we're getting you help, even if I have to physically drag you to the psychologist on Wednesday!"

Holy shit. If mellow, even-tempered Colby Morgan is yelling at you, then you know you done fucked up, son.

Colby takes a deep breath. He's visibly trembling. But when he finally speaks, he sounds calm again. "I set an alert on your phone. It's gonna go off in plenty of time to get you to your appointment on Wednesday."

I exhale with annoyance.

"Remember how messed up I was after my accident? I thought I could handle my nightmares and anxiety by myself, but Lydia insisted I see a therapist. And since I trusted her judgment, I went." He grins. "And also because I *really* wanted to get into Lydia's pants."

The three of us chuckle.

"But the point is, therapy really helped me. And I think it's going to help you, too. What do you have to lose? You're obviously miserable, Daxy."

Emotion rises inside me at the look of sincere concern on Colby's face. At the way he just now said *Daxy*. I swallow hard and nod.

"Thank you," Colby says. His broad shoulders relax. "And one more thing: for a full month, you're gonna stay clean and sober."

I roll my eyes. "I'm not addicted to anything."

"Then taking a month off from partying should be a snap for you. If you make it a month without ingesting so much as a beer, then we know you're right about not needing help. But if you can't do it, then I guess you'll have learned something important about yourself, huh? Something that'd be a damned good thing to know."

I throw up my hands. "Fine. If it'll make you happy, I'll be a Boy Scout for the next thirty days. Anything else, Master Yoda, or are we good?"

"We're good," Colby says. "As long as I have your word."

"You have my word."

"And if you can't do it, you'll immediately let me know."

I roll my eyes.

"Oh, quit scowling," Ryan says. "We all know you're secretly thrilled somebody's *finally* calling you on your shit."

I roll my eyes again, even though he's right.

"If you can't make it thirty days, you promise to tell me," Colby says. "Say 'I promise.'"

"I promise."

"Thank you."

I twist my mouth and mutter, "You're right about the calling me on my shit thing."

"Yes, I know," Ryan says.

I sigh. "Actually, you could smoke a Thanksgiving Day turkey up my ass from all the smoke that's been blown up there over the past few months."

My brothers laugh.

"I can only imagine," Ryan says. "You're like one of those skywriters at this point—trailing smoke out your ass everywhere you go."

We all chuckle.

"The other day in a radio interview, I told the stupidest joke—a legit *dad* joke—like, I think I made a pun out of slay and sleigh or something stupid like that—just because I was trying to make Colin and Fish groan in pain—and the woman interviewing us laughed hysterically like I'd said the funniest thing she'd ever heard."

"Holy hell," Ryan says.

"Right? It's shit like that that drives me up a wall. Like, dude, laugh if I'm actually being funny. I'm a vain motherfucker, as much as the next guy. I love getting a laugh. But if I'm not *actually* funny—if I'm lame as shit—then have the decency to roll your eyes at me. *For the love of God.*"

"Send that ass-kisser my way and I'll set her straight," Ryan says. "I'll tell her you're the least funny goat, by far. Not to mention, the least funny Morgan."

"Fuck you. I'm funnier than Colby, at least."

"Like hell you are," Colby says.

"Aw, you know he is," Ryan says. "What I should have said is Dax is the least funny Morgan out of the actually funny Morgans. It's a given he's funnier than you and Dad. You two don't count because you're so *not* funny, you're not even entered in the race."

"Are you high?" Colby says. "I might not be *Keane*-level funny. I grant you that. But I'm *funny*."

"*Keane*-level funny?" Ryan says. "You're implying Keane is the gold standard of funny in our family, not me?"

Colby and I look at Ryan like, *Duh.*

"It's an accepted fact that Keane is the funniest," I say, looking at Ryan. "Then you, Kat, Mom, and me, in that order."

Now it's Ryan's turn to be offended. "Keane's not funnier than me. Peen's problem is he's *too* funny. He never lets up. I, on the other hand, pick my spots. Plus, my humor is way cleverer than Peen's. His idea of funny is leaving a dick-and-balls doodle in some random place for Mom to find, and then telling her it's a rocket at lift-off."

Colby and I laugh, simply because, whenever Keane the Peen does that, it's hysterical. Quickly, our conversation devolves into the three of us reminiscing about the many, *many* times Keane's pulled the dick-and-balls-doodle prank on our darling mother, sometimes with all of us around to watch and laugh.

"Okay, that was a bad example," Ryan says, chuckling. "On second thought, I admit Keane's dick-and-balls doodles are hilarious. But, still, in the big picture, I'm funnier than him."

Colby and I disagree vehemently. Ryan insists, with equal fervor. We argue and laugh and back up our arguments with classic family stories. And through it all, I feel the stress and anxiety I've been wearing like a heavy cloak around me for so long becoming slightly lighter against my shoulders and back.

"Hey, do you guys remember Julia Fortunato?" I ask. "The girl who took my virginity at music camp?"

"And then promptly ghosted you?" Colby says.

"That's the one. Guess what? After eight years of ghosting me, she finally contacted me a couple months ago, out of nowhere."

"You're joking," Colby says.

"Nope."

"Gee, I wonder why she suddenly contacted you," Ryan says caustically. "Could it be your two number ones and two Top 20s?"

"Yeah, my agent called and was like, 'Hey, I got a voicemail from a girl who says she's a blast from your past. Normally, I wouldn't bother you with messages like this, but this one seems legit.'"

"What'd she say in her voicemail?" Colby asks.

Ryan interjects, "'Hi, Dax! Congratulations on your *two* number ones! Let's fuck!'?"

"Yeah, basically. She was like, 'Blah, blah you're so amazing. I've watched the 'People Like Us' video a thousand times and it's obvious you've learned a thing or two since we got together. Let's meet up so you can show me what new stuff you've learned.'"

Colby grimaces, but Ryan laughs.

"Well, damn, points for clarity," Ryan says. "So, did you take her up on her offer?"

"Hell no. I told my agent to call her and say, 'Sorry, I gave Dax your message, but he doesn't remember you.'"

"*Savage*," Ryan says. He hoots with glee.

"The crazy thing is, for years, I had this fantasy I'd see Julia Fortunato again—that I'd fuck her again, but next time, so well, *she'd* be the one begging *me* to stay in touch. I'd tell her, 'Sure, let's keep in touch, Julia'... but then, I'd ghost the hell out of her."

My brothers laugh.

"But the minute my agent told me the 'blast from my past' was Julia, and not this other girl, I felt nothing but disgust and disappointment. No desire to see her at all."

"What other girl?" Colby asks.

"This girl I met right before the tour."

"The one from Reed's party—the one you told us about at your going-away dinner?" Colby asks.

"Yeah, I forgot I'd told you guys about her. Honestly, that's what started my downward spiral. Finding out the 'blast from my past' was Julia and not that other girl."

"Violet?" Colby says.

"Wow. How'd you remember that?"

"I didn't. You kept babbling about her while you were barfing."

"Oh." I sigh wistfully. "*Violet Rhodes*. I haven't stopped thinking about her throughout the tour. If I'm addicted to anything, it's her. Before I got writer's block, I cranked out half an album's worth of songs inspired by her." I exhale a long, tortured breath. "It just sucks, you know? With Violet, I knew for a fact she liked me for *me*. There was never a doubt. But nowadays, all I've got are doubts when I meet someone. I can't help wondering, will I ever meet a hot girl again and know, for sure, she's genuinely into me? Or will I *always* have doubts?"

"Maybe you're not obsessed with this Violet girl so much as the *idea* of her," Ryan says. "Maybe she's become a symbol of what you're missing about your old life."

I consider that for a moment. "No, I'm pretty sure I'm just totally and completely obsessed with Violet." I rub my face. "But who knows? Fuck. I can't even clearly remember her face anymore. It's been so long. Plus, she didn't give me her number, so I might be in this on my own."

Colby says, "You think maybe it would help if you tracked her down, now that you're back?"

"Yeah, I'm already planning to do that, just as soon as I've had a few days to recharge my batteries."

Colby puts out his hand to Ryan, a smirk on his face. "Pay up, fucker. Told you."

Ryan rolls his eyes. "You asked him a leading question."

"So what? He answered it honestly. Pay up."

"What was the bet?" I ask.

Colby says, "After you were so smitten with Violet at your going-away party, I told Ryan, 'I'd bet anything he'll still be hung up on her when he gets back.' And Ryan said, 'No way. Dax is twenty-two and about to become the next big thing. He won't remember her when he gets back.' So, I said, 'A hundred bucks says you're wrong. He's gonna track her down within a month of getting back.'"

"Pay the man, Rum Cake," I say to Ryan. "Violet told me her

friend would be working at River Records by the time I got back from tour. So, I'm gonna go down to Reed's office this week and find the friend. I'd call, but I want to ask her some questions and feel her out. Plus, I need to talk to Reed, so I don't mind going down there in person."

"What do you need to talk to Reed about?" Colby asks. "The new album?"

"Yeah. That, and I just realized the other day I'm homeless now. I need a real estate agent or whatever. Probably an accountant, too. I'm sure Reed can hook me up with whoever."

Ryan whacks me across the shoulder. "Hey, dumbshit. Your real estate agent is sitting right here."

"You? But I thought you were a real estate *broker*. Don't you handle office buildings and stuff?"

"I can handle any kind of real estate transaction. If I were a lowly *agent*, I could only handle residential."

"But you don't even live in L.A."

"I'm licensed in California. I've been looking at L.A. locations for the bar." He's talking about Captain's, the chain of bars that have turned Ryan into a legit baller the past couple years. "You think I'd let some stranger help *my* baby brother find his first house? I won't even make you pay me a commission. That's how much I'm willing to help you."

"Wow. Now that's love."

He winks. "You know I love you the most, kid, even if you annoy me."

"Thanks," I say, even though we both know he's full of shit. As every Morgan knows, Ryan loves Colby the most, by far, followed closely by his love for Kat, and then Keane. Yes, he loves me. The dude would take a bullet for me, without a second thought. *Of course.* The same as I'd do for him. But Ryan understands me the least of anyone, for whatever reason. But, in this moment, the way Ryan's smiling at me, I could actually believe he truly means every word he just said. So, fuck it, I say, "I love you the most, too, Rum Cake."

Ryan says, "I've got a great accountant for you, by the way. And probably anyone else you're gonna need. I'll work on assembling a team for you."

"Thanks, Ry. You're the best."

"You bet."

There's a knock at the door. "Room service!"

Ryan pops up. "Holy hell, it's about time. I was just about to say let's kill the rockstar and eat him for a midnight snack. I'm starving."

TWENTY-ONE

DAX

It's early afternoon in my hotel suite now, an hour before I need to leave for the arena for soundcheck. Colin and Fish were here with my brothers and me earlier, hanging out and checking in, making sure I'm okay and have arms and all that. But Colin and Fish are gone now, and only the three of us Morgan boys remain. At the moment, Ryan is sprawled on the loveseat, researching the L.A. housing market on his laptop while Colby and I sit on the couch, video-chatting with Colby's son, Theo.

"What if you try modulating the key heading into the third chorus?" I say to Theo. And then, by way of explanation, I play him what I mean on my acoustic guitar.

Theo expresses extreme excitement about the idea. But then he surprises me by saying, "Or, I could modulate the key going into the *bridge*. Something like this." He plays what he's thinking on his guitar, and I'll be damned, it's a better idea than mine.

I tell Theo he's a genius, he says he's gotta go work it out, and we end the call.

But when I begin leaning my guitar against the side of the couch, Colby says, "Play us some of your new songs, Rock Star. You said you wrote a bunch at the beginning of the tour, inspired by your girl, right?"

I haven't played my new songs for anyone but Fish and Colin yet. But the idea of playing them for my brothers excites me, even though, admittedly, it makes me nervous, too. But since excitement is far outweighing anything else I'm feeling, I position my guitar, pause to gather myself, and then launch into playing "Hitwoman Elvis Disco Momma."

Much to my relief, my brothers go apeshit for the song. Emboldened, I play them a few others, one after another: "Island Girl," "In This Bathtub," "The Girl with the Dragonfly Tattoo," "Ultra Violet Radiation," and "Fireflies." And, with each new song, my brothers express nothing but extreme enthusiasm. I'm stoked, but not surprised. My brothers have never been a particularly tough audience when it comes to my music, the same as the rest of my family. Plus, I knew while writing this particular batch of songs they were magic, the same way I knew it when I wrote, "People Like Us."

"Are *all* those songs about Violet?" Colby asks. "Even 'Island Girl'?"

I chuckle. "Violet lives in Rhode Island."

Colby and Ryan laugh their asses off about that, and so do I, seeing as how "Island Girl" has a bit of a reggae vibe to it.

"My songs aren't necessarily literal," I say. "Violet's not a hitwoman, either. At least, I hope not."

"Have you written any songs that aren't about Violet?" Ryan asks.

"Yeah. I've got a bunch of random songs having nothing to do with women or sex. A 'rage against the machine' song. A 'why are we here?' song. A song about home. But the very best ones I've written lately—the ones I know for a fact are *magic*—they were all inspired by Violet. I've got this one that's not finished yet that's going to be the best of the bunch when it's done. It's called 'Caught Violet-Handed.' I started writing it and then got sidetracked by other songs. And then I got writer's block before I'd finished it. If I can just get unblocked and finish that one, I think it's a shoo-in to be the lead-off single."

"Couldn't 'Fireflies' be the lead-off?" Colby says. "It's so catchy."

"Same with 'Ultra Violet Radiation,'" Ryan says. "They're all great, but those two were my favorites. Also, that Hitwoman Elvis one is awesome."

"Thanks. I just wish I could get unblocked."

Ryan snickers. "If you play your girl any of those new songs when you track her down next week, I'm sure she'll 'unblock' the living hell out of you, Lionel Richie Style." Ryan's phone buzzes and he looks down. "Josh and Reed are in the lobby, on their way up."

"Josh and *Reed?*"

"They're picking me up for Henn's bachelor party tonight," Ryan says. "Reed's throwing Henn a poker party at his house."

"Didn't you party with Reed in Vegas a few months ago, too?"

"Yeah, unfortunately, partying with Reed on occasion comes with the territory of partying with Josh and Henn."

"You haven't warmed to Reed at all?" I ask. "Josh thinks the world of him."

Ryan scoffs. "I'll never be able to see past the way he salivated over Tessa in Maui. If we lived in a different century, I'd be chal- lenging Reed to a duel."

Colby laughs. "Tessa wasn't even your girlfriend at the time. Dislike the guy all you want because he's cocky or whatever, but I don't think you can fairly hold it against him that he made a play for your wife before she was even your girlfriend."

"Tessa was already mine in Maui. She just didn't know it yet."

Colby and I chuckle.

"All I know is, if I got hit by a bus tomorrow morning, Reed Rivers would be knocking on Tessa's door tomorrow afternoon, offering her a shoulder to cry on." Ryan's upper lip curls. "So, fine, I'll party with the guy now and again because Josh and Henn love him like a brother. But he'll never be a brother of mine."

There's a knock at the door, which Ryan answers, and five seconds later, our brother-in-law, Josh, is striding into the room with none other than Reed Rivers.

After a bit of small talk, Reed notices my acoustic guitar leaning against the couch. "Have you been writing?"

"No, I'm still blocked. I was just playing my brothers a few of the songs I wrote at the beginning of the tour, when things were still flowing."

Reed asks me to play him the songs I've got, but I balk, saying I want to fine-tune them before playing them for the head of my record label.

But Reed insists. "So play me your top two. I was just being polite by asking like you've got a choice in the matter. I own your ass, Golden Boy. Play me some fucking songs."

I exchange a look with Ryan. *Yeah, he's a kind of a dick.* But since Reed is right—he currently owns my ass—and, to be fair, he's a genius at what he does—I dutifully grab my guitar and play him the two songs my brothers said they liked best: "Fireflies" and "Ultra Violet Radiation." And thank God, Reed declares them both future smash hits. Plus, for what it's worth, my brother-in-law, Josh, says he loves the songs, too.

Reed rubs his palms together, his face aglow. "How many new songs you got?"

"Five or six that are totally finished and really good. Four that are finished and highly mediocre. And, thanks to the worst bout of writer's block I've ever had, three unfinished songs, one of which could be the lead-off single, if I ever finish it."

"Sounds like we're set without the unfinished songs," Reed says. "Why don't you come down to my office on Saturday to play me whatever you've got? I'm leaving for New York on Sunday for some business, and I want to get the ball rolling with the team before I go. We're going to release your second album in six months to keep momentum going, and I want the team to get going on promo and artwork and booking the tour dates as soon as possible."

I'm shocked. "You want to send us out on tour again in six months?"

"Six to eight. But as the headliner this time, obviously."

I don't speak.

"The real money is in touring, Dax. You know that." He pauses.

"Why do you look like I just punched you in the balls? You *love* performing."

I'm not sure how to articulate my competing thoughts. Reed is right: I do love performing. With all my heart. That forty-five minutes onstage every other night is what's given me life, more than anything else, these past eight months. And once 22 Goats is the headliner, not the opener, when we're no longer confined to a forty-five-minute set, I'll love performing even more. But, on the other hand, I'm exhausted. So fucking exhausted... And lonely, if I'm being honest, even though I'm constantly surrounded by people. And, oh God, if I'm still blocked six months from now, going into the next tour, I'm gonna have a legit nervous breakdown.

"I just want to make sure the next tour is a more manageable experience for me," I say. "I want things to be more tailored to my personality."

"The tour can be whatever you want it to be. Headliners are gods. You want to bathe in Evian? Fine. You want nothing but green M&Ms in your dressing rooms? No problem."

Colby says, "Reed, I think what Dax wants is more quality-of-life stuff. More downtime between shows. Full days built into the schedule where he's got no commitments and can shut himself away with his guitar and recharge, or hang out with visiting family. Dax is an extroverted introvert, Reed. He loves to perform more than life itself. But he can't be 'on' all the time, day after day, or he starts to crack."

I flash Colby a look of gratitude.

"Did I get that right?" Colby asks me.

"Exactly right."

Colby returns to Reed. "Daxy's been grateful for this tour. He knew going in the goats needed to prove themselves, and he was grateful to get the chance. But if you want him as your headliner, if you want the entire tour resting on his shoulders—because, let's face it, Dax is the reason those arenas are going to sell out—then you need to make damn sure our boy's got the space he needs—physically and mentally—to be at his best at all times."

"Absolutely," Reed says. "Half my artists are sensitive, like Dax. I totally get that personality type. Not all artists can command the kind of schedule you're asking for, because it elongates the tour and increases costs. But for Daxy, we'll structure the tour any way he wants it."

"Thank you," I say.

Ryan pipes in, "You'll also need to get Daxy tighter personal security than he's had on this tour. The way he's groped and clawed is ridiculous, Reed. That shit would start to wear on anyone, but especially a guy like Dax. Even in kindergarten, he felt the need to sit three girls down and tell them to chill the fuck out."

I smile at Ryan, thanking him for jumping in. For being the fixer, as usual. And also for referencing that particular story—a family favorite.

"I admit security was far more focused on Dean's needs this tour than Dax's, and that was a mistake," Reed says. "Dax had security, obviously, but, clearly, it wasn't tight enough for what he needs." He looks at me. "I'll tell Barry to give you his very best guys on the next tour. We'll make sure you've got all the space you need at all times."

"I don't care what color M&Ms are in the dressing rooms," I say. "I just don't want to have a nervous breakdown by the end of the tour. That wouldn't be good for any of us. Reed, I want to make obscene amounts of money for you and me and all of us, for years to come, by creating music I'm proud of. What I don't want to do is sell my soul to the devil to do it."

Reed smiles at me reassuringly, like I'm his golden goose and he doesn't want my feathers getting the least bit ruffled. "I'll talk to your manager and get everything nailed down. You just keep writing me hit songs like those two you just played me, and I promise, Golden Boy, whatever you want, literally, whatever it is, it's perfectly fine by me."

TWENTY-TWO

DAX

When I stride into my dressing room after soundcheck, flanked by Fish, Colin, and two new bodyguards, my family is here, hanging out and enjoying the Mexican food and margaritas my tour manager arranged at my request. When they see me, my family members bombard me with a torrent of hugs and tears and kisses. One by one, as I hug and kiss the ones I love the most, I apologize and grovel, asking for forgiveness for all my recent sins. And, thankfully, no matter which family member I'm talking to, or how I've dropped the ball, forgiveness is always mine.

After a while, my mother's voice, singing the birthday song, cuts through the din in the large room. I turn around to find my mother walking toward me with a cake, its candles ablaze. I make a wish and blow out the candles: *Please, let me track down Violet and feel those fireflies again—and, please, let her feel them, too.* Champagne is poured and distributed in plastic cups, although, given my promise of sobriety, I pass on the bubbly in favor of a bottle of sparkling water.

As cake slices are passed around, the guys from Red Card Riot pop their heads into the room, just to see what all the ruckus is about, and they're met with cheers and hugs and offers of cake and champagne, which they graciously accept.

It's not the first time the RCR guys have met the Morgans. It's actually the third. But both prior times were extremely brief hellos—backstage in New York and Seattle. Plus, my family members were star-struck as fuck on those occasions. This time, though, the vibe feels better to me—more like old friends reuniting than an official meet and greet.

The RCR guys tell my family the best G-rated tour stories, until, finally, it's time for the Morgans to head to their seats in the arena. When the last of them has left, I plop myself down in a sitting area with Fish and Colin and the four RCR guys—the six dudes I've seen every day these past eight months—and we all laugh about my loud and boisterous family.

"Your mom is hot," Clay says.

"Dude, watch yourself," Fish says. "That's what I always used to say when we were kids. And Dax wasn't pleased."

"I wasn't pleased," I confirm.

Fish continues, "Daxy's mom used to come out to the garage while we were rehearsing. Sometimes, she'd bring us sandwiches. Other times, she'd be getting clothes out of the dryer. And whenever she was there, I couldn't play."

"Hard to play bass with a boner," Colin says. "Right, Fish Head?"

"Dude," I say, grimacing.

"Dax finally threatened to beat me up if I said another word about his momma being hot," Fish says. "So, I cleverly transferred my crush to his sister—who, by the way, is the spitting image of her mother, so it was a genius loophole."

Everyone laughs, except me.

"Enough," I say. "No more drooling over my sister or momma, unless you wanna get pummeled."

"You know," Clay says, looking at Fish. "I couldn't help noticing Dax looks exactly like his sister and mother. You think maybe this crush of yours is actually on Dax?"

Fish shrugs. "Quite possibly. I've loved that boy since second grade. Maybe, somewhere deep, my love for him has transferred to his mom and sister, since they've got the working parts I'm wired to desire and also the face I've always loved so much. It's a sound theory, man."

God, I love Fish. The dude is straight. I know this for a fact. But I've always loved the fact that he feels no need to prove it to anyone. The fact that he's just so comfortable in his own skin—and so *not* homophobic—is why these sorts of questions and innuendos over the years have never fazed him.

Fish adds, "Unfortunately, over the years, the entire Morgan family has become my second family, so I can't pop boners for any of 'em anymore. It would just be too weird." He pauses. "Except for Dax's momma. She's still hot to me."

Everyone laughs, including me.

"Speaking of family," C-Bomb says, "my little sister is coming to the show tonight." He looks at us three goats. "And no drooling or popping boners allowed. She's hot, guys, same as Daxy's momma and sister." He winks at Fish conspiratorially. "But she's off-limits."

"I think that goes without saying," Colin says. "We've been on tour with you for eight months, C-Bomb. None of us would ever be stupid enough to make a move on any woman you care about, least of all your sister."

That's for damned sure. Behind C-Bomb's back, Colin, Fish, and I lovingly refer to him as The Caveman. Sometimes, The Hothead. He's the best guy in the world. An awesome mentor and surrogate big brother. But it's one of those situations where it's like, yeah, he's an asshole, but he's *our* beloved asshole. C-Bomb's not shy about being a dick if he thinks you deserve it. Oh, and he has anger management issues. And... he's super protective of his best friends and ready to fight at a moment's notice if he thinks someone is disrespecting them or himself. Turn the other cheek? Not Caleb Baumgarten. Nope. He's just too fixated on protecting the "honor" of the people he loves, whether that's his mother, sister, past girlfriends, or bandmates. I don't know specifics on some of C-Bomb's past bullshit, but the stories he's told about fist fights he's had in his youth always seem to have origin stories in some-body disrespecting someone he cares about, or somebody unwittingly poaching on a romantic interest of C-Bomb's or one of his friends'. But, hey, whatever. Now that I know the moral code C-Bomb lives by—now that all three of us goats do—we know exactly how to stay on his good side, so there's never been, and never will be, a problem.

To my surprise, Fish responds to Caleb's warning by saying, "Sorry, C-Bomb. I make no promises regarding your sister."

C-Bomb lowers his plastic cup and stares at Fish like, *Excuse me?*

Fish continues, "If your sister finds me irresistible, I can't control that. Get in line, sister."

It's a joke only Matthew Fishberger could get away with. And it slays. Everyone, including C-Bomb, laughs and laughs.

Just as our laughter is abating, there's a soft rap on the door, followed by our stage manager sticking her head inside the dressing room. "Hey, goats," she says. "Twenty minute warning."

"Hey, Greta," C-Bomb calls to her. "Can you do me a favor? My little sister just texted me. You know her, right?"

"Of course. I've met her a couple times on the last tours."

"She's standing at the VIP door and the dumbshit guard doesn't recognize her. She says she forgot to bring her ID and the dude thinks she's full of shit. Can you grab her for me and bring her here? I wanna introduce her to the goats."

"No problem, Caleb."

He calls to Greta's back. "And tell that dude guarding the door 'Caleb said fuck you.'"

"Not gonna happen."

When she's gone, C-Bomb leans back in his chair, chuckling. "Wow, our last show of the tour. I gotta say, watching you three goats skyrocket into the stratosphere has been a gas. What a ride."

"And it's all thanks to you guys," I say.

Dean scoffs. "Nobody gets two number ones and two Top 20s off a debut, simply because some other band said to their fans, 'Hey, check these guys out.'"

"Yeah, well, having Red Card Riot's stamp of approval certainly didn't hurt our chances," Fish says.

"As far as we're concerned, you guys are our brothers for life," Colin says.

"Amen," I say.

"Word," Fish adds.

But C-Bomb shakes his head. "You guys captured lightning in a bottle with that album. We were just pumped to be able to light *one* of the matches that *maybe* helped light the fuse to the dynamite."

Dean says, "But the dynamite was of your own creation."

"All we know is you guys have been amazing and we're forever grateful," I say. I raise my water bottle. "To brotherhood."

Bottles of beer and water are raised and clinked... and then Dean asks me something that makes my heart stop.

"Hey, are you down to write a couple songs with me?"

I can barely choke out the word *absolutely* fast enough.

"It's for an indie movie Reed's invested in," Dean says. "He said they need a couple big anthems for the opening and closing credits. Apparently, the movie's set in the seventies, so that ought to be a cool vibe. We can write something really retro for it. I'm thinking super crunchy guitars. Maybe a Hammond organ."

My heart is racing now. "Sounds amazing."

"We'll be writing the songs, but probably won't perform both. Reed said Aloha Carmichael might sing one. You and I will probably sing the second one together, billed as 'RCR featuring Dax Morgan.'"

I look at Fish and Colin, who are so obviously being left out of this invitation, and Colin winks at me, telling me he's cool. "Yeah, sounds good. Just happy to be a part."

"Caleb's coming to my house sometime next week, once we've all had a week to decompress and stop hating each other. Why don't you come with him and the three of us will jam and see what comes of it?"

"Cool."

C-Bomb says, "Do you need a place to stay, Daxy? I heard you telling Emmitt you're homeless, and I've got plenty of room. There's no sense in you staying at a hotel."

I'm electrified. I'm gonna write songs with Dean Masterson and bunk with C-Bomb? Ha! Life made. But seeing as how I've been around the block a few times at this point, I force myself to reply calmly, "Awesome, thanks."

There's a knock on the door behind me, and then a female voice says, "Caleb, your little sister is here."

"Booyah!" Caleb booms, popping off the couch.

I turn around, curious to see this supposedly "hot" little sister of C-Bomb's... the one whose honor he's defended repeatedly... and my heart... physically... stops.

No.

How is this... possible?

C-Bomb's little sister is...

Violet.

TWENTY-THREE

DAX

Violet is gorgeous. Even more so than I remembered.

I feel like my brain is short-circuiting. Physically jerking and jolting and smoking inside my skull. After all the times I've thought about Violet over the past eight months, she's finally here in front of me, in the flesh, instantly inciting fireflies in my belly again. *And it turns out she's C-Bomb's little sister?*

"Hey, sis," C-Bomb says, striding toward her. But then, to my massive relief, he stops short of Violet and embraces the woman standing next to her... a woman I immediately recognize as Violet's strawberry blonde friend from Reed's party.

Every cell in my body shudders with relief. *Oh, thank God.* But wait. *No.* What's happening now? C-Bomb is disengaging from the blonde and moving on to Violet with a wide, lusty smile.

"Holy shit, Vi!" C-Bomb booms. "You look good enough to eat. Come here." He wraps Violet in a fervent hug that makes me want to lurch across the room and physically pry him off her. The hug C-Bomb is giving Violet is different than the one he just gave to the blonde. This hug for Violet isn't about brotherly love. No, this one is dripping with stone-cold *lust*.

"Hey, Caleb," Violet mumbles into his broad shoulder. "It's been a while."

"Way too long."

C-Bomb nuzzles his nose into Violet's hair and pointedly inhales, instantly making me want to rip his head off. *That's my hair to smell, motherfucker.* I'm the one who's been sniffing Violet's pillowcase for the past eight months, for fuck's sake, even though, by the end, I'm pretty sure I was just imagining any trace of her flowery scent.

With one last inhale of Violet's hair, C-Bomb murmurs, "You smell so good, baby. As usual."

My stomach clenches. *Baby? As usual?*

I stare like a sniper at the pair, clenching my jaw and fists in equal measure. *This can't be happening.*

"God, you look good," C-Bomb says, pulling back from their hug.

But he's wrong about that. Violet doesn't look good. She looks amazing. Her dark hair is longer now, and she's dressed like a rocker's wet dream in dark, skin-tight leather pants and a shimmering, purple tank top with a plunging neckline. Why'd she pick that sexy top tonight? To show me what I've been missing out on for the past eight months or to show C-Bomb what he's been missing out on for however long? Did she come to see *me* tonight... or *him?*

"I was actually gonna call you after the tour," C-Bomb says. "And now, here you are. It's fate."

For the first time since Violet walked through the door, she glances at me. When her stormy, blue-gray eyes connect to mine, they say, *I'm sorry. I didn't mean for it to happen like this.*

I want you, I shoot back instantly. Reflexively. I'm letting instinct take over, even though I shouldn't.

Quickly, Violet looks away, her cheeks flushed, as C-Bomb addresses Colin, Fish, and me.

"Guys," C-Bomb says, "this right here is my little sister, Miranda. And this knockout is my ex, Violet." He shoots Violet a wink. "The one that got away."

Violet's already crimson face turns into a five-alarm fire. She steals another brief glance at me, her chin lowered, and mutters, "Caleb. *Please.*"

C-Bomb chuckles and says, "Ladies, this is Fish, Colin, and Dax. But I'm sure you already know that. These three goats haven't been keeping a low-profile these days."

Miranda and Violet say a polite hello to us, and we three goats return the favor.

The RCR guys converge on the girls and conversation ensues.

I watch from twenty yards away, my body shuddering with a riot of physical reactions to Violet's sheer proximity. My heart is exploding, my skin is on fire, my eyes feel magnetically pulled to her. And, most of all, my belly is alive with flapping wings and glowing lights that only this woman, and no other, ignites inside me. Holy fucking Christ. After all the times I've fantasized about Violet, all the songs I've written about her, all the times I've been drawn to women with dark bobs and bangs around the world... finally, when I'd already resolved to track her down in Rhode Island, the girl walks into my dressing room in L.A... *and turns out to be C-Bomb's "one that got away."*

It's a catastrophe. A crisis of epic proportions. Because now that I'm seeing Violet again, there's no doubt in my mind: *I want her.*

For months, out of sheer survival instinct, I've been telling myself Violet was nothing but the right girl on the right night. A symbol. A projection. The sexy girl who played fuck fairy and savior to me on the one night when I needed it most. I told myself I'd turned Violet into something supernatural in my mind, a unicorn she couldn't possibly live up to in reality... But now, seeing her again, I know I didn't exaggerate or misremember her at all. Standing here now, it's clear to me I've been addicted to a drug this whole time. *A drug called Violet.*

Colin has crossed the room and cluelessly joined the conversation with RCR and the girls—because, of course, he never laid eyes on Violet at the party and has no idea about the bomb that just now dropped on me. But Fish knows what's up. He's hanging back in the corner with me, watching the group from afar and shaking his head.

Fish whispers, "That's the 'Fireflies' girl, right?"

"The one and only."

"Please, tell me you're not feeling fireflies again."

"I am. A whole flock of 'em."

"Well, tell 'em to go away."

"I don't think it works like that."

Fish pauses. "This isn't gonna end well, Daxy."

I say nothing. Because I agree: if it turns out Violet wants me—which remains to be seen—then, yeah, this isn't gonna end well.

Fish says, "Well, at least you know now why she wouldn't give you her number the morning after the party. She wasn't rejecting you. She was *protecting* you from The Caveman's wrath."

He's right. Oh my God. Yes. Intense relief washes over me. Violet *did* feel fireflies every bit as much as I did. She was simply protecting me. "Yeah, and she was also probably protecting herself," I whisper to Fish. "She told me her first love went away for his job, cheated on her, and broke her heart. Now I know the guy's 'job' was a world tour. Obviously, she didn't want to put herself through that again."

"Her first *love*?" Fish whispers. "Aw, Daxy. This is bad. You've gotta stay away from this one."

I press my lips together and stare at Violet. I can't fathom staying away from Violet, any more than I can imagine not breathing or eating.

Lyrics.

Hallelujah.

For the first time in months, they're flooding me. My heart thrumming with excitement, I pull out my phone and take furious notes:

You caught me violet-handed, baby
And now I'm drowning in blue
No yellow fever burnin' up my skin
This sickness has a violet hue

. . .

"We'd better join the group," Fish says, forcing me to look up. "If we don't, it's gonna be weird." Without waiting for my reply, Fish grabs my arm and pulls me over to the group.

As we approach, Violet is saying, ". . . indie movie set in the seventies, so the costumes are especially fun. I'm just a lowly assistant on the design team. We're in pre-production now, so I'm only needed for occasional meetings. But in a month, I'll be pretty busy on-set."

"You're a freelancer?" Dean asks.

Violet's eyes flicker to me and then return to Dean. "Yeah. I did an internship my last semester at school, and that led to this job. Hopefully, this job will lead to the next one, and so on. That's how it works in the industry."

"Oh, I'm sure you'll get hired again," C-Bomb says. "They'll know talent when they see it." He winks at Violet, making me want to throttle him, and then says, "So, hey, ladies, we're having a little wrap party in Dean's suite after the show. Come celebrate the end of the tour with us."

"Of course!" Miranda chirps.

But Violet balks. "Oh, I'm going to the children's hospital bright and early tomorrow morning to deliver some superhero costumes. I think I'll head home right after the concert to get some sleep."

C-Bomb scoffs. "You can sleep when you're dead. We all wanna hear more about what you've been up to. Isn't that right, guys?"

The RCR guys dutifully confirm that, yep, they're all dying hear whatever Violet's been up to lately.

C-Bomb turns to Colin, Fish, and me. "You three goats are coming to the wrap-party, right?"

Without hesitation, Colin confirms that, yes, indeed, the three of us wouldn't miss it. And, fuck my life, I don't contradict him, even though I know my family is going to kill me when I don't show up at their hotel right after the show.

Violet doesn't look at me. She smiles at Colin. "Well, okay. I guess if you three goats are going to the party, I'll go for a little while."

I feel Fish stiffening next to me, freaking out about the way this thing is going. But I say nothing. What's there to say? *I want her.*

Caleb pulls out his phone. "I'll text you the suite number and the code for the private elevator. Do you still have the same phone number, baby?"

"No, I got a new one a couple months ago..." Violet's eyes flicker to me. "When I moved to L.A."

My heart lurches. *Violet lives in L.A.?*

Violet returns to C-Bomb. "And please don't call me baby, Caleb. I haven't been your baby in a very long time."

The RCR guys hoot at the burn. Even Caleb looks highly amused by Violet's sassiness. And me? I'm feeling like jumping for joy. *Violet lives in L.A. and she doesn't want Caleb to call her baby!* I look down and smile like a goof. Violet wants me. Every bit as much as I want her.

Miranda says to her brother, "Just text *me* the info, Caleb. Violet will be with me."

C-Bomb smirks. "I'd much rather text it to Violet."

"Yeah, well, life is full of disappointments, Caleb," Violet says, making everyone, including C-Bomb, laugh again. Violet addresses Colin, Fish, and me. "It was great meeting you guys. Have a great show."

Miranda echoes Violet's sentiments, and as she does, she looks directly at me and shoots me a quick, nonverbal apology, the same way Violet did a few moments ago.

I nod my acknowledgment. I don't know how this torturous situation came about tonight—my long-awaited reunion with Violet transpiring with Caleb standing mere feet away—but however it happened, it's clear to me neither of these girls envisioned it playing out quite this way.

The girls start to leave the dressing room to head to their seats, but C-Bomb calls out to them, pausing them in the doorway.

"Come backstage after the goats' set," C-Bomb says. "But come to our dressing room across the hallway, not this one. We'll hang out for a bit before our set. Have a beer."

"Sure thing," Miranda says.

C-Bomb looks at Violet, his features surprisingly earnest.

"There's something I really want to talk to you about tonight, Vi. In private. So, be sure to come."

Violet's cheeks flush. Her chest heaves sharply. She nods stiffly, making C-Bomb smile with relief, but the second he looks away, Violet's eyes flicker straight to me to issue yet another quick apology.

Same as before, I reply to Violet's nonverbal communication with one of my own: *I want you.* I know I shouldn't tell her that. I should tell her shit like, *We shouldn't. We can't. This is a nonstarter.* But, apparently, some things are out of my control. No matter what my brain tells me to do, my heart and body are telling me to get this girl.

Violet looks away from my blazing eyes to say her final goodbyes to the RCR guys and then she and Miranda follow one of the tour assistants out of the room.

The minute the girls are gone, I pull out my phone, my heart pounding:

No gray area, not tickled pink
No black sheep or blue ribbons, too
Yeah, everything is violet now
Everything is you
I want to roll around in a field of flowers,
All of 'em painted a light purple hue
I wanna kiss the sorry out of your eyes
Lick it off your slit and thighs
You've caught me Violet-handed, baby
And now I got them...
Whether I want them or not
I got the thing that's gonna be
My undoing, a catastrophe
I got them white-hot...
Heart beating, skin tingling
Oh, Violet, baby,
The one who got away from me
I got them Violet blues

"It's showtime, goats," our stage manager, Greta, says, appearing in the doorframe.

I stuff my phone back in my pocket and commence the usual pre-show rituals with Colin and Fish. We huddle up, make our usual goat sounds, and then follow all of it up with our usual chant—"one, two, three, *goats!*"

Thanks to my "clean and sober" promise to Colby, we skip our usual three-way tequila shots tonight, and instead head straight to fist-bumps and high-fives. And then, with typical pre-show adrenaline coursing through our veins, we stride toward the door to follow our waiting stage manager.

"Never gets old," Colin says, his voice juiced with excitement.

"This is the forty-five minutes I fucking *live* for," I say, my heart pounding.

"Best job in the world," Fish adds.

Just before we reach the doorway, C-Bomb calls to us, and when we turn around, we find him smiling like a shark.

"I think it goes without saying," C-Bomb says, "but I feel like I should say it, anyway. Everything I said about my sister—about her being off-limits? That goes triple for my ex." His gaze rests squarely on me. "Violet's hot as fuck, I know. But make no mistake about it, gentlemen: *that girl is mine.*"

D ax is supernatural on that stage. A shimmering god. He's
physically glowing up there, and not because of the stage
lights bathing him in supernatural light—but because he's
raw and pure and honest in his performance, so primal and sexy and
gorgeous and true, so *called* to do what he's doing, it's like the man
swallowed a floodlight, set to high.

I thought coming here tonight to see Dax would give me the
closure I've so desperately needed—a chance to finally, after all this
time, move on from this painful, stagnating ache. This physical
craving I can't stop feeling. But, instead, seeing him again in that
dressing room, even with Caleb unexpectedly standing there and
referring to me as "the one that got away,"—holy hell!—and, now,
seeing him on that stage—the only thing I'm feeling is physical
desperation for him. Like I've crawled across miles of cracked,
scorched desert and, finally, blessedly, reached an oasis. I'm an alcoholic who's been clean and sober for eight months and now, in a fit of
desperation and recklessness, has dipped her finger into a glass of
tequila and smeared the golden liquid across her lips.

When Dax finishes his song, everyone in the arena, including
Miranda and me, erupts in enthusiastic applause. Dax thanks the

crowd, takes a drink from his water bottle, and says, "When we three goats started this tour, nobody knew who we were. And now, look at you guys, holding up signs and singing along to every word." He salutes the audience with his water bottle. "We love you so much!"

The place erupts and Dax touches his chest, telling everyone he's feeling the love.

"I wanna give a special shout-out to my family. The Morgans. I love you guys the most!"

The crowd goes wild.

"Since it's our last show of the tour . . . Wow, I can't believe I just said that." He chuckles. "We want to do something extra special for you guys. Do you want to be the first people in the world to hear one of our new songs?"

The arena goes crazy.

"I'll take that as a yes," Dax says. "We haven't rehearsed this one yet. We only just decided to play it for you tonight. But fuck it. Sometimes in life, you gotta do something stupid, just so you don't have regrets later." He looks at his bandmates, briefly, collecting nods, and then, with a sexy little smile aimed at his audience, Dax peels off a guitar riff, leans into his microphone, and begins to sing:

Fireflies
You got me feelin' 'em
Never before or since
All my life
Been chasing butterflies
And in
Just one night
One perfect night . . .
Girl, you made butterflies
Your bitch
Oh, Fireflies
Oh, In your eyes

. . .

I look at Miranda. She mouths, *Oh my God,* and grabs my arm and starts shrieking. But I'm not having it. I swat at her and tell her to pipe down so I can hear every word of the coming verse:

Don't know if you're feeling it
These wings and lights
Or if everything's all in my head
But there's one thing I know
One singular truth:
I need you
I need you
Girl, I need you so bad
Back in my life,
In my bed.

The song barrels into another singalong chorus, and, finally, reaches a passionate, soul-stirring crescendo, at which point the drummer and bass player drop out of the song, leaving Dax all alone on his guitar, his stunning face awash in blue.

His chest heaving and his eyes sparkling, Dax leans into his microphone and delivers his final lyrics intimately, like he's singing them to directly me. Like we're naked in bed together after sex and, now, Dax is singing me a private, heartfelt lullaby:

Fireflies
Fireflies
You got me feelin' 'em
With you
And nobody else
You're a flower
A road
A destination

Would give my soul to the devil
My soul to the devil
To feel
Those
Fireflies
In my belly
Again

Dax stops strumming and drops his head. And the entire arena—everyone except for me, because I can't move—bursts into thunderous applause.

As I teeter in place, shocked and awed, Miranda grabs my arm. "A flower! A road! Oh my God, Violet! He's telling you he doesn't care about Caleb! He's saying he wants you, regardless!"

I crumple into my chair, the enormity of the situation dawning on me. How is this my life? I can't process this. When I left my apartment this evening, I had one actual guy to deal with, plus one fantasy rockstar—a rockstar I'd convinced myself had become completely out of reach to me. And now, in the space of mere hours, I've suddenly got not one, not two, but *three* actual guys to deal with:

One, the guy I've been dating recently. The only *actual* guy I had in my life when I left my apartment tonight. I've tried to want him, told myself to want him, but now I know it's impossible. Now that I've seen Dax again, and heard that song, I know with crystal clarity the guy I've been dating has been nothing but a placeholder—a way to distract my aching, bleeding heart while I've awaited Dax's return from tour.

Two, the guy I used to want, more than anything. My first love who went away and broke my heart, and just now shocked me by calling me "the one that got away" and then dropped the bomb he wants to talk to me, in private, after Dax's set.

And, three . . . ah, my lucky number three. I've got the glorious rock god on that stage. The only man I truly want. The guy who just now told me and this entire freaking arena, in secret code, that he wants me—a flower, a road—as much as I want him. Holy crap, he said he wants me in his bed *and in his life*! Oh, God, I'm losing my mind.

Of course, it's thrilling to hear Dax is still attracted to me, after all this time. Beyond thrilling. But once Dax is able to thoughtfully weigh the consequences of being with me, a girl he spent *one* magical night with months ago, will he really move forward with me? I can't fathom it. Plus, Dax only knows about Caleb at this point. Half the story. Once he finds out the rest, he'll have double the reasons to run for the hills. And, sadly, if I'm being honest with myself, I'll know in my heart that's exactly what he should do.

Go to http://www.laurenrowebooks.com/22-goats-fireflies to hear 22 Goats play Fireflies.

TWENTY-FIVE

DAX

"Why isn't she here yet?" I say to Fish. "My family keeps texting me, telling me to get my ass to Josh and Kat's suite."

"Is your family staying here at this hotel?" Fish asks.

"No." I tell Fish the name of my family's hotel—a ritzy resort across town by the beach. "I told them I have to show my face at the wrap party for a bit, or else the crew will think I'm a dick. But if I don't get over there to hang out with my family in an hour or so, they're gonna hunt me down and beat me. Maybe even drag my ass to rehab."

"*Rehab?*"

I roll my eyes. "They've seen one too many rockstar documentaries, I think."

"Or maybe they've seen the internet," Fish says dryly. "Photos of you partying like a rockstar are everywhere, Daxy. Hate to break it to you."

"Half the time in those photos, I'm just exhausted after a long travel day. Sometimes, the photo caught me blinking or whatever. And then they slap a click-bait headline on there, making me out to be some zombie, and everyone believes it."

"Yeah, I know that and *you* know that. But your family doesn't. Especially not after your arms melted off the other night. They're right to be worried after that crazy shit, Dax. You kind of threw lighter fluid on the 'rockstar cliché' narrative and then lit a match that night."

I mutter curses under my breath.

Fish says, "Just go to your family now, man. Nobody will be pissed if you skip out on the party."

I glare at Fish. He knows full well me not wanting to come off as a dick isn't the reason I haven't left this party yet. It's because I'm physically aching to see Violet again. Because my very molecules *need* to pull Violet aside and find out if she's thinking and feeling what I confessed to thinking and feeling in my song. Unfortunately, though, since I can't very well ask C-Bomb, "Hey, have you heard from your sister or Violet yet? *Are they still coming?*" I've got no choice but to stand here with Fish, sipping my sparkling water and staring at the door to the suite like a puppy awaiting his master.

I glance across the room to peek at C-Bomb. He's playing beer pong with Colin and Clay and a couple guys from the crew. I look C-Bomb up and down, and jealousy surges inside me. God, I hate feeling this way. Jealousy isn't my thing. But ever since C-Bomb hugged Violet like he wanted to sink his cock inside her—ever since he shoved his nose into her hair and *inhaled,* making it clear he wanted to do the same thing while camped between her legs, I can't stop imagining him doing all the things to her *I* want to do. All the things he's obviously already done with her, at some point in the past. Fuck! That's the shit that's making me want to rip Caleb's head and dick clean off his body. Knowing he's tasted her and wants to do it again. I'm not a violent dude, typically. I'm chill. Live and let love. And yet, standing here now, there's no doubt in my mind I'm fully capable of murder, under the right circumstances.

"Dax, you should go," Fish says. "Even if she winds up coming here, this party isn't the place for you to talk to her in private. Not with Caleb here. It won't end well."

"If she shows up, I'll be discreet," I whisper.

"It's not a good idea, man."

"I'll be careful. If I don't talk to her tonight, I'm gonna explode. I've at least gotta tell her I've been thinking about her this whole time."

"You already told her that in the song. The ball's in her court now. Let her make the next move. Clearly, she thinks this party is gonna turn into an episode of *Jerry Springer* if she shows up, so she's staying away. And she's most likely right about that. At least one of you is thinking clearly."

"You think maybe the song scared her off?"

"I think she's in an impossible situation. She can't come here and talk to you with *him* standing there. You know how he is. He's not a 'talk first, hit later' kind of guy. If he finds out about you two, he'll throw you off the balcony and ask questions later."

I glance at C-Bomb, and a wave of primal jealousy crashes into me again. The dude is ripped. Just the thought of him with Violet... Oh, God, I'm driving myself insane. What the fuck did he talk to Violet about earlier tonight, right after our set? I think I can guess. Unfortunately, when I got back to my dressing room after perform-ing, the door to the RCR dressing room was firmly closed. Were they already in there, talking? Or maybe even *kissing*? Or *worse*? There was no way for me to know what was going on in there, short of pressing my ear against the door, which I was tempted to do, but refrained. Somehow, I forced myself to shower in my dressing room and hang out and wait... just in case Violet sneaked in to see me after Red Card Riot went onstage. But, nope, she never came. And now, here I am, staring at the door of this suite, feeling like I've been stood up.

"I'm sure she'll contact you later," Fish says. "There's no way she doesn't want to talk to you after hearing that song."

"I'm not gonna wait around for that to happen. I'm seeing Reed tomorrow at Henn and Hannah's wedding. I'll ask him for Miranda's number then and connect with Violet that way. I can't wait another day."

"And then what?" Fish lowers his voice. "Are you willing to get with Caleb's ex—*after* finding out that's who she is? At Reed's party you didn't know. That was different. If you get with her now, it's gonna be World War III."

My stomach twists. "I just need to talk to her. If something were to happen between us, nobody would have to know about it. We could hook up on the downlow, just to see if the connection is still there. And if not, walk away without anyone the wiser."

Fish scoffs. "Wow, you've already thought this through, huh?"

I don't deny it.

"How ironic is it your family thinks you need rehab for some imaginary coke habit, and all this time, you've just been going through Violet withdrawals."

Lyrics.

Out of nowhere, they're here again.

I pull out my phone, intending to jot them down, but a voice calling my name forces me to look up. The voice belongs to a statuesque woman who's sauntering toward Fish and me. She's got a huge smile on her face like we're besties, but I have no idea who she is.

"It's me! Alexandria!" she says when she reaches us.

She air-kisses Fish and then me, like we're old friends. But, still, I stare blankly.

"Don't you remember me?" she says, laughing. "We partied together at Aloha Carmichael's party last year!"

Fish and I exchange a look of shock. *The star-fucker model.*

Blah, blah, blah, the star-fucker says. She's seen us in this video and that one, on that TV appearance and on such and such awards show. She says she watched our performance on the Billboard Music Awards with some model friends of hers, and told them proudly, "I know those guys! They're the sweetest!"

Fish and I look at each other again. *This girl's on crack.*

She grabs my arm. "Do you still have a girlfriend, Dax?"

"I do. Same one. We're stronger than ever. And she's still the jealous type."

We share a fake laugh.

She links her arm in Fish's, all smiles and flirtation. "And what about you, cutie pie? Have you been snatched up since I last saw you? For my sake, I hope not."

Fish makes an incredulous face. "You're joking."

She leans forward conspiratorially. "I follow you on Instagram. I know you were pulling my leg about being with Colin. You're so funny."

Fish looks pissed. "You're seriously gonna flirt with me *now*, like you didn't flat-out stiff-arm me at Aloha's party... and the only thing that's happened between now and then is that my band hit it big?"

She touches her chest. "I didn't stiff-arm you!"

"Um. Yeah, you did."

"Honey, no. *You rejected me.* You said you were with the drummer."

"*Because you stiff-armed me!*" Fish says. He gathers himself. "Look, you didn't have to slobber all over me at that party. I don't blame you for setting your sights higher than me. Especially back then, because I acted like a desperate idiot. But you certainly didn't have to be *mean* to me. You could have let me down easy. You could have been kind. You didn't have to treat me like a mangy dog."

"A mangy...? Fish, that's crazy. And, regardless, *hello*. I'm flirting with you *now*. That's all that matters, isn't it?"

"No, it's not all that matters. I'm exactly the same dude I was back then. If you thought I was unworthy then, I'm unworthy now. If I was ugly then, I'm ugly now. I'm in the same band. I've got the same friends and I make the same jokes. The only difference now is, for some reason, the world's decided I'm cool. Oh, and I'm loaded now, too. But I'm sure that fact hasn't escaped you."

The woman looks shocked. "Fish, I don't care about money. I was just hoping to get to know you. You're the one who rejected me that night and I've never forgotten it. Not the other way around."

Fish's jaw drops. "Okay, you're either a liar or crazy. But, either way, I want nothing to do with you. And you're absolutely right: it's not because I'm with Colin or any other dude. I do, indeed, like girls. *A lot.* But if there's one thing I've learned about myself these past months, it's that I'll take a genuinely nice, fun girl over a stuck-up, fame-chasing, bitchy model star-fucker, any day of the week. Come on, Dax. I'm done wasting my time here." With that, Fish saunters away like he's got the biggest dick in the room.

"You're my hero," I say when Fish comes to a stand in a far corner.

But, to my surprise, Fish looks bummed, not triumphant. "Was I too dicky to her?"

"What? No! You wielded the perfect amount of dick. Didn't it feel good to say all that to her?"

"Yeah, it felt amazing. But then, the look on her face as I was walking away made me think maybe I overdid it. I'm not used to being mean to girls. They're always mean to me."

I laugh. "Aw, Fish Taco. Don't backtrack now. All you did was tell her the truth."

Fish processes that for a long moment. "God, she's such a star-fucker."

"Yup."

He sighs. "Can I be honest with you?"

"Always."

"I'm sick of them. Star-fuckers. Groupies. I just want a girlfriend. A normal, nice girlfriend who actually likes me. This whole scene is starting to skeeve me out, man. I'm not cut out for it. I don't care if that makes me sound like a geek or whatever. I just want someone who likes me and not my bank account or clout."

I laugh. "What a concept." I clink his beer with my water bottle. "There's nothing geeky about that, brother. It's the truth. And the truth shall set you free. Always."

I reflexively peek at the door again, willing Violet to walk in. *The truth shall set you free.* I'm a firm believer in it. But what's the truth when it comes to Violet? Am I truly willing to destroy my friendship with C-Bomb to get inside that girl again? My body is saying yes, yes, yes to that question. But, of course, my brain is telling me no, no, no. Or, at least, my brain is telling me to slow down and *think* about it carefully. I've always respected the bro code. How many times has

Caleb mentored me? Been an amazing friend? More times than I can count. I mean, fuck! The dude just invited me to live in his house until I find a place to live.

My phone pings and I look down. It's a text from my sister, asking me where the fuck I am.

"I gotta go," I say to Fish. "If, by some miracle, Violet shows up after I'm gone, get her number for me, okay? Or give her mine. Either way, tell her I have to talk to her tonight, no matter what."

"Talk to who?" Colin says, walking up. But the look on his face tells me he knows the answer to his own question.

Before our set, Colin had no idea Violet was the girl from Reed's party, simply because he was off with his dancer by the time I laid eyes on Violet. But Fish and I told Colin the situation right after our set, while we were hanging out in our dressing room. We didn't get a chance to talk about it in detail, however, because, a minute after we dropped the bomb, some "VIPs" were escorted into the dressing room to take photos with us and we had to be "on." Welcome to my life. And then we came to this party with a bunch of crew all around us. So, all right, I guess we're finally gonna hash this out now.

"To Violet," I say evenly, even though I know Colin already knows that's who I was talking about.

"Don't use her name," Fish whispers, glancing around nervously.

Colin crosses his arms over his chest. "And what will you do after you talk to her? What's your big plan, Daxy boy?"

I exhale with exasperation, not sure how to answer the question honestly.

"The drummer still loves her," Colin says, avoiding the use of Caleb's name. "He called her the 'one that got away.'"

"Yes, I heard that."

Without warning, Colin gets into my face. "You sure you heard it? Because I don't think you did."

"Back off, man."

He doesn't back off. "If you heard it, you wouldn't be staring at the front door, waiting for her to show up."

I lean into his face. "Does *she* get a vote? Because I didn't get the impression she was into the drummer. Does that matter?"

"No, it doesn't," Colin yell-whispers. He assesses my face for a long, tense moment. And then he shakes his head. "You're planning to go after her. It's written all over your face. You're doing this, no matter the cost to all of us."

"The cost to '*all of us*'?" I say incredulously. "What the fuck do you have to do with it?"

Colin's dark eyes catch fire. "*Think*, Dax. You fuck her and we all get fucked. Our band has all the same fans as RCR. If there's a public feud between you and him, whose side will they pick—especially if you're the asshole who went after another guy's girl?"

Anger is rising inside me, heating my blood. "She's not his *girl*. She's his *ex*."

"Same fucking thing."

"No, it's not."

"Okay, what about *Reed*, then?"

"*Reed*?"

"RCR is rock royalty. A bigger cash cow than us. If C-Bomb told Reed 'It's us or them,' who do you think he'd pick?"

I roll my eyes. "Reed can't bounce us from his label, just because C-Bomb's decided he hates me for personal reasons. There are contracts to uphold. Big money at stake. There'd be lawsuits if Reed fucked us over like that."

"Don't be naïve. You think any of that would stop Reed from doing whatever the hell he wants to do? Reed's charming as fuck, but never forget he's a shark, man. A Viking. He pillages and plunders. Everyone knows he bounced that one band off his label, even after sinking a ton of money into them, just because their lead singer fucked his girlfriend. I'm sure they had a contract, too."

"But C-Bomb's ex—"

"Don't say names," Fish whispers.

I lower my voice. "But *the drummer's* ex isn't *Reed's* ex, you dumbass. Reed wouldn't give a shit who I fucked, as long as we're churning out hits. In fact, that's what he said to me this morning at the hotel. He was like, 'Just keep writing me hits, and you can have whatever you want.'"

"He didn't mean C-Bomb's girl!" Colin yell-whispers.

"No names!" Fish whispers.

"I'm sure, if asked, Reed would say he did," I say.

Colin exhales. "Okay, then, what about our brotherhood with *the drummer* and the rest of the band? The guy just invited you to stay at his house. And Dean invited you to write songs with him for a movie soundtrack. Do you think Dean Masterson needs you—or anyone else —to help him write two songs? *No*. He could do that all by himself in his sleep. He's spreading the wealth, man. Bringing you into the fold. Being your mentor and *friend*."

My stomach revolts, making me feel instantly nauseated. On this score, Colin is absolutely right. Both C-Bomb and Dean have been fantastic friends to me, personally, and also to our band. If I go after Violet—*assuming C-Bomb were to find out about it*—I'd become C-Bomb's mortal enemy. At least, according to him. And that would necessitate the rest of the RCR guys circling the wagons around him. They'd have no choice, because that's how bands—and brotherhoods —work. *Brotherhood*. Shit. Colin is hitting me where it counts on that front. He knows that's what I value most in this life—loyalty and fidelity to the ones I love the most.

Colin says, "Don't think with your dick, Dax. There are infinite girls in this world, and you can have anyone you want. Literally. So, why go after the drummer's girl?"

I grit my teeth, my blood boiling and my skin hot, and whisper-shout, "*Ex*-girl, whose body language told me she doesn't want him. He doesn't get to *claim* another person unilaterally. She's not his property."

"She's still off-limits and you know it."

I drag my hands over my face, feeling physically desperate. Breathless. *Pissed*. "Colin, listen to me. I concede there are a lot of girls in the world. I know this for a fact because I'm pretty sure I've fucked half of 'em during the tour, trying to recapture what I felt with *her*. But that's exactly why I can't just walk away from this one without at least talking to her. Because nobody else, no matter who they were, or how hot they were, has ever made me feel the way *she* did. The way she *does*. You know the lyrics to the 'Fireflies' song, man. 'Never before or since.' It's the truth."

Colin's fury ignites to a new level. He grunts with his anger. "God, I'm so pissed at you for busting out that goddamned song tonight without telling me the situation. I never would have agreed to play that song if I'd known."

Fish steps in. "We didn't purposely keep you out of the loop. There was no chance to tell you the sitch because Greta was walking with us as we walked to the stage."

My heart is raging in my ears. "At least I had the wherewithal not to play 'Ultra Violet Radiation.' You're welcome, motherfucker."

Colin scoffs. "I'm surprised you were able to think clearly about that, seeing as how your hard-on was drawing all the blood from your brain." He turns to Fish and pushes on his skinny chest. "I'm actually even more pissed at you about playing that song than Dax. I know why *Dax* was stupid enough to want to play it, but what was your excuse for going along with him? What if *the drummer* had watched our set?"

Fish rolls his eyes. "He never watches our set."

"But what if he did, just this once? And what if he listened closely to the lyrics of the song—a flower, a road—and put two and two together?"

"That's a lot of what ifs," Fish says.

"The lyrics are meaningless," I say, "unless you know exactly what you're listening for."

"Oh yeah?" Colin says, his dark eyes flashing with pent-up rage. "Well, what's gonna happen when the song comes out on our second album? Not to mention 'Ultra Violet Radiation' and that other one you've been working on with her name all over it? Are you willing to throw all those new songs in the trash heap or is this shit gonna hit the fan, one way or another down the line?"

"We'll cross that bridge when we get there," I say calmly, but my stomach is suddenly churning almost painfully.

"Whatever," Colin says caustically. He returns to Fish. "Either way, there was no excuse for you going along with him tonight. He's drunk on her, but you had no fucking excuse."

Now it's Fish's turn to explode. "No *excuse?*" he whisper-shouts into Colin's face. "My *excuse* was Dax has been obsessed with this girl for months! Writing songs about her. Chasing girls with the same hairstyle. Craving her like a drug. My *excuse* was that Dax has been miserable for months, Colin, and I care more about him, my *best friend,* than I care about the band or the fame or the money!"

Colin pushes on Fish's scrawny chest, hard, and whisper-shouts, "You think I care more about money and fame than I care about Dax? Well, fuck you, you piece of shit Shaggy motherfucker, if that's what you think of me. *Fuck you.*"

I get between them. "Stop it, guys. Nobody cares about anything more than we care about each other. We're all for one, one for all."

Colin turns on me, looking like a fire-breathing dragon. "That's what I used to think, until you two played a song, and took a risk, without telling me what was going on." He's seething. Furious. Utterly betrayed. "Obviously, you care more about re-fucking a one-night stand than you care about Fish or me or this band."

"Fuck you," I whisper. But my heart is breaking at the accusation. "And watch yourself, motherfucker. This is your last warning."

Colin scoffs. "I get it's your world and we're just living in it, Daxy. And I get that she rocked your world like nobody ever has. But give it a month—or a year or two—and it'll be over. But Fish and I— and, hopefully, our band—will still be here, making history, if you don't fuck it all up. Is it really worth possibly fucking over our band, our dreams, our future, our very friendship for what's probably gonna turn out to be a brief magic carpet ride with some girl's magic pussy?"

Oh, that does it. I can't control myself a second longer. In a frenzy of rage, I grab Colin and furiously push him against the nearby wall. I'm intending to beat the shit out of him, but before I throw the first punch, he pushes back, hard, throwing me off balance. Not hard to do. I suck at fighting and he's stronger than me. We scuffle briefly, before strong arms are suddenly bear-hugging me and peeling Colin off me.

Quickly, I realize it's C-Bomb who's holding me back—a twist I really don't need right now—while Dean holds Colin, and Fish is standing between us, his arms splayed out like he's refereeing a prize fight.

"What the fuck is this?" Dean shouts.

We three goats stare and seethe silently for a long beat.

Finally, Fish says, "We're just having a bit of a disagreement."

"Yeah, I can see that," Dean says.

My breathing is ragged. My skin is hot. I manage to say through clenched teeth, "I think we've got cabin fever after being together for so long."

"What'd he say to piss you off like that?" C-Bomb says to me. And when nobody answers the question, he looks at Dean and says, "It's like watching ourselves, right after our first tour."

Dean nods. "Caleb and I had a doozy of a screaming match after our first tour. Almost turned into fisticuffs."

"Almost?" C-Bomb says. "Dude, I threw a punch."

"Oh, yeah. Good thing you were so drunk, you missed." Dean nudges Colin. "It's always the drummers who are the loosest cannons in every band, huh?"

But Colin doesn't look the least bit amused.

C-Bomb says, "What the hell were you guys fighting about?"

I flash a pained look at Fish. *Say something. Do something. Help me.*

Fish says, "Some issues that have been lowkey bubbling under the surface came to a head. Colin gets tired of everything always being The Dax Show."

"And that's understandable," I interject. "I'm tired of it, too."

Colin visibly softens, ever so slightly.

"Different band, same shit," C-Bomb says, laughing. He looks at Colin. "Dude, listen to me. If it weren't The Dax Show, those videos wouldn't have gone viral like they did, and who knows if those songs would have blown up to high heaven. My advice? Look at all the zeroes in your bank account and get over it."

Colin takes a deep breath. "I've got no problem with The Dax Show. I'm stoked about the success of the band and how we got here. I love and admire Dax." He addresses me. His chest is heaving. His cheeks are flushed. "I shouldn't have said what I did about The Dax Show. That's not how I genuinely feel. And even if I did, Reed told us up front your face was gonna sell a fuck-ton of records for us. We knew what we were getting into from day one, and I'm stoked it's worked out the way it has. Honestly, I've got the best of all worlds. You're the one with the shitty end of the stick, if you ask me. I wouldn't want to trade places with you, if I could."

I swallow hard. "I'm sick of me always being front and center, too. Every bit as much as you are."

"But I'm not sick of it. That concept was all jumbled together with the other thing. But I was out of line in that other thing I said. I shouldn't have said that last thing. Not with those particular words. That was a straight-up dick thing to say."

"What'd you say?" C-Bomb says. "Things are finally getting good."

"Doesn't matter," I say quickly. "It's already forgotten."

"But what'd he say?" C-Bomb persists.

Fish addresses Dean and Caleb, deftly changing the subject. "What did you two fight about after your first tour?"

"Band politics," Dean says, at the same time Caleb says, "Girls."

"*Girls?*" Dean says, sounding genuinely surprised.

"You don't remember?"

Dean shakes his head.

"I said something shitty about Shaynee, and you shot back at me that I'd been an asshole to Violet and she deserved someone better than me. And I snapped."

I shoot Fish a look like, *Fuck my life.*

"Wow, I don't remember that," Dean says. He smiles at the three of us goats. "And that's what's gonna happen for you guys, too: you won't even remember what this fight was about in a couple tours.

Maybe even a couple hours. So, my advice to you is skip ahead to the part where you don't remember. You three are riding a rocket to the moon right now—having the kind of success most bands could only dream of in their wildest dreams. Don't let petty bullshit or jealousy or girls or anything else fuck it up. Ride this wave all the way to the moon for years to come."

Colin nods. So do I. And Fish breathes a huge sigh of relief.

"Now isn't that better?" C-Bomb says. "Smiling goats, yet again. Now make your stupid little goat sounds as a peace offering."

We all tell him no, not now, we only do that before shows, but he insists. So, finally, Fish makes the softest of goat sounds to get us started, a ridiculous little "maaah" that makes us all chuckle, despite ourselves, and Colin and I begrudgingly follow suit.

"Now bro-hug," C-Bomb commands.

Exhaling, we do it.

"There. Catastrophe averted," Dean says, clapping his hands together. "You're welcome."

C-Bomb whacks my shoulder. "Now, come with me, Golden Boy. I've got a catastrophe of my own I need to avert, and Dean is too sick of hearing me talk about it to be of any use to me. Come on. Let's smoke a blunt on the veranda and talk."

"I've actually gotta meet my family..."

But it's no use. C-Bomb is already gone.

Fuck.

I flash Colin and Fish a look that says, *Help me,* tap out a quick text to my sister to tell her I'm coming soon, I swear, and then drag my sorry ass to the veranda.

TWENTY-SIX

DAX

C-Bomb offers a lit blunt to me.

"No, thanks. I promised my brother I'd be clean and sober for a full month."

C-Bomb looks aghast. "*Why?*"

"My family is convinced I'm the second coming of Ozzy Osbourne, circa 1982. Or that I'm well on my way. I've got thirty days to prove them right or wrong. And myself."

C-Bomb leans over the railing of the veranda and inhales from his joint again. "Well, your family might have a valid point about the Ozzy thing. Wasn't it you who bit the head off a bat during your show in Philly?"

"I think that was a protein bar."

We both laugh.

C-Bomb takes a long suck off the joint again. "So, how's clean and sober living going, so far? Are you a new man, Mr. Morgan?"

"Absolutely. It's changed my life in every conceivable way, top to bottom. I mean, sure, it's only been thirty-six hours, but..."

Again, we laugh.

But even as I laugh with C-Bomb—or, rather, *pretend* to laugh— my mind is racing. What the fuck does he want to talk to me about on this balcony? What did he say to Violet when they talked in private after my set? How did she react? And, most importantly, did C-Bomb invite me out here to talk—or throw me off the balcony?

C-Bomb looks out at the twinkling lights of Beverly Hills for a long beat. Finally, he says, "Tonight I told Violet I still love her. That I'm ready to commit to her and only her." He puts the blunt between his lips, inhales, and speaks on his exhale, "And she said no, thanks."

My heart leaps. But, somehow, I manage to say, "Wow."

He looks out into the night for a long, unsettling beat. "I always assumed Violet would be there waiting for me when I finally pulled my head out of my ass. Yeah, I knew she was dating now and again, but I always figured those guys, whoever they were, were place-holders—a way to keep herself busy while she waited for me to figure my shit out. But it turns out I was wrong." He runs his hand through his mop of reddish-blonde hair. "I think that's what's torturing me the most. That there could possibly be some guy out there, some normal, boring guy she actually wants more than me. How could that be? We were *epic*. And she wants *him,* whoever he is?"

I feel physically ill. Like I'm either gonna barf or crap my pants. "She told you she's... seeing someone?"

"I asked her if she was with someone else, and she said, 'It doesn't matter. I wouldn't want to start up with you again, even if I wasn't.' So, of course, I was like, 'I'll take that as a yes.' And she got all flustered and pissed and said, 'It's none of your business. You're missing my point. *I don't want you, regardless.*' But she didn't say, 'No, I'm not seeing someone else, Caleb,' which would have been an easy thing to say, if it were the truth."

My head is spinning. My heart racing. Did Violet hear "Fireflies" tonight, right before talking to Caleb, and decide, right then and there, to give me a shot? That's what the song asked her to do, after all —to return to my bed and my life. Would Violet have said yes to Caleb, if it weren't for me singing that song? Oh, God, my head feels like it's going to explode.

Caleb stubs out the remnants of his joint on the metal railing.

"All I can think is it's gotta be someone I know. Otherwise, she'd just tell me about him."

My heart stops. *Holy shit.*

Caleb sighs and leans over the railing again. He's silent for a long, tense moment before saying, "I really fucked up, man. That girl loved me. Like, for *real.* She loved Caleb. Not C-Bomb. She wanted me before all the fame and money. She wanted me for *me.*" He grunts. "And I threw it all away."

I lower my head to hide the look of anguish that's surely over-taking my features. *This. Is. Fucking. Excruciating.*

C-Bomb continues, "The worst part is that I'm a day late and a dollar short. She told me, 'If you'd said these things to me a year ago, I would have said yes. But things are different now. *I'm* different. I've moved on. And so should you.'"

"Wow," I say lamely, my heart exploding. "That's..." I don't complete the sentence, probably because, the only word coming to my mind is: *fantastic.*

Caleb hangs his head for another long moment. But when he lifts it again, there's fire in his eyes. "You know what? *Fuck that.* If she wanted me a year ago, then I can make her want me again. Whoever the new guy is, he can't compete with me. Nobody can." He beats on his hard chest and his green eyes ignite. "I'm *me,* man. A beast. When I want something, *I get it.*"

Not this time, Caleb. You're not even close to the right guy for her. The right guy for her is me.

"She just wants me to fight for her!" He straightens up. "She wants me to prove I've genuinely changed."

Caleb looks at me like he's expecting me to say something. But that's not gonna happen. My brain is melting. Should I confess my sins, right here and now? Because no part of me wants to do that. Should I encourage him? Because I don't want to do that, either. I open and close my mouth, but nothing comes out. *This is a nightmare.*

Apparently, my silence doesn't register with C-Bomb. He's a new man. His face aglow, he claps my shoulder. "Thanks, Daxy boy. I really needed to talk this through with someone I trust and Dean would have thrown a punch if I'd mentioned Violet's name again." He takes a deep, cleansing breath in the night air. "You know what? I feel good. I've got clarity. I know what I want, and I'm gonna go after it. All I have to do is worm my way back into her life, slowly but surely, until the time is right to... *pounce.*"

He raises his fist and I jerk back, thinking he's going to hit me. But when I realize he's only expecting me to bump his fist with mine, I do it reflexively, even though the last thing in the world I want to do is give Caleb the slightest encouragement.

Chuckling, Caleb says, "You're a damned good listener, Daxy Morgan. And a damned good friend. Thanks."

TWENTY-SEVEN

DAX

When I walk onto Reed's twinkling patio for Henn and Hannah's wedding, the same patio where I kissed Violet all those months ago, the ceremony is already underway. There are about seventy-five guests here, I'd estimate, based on the rows of chairs. I spot my family in the second-to-last row and slide into a seat between my mother and Colby.

As I take my chair, my mother pokes my thigh with an angry index finger and glares at me for being late.

Sorry, I mouth. I motion like I'm playing guitar and she rolls her eyes. She knows exactly what that gesture means: I got caught up writing a song and lost track of time. It's not the first time. And, surely, it won't be the last.

I turn my attention toward the ceremony at the far end of the patio, where the bride, Hannah, is in the midst of saying her vows to her besotted groom, Henn. To Hannah's left, her three bridesmaids—my sister, Kat, Kat's best friend, Sarah, and the bride's sister, Maddy—the cutie who's now wearing Keane's engagement ring—are all clad in dark blue mix-and-match dresses. Henn, for his part, is accompanied by his three groomsmen—Reed Rivers, my brother-in-law, Josh Faraday, and Josh's twin brother, Jonas—all dressed in sharp dark suits. Every last person up there is wearing happy smiles, blissfully unaware I'm sitting in the second to last row, imploding.

After bailing on the wrap party last night, Violet hasn't contacted me. And since I don't have her phone number, I haven't been able to do anything about it. I swear, the minute this ceremony is over, I'm going to pull Reed aside and get Miranda's phone number. Not sure what I'll say to Reed to make my request seem innocuous, what bullshit I'll spew to keep Reed from telling C-Bomb I'm apparently planning to hit on C-Bomb's little sister. But I'll figure it out.

The bride's voice draws my attention back to the ceremony. Hannah is looking at Henn, saying, ". . . and that's the precise moment I knew you were the perfect man for me."

Everyone around me chuckles at whatever humorous thing Hannah just said. But, of course, the joke is lost on my wandering brain.

"You're my best friend, Henny," Hannah continues, her eyes and hands locked with her groom's. "My Prince Charming. I promise to love and cherish you. To be the best wife and friend I can be to you, forever."

Henn visibly vibrates with joy and everyone swoons and chuckles at his reaction.

As Henn begins saying his vows, my gaze drifts to the far corner of the patio, to the spot where I sat with Violet eight months ago. Instantly, my mind conjures my image and Violet's, sitting together on a loveseat. She's dressed like Elvis reimagined. I'm wearing a goofy smile. I see us talking, laughing... and, finally, *kissing*.

Fireworks.

I feel them now, just *remembering* that amazing kiss, every bit as much as I felt them back then.

But, suddenly, my happy memories are invaded by images of Caleb's face. He's smiling at me on that balcony last night. Thanking me. *Trusting* me.

I return to the ceremony again, my chest heaving, to find Henn in the middle of saying his vows. Henn is saying, ". . . and when our eyes met that first time, I instantly felt like I was home in your eyes. And

I've been feeling at home with you—wherever we are and whatever we're doing—ever since."

Everyone around me swoons. And all I can think about is Violet, yet again. The way I felt at home in her eyes, the minute she smiled at me across that crowded party. No, the minute she *scowled* at me like she was pissed I hadn't approached her quickly enough.

I look at my mom and dad next to me. Their hands are clasped. I peek at Colby and his wife on the other side of me. Then Ryan and his wife. Every couple is holding hands and looking sentimental. Reliving their own vows, I'm sure. Remembering how they felt at home in their own spouse's eyes, the moment they met.

You can't have her, Dax. It's too complicated. Too fucked up. You barely know her. You're projecting. The feelings aren't real. You can't betray Caleb.

But nothing my brain screams at me is convincing my heart in the least.

My eyes drift toward the front of the patio again. I'm intending to peek at my sister and her husband up there, to see if they're looking as sentimental as the other spouses in my family... but my attention is sharply diverted by a woman in the second row.

Who the fuck is that?

My heart stops.

I can't see the woman's face, only the back of her dark head, but... *Oh my fucking God!* It's Violet! She just turned her head, ever so briefly, and I could plainly see Violet's profile!

I'm instantly on fire. Every cell in my body wants to bolt out of my chair and sprint to her, but since the goddamned wedding ceremony isn't over yet, I'm forced to sit in my seat, fidgeting and rocking like a kid in need of a toilet.

My mom puts her hand on my leg and squeezes. And when I look at her, she's glaring at me like, *What the hell is wrong with you?*

I shake my head. *Don't even start with me, Mom. Not now.*

The officiant says, "Henn and Hannah, by the laws of the State of California, I now pronounce you husband and wife. Henn, you may kiss your bride."

The place erupts in applause while I sit on my hands. *How is Violet here?* Is she friends with Hannah, the bride? That's got to be it. Hannah works in PR for a movie studio and I overheard Violet saying something about designing costumes for a movie...

The officiant introduces the happy couple and they march down the center aisle.

I bolt to standing, intending to barrel out to the side aisle and run as fast as my shaking legs will carry me. But, fuck my life, when I stand, everyone around me stands, too. Because, yeah, it's a wedding —and this is the moment when they're supposed to applaud the newly married couple. Fuck! I clap, along with everyone else, just so I don't look like a serial killer. And, finally, Henn and Hannah pass by, followed by Reed and Maddy, and then Josh and Kat, and Jonas and Sarah.

Hyperventilating, I tap Colby's shoulder to let me pass and then stumble over his feet when he doesn't react fast enough. "Sorry, sorry, sorry," I say as I trip over my family members' feet down the row.

"What the hell is wrong with you?" Ryan barks behind me.

But Captain Morgan can kiss my ass.

Violet.

I'm a horse running for the barn now. Charging toward Violet, weaving through people who are converging to hug and talk... but, no, no, no, she's striding away from me, heading down the center aisle, on her way to say hello to the bride and groom. My chest heaving, I loop through the area where the ceremony just happened and begin loping down the center aisle behind Violet... and then stop dead in my tracks.

No.

She's reached her destination. And it's not Henn and Hannah. *It's Reed.* A fact that just became clear when Violet reached Reed and he immediately slid his arm affectionately around her shoulders, like he's done it a thousand times. *Like she's his.* He pulls her close. And my heart explodes with jealousy. *Violet is dating goddamned motherfucking Reed Rivers?* No wonder she didn't want to tell C-Bomb the name of the guy she's seeing. *It's yet another catastrophe.*

I stare like a sniper, adrenaline, jealousy, outrage coursing through my veins. Violet's wearing a sultry gown tonight—a sleek silver number with a low-cut back that flatters her curves. Did she wear that sexy gown especially for Reed tonight? Did he buy it for her? Is he planning to peel it off her later tonight?

Mere hours ago, I laughed at Ryan for holding a grudge against Reed—for being pissed at him for hitting on Ryan's wife before she was even Ryan's girlfriend. But now, I get it. Oh, God, I get it. Because all of a sudden, I want to rip Reed Rivers limb from limb, my record deal be damned, for touching the woman who's *mine, mine, mine*—even if she doesn't know it yet.

I watch Reed lean into Violet's ear to whisper. She nods and holds his gaze with an adorable, sexy smile. And that's when I see it. *Mutual affection.* Holy fuck! Violet's not simply Reed's sexy plaything, and Reed's not simply the rich, powerful guy who's showing Violet a good time. *They actually like each other.* Maybe even... No. I can't believe it. Although, there's no denying, just this fast, I'm seeing something on that cold-hearted bastard's face I've never seen before, not in all the times I've seen him with a woman on his arm.

I begin moving slowly forward, drawn to my own decimation like a moth to flame. My brain is telling me to turn around and save myself. It's telling me I'm the *Titanic* and Violet is the iceberg. It's telling me to think of Colin and Fish and Caleb. To remember this is a losing proposition for me. A terrible idea. But I can't stop myself. I need to see if she clutches Reed tighter when she sees me... or jerks away from him.

Just as I close in on Reed and Violet from behind, a photographer approaches their group and says she's ready to photograph the wedding party now.

Reed gives Violet's shoulders a little squeeze. "You wanna come with, or...?"

"No, no, I'll grab a drink and listen to the band," she says.

"I'll introduce you around when I'm done."

"Should be about thirty minutes," the photographer says.

"I can't wait for everyone to meet you, baby," Reed says as he leaves.

"Sounds good. I'm excited."

The second Reed is gone, I lurch toward Violet and touch her shoulder. "Violet."

Startled, she turns around... and gasps at the sight of me like I just popped out from behind a tree. "Dax," she says, clutching her heart. "What are you doing here?"

My pulse throbbing in my ears, I manage to say, "The bride and groom are family friends. My whole family is here. *You're dating Reed fucking Rivers?*"

She looks over her shoulder, her eyes flashing with panic. "We can't talk here. Follow me and stay five paces behind."

TWENTY-EIGHT

VIOLET

My heartbeat raging in my ears, I stride past the table rounds set up for dinner, past a jazz trio playing for cocktail hour, and a bow-tied bartender. I pass a three-tiered wedding cake with a plastic bride and groom on top, and a waiter carrying a tray of champagne flutes. I turn on wobbly legs into a short hallway, feeling like I'm about to hyperventilate, pass a bathroom, and then the spare room where Reed's live-in housekeeper, Amalia, stays during the week, and, finally, hurl myself into a laundry room. If, by some slim chance, Reed comes looking for me after the photo shoot with the bridal party, I've got to think his laundry room will be the last place he'd look.

Dax enters the small room on my heels—so much for keeping five paces behind me—and shuts the door as I whirl around.

"You can't date Reed Rivers!" he shouts the moment the door is closed. "He's a player, Violet. A dog. I don't know what he said or did to dupe you into looking at him like he's some knight in shining armor, how many private planes he's flown you on, but—"

"You think I'm a gold digger?" I roar, instantly livid. "You think I'm dating Reed for his money or lifestyle?"

Dax blanches. "That came out wrong. I just meant he's not the guy you think he is, not when it comes to women, and I'm not gonna stand here and let you—"

"You're not gonna *let* me? Excuse me, but one night of fucking me eight months ago—"

"Okay, let's rewind."

"—doesn't give you the right to tell me—"

"Can we rewind, please?"

"—who I can and can't date, especially when we both know, thanks to the goddamned internet—"

"Don't believe everything you see on the internet."

"—you partied like a rockstar during the entire tour."

"Not the entire tour. And not nearly as much as it appeared."

"But I didn't hold it against you! You were single and the entire world's fantasy-boyfriend! But don't you *dare* think you can party your ass off for all of Instagram and *TMZ* to see and then come back here and tell me I'm not *allowed* to date Reed or anyone else during the same time. I've been single, too, Dax! Have I not been allowed to date because I'm a woman? Or because I'm not a rockstar?"

"Violet, forget all that. No matter what photos you saw, I never stopped thinking about you during the tour. Pretty much everything I've done, I've just been trying to forget you. To survive."

"Well, maybe I've just been trying to survive, too."

His chest heaves at my admission. He swallows hard. "Violet, I'm not slut-shaming you, okay? I'm the last guy in the world who'd do that. What I'm saying is I can't stand seeing you with Reed or anyone else, because..." He takes a step forward, his eyes blazing. Sex is wafting off him. "Because I want you for myself." He takes another step forward. "I can't stand the thought of another man's hands on you, Violet. Because I'm *jealous*."

My breathing is shallow. My head is spinning with desire. Every molecule of my body wants to touch him. Kiss him. Rip his clothes off and invite him inside me.

He takes another step, closing the gap between us. "Do you love him?" he whispers.

I pause. "Yes."

Dax freezes. Shock. Pain. Anguish. Regret. All of it flickers across Dax's gorgeous face in the blink of an eye. And I'm not gonna lie, I'm feeling immense pleasure at the sight of all of it. But I've had my fun. I'm not a sadist. Time to straighten the poor boy out.

"Yes, I love Reed. *Because he's my brother.*"

Dax's jaw hangs open.

"I've told you the whole story. Reed and I have the same shitty-ass father."

Dax closes his eyes and lets out a long exhale... and when he opens his eyes again, a switch has flipped inside him. In a blur of desire and need, he pitches forward, wraps me in his arms, and crushes his soft lips against mine. And even though my brain knows Reed being my brother, rather than my lover, doesn't clear the way for us—that, in fact, the smart thing for Dax to do would be to stay far away from me—my body in this moment doesn't care about pesky things like caution or consequences. All my body cares about is the white-hot desire wracking my every nerve ending and pooling almost painfully between my legs.

Even though I know I shouldn't, I surrender to Dax—to desire—throwing my arms around his neck and returning his passionate kiss with everything I've got. Our tongues tangle and dance. Our lips devour and consume. His body shuddering, Dax backs me up and pins me against the washing machine. With a deep groan, his every breath relaying his desperation, he grinds his hard bulge against me, right into my bull's-eye, and kisses me with a passion I've never experienced before. I'm oxygen and he's a drowning man. I'm a lifeline thrown to a sailor swept into stormy seas. I'm the very blood coursing through this boy's hot veins.

Oh, God, I'm enraptured, utterly enthralled. Feeling like I've been on life support for eight months, and suddenly springing to full health. I thought I remembered what it felt like to kiss this beautiful boy, but I was wrong. The pleasure I'm feeling, the riot of emotion and arousal and *need* flashing across my heart and soul and nerve endings and skin and nipples and clit... all of it is so much more than fireflies in my belly. It's an electrical storm—an explosion of heat and lightning, of lust and sense memory and hope, enough to power a sky full of stars and send my aching heart beating fully, *joyfully*, once again.

As we kiss, passion consumes us like a pyre. There's no turning back now. Frantically, Dax hikes up my dress, yanks down my panties, and slides his fingers inside me, making me moan and gyrate against his hand. With his free hand, he unzips his pants and pulls them down slightly, along with his briefs, enough to free his hard cock. His chest rising and falling sharply like he's running a marathon, he pulls a condom out of his pants and gets himself covered. And with his dick straining between us, he slides his wet fingers to a new spot deep inside me—that same, deep spot he stroked during our night together, the spot that gave me orgasm after orgasm, each one better than the last. I tilt my head back and moan and shudder and hump his hand, awaiting the tsunami that's surely going to crash into me.

When I come, it's hard and full of emotion and relief. I come so hard, in fact, with such force and greed, I gyrate against the washing machine like I'm having a seizure.

As I moan and shake, Dax twists the dial on the washer and pounds his fist against the buttons—and, two seconds later, just as the machine begins vibrating deliciously against my bare ass, Dax plunges himself inside me.

We both growl and moan at the sensation of him filling me and the washing machine vibrating against me. Did it feel *this* good before to have Dax inside me? Because having this man filling me up feels like something supernatural. No, it feels like fate. Destiny. Like the entire universe is sighing with relief at his penetration, not just me.

Dax presses his lips against mine and grabs my breast and begins fucking me against the vibrating washer like a beast. And I'm instantly transported to the brink. I'm a rubber band about to snap. A heart about to burst. I grab at Dax's shoulders and neck and hair. I claw at him, clutch him, feeling like I'm rocketing toward some sort of pleasure-induced delirium. Pure ecstasy. Wanton addiction.

Dax growls out my name, and, a moment later, my innermost muscles begin squeezing and rippling fiercely, which immediately pushes Dax into a release of his own.

When our bodies come down, Dax kisses me slowly, his breathing ragged. He rests his forehead against mine and sighs. "Even better than I remembered."

I'm shaking. Overwhelmed. These intense feelings I'm having make no sense, given the timeline of things. "That song," I whisper hoarsely, my heart beating wildly. "It was incredible, Dax."

He smiles. "You liked it?"

"*I loved it.*"

"I was hoping it would turn you on, but... *wow.* I should sing you songs more often."

I smile. "Please do."

With a sigh, he pulls out of me and peels off his condom.

I bend down to pick up my undies, my body trembling, and when I straighten up, Dax surprises me by grabbing them out of my hand and sliding them into his pocket.

With a wicked smile, he says, "I stole a pillowcase you'd slept on and brought it around the world with me, but your scent wore off months ago."

I stare at him for a beat, not sure if he's serious. "You took the pillowcase I used from the hotel?"

He smiles and nods.

My heart leaps. "And you've been... *sniffing* it all this time?"

"Every night. Scent is a big thing for me. It really turns me on. And yours turns me on like nothing else. Your hair smells like flowers. Like *violets.*" With that, he reaches behind me, unzips my dress, and pulls it down until it's crumpled on the ground around my feet. His eyes on mine, he lifts me up and places my bare ass onto the vibrating washing machine. And then, without hesitation, he grips my hips and pulls me into his waiting face.

For a long moment, Dax nuzzles me with his nose, pointedly inhaling like he's enjoying a bouquet of flowers, and when he's got me physically shivering with anticipation and arousal, he begins licking and sucking at my folds while fingering me... until, finally, going in for the kill. As he swirls his tongue against my clit and strokes my G-spot, I rapidly lose my mind. I place the soles of my feet onto the washing machine and spread my legs wide, offering him every inch of me, and he accepts my invitation without hesitation. As the washing machine moves underneath me, Dax works me with enthusiasm. I grip his long hair, feeling like a wild animal in heat, until, finally, a powerful orgasm slams into me—an orgasm of such intensity, it brings tears to my eyes.

Dax emerges from my legs, smiling. His face is flushed. His lips shiny. He's stunning. He says, "I thought I remembered how good you taste. How hot you are when you come. But my memories were nothing but a blurry snapshot. This, right here, this is living color. This is high def."

Again, my heart feels like it's exploding with joy. But I run my fingers through his hair and say the responsible thing. "We can't do this, you know."

"We just did."

"But not for real."

He doesn't reply. And I'm not gonna lie, a jolt of pure elation hits me when he doesn't agree with my assessment. Could he seriously be considering getting involved with me, despite everything? He probably shouldn't do it, knowing Caleb. Not to mention Reed. I shouldn't let him do it... *But, oh, God, I want him to do it.*

I close my legs. "I'd better get out there. Reed's going to wonder where I am pretty soon."

"Yeah, my family, too."

I hop down from the washer, grab my dress off the floor, and begin getting dressed. "Can I have my undies, please?"

"They're mine now."

I don't argue... because, truth be told, I'm insanely turned on knowing my undies are sitting in Dax's pocket, and that I'm wet and bare underneath my dress.

I turn my back on him, nonverbally asking him to zip me up—and his fingers slide along my bare back, making me shudder.

Dax says, "I heard Reed say he wants to introduce you around...?"

I turn around to face him. "Yeah, he asked me to come as his plus-one tonight so he can introduce me to his friends. That party for Aloha was the very first time I'd entered Reed's world. Tonight is the second. Now that I'm living in L.A., my brother finally feels ready to merge his 'two worlds' a bit. He said he's excited to introduce me to 'Josh's in-laws.' That's your family, right?"

"Yep."

"He said he thinks I'll like them all, but someone named Maddy might be someone I could become friends with here in L.A."

"Maddy is my brother Keane's fiancée. The maid of honor."

"Oh, she's adorable." I sigh. "Reed is so good to me. I told him the move has been tough on me—that I miss my friends from school. It's been a lot lonelier moving here than I expected, only knowing three people in town."

"Three?"

"Reed, Miranda, and..." I press my lips together, my stomach tightening. But then quickly decide, screw it, I've got nothing to hide or be ashamed of. I've been a single woman all this time. "And this guy named Ethan. I've been dating him casually since I moved to L.A. But after I saw you last night, and heard 'Fireflies,' I drove straight to Ethan's house and broke it off with him. That's why I didn't go to the wrap party. Well, among other reasons. I was also having a nervous breakdown at the thought of being in the same room with you and Caleb again."

"Do you love him?" Dax asks, his voice tight.

"No. It was casual, like I said. And a bad idea. He's a movie producer. He helped me get an internship my last semester of school, which led to my current gig. I just got hired to work on the design team for one of the movies Ethan's producing. Being romantically involved with him is a bad idea, since he's my boss's boss. Well, actually, he's my boss's *boss's* boss. But, whatever, none of that matters now because I went to his place last night, after the concert, and told him I want to keep things professional. We weren't even exclusive,

Dax. And he's got his pick of women. He's actually quite the ladies' man. Surely, he'll survive the rejection."

Dax looks upset. "When C-Bomb said you were seeing someone, I was thinking that meant me."

I'm instantly too freaked out to address Dax's misunderstanding, which is actually kind of cute. I blurt, "*You've talked to Caleb about me?*"

"*Whoa.* Calm down. He doesn't suspect anything. He was using me as a sounding board last night at the wrap party because"—Dax grimaces—"he needed a friend. Oh, God, I'm going to hell. Caleb is a good friend of mine. He told me he still loves you, and I said nothing about us." Dax drags his hands over his face. "And now I just fucked you and ate you out."

My heart physically hurts, along with my stomach. What girl wants to see the dude she just fucked looking like this—like he's full of regret for what he just did? "Yeah, and Caleb is only half of the problem," I say, feeling defeated. "Don't forget Reed is my brother."

Dax scoffs. "I don't care about Reed being your brother. He can go fuck himself if he doesn't like us being together. Caleb, on the other hand? That's a major complication for me. I mean, he can go fuck himself, too, at the end of the day, if this turns out to be..."

I can barely breathe. I wait, my heart thumping. But Dax doesn't finish his sentence. "If this turns out to be... *what?* Finish your thought."

"I don't know what the end of that sentence should be. That's why I stopped. Worth it? Worth fucking Caleb over and turning RCR against me and my band?"

I nod slowly. "Yeah, I think that about covers it."

He throws up his hands. "Just being straight with you, Violet. If it turns out this thing between us isn't gonna last, if it's not gonna be something lasting or enduring, then I'd sure hate for Caleb to find out about it. Why hurt him if it's not necessary?"

I consider that for a moment, and finally nod my agreement. "You're right. If this thing turns out to be nothing but lust—"

"It's not lust. It's much more than that and we both know it. The question is: how much more?"

I process that for a beat. "Okay, then, if this turns out to be, I don't know, *infatuation,* then I agree it'd be best for everyone, ourselves included, if Caleb never finds out about us."

Dax looks tortured. But he nods.

"Just to be clear, though, Caleb doesn't own me. He's not my boyfriend, and I'm not cheating on him. I'm a single woman and I can do whatever I want."

"I know that," he says. "You've done nothing wrong. I'm the one who's betraying a friend."

I stare him down. Clearly, this is his decision to make, not mine, and we both know it.

Dax exhales. "But what if... what if this thing *isn't* infatuation? What if it turns out to be... *the real deal?*"

My heart skips a beat.

"If that's the way this thing ends up," he says, "then I'm sure as hell not gonna skulk around in secret with you *forever.* At some point, I'm gonna want to show you off and shout from the highest rooftops you're mine."

My heart is racing now. "So what are you saying? You're willing to skulk around in secret *for a while?* Just long enough to determine if this thing between us is something more than infatuation?"

"Yeah. That's exactly what I'm saying. I'm willing to skulk around long enough to figure it out."

"How long is that?"

"I don't know," he says. "I'll know it when I get there, I guess."

I pull a face.

"Do you have a deadline?" he asks.

A deadline? The thought hadn't even occurred to me. All I know is I want him. And that I'm too far gone now to give him up or not go along with what he's proposing. In reality, what choice do I have, other than to go along? I want him any way I can get him. But, honestly, I have no idea how long I'll be willing to pursue this so-called romance of ours in secret. A couple months, maybe? Right now, my answer to whatever Dax is proposing, whatever it is, is *yes.*

When I don't speak, Dax touches my shoulder. "Violet," he whispers. "I just need a little time to make sure I can trust these intense feelings. It's a whole lot I'm feeling in a ridiculously short amount of time."

I nod. "Yeah, I know. I'm freaking out at the insane speed of things myself. I'm in. Skulking around in secret, it is."

He exhales in relief.

"Although, I've got to think 'skulking in secret' with you is going to be a tall order. Anywhere you go, it's fifty-fifty paparazzi or fans will snap photos of you. Last I checked, that 'Dax in the Wild' Instagram account had, like, twenty million followers."

He looks at me blankly.

"You haven't seen 'Dax in the Wild'? It's an account dedicated exclusively to fan photos of you, taken 'in the wild.'" I pull out my phone, swipe into Instagram, and find the account. "See? It's all you, all the time. If a fan snaps a shot of you, anywhere in the world, they send it to this account and it gets uploaded."

Dax looks at my screen and rolls his eyes. "What the hell is wrong with people? Look at this one. I'm just sitting there, drinking a coffee. Oh my God. It's the same in all of these shots. I'm doing nothing but living my life."

I shrug. "People are obsessed with you. Which, I must admit, I can understand. But the point is, if we're seen in public together, there's a good chance it'll take thirty minutes before you're hearing from Reed or Caleb, or both, asking what the hell you were doing with me. And what will you say? 'Oh, I, uh, had some questions about costume design'?"

"Okay, then, we'll just have to be crazy-careful. We'll meet in hotels."

"Until?"

"Until one of two things happens: one, we're both so sure this thing is the real deal, we don't care who knows about it, or, two, one of us decides they're done."

My stomach clenches at the thought of that second scenario coming to pass. In fact, the idea of it makes me want to burst into tears. I take a deep breath and clear my throat. "Reed being my brother isn't the big nothing-burger you're assuming. It's only slightly less of a clusterfuck than Reed being my boyfriend. After everything that happened with Caleb, Reed told me in no uncertain terms not to get involved with any of his artists, ever again. When I went to Reed's party for Aloha, he even showed me photos of the guys coming to the party so I'd know to stay away from them."

"He didn't know Fish, Colin, and I were coming. Like I told you, we were at the party through our friend, Zander." Dax crosses his arms over his chest. "Why the hell does Reed care who you mess around with? He's your brother, not your keeper."

"Reed doesn't care if I date, in general. He's not a lunatic. But the guys signed to his label are off-limits. If someone on Reed's label were to treat me like shit or use me or, God forbid, break my heart, Reed says he's not sure he'd be able to keep himself from going scorched earth on the guy's ass, and he *really* doesn't want to be put in that position. When Caleb broke my heart, Reed wanted to ruin his life until I convinced him not to do it. That's why I interrogated you at the party about how you got through the front door: because I'd promised Reed I'd stay away from his artists."

Dax sighs. "I didn't tell you about my band being signed to Reed's label because I wanted you to like me for *me*."

"Well, mission accomplished."

We share a smile.

Dax says, "I did my own interrogation of you, too, you might recall. I wanted to make triple sure you weren't connected to Reed in some way. The last thing I wanted was to get involved with a girl Reed had dated or had his eye on."

I roll my eyes. "I didn't mention I was Reed's sister because I thought you were an aspiring musician, and I didn't want you to pretend to like me to get to Reed."

"Oh, man." Dax shakes his head and smiles adorably. "We were quite the pair that night, huh?"

My heart skips a beat at his beautiful smile. "Yes, we were." I bite my lip, overwhelmed by that bursting feeling in my heart. "So, are you willing to give this a whirl, even if it means at the end of the day, you *might* wind up pissing off *both* Caleb *and* the head of your record label?"

"I don't care about Reed."

"Well, I do. If things don't go well between us at some point, I don't want the added pressure of feeling like I've somehow screwed up your career."

"I have no particular desire to tell Reed what's going on with us," Dax says. "It's none of his business. Plus, I don't want Reed saying anything to Caleb."

"Reed wouldn't betray me by saying something to Caleb. My brother loves me."

Dax's face softens. "Of course, he does." He touches my face. "I meant I don't want Reed saying something off the cuff, without realizing the implications. That's all I meant." He looks deep into my eyes. "Violet, I can't stand the thought of you with someone else. I need this thing between us to be exclusive. I want you all to myself, and you've got me the same way. Roger?"

My heart is exploding in my chest. I feel vaguely faint. "Roger."

He flashes me a radiant smile. "No, sweetheart. In my family, the required response to 'Roger' is 'Rabbit.'"

I giggle. "*Rabbit.*"

Dax looks giddy. He pecks my lips. "I'll book a hotel room for this entire week. After the wedding, go to your place and pack whatever you need for a week and meet me there. I'll text you the info."

My breath catches. "You want me to stay with you for a whole week?"

Dax pulls out his phone. "No, I *need* you to stay with me for a week. What's your number so I can text you the hotel info?"

I tell it to him, and two seconds later, receive a text from him.

. . .

> *Hello, Hitwoman Elvis Disco Momma. You're gorgeous and delicious and I can't wait to eat your pussy again.*

Laughing, I say, "You'd better put me into your contacts with a code name. We don't want anyone peeking at our text messages and figuring us out."

"I'm one step ahead of you. I've already given you a code name."

I tap some buttons, saving Dax's number into my phone. "Okay, I saved you in my contacts as 'DJ.' What's my secret name?"

Dax grins. "You can't guess?"

I shake my head.

Dax drags his teeth across his lower lip and smiles adorably. "*Firefly.*"

TWENTY-NINE

DAX

"**W**ait fifteen minutes before you come out," Violet says, smoothing her hands down the front of her silver dress. "From now on, this is nothing short of a covert military operation." She flashes me a naughty smile. "We're fuck-spies on the run, baby. *Ooh.* That's kinda kinky, huh?" With that, she winks and slips out the door of the laundry room, leaving me smiling from ear to ear.

A minute later, my phone buzzes with a text from Kat.

Kat: Where the FUCK are you?

I pause. I probably shouldn't tell Kat the truth, seeing as how Violet and I just decided we're "fuck-spies" and all. But then again... Kat's my confidante, and I'm hers. We're the Wonder Twins. Kat's certainly told *me* plenty of stories about felony-stupid fuckery *she's* engaged in, just because she couldn't resist. Yeah, fuck it. I can't keep something this awesome from my sister.

Me: I'm in Reed's laundry room, hiding out for a few minutes so nobody suspects I was just in here making out with a purdy girl.

Kat: WHAT?!! WHO?!!!!

Me: Come here and I'll tell you...

I describe the laundry room's location and two minutes later, the door flies opens.

"Did some valet parker slip you a note as you walked in?" Kat says, her blue eyes sparkling. "Or was it a *bartendress? Who, who, whooo?*"

"Shut the door behind you, owl girl. And no to both."

Kat shuts the door and bounces toward me, and I help her up onto the dryer to sit next to me, our thighs touching and our legs dangling off the machine.

"Okay, Blabbermouth," I say. "What I'm about to tell you is one thousand percent confidential. Highest-level top secret. Roger?"

"Rabbit."

"You can't tell *anyone,* not even Josh."

Kat rests a palm on her heart and raises her other hand. "I swear, on our Wonder Twin powers, to keep this secret." She lowers her hand. "Although, we both know I'll break down and tell Josh in the throes of passion."

I laugh. "You can't tell Josh. *Especially* not Josh. He's too close to the enemy."

"The *enemy?* What the heck does Josh have to do with this?"

I pause. "Five minutes ago, I was making sweet love to a beautiful girl named Violet in this laundry room—against that very washing machine. A girl named Violet who's none other than Reed Rivers' little sister."

"Holy shit." Kat laughs. "Okay, first off, thank you for sitting me atop the *dryer.* And second off, I didn't even know Reed had a sister!"

"Half-sister, actually. They share a father. And, oh, God, Jizzy Pop, she's the hottest girl who ever lived."

"But is she *intriguing?*"

"She is. Very much so."

Kat giggles. "Holy Rock Star Perks, Batman. Talk about using your newfound celebrity status to your fullest advantage."

"No, you dork. I didn't just meet some *intriguing* girl at a wedding and, five minutes later, bang her in a laundry room. I already knew Violet from before the tour." I briefly tell Kat the Story of Violet, including the unfortunate complication I learned last night.

"Holy hell," Kat says. "You're playing with fire here, Daxy. Careful you don't get burned."

"Violet and I have already agreed to skulk around in secret for a while—you know, like classy people do—until we're sure it's worth it to both of us to blow shit up. I mean, in reality, Violet and I barely know each other. All we know is we can't keep our hands off each other and we're both dying to get to know each other a whole lot better." I smile. "Inside and out."

"Just be careful, Dax. No sense unleashing the kraken for a fling. A hot fling, it sounds like, but, still."

"I got this. We've decided we're fuck-spies on the run."

"So what will happen if it becomes more than a fling? What then?"

"Then... we'll... see what we want to do."

"From what I've seen, you've gotten really close to RCR's drummer."

My stomach flips over. "I can't think about him right now. I'll cross that bridge when and if I get there. Until then, I'm just gonna enjoy the ride... in secret... until I know for sure our chemistry will survive out there in the real world."

"But how can you know that unless you go out into the real world with her? I mean, sorry to be a Debbie Downer here, but having amazing chemistry while banging someone in a hotel room or laundry room is a lot easier than holding onto that chemistry through the trials and tribulations of real life. Being in Vegas with Josh in the beginning was sexy and exciting, but we were in a bubble. Neither of us could be sure our feelings were real until I went to his house and met his friends and he came home with me to meet you guys."

I exhale with exasperation. "Kat, if I so much as walk down the street with Violet, there's a good chance someone's gonna snap a photo of us and post it online. There are Instagram accounts where people upload photos of me, just living my life."

"Yeah, I know. The biggest one is called 'Dax in the Wild.' It's actually kind of creepy."

"Right? What the hell is so interesting about me sitting in a chair, reading a book?"

"Dax. Honey. Every breath you take is interesting to people at this point."

I run my hand through my hair. "Which is exactly my point. There's no reliable way I'm gonna be able to test out my chemistry with Violet in the real world without C-Bomb and Reed finding out about it."

Kat puts her arm around me. "It's okay, Daxy-pants. Just enjoy the ride and see where things lead. Cross the 'real world' bridge if and when you get there."

I lean into Kat and touch the side of my head to hers. "Now see? That's why I love you the most, Splooge."

She pats my arm. "Now, *please* tell me you turned on the washing machine when you screwed your girl against it, or I'm gonna bitch-slap you for missing a fantastic opportunity."

I laugh. "Of course, I did. I'm a Morgan, dude. We're smart like that."

"Good boy." But before Kat says another word, the laundry room door opens and our mother pops her head into the room.

THIRTY

DAX

"I thought I heard your voices in here!" Mom barrels into the laundry room like a drug-sniffing dog. "What are you two doing in a *laundry room,* when everyone else is out there, chatting and enjoying cocktails?"

"I'm not 'enjoying cocktails' these days, remember?" I say. "So I came in here to make a phone call."

"And then I went looking for a bathroom and heard Dax's voice," Kat says, "and decided to come say hi."

Mom narrows her eyes. "Okay, cut the crap, you two. This ain't my first time at the Kat and Dax rodeo."

We laugh.

"It's not normal to hang out in a laundry room at a wedding when everyone you love the most is out there, having fun." Concern flickers across Mom's face as she looks at me. "Tell the truth, Dax. Did you come back here to snort drugs?"

I roll my eyes. "No, I didn't come back here to 'snort drugs.' I'm not in need of rehab or any other kind of intervention. Well, I mean, yeah, I snorted the tiniest bit of cocaine off Kat's stomach when she first came in, but it was such a small amount of blow, it hardly counts."

Mom rolls her eyes. "If you're not on drugs, then tell me what's going on with you. You couldn't even sit still during the ceremony. I googled it, and that's exactly how people on drugs act—like they've got ants in their pants."

"My problem isn't a chemical one, Mom. Unless you count hormones as a chemical." I sigh. "If you must know, I'm obsessed with a girl. She's the reason I've got ants in my pants."

Mom sighs with relief. "Is that who you came back here to call?"

I pause, simply because I'm the world's worst liar. "Yes."

Mom narrows her eyes. "Why are you lying to me, David Jackson?"

"I didn't lie to you, mother dearest."

"Dax, you're the worst liar in the family, next to Colby."

"It's true. You are," Kat says. She smiles proudly. "And I'm the best."

"Wipe that smile off your face, Kitty," Mom says. "You shouldn't be *proud* of being a fantastic liar."

Kat laughs. "Perhaps not. But I am."

Mom says, "What part is the lie? The girl? The call? The hormones?"

"Okay, you got me, Mom. The truth is I came back here to 'snort drugs.'"

"Just tell me what's going on."

"Nothing. I just needed to make a call."

"Well, whoever she is, I hope it's not serious. Because I think I just met the girl of your dreams ten minutes ago."

"Oh, God, Mom. *No.*"

"*Yes.* That's why I came looking for you. Because I want to introduce you."

"Gah."

"Yes, I'm fully aware you've got your pick of girls these days. That much is abundantly clear." She rolls her eyes. "But from what I've seen, you've been surrounding yourself with women who kiss your butt. And that's not you. You need a woman of *substance.* And I think I just met someone exactly like that. When I started talking to her, I instantly thought, 'Where the heck is Daxy? He would flip out over this amazing girl.'"

"Who is she?" Kat asks.

"Don't encourage her."

"Her name is Violet," Mom says. "She's Reed's sister and I'm just... *What?*"

"Nothing," Kat says, trying to hold back her laughter. "You're just the cutest, Mom. Continue."

Mom eyes Kat suspiciously for a moment. "She's very beautiful, this girl. The artsy type, which I know you've always liked, Daxy. She's even got a tattoo and a little stud in her nose, both of which I know are your kryptonite. But the best part is she seems to be a very interesting person. Highly intelligent and kind. Reed was telling us about... *What?*"

"Who put you up to this?" I ask, crossing my arms. "Was it Rum Cake? Did he connect the dots and send you in here to punk me?"

Mom looks genuinely confused. "Ryan? No. Reed introduced his sister to our family just now. He said she just graduated from an art college back east with a degree in fashion design and that she moved to L.A. to become a costume designer and start a non-profit to help kids with cancer. So Maddy and I started chatting with Violet, and it turns out she designs *superhero* costumes for kids with cancer." Mom looks emotional at the thought. "Reed said she's been doing it for years, every single week, without fail." Mom pauses, shaking her head. "Maddy offered to go to lunch with Violet some time, to show her around L.A., and Violet seemed genuinely appreciative, because she said she doesn't know a lot of people here. And that's when I started looking around for you, because I thought, 'Dax is back in L.A. now. Maybe *he* could take this sweet, pretty girl to lunch.'" Mom puts her hands on her hips. "Okay, *what?* You're mad at me for playing matchmaker? Is it because she's Reed's sister? Because, honey, I don't see why that should matter. If the two of you were to hit it off and—"

"Mom," Kat says. "Slow your roll, dude. I can't take it anymore. Reed's sister is the girl."

"Kat!" I shout.

"What girl?" Mom says.

"What happened to swearing on our Wonder Twin powers?"

"Oh, Daxy, come on," Kat says. "At this point, Mom is less of a liability if she knows the truth. God only knows how hard she'll work to push you two together tonight if we don't tell her, and that would be bad."

Mom shouts, "*What* truth? What girl?"

I sigh. "Mom, the girl I've been obsessed with is Violet. *She's the girl.*"

Mom furrows her brow. "But why would you come back here to a laundry room to *call* Violet when she's standing out there?"

"Because I didn't come back here to make a phone call. That was a lie. Violet and I came back here to talk and kiss. She left the room before me so nobody would notice we'd disappeared together— because we don't want Reed to find out about us yet, if ever—and Kat found me in here and I've been telling her all about it. Happy now, you freaking bloodhound?"

"In other words, Mom, your son is a horn dog," Kat says.

"Well, I already knew that. In kindergarten, he had three girl-friends, for Pete's sake. *That I knew of.*"

"Mom, please. This is not a conversation I want to be having with you." I glare at Kat. "Thanks a lot, Kat."

Mom chuckles. "Oh, slow your roll, Dax. I've raised four kids before you—one of them *Keane.* Trust me, when it comes to boys and raging hormones, nothing shocks me anymore."

I grimace. "Please, Mom. Move along."

Mom tucks her blonde bob behind her ear. "It always amazes me any of you think you can get away with lying to me. How many times do I have to tell you kids: I'll *always* sniff out the truth, one way or another."

Kat and I exchange a look of pure amusement. As we both know, our darling mother doesn't know half of Kat's secrets and never will.

Mom says, "Now tell me, how long have you been dating Violet?"

"Dating? Oh, um... since... today, I guess. Officially. But I met her right before the tour. She's the one I wrote 'Fireflies' about—that new song I played at the concert last night."

Mom is giddy. "You wrote *that* one about Violet? Oh, Dax! You must really like her."

"Swoon, right?" Kat says.

"Swoon," Mom agrees. She clutches her heart. "Ha! I'm a genius."

"Let's not get ahead of ourselves, okay? This thing with Violet is brand new. I'm still figuring things out. So, please, nothing leaves this room."

"Because of Reed? Because, honey, I don't think you should worry about him. Reed likes you. And you come from a *fantastic* family." She winks.

"It's not just Reed." I describe the situation regarding Caleb and my mom gasps and palms her cheeks.

"Well, that's definitely a twist," she says. "Oh, Dax. *Ugh.*"

"Yeah, I know. So, now you see why Violet and I want to keep things under wraps for now."

Mom clutches her stomach like she feels vicariously ill for me. "What a... what's the word you always say, honey?"

"Clusterfuck."

"Yes," Mom says. "Exactly."

"So now you see why I don't want you saying anything to anyone, okay?"

Mom puts her palm in the air and solemnly swears to secrecy. "But can I tell your father?"

"As long as you tell him he can't... Actually, never mind. Yeah, you can tell him."

There's no need for anyone to muzzle my father. That dude wouldn't tell anyone a damned thing about my love life, or any of his kids' love lives, whether he'd been sworn to secrecy or not.

"Hey, if Mom's telling Dad, then can I pretty-please tell Josh?" Kat says. "He won't tell Reed. On something like this, his loyalty will lie with me and his beloved Morgans."

"Sure, fine. Whatever. Just make sure he understands he can't tell Reed."

"He'll be a locked vault."

"Can I tell Colby, then?" Mom says. "When I asked him if he'd seen you, I told him I wanted to find you to introduce you to Reed's sister, Violet. And he said, '*Reed has a sister named Violet?*' So I pointed her out and, the minute Colby saw Violet, he threw his head back and laughed. And then he beelined straight to Ryan."

"Oh, for the love of..." I mutter.

"Hmm," Mom says, her mouth twisting adorably. "Now that I know what's going on, I'm thinking Colby must have figured out you're dating Violet."

"Colby and Ryan know I've been obsessed with a girl named Violet since before the tour—a girl with dark hair and bangs. But they didn't know Violet was Reed's sister and Caleb's ex."

"Well, Colby's obviously connected the dots and told Ryan," Mom says.

Kat adds, "And I'm sure both guys have already told their wives, too."

I'm appalled. "Why would they do that?"

"Because Lydia and Tessa were both swooning like crazy when you sang 'Fireflies' at the concert, and I overheard Ryan telling them it was about some girl named Violet. I can't imagine the guys didn't feel compelled to point Violet out as your muse. They don't know she's forbidden fruit."

"Jesus Christ, this family," I mutter, rubbing my forehead. "Look, it's imperative everyone knows not to say anything to Reed. I don't think he'd say anything to Caleb, but I'm not sure about that. I'm also not positive at this point Reed wouldn't be pissed at me for messing with his sister."

"I'll make sure the Morgan Mafia is activated," Kat says.

"We'll all be a locked vault," Mom says, winking.

I chuckle. "Thanks." I stride to the door and open it for my mom and sister—the two women I love the most—more than words could ever say. "After you, ladies. I'm sure everyone is wondering where we are and I, for one, don't want them finding out Mom was in here doing blow off Kitty's stomach."

THIRTY-ONE

DAX

When I head into the party with my mom and sister, the pre-dinner cocktail hour is in full swing. I spot Reed in conversation with a group that includes the bride and groom. Across the room from Reed, Keane is standing, drink in hand, with the rest of our family—Colby and Ryan, their wives, and our father. And, lo and behold, Violet, the woman who gets my motor revving like none other, is sitting at one of the table rounds with Keane's adorable fiancée, Maddy, engaged in what appears to be a particularly enthusiastic conversation.

When Mom spies Violet and Maddy together, she cocks an eyebrow. "Why don't you say hello to your future sister-in-law, Daxy? You haven't seen Maddy since she and Keane got back from Australia, right?"

Kat links arms with our mother. "Isn't it delightful when the universe helps a brother out? Come on, Motherboard. Let's go tell everybody all of Daxy's salacious secrets."

After my mother and sister are gone, I approach the table where Violet and Maddy are huddled together, but when I'm close enough to hear their conversation, it's too cute to interrupt, so I hang back and eavesdrop.

"I love it so much!" Maddy gushes, looking at something on Violet's phone. "Did you ever make the actual dress?"

"No, just the sketch. I'm just showing it to you because it seems close to the wedding dress you've described."

"*Close?* Violet, no, this is *exactly* what my dream dress would look like. Would you send this to me so I can show it to salespeople when I go shopping with my mother?"

"Of course." Violet swipes at her phone and hands it to Maddy. "Type in your number."

Maddy starts typing. "I think it was fate we met tonight, Violet."

"I think so, too. I truly think something like this sketch would be perfect for your body type and energy."

"Oh my God, Violet. Will you *please* come wedding-dress shopping with me? I need your expertise."

Violet lights up. "I'd *love* to. I'm actually kind of obsessed with wedding dresses."

"I'm going shopping with my mom this week. My mom is heading back to Seattle on Friday, so she's insisting we go shopping before she leaves."

"You sure I won't be a third wheel?" Violet asks.

"Of course not. And you'd be doing me a huge favor. If my mom gets her way, my wedding dress will be an exact replica of Princess Diana's—only with poofier sleeves and a way longer train."

Both ladies giggle. And my heart skips a beat. Clearly, this is a match made in heaven.

"Just let me know the day and I'll make it work," Violet says. "My new job hasn't really kicked in yet, so I've got a pretty wide-open schedule."

Except that you're going to be fucking me all week, I think.

I take a couple steps forward and greet the ladies.

"Daxy!" Maddy says, popping up. She lopes over to me and hugs me. "Welcome home. Sorry I missed your show last night. I was with Hannah for her last night as a single lady. I heard the show was amazing."

"You saw the same show in Seattle. Welcome home to you, too. And congrats on the engagement. Let's see the ring, sister."

Maddy gleefully shows it to me and I tell her Keane knocked it out of the park, which he did.

Maddy motions to Violet. "Dax, this is Reed's sister, Violet. Violet, this is my soon-to-be brother-in-law, Dax Morgan—my fiancé's little brother."

My heart swells. It's been a long time since anyone introduced me in relation to my family, as opposed to saying something regarding my band. Growing up, I used to hate being introduced as Keane's younger brother all the time, back when Keane was a star athlete and I was nothing but his introverted, longhaired little brother who skateboarded, smoked weed, and preferred shutting myself into my room to play guitar over being the life of a big party. But now, suddenly, being introduced as Keane's little brother feels good. Like a badge of honor. Maybe even a salve for my soul.

"Hey, Violet," I say, hugging her politely and stealing a quick sniff of her hair. "Nice to see you again."

"You, too. Great show last night."

"Oh, you two have already met?"

"Last night," Violet says, her cheeks blooming. "My best friend, Miranda, and I were lucky enough to go backstage before the concert."

"One of the perks of having Reed Rivers as your brother," Maddy says.

"Actually, no, it was Miranda who arranged it," Violet says. Her eyes flicker to me. "Miranda's brother is the drummer for Red Card Riot."

And the guy who called you "the one that got away" and hugged you like he wanted to fuck you. Oh, and then took me onto a balcony to tell me he still loves you and plans to win you back.

Violet smiles at me from underneath her lashes. "I loved that new song you played last night, Dax. It gave me chills."

"It poured out of me from the depths of my soul."

Violet's eyes sparkle. "I could tell."

Maddy looks from Violet to me for a beat, like she's catching a whiff of the chemistry passing between us. "Everyone keeps talking about that new song you played last night," Maddy says. "I'm bummed I missed it."

I peel my eyes off Violet's. "I'll sing it for you whenever I've got my guitar. Now, sit down and tell me about Keane's proposal. I saw the video, but tell me about it from your point of view."

The three of us sit at the table, with Maddy in the middle, and Maddy launches into telling her story. But I can barely process a word she says. I'm just too overcome by Violet's proximity to concentrate... by her lips as she licks them... and the fact that I can still taste Violet's sweetness on my tongue. Plus, I'm pretty turned on to have Violet's G-string burning like ultraviolet radiation in my pocket. In fact, as I sit here, my dick is tingling and my palms sweating.

Our conversation twists and turns from Maddy's story, until, soon, Maddy gets Violet talking about the nonprofit she's recently started in L.A.—The Superhero Project. At Maddy's request, Violet pulls out her phone and shows us some photos of her efforts. As I peek over Maddy's shoulder, Violet scrolls through images of kids, some of them dressed in full-blown superhero costumes worthy of a Marvel movie, others clad in simple hospital gowns. In each photo, the kid is beaming, despite their illness, their joy at their new superhero costume obvious.

Suddenly, the enormity of what Violet's been doing all these years hits me. The kindness of it. The fact that she gives her heart and soul and time to kids she doesn't even know—for no other reason than she wants to spread a little joy and hope and love to people in need.

Emotion rises inside me. Admiration, too. Before this moment, I knew Violet was a woman of substance, like my mom called her, beyond her obvious sex appeal. But, all of a sudden, I'm appreciating the goodness of Violet's heart. There's no doubt about it, she's the kind of girl I'd take home to meet my family... which is a mighty good thing, seeing as how Violet's going to meet all of them tonight, if she hasn't already.

"And this is Ashley," Violet says, her voice laced with particular affection. *"Puppy Girl.* I had to design a hospital gown for her because she was stuck in the hospital for months."

"Puppy Girl?" Maddy asks.

"All Ashley wanted was to run and play with a new puppy." She swipes to the next photo and a truly breathtaking smile spreads across Violet's face. "Look what Ashley's parents sent me, just last week. Puppy Girl got her wish!"

Maddy and I both gasp at the sight of Ashley, this time with short hair, instead of a knit cap. Her little body looks far more robust than in the prior photo. *And she's rolling around on green grass with a chocolate Labrador puppy.*

"I cried when I got this photo," Violet says.

"I'm crying about it, too," Maddy says, wiping her eyes. "Do you keep in touch with all the kids you design costumes for?"

"No. Hardly ever. Ashley just touched me, extra deep. Whenever Ashley's feeling up to it, Reed said he'd send her and her family to Disneyland, all expenses paid, as my birthday present."

"As *your* birthday present?" Maddy says. She glances at me, and it's plain to see she's deeply impressed with Violet. And I must admit, so am I... in a whole new way.

"Reed is always really generous with me," Violet says. She shoots me a pointed look that tells me she didn't appreciate my earlier unkind words about her brother in the laundry room. She returns to Maddy. "I was just about to turn fifteen when I met Reed for the first time. He'd just turned twenty-five and had never had a sibling before. So, taking on a little sister was an adjustment for him. But he's been a prince to me since day one."

"You and Reed have the same father?"

Violet nods. "Our father passed away when Reed was nineteen and I was nine. Reed's mother has a history of mental illness, and his childhood was chaotic and unstable. Frankly, it was horrible. So, I think, when we connected, Reed was as grateful to find someone to love unconditionally as I was." Again, she looks at me in a way that tells me I've got Reed all wrong. "Reed didn't have to be a big brother to me. He *chose* to do that. I know in other aspects of Reed's life, in his romantic life, maybe, he has a hard time trusting or forging deep bonds. But with me, he's always been true blue. He funded The Superhero Project. He paid for my schooling. And since I moved to L.A., he's been letting me live rent-free in one of his best apartments with my best friend, while I try to get my so-called career off the ground. And he's not just generous with me financially. He protects me and cares for me." She shoots me yet another chastising glance, just in case I haven't gotten the message yet.

"How did you and Reed finally connect?" Maddy asks.

"Reed reached out to me after the death of my little brother. He died of leukemia at age three."

Maddy looks stricken. "Oh, Violet. I'm so sorry."

Oh, the look of pain flashing across Violet's face is cracking my heart.

Maddy says, "That's why you created The Superhero Project?"

"Yes. In Jackson's memory. It's all for him."

Maddy touches her heart. "What a lovely way to honor your brother."

"And channel my grief," Violet says softly. "Helping those kids is what keeps me going."

Maddy hugs Violet and whispers condolences—and as I watch the exchange, I feel overwhelmed with respect and adoration for Violet. Violet already owns my dick. But in this moment, Violet just reached into my chest cavity, pulled my beating heart out, and stuffed it firmly into her pocket.

"Hey, hey!" Keane says, approaching, and the girls break apart from their embrace. Keane takes a seat next to me at the table and introduces himself to Violet. "Am I interrupting something?"

"Not at all," Violet says. "I'm excited to meet you. Maddy was telling me earlier about your *Ball Peen Hammer* videos. I can't wait to binge-watch all of them."

"Get ready to roll your eyes at Keane *a lot*," I say, laughing.

"But in the best possible way," Maddy adds. She smiles at Keane, her beloved new fiancé. "Guess what, Honey Boo Boo? Violet's coming wedding-dress shopping with me this week."

"Awesome."

"I'm actually obsessed with wedding dresses," Violet says. "Not for myself to wear, just to be clear. I love *designing* them. I'm also excited to meet someone nice in L.A.—someone who could be my actual friend, as opposed to someone who's secretly interested in getting access to Reed."

"Oh, man, I imagine that happens to you a lot in this town," Maddy says.

"It happens all the time," Violet admits. "The only true blue friend I've got here in L.A. is my childhood friend, Miranda. We're roommates, which is awesome, but she's working full-time at River Records and traveling a bunch for her job, so she's not around much."

"I don't have a whole lot of close girlfriends, either," Maddy says. "Besides my sister, there's only Aloha. But she's super busy and always traveling. And even when she's around, she can't really do 'normal girlfriend' things, like shopping for a wedding dress, just because she attracts way too much attention."

Violet's eyes widen. "Your friend is Aloha... *Carmichael*?"

Maddy nods. "Keane's best friend, Zander, is her bodyguard, so we connected that way. One thing led to another, Keane and I joined the tour for a few weeks in Australia, and now Aloha and I are soul sisters. Hey! I bet she'd love to hear about The Superhero Project. Aloha often visits children's hospitals in cities on her tours. Why don't I introduce the two of you?"

"Oh my gosh, Maddy. That'd be incredible! My ultimate goal is to raise awareness and money not just for the kids' costumes, but for their families. You know, so parents don't have to worry about their jobs or rent or putting food on the table while their kid is going through treatments."

"Oh, Violet, that's amazing. Would it help you if Keane and I were to feature you on our web show?"

Violet expresses excitement and gratitude. Keane says it's a great idea. And, once again, I'm drowning in not only white-hot sexual attraction, but also extreme adoration and respect.

"I'm texting Aloha now," Maddy says, tapping on her phone. "No promises, of course. But I'm sure she'd love to meet you and hear about the amazing things you're doing and how you want to expand your mission. If you're lucky, maybe she'll get on board somehow or, at least, tweet about it."

"Oh, God. I'm freaking out. I've always idolized Aloha. I might fangirl pretty hard, so I apologize in advance if I do."

"I'm surprised Reed hasn't already introduced you, if you're a fan," Keane says.

"Reed offered when I went to a party he threw for Aloha at his house last year. But she was partying with her friends, celebrating the kickoff of her tour, and I didn't want to bother her. Also, confession? One of my dreams is to design a costume for Aloha one day—for a music video or something—and I didn't want to meet Aloha through Reed and have her feel any obligation to take a look at my designs."

Keane's smiling like the cat who swallowed the canary. "I *knew* I recognized you from somewhere, but I couldn't place you. Even when I heard my mother and Kat over there, talking about you and Dax, I still couldn't figure it out. But just now, when you mentioned Reed's party, it clicked. You're the girl in the white pantsuit from Reed's party—the one who was macking down on Daxy on the patio!"

Violet and I look at each other and blush.

Maddy furrows her brow. "But... Violet said you two met for the first time last night."

Violet and I exchange a look that says, *Busted.* I address Maddy. "Violet and I met the night of Reed's party. That new song everyone's been talking about? I wrote it about Violet. When Violet said we met last night, she was just sticking to our agreed-upon script. I hadn't had the chance to tell her my entire family was in the process of finding out about our secret across the room." I explain to Violet how and why I told my mom and sister about us in the laundry room, and that, sorry, that most likely means my entire family knows about us by now.

"They do," Keane confirms. "Everyone was talking about it over there. But don't worry. We all understand it's top-secret, classified intel."

"But *why* is it top-secret?" Maddy says.

I explain The Caleb Situation to Maddy and she grimaces, the same way my mother did in the laundry room.

"Also, I'm not eager to tell my brother about us," Violet says. She explains the gist to Keane and Maddy and adds, "When Caleb cheated on me during RCR's first tour, Reed was ready to drop the band from his label if they didn't drop Caleb as their drummer. Can you imagine?"

I feel like I've been punched in the gut. "*Reed wanted RCR to drop Caleb?* But Caleb is the best drummer out there! And RCR was blowing up like crazy on that first tour."

"Crazy, right?" Violet says. "Maybe it was all talk. Maybe Reed was just trying to demonstrate loyalty to me, his new sister. Who knows? All I know is Reed said it, and I believed he meant it, so I lied and told him the stories about Caleb cheating on me weren't true. I swore up and down Caleb had broken my heart by seeming distant with me, but nothing else. I swore I'd broken up with Caleb first, and that he was simply trying to numb the pain with those groupies." She rolls her eyes.

I can't believe my ears. My breathing is shallow. "Lemme get this straight. C-Bomb cheated on *you*, and yet, you bent over backwards to protect *him*?"

Violet shrugs. "Dean didn't cheat on me. And neither did Clay or Emmitt. I didn't want those guys to suffer for something Caleb did. Those guys had worked their asses off to get where they were and I wasn't going to let Reed or anyone take it away from them, especially not on account of me. Plus, even though Caleb had broken my heart, I still wanted his dreams to come true. His dreams were mine. I met Caleb when I was thirteen and he was sixteen, back when I was nothing to Caleb but his little sister's dorky friend. After Reed came into my life, I pestered him relentlessly to catch an RCR show in San Diego. He finally did it just to shut me up, I think." She laughs. "Reed signed RCR the very next day, and I felt like it was happening to *me*. Just because my romance with Caleb ended badly, I wasn't about to let my personal heartbreak get in the way of watching those boys fulfill their dreams—their *destiny*."

I feel like I'm physically staggering as I sit here. Violet is... amazing. Caleb *literally* owes everything to her. And yet, he betrayed her. And when he did, she put his dreams, and the dreams of his band-mates, above getting any kind of sweet revenge.

"So, that's why I've got no desire to tell Reed about Dax and me," Violet says. "If things aren't destined to work out for us, I don't want to feel stressed about Reed getting pissed at Dax for sins, real or imagined, and taking it out on Dax or 22 Goats."

All at once, everyone turns to look at me. And I suddenly realize a weird, guttural whimpering sound just came out of me. A kind of tortured groan, like my very soul is straining to fuse with Violet's. But when I say nothing in response to the three pairs of eyes on me, Keane and Maddy resume the conversation.

"Did you know right away Red Card Riot was destined to blow up as big as they have?" Keane asks.

"Nobody could have predicted how big they've become," Violet says. "But I knew they were destined for huge success. I became friends with Miranda in middle school, and whenever I'd go to her house, I'd see her big brother, Caleb. He was in high school and the drummer in a rock band, so I was in awe of him. Our age gap felt huge back then, though, so he paid no attention to me. I was just his kid sister's dorky friend who was always hanging around, like a gnat, watching the guys rehearse."

"Until...?" Maddy prompts.

"Until one day, a week after I'd turned sixteen, he finally noticed me."

My stomach knots as my mind provides the obvious visual: Caleb kissing Violet—and Violet being thrilled about it.

Violet says, "We were in a relationship for a year, right up until

RCR went off on their first tour. I spent about six months licking my wounds after we broke up, and then went off to college three thousand miles away and started a whole new life."

My mind is suddenly teeming with thoughts. If I'd been nineteen during this tour, and I had my first love waiting for me back home, would I have stayed true to her? I like to think I would have, because I'm a Morgan and we don't cheat. But having just been through the eye of the storm, I think there's a chance I would have let myself—and my first love down—the way Caleb did. No wonder Violet said she was doing me a favor eight months ago when she sent me off, completely unattached. She knew what I was in for in the coming months on tour, better than anyone. She knew I was going to get sucked into a hurricane with no parallel in the real world. Something nearly impossible to weather in one piece. And she didn't want to sit around, waiting by the phone, while I inevitably lost my way for a bit and fell apart... and left her in the dust.

The singer of the jazz trio in the corner says, "I've just been advised dinner is about to be served. Everyone, please find your assigned tables now. Thank you."

"I'll see you after dinner," I say to Violet, as she rises from her chair, well aware she's assigned to a table with Reed and the bride and groom, while I'm assigned to a table with my family.

"I'll see you on the dance floor," she replies. "I'm in the mood to shake my money-maker tonight, baby."

"Oh, Dax doesn't shake his money-maker," Keane says. "Not unless he's onstage with his guitar or blitzed out of his mind at a family wedding." He gestures to the water bottle in my hand. "If you can get Daxy to dance tonight, sober as a judge, that'll be a family first."

Violet cocks an eyebrow. "Challenge accepted." With a cute little wink, she turns to walk away... and runs smack into Reed's chest.

"Ho!" Reed says, laughing. He grabs Violet's shoulders to steady her. "I was coming to escort my pretty plus-one to our table."

"How chivalrous of you." She shoots me yet another scathing look in defense of her brother, before addressing Reed again. "You were right about Maddy being my spirit animal. We've already made plans to go wedding-dress shopping this week."

"I knew you two would hit it off," Reed says. "Did you know you two are roommates in a parallel universe?" He addresses Maddy. "When you and Hannah moved out of your unit, I gave it to Violet and her best friend."

"No way! Which bedroom is yours, Violet?"

"The one on the right."

"That was mine, too!"

The ladies laugh.

"Hey, I've had sex in your bedroom, Violet," Keane says. "If only those walls could talk, they'd scream 'Yes, yes, *yessss!*'"

As everyone else laughs, Maddy whacks Keane on his shoulder.

"Who lives in the apartment across the hall nowadays?" I ask Violet. "Fish, Colin, and I lived there before the tour, while we were writing and recording our album."

"I just installed a new band in there last week, actually," Reed says. "They're going to be writing and recording their debut for the next several months."

"Whoa, it really *is* a parallel universe!" Maddy says, laughing. "Is the new band a trio?"

"They are. And the lead singer has long, blonde hair."

"*He does?*" Maddy says, gasping.

"*She* does." Reed chuckles and looks at me. "I heard you're crashing at Caleb's these days, while you look for a place?"

My stomach twists. "No, I decided to stay at a hotel."

"Whatever works. You can stay here for a few weeks, if you get sick of hotels."

"Thanks, but I realized I'd rather just chill by myself for a little while."

"I get it. Standing offer, though."

"Thanks."

Reed puts his arm out to Violet, who's right now shooting me yet another chastising look in reaction to Reed's offer of a place to stay.

"Bye, guys," Violet says, taking her brother's arm. She looks at me. "I'll see you all on the dance floor after dinner." With that, she sashays away with Reed, swinging her ass like she knows full well I'm staring at it as she retreats... while thinking about the fact that it's bare underneath that dress of hers, because her fire-red undies are burning a hole inside my pocket.

Lyrics.

Oh my God.

I pull out my phone and begin furiously jotting them down.

Keane watches me for a moment. "Lyrics?" he says.

"Mmm hmm."

"About Violet?"

"Uh huh. Shh, Peenie."

"Oh, man, you're a goner, aren't you? In your world, a girl who inspires lyrics is even hotter than a girl who can suck an orange through a garden hose."

"Shut up, dude. I need to listen."

"To what?"

"The song in my head."

Oh, God, I'm euphoric. The muse is back! Finally, after months of writer's block, I'm officially cured.

When I've got all the words down, I look up from my phone and discover Keane and Maddy smirking at me.

"Oh, Daxy," Maddy says. "Someone's falling fast and hard."

I shove my phone into my pocket. "It's way too soon to be making proclamations like that, Mad Dog. One day at a time." But even as I say the words, I know I'm full of shit. Maddy's right. I'm falling fast and hard. Faster and harder than I've fallen for any girl in my life. "Come on, guys. Mom is giving us the stink-eye over there. Let's bounce."

"Giving *you* the stink-eye," Keane corrects. "Maddy's the maid of honor, remember? We're sitting at the bride and groom's table with the cool kids. Have fun at the ghetto table, sucka."

"Aw, man. I'm jealous you're sitting with Violet. Don't forget to keep mum about Vi and me."

"We gotchu, Rock Star," Keane says with a wink. "Kat activated the Morgan Mafia."

With a grateful smile, I begin walking toward my assigned table, but Keane's voice calling my name stops me. I turn around, a question on my face.

"When was the last time a girl inspired lyrics the way Violet does, brother?"

I look at Violet across the room for a long moment. She's shaking hands around her table, flashing radiant smiles. Winning hearts. Lighting people up the way only she does. And I feel like a sunflower stretching, bending, *twisting* to bask in her beautiful, golden light. "The way Violet does?" I say, my eyes fixed on my glorious muse. "It's never happened before. She's my first." My heart skips a beat. "My only."

THIRTY-TWO

DAX

Every member of my family—including Colby and me, believe it or not—are out here on the dance floor, cutting loose, right alongside the bride and groom and Violet and Reed and every other person at this awesome wedding. I'm completely sober, of course, thanks to my promise to Colby. Which is more than I can say for Colby. The boy is definitely tying one on tonight. But Violet's drinking nothing but water, in solidarity with me, so that's made it easier for me to stay the course.

And yet, sober as I am among a room full of drunkards, I feel shit-faced. High as a kite, in fact. Like I'm dancing ten feet above the ground. Because tonight, I'm not Dax Morgan of 22 Goats. I'm just Dax, the fifth Morgan kid. The guy whose dad didn't give a shit what the hell he was called. I'm not the guy who gets offered blowjobs at every turn, or the world's "fantasy boyfriend" or "celebrity crush." I'm not the guy with the ass from that music video that went viral. I'm just a dude who's having a good time with his family and friends while trying his damnedest to impress the most electrifying girl he's ever met.

When the current song ends, everyone exchanges "let's take a break" gestures all around me. And off my core group goes, exiting the dance floor in a slow-moving herd that wordlessly sweeps Violet along with us, like it's already understood at a cellular level among my people: *this girl is one of us now.*

Our group takes seats around two tables shoved together, with Violet plopping herself down next to me, with Maddy on her other side. A roving cocktail server comes by and takes orders. I'm a bit annoyed to have to order water from this woman *again,* as opposed to the whiskey or tequila I'd much rather be drinking. But it's not the end of the world, especially with Violet ordering water, too. I told Violet she doesn't have to abstain from drinking tonight on my account, but when she heard what I was doing, and why, she said she was excited to do it with me, for however long. Not gonna lie, it made me like her even more, if that's even possible.

When the server leaves, Kat says, "I can't believe all four notorious 'non-dancers' in my family have been dancing like fools tonight, Lionel Richie Style." She's referring to Colby, me, Dad, and her brother-in-law, Jonas. Kat adds, "Is there something in the water tonight? You four didn't dance this much at *my* wedding." She winks at me, letting me know she's well aware what's brought me onto the dance floor tonight, and I respond by winking back like a thief with a pocketful of stolen cookies. Or, more accurately, a pocketful of stolen undies. Fire-red, stolen undies that smell like heaven. Just knowing they're in my pocket, I've been popping random boners all night.

Maddy says, "Whatever's gotten everyone out there dancing, Keane and I want to duplicate it at our wedding. This is so much fun."

Mom's eyes light up. "Does that mean you and Keaney have started making wedding plans? Is there a proposed date? A location?"

"Take a chill pill, Momma Lou," Keane says. "There are lots of moving parts here, with everyone's crazy schedules."

"Well, while we're all sitting here, let's nail down a date," Mom says.

The entire table starts talking about possible dates for Keane and Maddy's wedding, but I tune them out, opting instead to focus on my hand—which, at the moment, is resting on Violet's bare thigh underneath the table.

I pull up Violet's dress even more and slide my palm higher onto Violet's bare thigh, making my intentions abundantly clear. *I'm going in.* And to my thrill, Violet widens her legs at my touch, inviting me to go all the way. Just to be sure I'm understanding her signals, though, I look at Violet pointedly, my eyebrows raised, and, hot damn, my sexy girl glances away nonchalantly and yawns... while spreading her creamy thighs even wider and jerking her pelvis slightly forward, as if to say, *Come and get it, baby.*

She doesn't have to ask me twice.

As everyone around me starts talking about the possibility of a destination wedding for Keane and Maddy, I slowly graze my fingertips up Violet's soft inner thigh toward The Promised Land. Up, up, up, my greedy hand goes, sending blood whooshing straight into my cock.

Just before my fingers reach their warm, wet destination, my eyes happen to meet Reed's across the table. He juts his chin at me, acknowledging my gaze, and I smile at him brightly in return, just as I sink two fingers inside his little sister.

"A destination wedding would be a dream come true," Maddy says. "But maybe a one-night party, like tonight, would be easier for everyone?"

When Reed's dark eyes leave mine, I begin finger-fucking Violet in earnest.

Reed says to Maddy, "You can have the wedding here, if you'd like."

"Oh, that's such a sweet offer," Maddy says. "But I think doing it here would feel like a redo of my sister's wedding—a bit like *Groundhog Day.*"

I nod like I'm listening to Maddy's comment. But, oh fuck, I'm hard as steel and dripping with arousal underneath this table. Getting more and more turned on as Violet gets wetter and wetter around my thrusting, hungry fingers.

Violet shifts in her seat as her arousal becomes palpable. When she lifts her water glass to her lips, her hand is trembling, ever so slightly.

I look away from Violet's shaking water glass, my fingers still working her, and shift in my seat, trying to relieve my straining hard-on. But moving around in my seat isn't doing the trick. I'm throbbing down there. About to explode.

My cock aching, I begin sliding my fingers from Violet's wetness to her hard, swollen tip, and then back again. Back and forth, my fingers go, as I coat that magical bundle of nerves with her slickness— the sweet wetness that tells me she's aching and ready for me.

When Violet lets out a long, soft moan, I zero in on her tip in earnest. Around and around I massage that hard bud, in firm, confident, unrelenting circles. After a minute, Violet lets out a little squeak and abruptly bows her head. Her chest heaves. She presses her pelvis fervently into my fingers underneath the table and quivers at my touch.

I glance around, worried we're going to get caught, but nobody's paying attention to Violet or me, not with the DJ playing music behind us and animated conversation dominating the table.

"Okay, here's the plan," Josh says. "We're going to do a destination wedding, all expenses paid by me. It'll be my wedding present to you two and my Christmas present to the family."

Everyone gasps and expresses amazement at Josh's generous pronouncement, and I use their excitement as cover to go in for the kill. I increase the speed and intensity of my assault on Violet's clit and, in response, she grips the tablecloth and moans again, this time a little bit more loudly, and I know she's right on the bitter edge.

Keane and Maddy are saying all the right things to Josh about his offer. Things like "We couldn't possibly accept." And Josh keeps insisting. Around and around they go, just like my fingers on Violet's clit. And finally, just as Josh's gift is accepted with gratitude and excitement, Violet comes like a rumbling freight train against my hand. She's rippling. Clenching. And it's glorious.

Timing. That's what they're talking about at the table now. Trying to nail it down.

But I'm too turned on, too hard and dripping, to focus on anything being said. I'm not done with Violet yet. I want more. *I want to make her mine.* Did Caleb get her off the way I do? What about that guy she dated while I was gone? Has anyone ever made Violet's eyes roll back into her head, over and over again? I feel desperate to be the top of the heap to her. The best she's ever had. In my song last night, I told Violet she's like nobody else to me. *Never before or since.* I feel ravenous to be her one and only, too.

When Violet realizes I'm not letting up, despite her climax, her breathing hitches sharply. She visibly digs in, preparing herself for what's sure to be an even more intense orgasm the second time around.

Scheduling.

That's what everyone at the table is talking about. Keane's upcoming shooting schedule for his TV show. The documentary Maddy is gearing up to make about Aloha. The grand opening for the next Captain's location—the chain of bars Ryan and his wife run together with Josh and his brother. As the people around me talk and talk, I buckle down, determined to pull lucky number two out of Violet within the next minute.

I try a new motion with my fingers. A new rhythm. And by the way Violet reacts to it, it's clear I'm on to something.

The Bahamas.

Josh just suggested it as the location for Keane and Maddy's destination wedding, and everyone is expressing enthusiasm.

I shift to using the pad of my thumb. I press it against Violet's clit, in firm pulsing motions, and... *yes.* There we go. Violet digs her fingernails into the top of my hand underneath the table, bows her head, shifts in her seat... and comes hard against my fingers. Harder than the last time, I can plainly tell. It's an incredible sensation, feeling those muscles ripple and grip so forcefully. Knowing Violet's got to be desperate by now to get fucked—every bit as desperate as I am to fuck her.

"...next tour, Dax?"

I jerk my head up at the sound of my name.

Keane repeats, "When's your next tour, brah?"

"Reed?" I say, doing my best to sound calm and collected. But even as I say it, my fingertips are gently brushing up and down Violet's slit, making sure she stays aroused and ready for me. "You wanna tell 'em about my touring schedule?"

Reed tells everyone that 22 Goats will be back on the road again, this time as the headliner, in six to eight months. "But we can carve out a week from the tour for Dax and the boys to go to the wedding, just as long as we have the dates in advance."

My sister-in-law, Tessa, volunteers to start scouting locations and nailing down the dates. Everyone around me agrees Tessa's the right woman for the job.

I slowly pull Violet's dress down to cover her thighs and lean into her ear. "Meet me in the bathroom in five. The one down that hall." I indicate with my chin.

Violet glances across the table—at her brother—and it's instantly clear she's worried he'll notice both of us leaving at the same time.

"I'll create a distraction," I whisper. "Just go. If I don't fuck you, I'm gonna come in my pants."

Violet rises and excuses herself—but nobody bats an eyelash, since they're now enthusiastically talking about the size of Keane and Maddy's guest list.

Casually, I pull out my phone and tap out a text to Keane.

Me: You got weed?

When Keane doesn't immediately pull out his phone, I catch his eye and hold up mine, telling him that buzzing in his pocket was me. Thankfully, Keane and I have had secret text conversations in groups many times, so he knows what's up. He pulls out his phone and glances down, and immediately pulls a face. Two seconds later, I get his reply text.

. . .

Keane: If you smoke tonight, Colby's gonna drag your ass to rehab tomorrow.

Rolling my eyes, I tap out my reply and press send.

Me: Not for me. I wanna meet Vi in the bathroom and I need you to distract her bro. I'm thinking a celebratory joint with the groom and his buddies on the patio...

Keane's gaze flickers to Violet's vacant chair. A half-second later, I receive a single-word reply from him.

Keane: Roger.

Of course, I reply as Morgan law requires me to do.

Me: Rabbit.

And then I look around casually, like I'm thoroughly engaged in the conversation.

I watch Keane lean over to Henn and whisper to him, and then grin as word of Keane's invitation visibly spreads among Henn and his closest crew. In short order, the precise group of softcore tokers I would have predicted—Reed, Henn, Josh, and Ryan—rise from the table with Keane and follow him to the patio.

Colby catches my eye and winks at me as the guys depart,

acknowledging I didn't join the party, like I normally would, and I raise my empty water bottle to him like, *Yeah, fucker, a promise is a promise.*

My path now cleared to join Violet in the bathroom, I begin rising from my chair. But when my eyes happen to catch my mother's blue gaze, I freeze. I can't tell if it's sheer coincidence she's staring at me right now, or if she knows she's catching me with my hand in the cookie jar. Either way, I slide my ass back down into my seat.

She smiles sweetly, glances at Violet's vacant chair, and looks at Keane and Maddy.

Well, fuck. I don't need my mother's eyes on me as I disappear into a hallway to bang Violet. I mean, yeah, my mother knows *generally* that I'm hot for Violet. And she knows *generally* I'm a horny dude. But does my darling mother really need to know, for a *fact*, I'm disappearing to bang Violet for a second time tonight?

Okay, obviously, I need a distraction. I need my Wonder Twin. I pull out my phone again, but before I've begun tapping out a text to Kat, it buzzes with an incoming text from... Kat.

Kat: Wonder Twin powers, activate. I'll distract Mom. Wait for my signal.

When I look up from my phone, Kat is smiling devilishly at me. With a cute little wink, she gets up from the table and strides to the DJ across the room. Two seconds later, the guy announces, "I've had a request for the bride and all the ladies to come the dance floor! Come on, ladies, show the fellas how you shake it!"

The song switches to "Dancing Queen," and pretty much every woman in attendance at the wedding, including my beloved mother, leaps up and giddily gallops onto the dance floor, as requested.

A huge smile on my face, and my heart thumping wildly, I shoot a grateful text to Kat.

. . .

Me: Best. Sister. Ever.

And then I get up, my hard cock throbbing and my body on fire, and walk briskly toward the bathroom.

THIRTY-THREE

VIOLET

When Dax turns around from locking the bathroom door, he grimaces. "I just realized I don't have a condom."

I hold up a foil packet, a naughty smile on my face. "I pilfered one from Reed's nightstand. He's got a huge box of them. He'll never miss it."

"You're a goddess." He lurches at me. His breathing ragged, he turns me around. Hikes up my dress. He unzips his pants and gets himself covered, pins my belly against the sink, and plunges himself inside me from behind.

Heaven.

I groan at the invasion of Dax's body and sigh as my body molds to his—as my *soul* molds to his. He unzips me and slides his hand inside my dress. He cups my breast as he fucks me. Pinches my nipple. And, all the while, he stares over my shoulder at my eyes in the mirror as he fucks me. Intense energy courses between us. This connection is like nothing I've felt before.

I grip the sink as Dax thrusts in and out of me, his blue eyes locked with mine.

"You feel so good," he whispers, moving in and out of me, fondling my breast under my dress. "I'm addicted to you, Violet." He begins working my clit as he fucks me. He kisses my neck and bites at my ear. "I want you."

"You've got me."

"I want more."

I shudder with pleasure. I don't know what that means, exactly. But the way he said it sent shivers zapping across my nerve endings.

Dax is growling now. Grunting like he's in the zone. Our hips are rocking together in perfect rhythm. We're spiraling into a frenzy, the two of us. Turning into wild animals.

I reach my arm around his neck behind me and turn my head and he devours my lips.

A flash of pleasure zings my clit underneath Dax's talented fingers, making me gasp. I abruptly disengage from our kiss and grip the sink, readying myself for what's surely going to be a body-quaking orgasm.

"Oh, God, Dax," I choke out.

He sucks my earlobe like it's my clit, and I lose it. Warm, delicious waves seize me, making me cry out and crumple into the sink. As my body undulates and warps, Dax stiffens behind me and comes like a rocket inside me, my name on his lips. And, lucky me, I get to witness the whole thing in the mirror—the look of pure rapture on Dax's gorgeous face as he reaches orgasm. It's the same primal look that overtook his face several times last night while playing his guitar. The look of a man in the throes of pure ecstasy.

As Dax's body shudders and quivers, he covers my mouth with his hand and I lick and bite at his fingers, still ravenous for him.

We're both breathing hard. Coming down from the high. He turns me around, grabs my face, and kisses me deeply, making my very soul lurch and bound and leap inside me.

I return Dax's kiss, clawing at him, grasping, needing, and finally leave his mouth to nip at his neck and jawline. I nuzzle his glorious hair and inhale his delicious scent. I lick his neck and grab his ass. I feel addicted to this boy. Drugged. I've never felt this kind of high with someone. This kind of *desperation*.

When Dax leans back, his eyes are blazing. "Those fireflies are fire-breathing dragons now. A fucking Phoenix on the rise."

I nod, as excitement surges inside me.

He zips his pants. "You head back out there first. I'll wait five minutes and then come out and say my goodbyes. Meet me at my hotel as soon as you can get away. I texted you the info. Come as soon as you can, okay? I can't stand the thought of being apart from you." He's trembling. Like he's giving me instructions to board a lifeboat on a sinking ship. "And don't forget to swing by your place and get a week's worth of stuff. I want you in my bed for a solid week, Vi." He touches my face, his blue eyes smoldering and his body language verging on manic. "I feel like I've waited my whole damn life to be with you again. Like I rubbed a magic lamp and made a wish, and now you're finally here."

I nod profusely and try not to whimper.

He kisses me again, passionately, before finally peeling himself away from me. "Okay, go on, baby. The sooner we get out of here, the sooner we'll be naked and my tongue will be inside you."

I shudder with excitement as I pull myself together. "See you soon."

"See you soon, disco momma." His chest heaves with excitement. "Oh, God. A solid week. Talk about *flow*. This is gonna be *epic*."

THIRTY-FOUR

VIOLET

The alarm on Dax's phone goes off, yanking me out of sleep.

"What the fuck?" he says next to me, rolling over and reaching for it. He looks at his screen. "Aw, come on! Fuck you, Colby. Asshole. Fucker. *I hate you.*"

I laugh. "What?"

"I forgot Colby made an appointment with a therapist for me today. Fuck!"

I giggle and touch his bicep. "Maybe therapy will be good for you."

"You're all the therapy I need, Violet Rhodes," he says, pulling my naked body to his. "You've helped me talk through all my shit these past couple days, and you've done it naked. Sometimes, in a bathtub. Can a therapist say that?"

"God, I hope not."

"And not only that, you've got therapeutic tools at your disposal this guy couldn't possibly have. Amazing, healing stuff like *this*." He grabs my ass and squeezes. "And *this*." He grabs my breast. "And *this*." He brushes his hand between my legs, making me jolt with arousal. "All this is the best therapy I've ever had."

"You've had therapy before?"

"No."

I roll my eyes.

Laughing, he kisses my cheek. "I don't need actual therapy to know your brand of it is way better than anything else on the market. I've never felt better in my life than I do right now after spending two days and three nights here with you. Any problems I was having toward the end of the tour, they're all gone now, thanks to you and all your amazing"—he grabs my ass again—"*therapy*."

I press my nose into his. "Anybody would feel like they don't have a care in the world after talking and fucking nonstop for two and a half days. The problem is you can't stay in this room, talking and fucking with me, forever."

"I don't see why not."

"Babe, seriously. Therapy will help you figure out how to feel this happy"—I grab his hard-on—"out there, in the real world."

"You sure you want me to feel *this* happy out there? Because I think that's a public lewdness charge waiting to happen."

I giggle. "And Ryan thinks *he's* the funniest Morgan. Ha."

"When did he say that?"

"At the wedding. He and Keane were having a debate, and I happened to be sitting at the table, watching them. Highly amusing. It was a fight to the death."

"Who won?"

"Keane, I'd say."

"And rightly so. Where was I?"

"Dancing with Kat." I smile. "Being adorable and sexy and yummy from afar."

He kisses me. "*You're* adorable and sexy and yummy. Especially right now." He begins stroking between my legs again. Kissing me passionately. And, quickly, I'm ramping up to full-throttle.

Suddenly, Dax's phone starts chirping again, and he abruptly pulls away from me with an annoyed groan.

"Goddamned Colby. He added a second alert!" He shuts off the sound. "You know what? I'm not going. I don't need therapy. I'm cured."

"Go, Dax. It'll be good for you."

He nuzzles my nose. "But I'd rather stay here with you and fuck you again, all day long."

"Well, that's not gonna happen, regardless, because I'm going wedding-dress shopping with Maddy and her mother today."

"Today?"

"Yep. So I guess you might as well go to your appointment, even if it's just to humor Colby."

"When are you going?"

"I'm meeting them at eleven thirty. What time's your appointment?"

"Eleven fifteen."

"See? Perfect timing. It's fate."

"You're coming back here after shopping, though, right?"

"Of course. And I'm sure I'll be rarin' to go, sexy boy. Wedding dresses get me all hot and bothered."

"Perfect. I'll do some writing this afternoon while you're gone—which always gets my juices flowing. So when you get back I'll be desperate to impale you with my hard songwriter's cock."

"Oooh. You're gonna impale me with your hard *songwriter's* cock? Sounds like ecstasy." I grab his hard-on under the sheet again. "Maybe you should show me how you're gonna do it now, real quick, just so I know what I'm looking forward to."

"Gladly."

His lips crush mine. His hand slides between my legs and inside me. And soon...

"Oh, God," I grit out. I make a tortured sound, arch my back, whimper... and then... *heaven*. My deepest muscles begin rippling against Dax's fingers inside me with a delicious orgasm. Oh, God, he's good. And he's only gotten better and better as we've gotten to know each other's bodies over the past three days. As we've had candlelit meals in our suite and talked the nights away about anything and everything.

Wordlessly, Dax climbs on top of me and burrows himself inside me, without a condom. We talked about it yesterday and decided to go for it. I'm on the pill, and we're exclusive, so we're taking the plunge. And I must admit, having Dax inside me, bareback, makes me even more ravenous for him than ever. Just knowing he's feeling every ridge and muscle of me, that there's absolutely nothing to dull his pleasure and there's nothing between us, no matter how thin, feels like a metaphor for how close we've become, just this fast.

As Dax thrusts, he grinds his hips against my pelvis with gusto—and I receive him enthusiastically. When we get going like crazy, I wrap my thighs around his torso and dig my fingernails into his shoulders like I'm hanging onto the edge of a cliff, and I moan and groan and babble his name. Oh, God, yes, I do. I bite and kiss and suck on his neck and lips, every cell in my body alive with my delicious addiction.

With a loud, lusty moan, I arch my back underneath Dax, dig my nails into his back again, nice and deep, and come, prompting Dax to jerk on top of me and release inside me... just as Dax's phone begins blaring loudly for a third time.

Dax jolts on top of me at the unexpected sound. "Fuck!" He rolls off me, grabs his phone, and turns it off with annoyance. "Yes, Colby. I'm going to the appointment. Now leave me alone, you asshole."

"He's a very sweet and protective asshole."

Dax returns to me and smiles. "Yeah, he is. He's the best."

"Where's the therapist's office?"

"Beverly Hills."

"You should be good if you go down Wilshire."

"Yeah, that's what I'll do." He rolls onto his back. "Colby said this guy specializes in celebrities. Apparently, my family doesn't think I'm dealing with the 'overnight fame' thing all that well."

"I would tend to agree with them. Wouldn't you?"

Dax turns his head to look at me, his brow knit. "Why do you think that?"

"Because I can see it on your face. And also because I know, from watching the RCR guys implode that first year, all in different

ways and to varying degrees, that overnight fame is a huge adjustment. Let alone becoming a cultural phenomenon the way you
have."

Dax looks surprised. "I'm a 'cultural phenomenon'?"

I pause, not sure if he's serious. "Yeah. Definitely. Nobody has
made more of a splash this year than 22 Goats. You, in particular."

Dax makes a cute face that tells me he truly doesn't comprehend
just how famous he's become. "Yeah, maybe seeing this guy will be
good."

"I think so. Therapy is a good thing. Nothing to be ashamed of.
I've had a ton of it, and I'm not ashamed of that. It's helped me a lot."

"Yeah, maybe there are a few things I could talk through." He's
quiet for a moment, staring at the ceiling. "Remember that girl I told
you about—the one from summer camp who rocked my world and
then ghosted me?"

I slide my palm onto his bare chest and cuddle up to him. "Julia
Fortunato."

"Wow, amazing memory." He makes a face of disdain. "She
contacted me a couple months ago."

My heart stops. I lift my head and stare. If Dax did the thing he
told me he's always fantasized about doing to her—fucking her brilliantly before ghosting her—I truly don't want to hear this story.

Dax continues, "I think that's when I realized, with full clarity,
I'd opened a door I'd never be able to shut again. For years, I fantasized I'd see Julia again and turn the tables on her. But in reality, I
didn't even want to touch her. Having her come out of the woodwork,
only because my band had hit it big, was just too repulsive to me. It
was just so symbolic of what my life had become. I realized the entire
world was filled with Julias, and all I wanted, the only thing, was my
one, true-blue Violet."

I release the breath I've been holding. "You didn't sleep with
Julia?"

"Nope. I told my agent to tell her I got her message but, sorry, I
didn't remember her."

My heart is soaring. "Oohh, that makes me happy." I snuggle into him and kiss his cheek. "Make me even happier and tell me more about how you wanted me, and not her."

He chuckles. "I was aching for our genuine soul connection. I wanted a girl who'd like me, even if the fame and money went away."

I touch his chiseled face. "I would, you know—want you if the fame and money went away."

"I know. There's no doubt in my mind."

We share a huge smile.

"Therapy helped you?" he asks.

"It did. I did it throughout all four years of college. But still, full disclosure, if I were a cake, and therapy an oven, I'm only half-baked now."

He chuckles.

"I'm still a lowkey shit show in some ways. I'm just not as *massive* a shit show as I might otherwise have been. I'm definitely not cake batter anymore, though, so I count it as a win."

"Violet, you're one of the most together people I know. I'm more of a shit show than you are."

"Good thing you're going to therapy, then, huh? Seriously, though, I know you're infatuated with me right now, because you've been fucking me for, like, sixty hours straight, but I feel the need to warn you: I'm still a work in progress."

"Of course, you are. Everyone is."

"I just don't want you projecting this 'perfect girl' thing onto me. I'm not perfect. I've definitely got flaws."

"What are your flaws? Tell me a single one. As far as I can tell, you're literally perfect."

"See? I don't want you to do that. I'm not even close to perfect."

"So, tell me a flaw."

"You tell me one first. I want to see how dark we're gonna go here before I drop too big a bomb."

He chuckles. "Well, I'm moody as fuck. Moo-fucking-*dee*, dude. I overthink things to the *extreme* sometimes. I'm selfish on occasion, especially when the muse strikes. There's more, I'm sure. But that's the stuff that comes to mind, right off the bat. Your turn."

I twist my mouth. "Well, off the top, I'd say I have major trust issues. Fear of abandonment. And those issues come out in ways I don't always understand completely. Sometimes, I push people away, when it's the last thing I consciously want to do. And then I'm sad when they go away, as requested. Lovely, huh?"

"All of that is perfectly understandable, considering your background."

I'm quiet for a moment. "I saw the way your father looked at your mother at the wedding, when she was flitting around, being silly and dancing and drinking champagne... And I was just so in awe of him. He's just so obviously *in love* with your mother, you know? He's nothing like her, that's plain to see, but he *gets* her."

"Yep. They're a perfect balance."

"I realized watching them—actually, stalking them—that I've never seen a couple like them before. Even in the best of times, my mother and stepfather's marriage wasn't like your parents'. They loved each other, I think, but they didn't *get* each other like yours do. Plus, their marriage only lasted four years and ended horribly. Your parents have been together...?"

"Thirty-four years. And they're still obviously in love."

"See? Relationship goals. But not just that, *family* goals. All you kids so obviously love your parents. And they love you guys. And it's just so..." Tears unexpectedly prick my eyes and I wipe them. "Sorry. I don't know why I'm suddenly feeling emotional. Seeing your family just made me realize how screwed up my life has been. How much I've missed out on. And, if I'm being honest, it made me feel kind of insecure around you. Like, how could I possibly be right for someone like you, when you come from that kind of stability and love?"

He puts his palm on my cheek. His blue eyes are blazing. "Violet, do you have any idea how good a person you are? Everyone can see it. My mother fell in love with you the minute she met you."

I sniffle. "She did?"

"She wanted to fix me up with you. I mean, what kind of girl inspires a *mother* to want to pimp out her son?"

I giggle through tears.

"I know my family is a bit overwhelming. My parents are one in a million. I've got all these siblings and we're all in each other's business. Privacy is nonexistent. Case in point, this therapy appointment I've got to run off to in exactly two minutes. But don't you see? Our different backgrounds are probably why we both feel the connection we do. Yeah, I come from a 'perfect' family. And yet, my whole life, I've felt an ache in my soul I can't quite shake—a homesickness— unless I've got a guitar in my hands. And then there's you. You come from pain and abandonment and loss. And yet, you light up every room you walk into. As far as I'm concerned, that makes us a perfect fit."

My breathing catches. My heart palpitates. "I'm not always happy," I confess. "I get blue sometimes."

"If you're blue, it's because you're perfectly human, not because you're broken," he whispers.

Tears well in my eyes. "Thank you. I think I am broken, though. Way deep inside. I've worked hard to fix the broken shards and glue them back together—the same way you glued your mother's vase back together. But, like that vase, if you were to look really closely, you'd see the cracks and lines."

He kisses me. "The lines and cracks make you beautiful." He strokes my face. "Just promise me something. You won't push me away because you're scared. Just keep showing me your lines and cracks, baby. Because they turn me on. And not just physically."

I swoon and nod. In truth, though, I'm not sure how much longer I can keep letting Dax tear down my walls without, at some point, surrendering to my instinct for self-preservation. When Dax first suggested this arrangement, I pictured myself rolling around naked with him, in secret, for a whole lot longer than a week. Indeed, I thought I could do it for months. But now, I'm feeling like I won't be able to hand him my heart on a silver platter without first securing his. Without knowing, for sure, Dax won't smash my heart if I hand it over.

Dax's phone rings with an incoming call. He looks at the phone, mutters, "Jesus, Colby." And picks up. "Hello, Colby. Yes, I'm going to my appointment." He pauses. "I know. I will. Thanks. Bye." Dax ends the call with a chuckle. "Fucking Colby."

Stuffing down the vague feeling of dread that's beginning to nip at my happy little bubble, I force a smile. "You'd better get moving, babe. You don't want to be late."

Dax's smile is beaming and glorious. "He said I need to remember I've never experienced fame while not on tour," he says. "He said I'm probably subconsciously equating fame with the intense version of it I experienced on tour—getting physically mobbed *everywhere* I go. But he said now that I'm back in LA, I'll be able to carve out a much more normal existence for myself, relatively speaking."

We're sitting across from each other in the large, Jacuzzi bathtub in our hotel bathroom, lit candles around us, while Dax tells me about today's therapy session. Of course, I told him he didn't need to tell me anything about it, if he didn't want to share. But Dax said he wanted to tell me about it because he was blown away by how much he liked it.

"I'm so glad you went to him, Dax. Sounds like he knows what he's talking about."

"He does."

Dax continues talking and talking, telling me everything the guy helped him with in just one session. Finally, in wrap-up, he says, "I liked the guy so much, I made another appointment with him for next week."

"Fantastic."

He rubs my leg under the warm water. "Toward the end, I told him about you."

"Me?"

"Yeah. We're gonna talk in detail about you next time."

My stomach wrenches sharply. Will Dax and the therapist talk through the "pros and cons" of him entering into a relationship with me? And if they do, will Dax decide I'm worth the headache... or not? I swallow hard. "Sounds like a great idea."

Dax smiles, apparently unaware of my clenching stomach. "What kinds of stuff did you talk about in therapy?"

"Everything. Jackson. My father and stepfather. My mother cheating on my stepfather. Caleb." Dax's features stiffen subtly at the mention of Caleb's name. *Shit.* Why did I mention Caleb's name? I squeeze Dax's leg underneath the water. "So, what did you do after your therapy session while I was shopping for wedding dresses?"

"I thought I was going to shut myself away to write, but I wound up hanging out with Fish. He rented a condo right on the beach in Santa Monica, thinking he might want to buy it eventually, so I went to see it. We played video games. Talked about nothing in particular. It was just like old times, only with an ocean view."

"Colin wasn't there?"

"He went to see a girl—one of Aloha's backup dancers. He met her before the tour at Reed's party and she just got back from Australia last night."

"Where is Colin living?"

"With one of his cousins for now. He told me to keep an eye out for him when I go house hunting with Ryan."

"When are you doing that?"

"Friday."

"I love house hunting," I say lamely, and instantly regret it. Crap. If I'm trying to get Dax to invite me to join him, it's a nonstarter and I know it. I might *feel* like Dax's girlfriend after spending so much time with him these past three days in this hotel room, but I have to remember I'm still his dirty little secret. The girl he can't be seen with *out there.*

"I've never done it before," Dax says, seemingly oblivious to the subtext of my comment. "Ryan's gonna show me what I can afford and help me decide what to do."

"Cool."

There's an awkward beat.

"So, tell me about your shopping trip with Maddy," Dax says, caressing my leg again. "Did you have fun?"

I tell him about my day, building up to the exciting news that, after not finding exactly what she wanted in the stores we visited, Maddy hired me to create her dream wedding dress. "It's a dream come true," I say excitedly. "When I was a kid, I sketched wedding dresses all the time and made them for my Barbies. Even today, whenever a celebrity is getting married, or there's a royal wedding coming up, I love sketching what I think the bride should wear and then waiting to see if I was anywhere close. It's my idea of the Super Bowl."

Dax laughs. "You're so freaking cute when you talk about this stuff."

"I get excited."

"You know, Maddy's a bit of a celebrity. Keane's the star of their videos, but everyone loves Maddy Behind the Camera. You'll probably get some good publicity over this if she posts videos of the finished product after the wedding."

I squeal with glee. "Do you think she'd do that?"

"I'm sure she would. Their engagement video got something like fifteen million views. The whole world is following their love story."

I drag my hands over my face, overwhelmed with excitement. "I can't believe this is my life. One of my dreams is to design wedding dresses for a living. Like, to have my own brand. If I could design two things—wedding dresses and costumes for pop divas like Aloha Carmichael—and nothing else, for the rest of my life, I'd be a very happy designer."

"Have you ever sketched a future wedding dress for yourself?"

"Ha! No." I snort. "I'm never getting married."

Dax looks surprised. "Why not?"

"I don't see the point."

He's quiet.

I feel my cheeks bloom. "You see the point?"

He shrugs. "I think finding that one person to share your life with, pledging forever to one special person, seems really cool."

"But you can pledge 'forever' to someone without getting married. And then, *voila,* if 'forever' turns out to be a bit bigger commitment than either person can manage, you can both be on your merry way. No harm, no foul, and no lawyers."

Dax pulls a face. "This from the girl who loves designing wedding dresses?"

"I'm just saying you can pledge forever to a girlfriend. No need to make her your *wife.*"

"Yeah, but the thing is I get off on the word *wife.*"

All at once, my heart skips a beat and arousal whooshes between my legs.

Dax flashes me a crooked smile. "My whole life, I've heard Colby and Ryan talking about their various girlfriends, but now that they've both got a one-and-only *wife,* it feels... different. Sacred. They've *chosen* to bring Lydia and Tessa into our family. They've *chosen* to pledge forever to them, in front of the world. I don't know, I don't want to miss out on getting to experience that brand of magic. I mean, only if I find the right girl, of course. But if I do, hell yeah, I'll want to make that woman my wife."

My heart is melting like an ice cream cone on a hot sidewalk. This boy. He's not like anybody I've ever met before. He certainly doesn't fit the stereotype of a "rockstar."

"You're absolutely *positive* you'll never get married?" he asks. "Like, you're dead-set against it, no matter what?"

My breathing is shallow. "Well, no... I wouldn't put it that way. I'm not absolutely dead-set *against* it. I've just never *pictured* it for myself."

Well, that's new. It's the first time I've equivocated on the topic in my life. Up until now, in every conversation I've ever had about the concept of marriage, I've firmly stated it's simply not for me. No way. Never. But now, looking into Dax's blue eyes, sitting here naked with him in this warm tub, when I'm feeling so open and light and happy and *adored*, I can't deny the word 'husband' has a certain appeal. "I grew up with a single mother," I say. "So that's always seemed normal to me. I think I've always assumed I'd become a single mother one day, too, just like my mom."

"But is that what you'd *want*, if you could pick?" Dax says. "I mean, why would anyone *want* that, if they had a choice?"

Anger flashes inside me, but I force myself to keep my tone measured. "Every day of my life, my mother's told me having me was the best decision she ever made. My father was an asshole and a liar. He cheated on his wife and defrauded hundreds of people out of their life savings. He demanded my mother abort me, and when she wouldn't do it, he paid her off and sent her packing. Was she supposed to pick him over me because being a single mother is so horrible? Is that what you're implying?"

"Whoa, Vi. I wasn't making a moral judgment about unwed mothers. Dude. Come on. You really think that's where I was coming from? I was simply making the observation that it seems like it'd be tough to have a kid alone. That, if given the *choice*, I'd think anyone would want to do it as part of a team. I've got a slew of nieces and nephews and I've seen firsthand how much work babies are."

Dax looks earnest. Beautiful. Sweet as can be. And I suddenly realize I've just revealed myself to be an overly sensitive lunatic. At least, regarding this topic. "I'm sorry. I've watched my mother get treated like a second-class citizen my whole life for being an unwed mother. Sometimes, it's not overt. People make comments or ask questions cloaked as concern. But the judgment is constantly there."

"I know I come from Perfect Family USA, but I certainly don't think my family is the only kind of family. Obviously, your mom was a badass for choosing to have you and raising you on her own. Especially, so young. She's got my full respect."

I take a deep breath. "Thank you. I'm sorry I got defensive."

"I'm sorry if I said anything that came off like a preacher at a Baptist revival."

I giggle. "You didn't. Not at all. I'm just a lunatic." I suddenly feel the need to make amends for jumping down his throat. I drift across the tub, slide my arms around his neck, and skim my hard nipples against his chest. "What about you?" I say softly. "Are you gonna have kids to go along with this magical wife of yours?"

"Just one. Sometimes, I imagine myself onstage, with my wife and kid out in the audience. My kid has those big earphones on—the ones that protect little kids' eardrums from loud music? And my wife is smoking hot and the coolest person, ever, and she's out there, holding our kid, looking hot. And I look out into the crowd, at my wife and kid out there, and my band is onstage with me—Fish and Colin, of course—and maybe their wives and kids are out in the audience, too, as long as this is a fairytale—and, fuck it, my whole family's out there, too, enjoying the show—and in that moment, I know I've truly managed to have it all."

His cock is hard against me. I slide myself onto it and take him into me and he groans his appreciation. But then he says, "Just to be clear, I don't want this fairytale baby any time soon. This baby in headphones is years off."

I smile as I fuck him slowly. "I take my pill religiously. I'm not looking to get knocked up and become a single mother any time soon. I promise."

He looks relieved. He starts fucking me in earnest. As we move together in the water, we kiss and caress. We whisper. We suck each other's lips and bite each other's necks. And through it all, I feel myself doing the one thing I've promised myself I wouldn't do, not unless Dax does it first: falling head over heels in love.

THIRTY-SIX

DAX

Violet's alarm goes off, ripping me out of an awesome dream. I peek at the clock on the nightstand and groan. *9:00.*

"Why so early?" I choke out.

"Nine o'clock is early?" Violet says next to me.

"It's the crack of dawn."

Chuckling, she pats my bare chest. "Go back to sleep, rockstar. I'll be quiet as a mouse."

I grab her arm to stop her movement. "Where are you going?"

"To the children's hospital. I'm interviewing kids for a new batch of superhero costumes."

"Can I come?"

She looks as shocked as I feel. Why did I say that?

"How would that work?" she asks, looking like her heart is beating a mile a minute. "I mean, aren't we still... secret fuck-spies?"

I swallow hard. *Shit.* I asked to come reflexively, not because I've consciously decided it's time for our official coming-out party. But now that I've said it, I don't want to take it back. "If we get spotted, we could say you told my family and me about The Superhero Project at the wedding and I was so impressed, I asked to join you the next time you went to the hospital."

Violet looks vaguely disappointed. She shakes her head. "That's too risky. If we're together, just me and you, any photo captured will tell a story far more salacious than any spin we might try to put on it later." She pauses like she's waiting for me to disagree. When I don't, she sighs and rolls toward the edge of the bed.

"We could call Keane and Maddy and ask them to come with us."

She pauses at the edge of the bed. I've got her full attention now.

"If we get photographed, we'd say your new bestie, Maddy Behind the Camera, is making a video about The Superhero Project."

"Actually, Maddy said she was interested in doing exactly that. She said it at the wedding."

"Perfect. So, we'll say Maddy and Keane came along with you to do the video, and Keane invited me, his little brother, just for kicks. Sounds believable to me."

Violet lights up. She crawls back to me on the bed. "I think that could work. Keane and Maddy will be our beard."

I grab my phone. "I'll text them now. What time should they meet us at the hospital?"

"Ten thirty. But, don't forget, you and I will have to drive separately."

I scowl, annoyed at the idea. "New plan," I say. "We'll have Keane and Maddy come here and we'll all go to the hospital together. I don't want to drive separately. I'm hopelessly addicted to you, baby. I need you in reach at all times."

"Glad to hear it, because I'm hopelessly addicted to you, too." She surprises me by straddling me on the bed. She's naked. So am I. And I know exactly where this is headed. "What the hell are you doing to me, David Jackson?" she purrs as I grab her breasts. "We said we were gonna be super-secret fuck-spies, remember? And you're already looking for loopholes?"

I slide my palms down her torso and grip her bare ass as she rubs herself against my hard-on. "I just can't stand being away from you, that's all."

She shudders as my fingers stroke her bare ass. "I don't think super-secret fuck-spies look for loopholes so they can visit kids in cancer wards together."

"Sure, they do. Anything for the mission."

She giggles. "I'm not complaining. I'm excited you're coming. But just so you know, after the hospital, I've got to go to a quick work meeting in Burbank. We're still in pre-production for the movie, so I'm only doing meetings once a week at this point. Maybe you can do something with Keane and Maddy while I'm at the meeting?"

I rub her thighs, aching to get inside her. "Will that bastard asshole be at the meeting?"

"What bastard asshole?"

"The one you dated until mere days ago, when you came to your senses."

She rolls her eyes. "He's not a bastard asshole. He's a really nice guy. A bit of a player, but up front about it. And no, he won't be there. But if he was going to be there, it wouldn't matter because I'm smitten with a certain secret fuck-spy."

"Do you think he's going to try to seduce you? To win you back?"

She laughs like that's the stupidest thing she's ever heard. "No. He took it *very* well when I told him I wanted to keep things professional. I actually think he was relieved. I don't think he was all that into me, any more than I was into him. But if he *did* try to seduce me, do you know what I'd say? I'd tell him I've only got eyes for one man —my hot super-secret fuck-spy baby."

My stomach somersaults unexpectedly. I know she's being silly, but for a split-second, I wanted nothing more than to hear Violet call me her hot *boyfriend* in that sentence.

She smiles at my salty expression. "Aw, you're *jealous?*"

"Hell yeah, I'm jealous. I don't believe for a minute he's not into you."

"He's not. And if he was, so what? It's not like he was the great love of my life. He was a distraction."

"For how long?"

"For how long what?"

"Did you let him *distract* you?"

"It's hard to say because it was off and on."

"Estimate."

"You *are* jealous."

"Very."

She gyrates on top of me, rubbing herself against my hard dick, and I fondle her tits.

"Well, let's see," she says. "At first, when I was in college and it was a casual long-distance thing, I hardly saw him at all. Just a handful of dinner dates in New York. Then, when I moved to LA two months ago, we started seeing each other pretty regularly. But we never got serious or exclusive."

"Where'd you meet him?"

"Why the hell are you asking me so many questions about him?"

"Because I'm being a jealous asshole."

"You really are."

"Just tell me where you met him and I'll shut up."

She rolls her eyes. "At Reed's party for Aloha. Minutes before I met you."

"He's that GQ motherfucker in the suit?"

She giggles. "That's him. We talked briefly that night. He said he produced indie movies. I said I was studying fashion design and had recently become interested in costume design. And then he shocked me by texting me a few days later and inviting me to dinner in New York."

"Jesus fucking Christ. *Asshole.*"

She giggles. "Might I remind you, I kept staring at you the whole time he was hitting on me, trying to get you to come over to say hello. Now come on. Stop being a jealous asshole and fuck me. You weren't a monk on tour, so shut the fuck up, you hypocrite. I had to do *something* so I wouldn't sit around, obsessing over the guy I saw *everywhere* in that damned music video."

That brings a huge smile to my face. "You were obsessing over me?"

"Relentlessly. Every time I thought about you, every time I dreamed about you or touched myself and fantasized about you—or wished someone else was you—I watched that music video." She smiles wickedly. "Which means at least half of the billion views on that thing are mine."

I grip her hips and guide her onto my cock. "If you had a music video, I'd have run up ten billion views during the tour. I swear to God."

She bites her lip as she fucks me. "I believe you. So, let's agree the past is the past. No more jealousy. *Onward.*"

I nod. "Onward."

She starts fucking me in earnest, and, soon, I'm not thinking about anything or anyone but my baby and me and her gorgeous tits and magical pussy... and how, fuck you, Caleb and GQ Mother-fucker, the beautiful goddess riding my cock is all *mine, mine, mine.*

THIRTY-SEVEN

DAX

The little girl in the pink knit cap loses her ever-lovin' mind as Aloha Carmichael enters the hospital room and strides toward her bed. She's the sixth kid in this cancer ward who's instantly recognized Aloha. Not surprisingly, seeing as how Aloha's a household name, especially with little girls. One kid recognized me, even though I wouldn't consider kids my demographic. When I entered his room, he blurted, "My mom loves you!" Yeah, everyone laughed pretty hard at that.

And by "everyone" I mean Keane, Maddy, Zander, Aloha, and Violet. When I called Keane and Maddy earlier to ask them to come to the hospital with us, they happened to be sitting at breakfast with Zander and Aloha, who'd just come back from Australia yesterday. And so, rather than ditch their jetlagged breakfast companions, Keane and Maddy dragged them along. And now, all six of us are making the rounds, meeting a whole bunch of cuties in hospital gowns and knit caps.

I gotta say, the entire experience has been deeply moving to me. The smiles we're getting from these kids... wow. They're fueling my soul. Not to mention, making me realize my so-called problems are actually miniscule in the big picture.

As Aloha has been dazzling the kids, and Keane and Zander have been charming their hair off—that's a little cancer humor one of the older kids taught us—and as Maddy Behind the Camera has been filming every interaction—Violet has quietly steered each conversation and gathered information for her superhero sketches. And every time Violet has turned her sketch pad around for the big reveal, my heart has skipped a beat at her latest lovely creation.

In this particular hospital room, I'm standing with Zander and Keane in a corner, watching a little girl in a purple knit cap giggle with Aloha, chat easily with Violet, and mug for Maddy's camera.

As the three of us dudes stand by and watch the girl-party across the room, Zander says, "I like Violet. She's a keeper."

"Maddy loves her," Keane says. "She couldn't stop talking about her yesterday when she got back from their shopping day."

"I can tell Aloha likes her, too," Zander says.

I look across the room at Violet and my heart swells at the way she's laughing with the little girl. "Yeah, Violet's amazing."

"Weird she's Reed's sister," Zander says. "She doesn't remind me of him at all."

"They're half-siblings," I say. "They have the same father, and they didn't grow up together. It's a long story. I'll tell you later."

Violet squeals across the room, drawing our attention. "Awesome, Aloha! I'll ask Dax!" She puts down her sketch pad and bounces over to me, her face aglow. "Babe! Aloha just invited us to come to her place for dinner tonight with Keane and Maddy! Can we go?" Her blue-gray eyes are pleading. Clearly, she's dying to go.

"Sounds fun," I say.

Violet squeals and pecks my cheek. "Don't worry. We'll drive over there separately, so nobody will spot us together." With that, she floats away, back to the ladies.

As Violet leaves, I feel some serious "disapproving dad" energy coming from Zander, so I don't look at him. But sure enough, Zander breaks the thick silence by whispering, "How long are you planning to treat that fine woman like a side piece, Dax Morgan?"

I sigh. "It's a complicated situation, Z. We're figuring things out slowly."

"Maybe *you're* figuring things out slowly," Zander says. "But Violet isn't. Obviously, she knows exactly what she wants."

"Yup," Keane says. "Head, nail, *hit*."

I sigh.

"Seems to me, the ball's in your court," Zander says. "That look she just gave you said more than words could. She's all-in."

"If you need words, though, let the record reflect she called you 'babe,'" Keane says.

"Guys, stop," I say. "Violet and I talked about the game plan together. She agreed to keeping things secret." A wave of anxiety rises up inside me. "Violet's no shrinking violet, guys. If she's got a problem with our arrangement, she'll let me know."

My phone buzzes with an incoming text and when I look down, my stomach constricts. It's a text from Caleb.

Caleb: You still good living in a hotel? I've got that spare bedroom, just sitting there.

My stomach somersaulting, I tap out a reply.

Me: Thanks, I'm good. Just easier this way.
Caleb: Do you and the goats wanna come over tonight to hang out and shoot some pool?

"Shit," I say, my heartbeat quickening. "*Fuck*."

"What?" Keane says.

"C-Bomb," I whisper. "He's inviting me to come over and hang out tonight."

Keane says, "Tell him, 'Sorry, dude. I'm gonna be busy fucking your girl tonight. How about tomorrow? Oh, wait. No. I'll be fucking her then, too.'"

"Shut the fuck up, Peenie. She's not his girl."

My stomach revolting, I tap out a reply.

Me: Sorry, can't make it. My buddy just got into town last night. Having dinner with him tonight.

Caleb: No prob. Dean was asking when you wanna do that songwriting sesh? How's Friday or Saturday looking?

Me: Going house shopping with my brother Friday. Saturday meeting with Reed.

Caleb: Cool, Saturday, it is. After your meeting with Reed. I'll tell Dean. Just come after your meeting, whenever that is. Good luck house hunting tomorrow.

I stare at my phone, panicking. Not knowing what to reply. Feeling like I'm going to hell. How the fuck am I going to sit across from Dean and Caleb and write songs with them on Saturday? I can't do it, obviously. But, oh God, I want to do it. Writing a song with Dean would be a dream fulfilled.

Violet's phone chirps in her pocket across the room. She pulls it out of her pocket, looks at the screen, and scowls. Without replying, she shoves it back into her pocket.

Shit. I bet that was Caleb texting her. Did he invite Violet to come over tonight, right after I turned him down? Or did he just play it cool and send her a "thinking of you" text?

Adrenaline surging inside me, jealousy, panic, I shove my phone into my pocket without saying a word to Caleb. A moment later, Violet turns her sketch pad around to reveal her latest masterpiece to the latest little girl. I can't see what's on the pad from here, but whatever it is, it's thrilling the girl. Not to mention Maddy and Aloha, too.

Goddammit. I feel like I'm leading a double life. And that's not something I'm wired to do. I'm not a guy who lies to his friends. I am who I am. And now I'm the piece of shit asshole who's sneaking around behind my buddy's back—and not only that, acting like the best girl in the world is a goddamned side piece, just like Zander said.

Violet gives the little girl a big farewell hug and Aloha and Maddy follow suit. Keane, Zander, and I wave our goodbyes and we all move, as a group, into the hallway to head to the next room. As we file out of the room, we find ourselves in front of a busy nurse's station. Predictably, several nurses pull out their phones. Most are pretending to check their phones at the precise moment we enter the hallway, but I know they're taking photos or videos of Aloha or me. Maybe both of us. I've seen this same maneuver before, many times.

After a moment, a nurse approaches and sheepishly asks for a selfie with Aloha and me. And when we oblige her, the kraken is unleashed. All at once, several more nurses ask. And then several more. So, of course, we oblige them all and wind up taking several big group shots when one of the nurses recognizes Keane, as well.

When Aloha begins chatting at length with a group of nurses, I step back and ask Violet to show me her sketch for the last little girl. And when she shows it to me—a rendering of a superhero called "Karate Chop Katie"—I'm so overwhelmed by the sheer beauty of it, the hope brimming off the page, the kindness, the love, I take Violet's face in my hands and kiss her deeply, right in the middle of the hall-way, in front of everyone... including one particular nurse who's been brazenly aiming her phone at me for the past ten seconds.

THIRTY-EIGHT

DAX

Violet, Maddy, Keane, Zander, and I are at Aloha's impressive house in the Hollywood Hills. For the past couple hours, we've been sitting on her patio in the warm evening, talking, laughing, and eating Mexican food. We've talked about a lot of different topics tonight. At the moment, Violet is answering Aloha's questions about Reed, Red Card Riot, and her upbringing in San Diego.

"Holy crap, Reed owes everything to you," Aloha says. "Red Card Riot put River Records on the map."

"Yeah, Reed calls me his lucky charm. One of his tattoos is this little violet-colored four leaf clover."

"Well, tattoos are nice, but did he give you a finder's fee or something?" Aloha says, laughing.

"A *finder's fee?*" Violet says, waving at the air. "Oh gosh, no. That would be ridiculous."

"If Reed gave you even one percent of what he's made off RCR, you'd be a very wealthy woman."

"I wouldn't accept money from Reed. Not like that. But he's always been ridiculously generous with me. Not because he *owes* me anything, just because he says he wants to take care of me."

"Hey, whatever he's done for you—the girl who had to *beg* him to come see a Red Card Riot show—it's the least he can do," Aloha says, chuckling.

It's clear Aloha intends her remarks lightly—with no malice whatsoever—but I can also plainly see Violet's shoulders have tightened with defensiveness, the same way they did when she thought I was bagging on single mothers.

Violet says, "Reed's also offered to help my career—to introduce me to people. But I've always said no. I don't want anyone thinking I'm riding his coattails for personal gain."

"Violet wants to do costume design, Aloha," Maddy interjects. "She's helping design costumes for an indie movie now, but you should see some of her sketches for this 'Icons Reimagined' project she did for school. Show her some of your sketches, Vi."

"Are you sure?" Violet asks, looking adorably shy.

"I'd love to see them," Aloha says. "Let's see."

With obvious excitement, Violet pulls out her phone and begins showing sketches to Aloha—and as she does that, I covertly check that "Dax in the Wild" Instagram account *again*, looking to see if any of the photos from today's visit to the hospital have made their way there. Holy shit. There's a shot from today uploaded on the account— one of Aloha and me and one of the nurses. *But no photo of me kissing Violet.* Not even one of me standing next to her, looking at her adoringly.

Acute disappointment washes over me. And that surprises me. Why the hell am I feeling *disappointment*? Shouldn't I be feeling *relief*? Obviously, I got lucky today and I should be happy about that. I was reckless to kiss Violet in that hallway and I dodged a bullet. Even as I did it, I knew I was taking a huge risk. So why am I not feeling unadulterated glee that I most likely got away with it?

I tune back into the conversation at the table, just in time to hear Aloha say to Violet, "If I tell you what I'm envisioning, would you be willing to take a stab at designing something like that for me?"

Violet bounces in her chair with effusive excitement. "I would *love* to, Aloha. Thank you so much for the opportunity!"

Oh, my heart. Sweet Violet is smiling like a kid on Christmas. It's enough to make my heart feel like it's swelling to three times its normal size. I take Violet's hand. This girl makes me feel high. *Drunk.* She's better than any shot of tequila or whiskey.

Speaking of booze, I look around the table at the empty beer bottles... and, just for a moment, feel annoyed at Colby. Not because I need a drink. I don't. I'm not in any danger of breaking my promise. But because beer is damned good with Mexican food and I'm pissed I didn't get to enjoy that simple pleasure tonight, all because Colby's being an over-protective nut job. But, whatever, when I look at Violet again, at the excited smile on her face, and the water bottle in front of her, the impulse to taste the deliciousness of a beer—and also to pummel Colby for being overly protective—passes.

"Hey, guys," Keane says, looking at his phone. "One of the gossip sites has a photo of us from the hospital today."

My breathing catches. *This is it.* "Let me see." I grab my brother's phone. And there we are, all six of us, huddled together in a shot the hospital administrator took of our group when we first arrived. Violet's not even standing next to me in the photo. She's way on the outside, cuddling with Maddy. Again, I feel disappointment, not relief.

"Phew," Violet says, peeking at Keane's screen. "Nothing scandalous." She smiles thinly at me, but I swear I see disappointment in her eyes. "We dodged a bullet, huh?"

"We sure did." I return her smile weakly, even though my heart is panging.

"We should be more careful next time," Violet says. She holds my gaze for a beat, and I can plainly see hurt in her stormy eyes. When she looks away, I look away, too. Only to find Zander looking at me like he thinks I'm a twat. I look away from Zander and catch Maddy looking at me the same way. Like she also thinks I'm a twat. And so, with nowhere to safely look, I look down at my lap.

THIRTY-NINE

VIOLET

"San Diego was cool when we blew through there on the tour," Dax says.

We're lying naked in bed together, on our sides, nose to nose. We banged like animals the minute we walked through the door from Aloha's house. And now, we're lying here talking about my hometown.

Dax says, "I'd never been to San Diego before that, but the RCR guys were all stoked to be back in their hometown. They kept going on and on about how great it is."

"It's 'America's Finest City.' That's San Diego's slogan."

"Yeah, so the guys told me. Over and over again." He chuckles. "The day after the show, we had some free time before our evening flight. So, Colin, Fish, and"—Dax pauses—"and I packed into a limo and took a little tour of the highlights."

Caleb.

That's the name Dax just left out of his story. Because, of course, *Caleb* would have been the one to show his friends the highlights of his beloved San Diego. I take a deep breath, stuffing down my anxiety. God, I hate seeing Dax perform mental gymnastics to manage the guilt he so obviously feels about betraying his good friend. And I hate having a third wheel in my relationship with Dax—or, whatever this thing I've been doing with Dax should rightly be called.

I sigh and stuff down my insecurities. "So, what sights did you see in San Diego?"

"Um, let's see. I was pretty stoned that day, as I recall. But I remember we went over this really cool bridge to this cool island..."

"Coronado."

"Yeah! And we saw this famous hotel..."

"The Hotel Del. Or, 'The Del,' as we locals call it."

"That place was sick. Did you know one of the rooms is haunted?"

"By a young woman named Kate Morgan. Hey, maybe she was your ancestor."

"Whoa. That's cool."

"Did you know a famous movie starring Marilyn Monroe was filmed at The Del? *Some Like It Hot.*"

"Look at you! My own personal San Diego tour guide."

I shrug. "I'm a local, baby. I know all the things."

"Clearly, you would have been a much better tour guide than... our driver."

My stomach clenches. There he is again: *Caleb.* But I ignore his obvious presence in this conversation—in this relationship—in this *bed*—and say, "You ever want a personal tour of San Diego, then I'm your girl."

Shit. Why did I say that? Obviously, we can't go to San Diego together, and I can't give him a personal tour of my hometown, *because he won't be seen in public with me.* Because Dax cares more about not offending Caleb than getting to be with me, out there in the world. Holy crap. My stomach clenches. I didn't realize I was thinking about it that way—that Dax is *choosing* Caleb over me. But... it kind of is what he's doing... right? Goddammit. This secret fuck-spies thing is so much harder than I thought it'd be! A total mind-fuck. With each passing day in this hotel room, we're beginning to feel less like secret fuck-spies and more like secret fuck *buddies*... And that's not something I've ever wanted to be with anyone.

If Dax wanted to keep things on the down low because he's famous and doesn't want his private life to become fodder for gossip sites, just on principle, that'd feel different to me than this present situation. Indeed, I wouldn't feel slighted or insecure about that. But knowing he legit *won't* be seen with me because we're doing something illicit, something that makes him feel guilty and smarmy... something he's *ashamed* to be doing... well, shit. That's a whole different kettle of fish. Something that's starting to make me feel like my mother. *And I don't like feeling like my mother.*

When I tune back into Dax, he's saying, ". . . and then we saw some seals, lying around on this beach. It wasn't a zoo. They were just there, in the wild, and everyone was taking photos of them." He laughs. "Hey, those seals were just like me! Out in the wild, getting their picture taken."

I want to laugh with him, but I can't. I'm too caught up in my thoughts.

"Do you know what that beach is called?" he asks. "The one with the seals?"

"La Jolla Cove."

"Yeah, that's right. God, I was stoned that day. I can't remember anything."

"No one knows why the seals chose that particular spot. But they're there every year."

"Where did you grow up in relation to that seal beach?"

"A few miles south in Pacific Beach. Our condo was a block from the beach."

"Nice."

"That's what happens when you get knocked up by a rich man who wants to get rid of you so his wife won't find out. He buys you a nice condo a block from the beach."

There's an awkward beat.

What am I doing? I'm coming across like such a Bitter Betty right now. I clear my throat. "So, tell me about your hometown. I've never been to Seattle."

"Ah, the Emerald City," he says reverently. "I love her so." He tells me a bit about his beloved city. And then he says, "It rains a ton, though. And it's freezing, compared to Southern California. If you come, no matter what time of year, make sure you bring a jacket and wear layers. Tourists are never prepared."

There's another awkward beat. That didn't sound like a personal invitation to come to Seattle. It was more like a travel advisory. Okay, I'm suddenly feeling like I'm drowning here. Like I'm way more into Dax than he is into me. Like maybe, when it comes down to it, he's going to decide moving ahead with me, moving beyond fuck buddy status, simply isn't worth the headache.

I pull away from Dax's embrace in the bed and look out at the night sky through the window, suddenly feeling anxious. Insecure. Rejected. If I'm being honest with myself, this situation is beginning to feel too stressful to enjoy. I can't get enough of this boy. I'm addicted to him in a way I've never experienced before. But I'm beginning to realize I want him for real. Not like this. I know *why* we agreed to keep things on the down low. It sounded like a perfectly rational idea at the time. But, slowly, I'm beginning to feel like Dax and I are staving off the inevitable. Hurtling at the speed of a snail toward a brick wall—a brick wall that's undoubtedly going to smash my heart.

"Is something wrong?" Dax says.

I pause, trying to decide how to explain the rising dread I'm feeling. The certainty slowly descending upon me that he's ultimately going to hurt me. Leave me. Not want me. *Shatter me.* "I think I'm having a bit of a harder time with this fuck-spies arrangement than I thought I would," I admit softly, still looking at the moonlit sky through the window.

Dax strokes my hair. "I just need a little more time, Vi. It hasn't even been a week. "

Of course, when Dax puts it that way, my brain knows it's objectively unreasonable for me to be feeling this sense of doom—for me to think, even for a minute, he's dragging his feet or stringing me along. Frankly, it's verging on crazy for me to even hint that he should be willing to shout about his feelings for me from the rooftops this soon, especially in light of the potential consequences. But my heart feels ready to take this thing public *now*. And knowing he doesn't feel the same way is killing me. "I guess it just feels like it's been a lot longer than a week to me," I say. "I feel like I've known you for months. Years, even."

I look at him. He looks stressed. Beautiful. Earnest. Like he's holding his breath.

And I suddenly realize I'm being unreasonable. Clingy. Surely, I'm letting my abandonment issues get the best of me. Dax is between a rock and a hard place and simply trying to find his way. I need to give him the time and space to do that. I touch his stunning, moonlit face and smile. "Pretend I never said anything, okay? I'm good."

"You sure?"

I nod. "I was just overthinking things." I pause, trying to get a grip on a thought niggling my brain. "I think maybe I got a bit triggered when Aloha said Reed's made so much money off RCR, he should have paid me a finder's fee. That kind of stressed me out."

"Yeah, I could tell. But she wasn't being literal. She was just saying Reed owes you so much for finding the band that put his record label on the map, that's all. She just meant he lucked out, big-time, that you pestered him like that."

"I know she didn't mean anything. She just hit a nerve, that's all. Reed and I barely knew each other back when I took him to see that RCR show. Sometimes, I wonder if Reed would have stuck around to become my big brother the way he did if he didn't feel like he owed me something. Did he love me, just for me, or did he love me for finding his first big golden goose?"

"Oh, sweetheart. Of course, Reed loves you. I saw the way he looked at you at the wedding. He adores you."

"All this time, I've had this fairytale in my head about my relationship with Reed. He swooped in when I needed him most. When I needed *someone* to take care of me. He's the one man in my life who's never abandoned me. Not yet, anyway." I swallow hard. "But, sometimes, I do wonder why he's done so much for me. All this time, I've thought he was so generous to fund The Superhero Project and my schooling. To give me a rent-free apartment and pay my bills. But in comparison to what he's made off RCR, I'm sure it's hardly anything. I'm not saying I deserve more, not at all, or that he owes me anything... I'm saying maybe he thinks it's the least he can do, not because he loves me, or wants to help me out of love, but because he feels he owes me something, and by doing these things for me, and spending time with me, he's actually getting off comparatively easy." Tears prick my eyes at my startling admission. I've thought about all this before, secretly, but I've never admitted any of it out loud, not even to Miranda or my therapist.

"Oh, Violet. No," Dax coos. "Baby, no."

I wipe my eyes. "I sometimes wonder about Caleb, too. He and I got together only *after* Reed came into my life. Would Caleb have made a move on me if I didn't suddenly have a new big brother with a record label?"

Dax looks anguished. "Violet. Caleb loved you. He still does. He told me so himself."

"I've never said any of this out loud," I confess. "Not about Reed or Caleb. Not to anyone. But I've thought it."

"Baby," he whispers, pulling me to him.

A dam breaks inside me. The insecurities I'm feeling about my relationship with Dax mingle with the ones I've felt for years in other aspects of my life, and I suddenly lose it. "I just don't understand why nobody wants me," I blurt, tears streaming out of my eyes. "Why I'm never enough."

Dax looks horrified. "What are you talking about? *Violet.* You're the most amazing girl I've ever met."

"I just want to know that someone, at some point, is going to go all-in with me because they love me. Because they *want* me and only me. I want someone who's going to stick around and not leave and not be ashamed of me. I don't want to have to sit by the phone and wish and hope to get a call. I loved my stepfather and he disappeared from my life. I thought he wanted to be my father, forever, and then, he just... left. I understood why, but it still hurt so much. And now, here I am, doubting my brother, too? But I can't help it. Everyone says he's a player and a dog. That he's ruthless in business. And I always say, 'You don't know him like I do. He's a sweetheart. So generous. So kind.' But does he really love me, unconditionally, the way I love him? Or does he love me because I'm the girl who brought him his first big fish?"

Dax grabs my face. His eyes are fierce. "Sweetheart, listen to me. Listen to my voice. You're worthy of love. Reed loves you. That's why I thought he was your boyfriend. That's why I was jealous. Because he looked at you in a way he's never once looked at any of the women I've seen on his arm. He looked at you like he adores you. Respects you. Admires you. *Loves you.*"

I start crying harder. Not about Reed, really. Not about Caleb or my stepfather or father. Not even about Jackson, specifically. About everything. About my life. My heartache. This constant feeling of rejection and doubt and loss. I'm just so stressed out by this state of limbo I'm in with Dax. This weird *audition* I'm on. Will Dax pick me to be his girlfriend or not? Will he decide I'm not worth the trouble or will he decide I am? I feel like I'm in a pressure cooker and I'm not holding up well. *I want Dax.* I want him like I've never wanted anyone in my life. In fact, no, I don't just *want* him. *I need him.* But I can't be the reason his band falters. Or his friendships falter—not just with Caleb, but with Dean and Clay and Emmitt, too—and then, if things turn to shit, perhaps, with Fish and Colin, as well. What if Dax chooses to be with me, and his next album bombs? Will he blame me for that? Will he say it's because RCR's fans turned on them? Am I damned if I do and damned if I don't here? I'm beginning to feel like this is a futile situation.

"Sweetheart, why are you crying like this?" Dax says. He looks panicked. "I don't understand."

"It's too complicated to explain. I'm just... tired. There's an egg timer on me, Dax. Tick-tick-tick! Will you decide you like me *more* than you like Caleb and Dean and Clay and Emmitt? I want you to want me, but not if being with me is gonna fuck up your life or make you feel like an asshole."

He looks stressed. "Please, just give me some more time, sweetheart. Until Wednesday. I'm seeing my therapist then, and I'll talk everything through with him then. Give me that."

"This isn't an ultimatum, Dax. This is just me, being honest with you about my insecurities and feelings. I don't know if all my feelings are fair or rational. All I know is what I feel. You asked what's wrong and I'm telling you the truth. I'm struggling to figure out how this is gonna end, and thinking about it ending without me being with you, out there in the real world, is breaking my heart."

He clutches me. "Violet, I want you, too. Can't you see that? Don't you understand? You're the most amazing girl I've ever met. I can't get enough of you." He wipes my tears. "God, you've been through a lot in your life, haven't you?"

I nod and sniffle.

He pulls me to him and kisses my hair and cheeks. He whispers everything is going to be all right. He tells me I'm a beautiful, gentle soul and I light up every room I walk into. "Violet," he says, "everyone who meets you falls in love with you at first sight."

Oh, for the love of fuck. I know Dax didn't meant to do it, but he just mind-fucked me some more. *Everyone* falls in love with me at first sight? *Including him?* Or was that merely a figure of speech?

But since there's no way I'm going to ask for clarification—and since that was surely the closest thing to a declaration of love I'm going to get from this boy any time soon—I kiss him and clutch him to me and try to force my brain to stop thinking so much.

In reply to my desperate body language, my obvious need, Dax cradles me and strokes my back. And, finally, when he begins softly singing "Fireflies" to me... my salty tears dry... my ragged breathing slows... and, soon, I drift off to sleep in Dax's arms, his soulful voice a lovely Band-Aid over my aching heart.

FORTY

DAX

"**D**ude, I'm not a forty-year-old accountant with a wife, three kids, and a mini-van," I say as we head up the walkway to the latest house.

"Don't judge it by the outside," Ryan says.

"There's no cool factor at all."

"The inside is cool."

"But it's nowhere near the beach," I say.

"I just want you to see what you can get in your price range, if you're willing to move twenty minutes inland. Lots of celebrities live over here, Dax."

"Do the celebrities gather for bingo and shuffleboard in the club-house? Because this place looks like a fucking retirement community."

"Jesus, Rock Star. Stop acting like a twat."

"I told you I wanna live near the beach."

"For the hundredth time," Ryan says. "I want you to see what your budget can buy you so you can make an informed decision at the end of the day. Your money stretches like crazy over here. Yes, you're making a shit-ton of money *right now*. And I hope that continues for you. But if it doesn't—if your second album doesn't smash—then you're gonna need to be extra smart with your money. You're twenty-three, Dax. What if the well has run dry by the time you're thirty-three? You might need to live off this first album's success for a long time. And if not, if the train keeps rolling down the tracks, then, great, you can upgrade—get a house like this one, but by the beach. But for now, we're gonna keep to the budget we talked about. And that means you can afford a tiny condo right on the beach or a big-ass, sprawling compound out here."

"A tiny condo is fine with me. Something like Fish's place."

"You need more security than Fish. Plus, I know you. You're a homebody. You're gonna want your place to be the hang-out."

"He's right about that," Keane says. "You don't get FOMO, brah. You get *JOMO*."

Zander and Fish agree.

Ryan says, "Just give it a chance. It's got a home theater, a home gym, a full basketball court out back, a pool and Jacuzzi. A game room with a pool table and a bar. State of the art security system and cameras. You might not want all that stuff, but I wouldn't be doing my job if I didn't show you this kind of place, just in case. Now stop being a whiny little rockstar bitch and let me do my job." He turns to the group. "Tell my rock star brother to stop being a whiny little rock-star bitch, please."

"Stop being a whiny little rockstar bitch," everyone chants in unison.

And by "everyone," I mean the entourage that's accompanying Ryan and me on today's house-hunting expedition: Zander, Keane, Maddy, Fish, and... my beautiful, sexy addiction. *Violet Rhodes.* Goddamn, I'm addicted to this woman. So much so, when it came time for me to leave Violet in the hotel room today, I simply couldn't do it. And not only because I've become physically addicted to her, but also because I just plain respect her opinion.

Which is why, when Ryan came to pick me up at the hotel, I invited Violet along... and then quickly invited Keane and Maddy, too, employing the same strategy we used for the children's hospital.

From there, Keane invited Zander, just because he loves him

more than life itself and has been missing him so much. I invited Fish and Colin, for the same reasons. Fish said yes, but Colin had plans with his dancer today. And that's how today's house-hunting posse was formed.

We reach the front door of the sprawling house. Ryan straightens his tie and knocks. A dude in a designer suit answers and greets us. Ryan acts all businesslike and shit, saying I'm his client and we appreciate the showing and blah, blah, blah. The dude fawns over me for a moment, telling me he loves this and that song—the same way the real estate agents at the last few places have done. I thank him, same as the others. And, finally, the dude says, "Let me give you a tour."

I take Violet's hand. "Lead on."

We snake through the compound, looking at all the bells and whistles and amenities. And I must admit, the place is damned impressive. Regardless, though, it feels like too much, too fast for me. Talk about adulting. If I lived here, I'd need to hire a pool guy. Dude, I'm not ready to have a pool guy. I'm twenty-three.

When we reach the basketball court, Keane picks up a ball and elegantly dunks it. Because he's a freak of nature. And, of course, that prompts Maddy to pull out her camera and tell Keane to do it again. "Fish, get in there. You two should play a little one-one-one."

"I suck at basketball," Fish says.

"Yeah, exactly. Have I ever mentioned this is a comedy show?" Maddy says.

"Ah."

And away Keane and Fish go, acting like goofballs while getting footage for "Ball Peen Hammer's Guide To a Handsome and Happy Life," the YouTube show starring Keane, produced by Maddy, that's become their precious baby. In addition to providing tons of fun and laughs for Keane and Maddy, the show has turned out to be a fantastic platform for Keane as he continues chasing his big Hollywood dreams. Plus, from what Keane's told me, it's a bit of a cash cow for the pair, as well.

"And, of course, there's a full security and surveillance system," the agent says as we walk away from the basketball court, leaving Keane, Maddy, and Fish out there, fooling around.

"Oh, I'd like to hear more about that," Zander says, and Ryan chimes in to say he's interested, as well.

Zander asks the guy a few questions that display his newfound knowledge of home security—which makes sense, given that he just finished upgrading Aloha's to the nines. And off the agent goes with Ryan and Zander to who-knows-where to show them the goods.

"You coming?" Ryan says to me.

"No, I think we'll wander a bit, if that's okay." I squeeze Violet's hand. "I could use a little alone time to gather my thoughts. You know, try to picture myself living here."

"Great idea," the agent says. "Take as much time as you need, Dax."

"Thanks."

As Violet and I walk away, hand in hand, I turn to her, a wicked smile on my face. "It's been far too long since I've kissed you, Violet Rhodes. I need my drug, baby."

She arches an eyebrow. "No argument from me."

I look around. "Come on." I grab her hand and lead her through the maze of the big-ass house, until we come upon a home gym. Once inside, I take her face in my hands and kiss her passionately... which quickly ignites me like crazy. As our tongues continue swirling, I pull up Violet's skirt and slide my fingers inside her panties, and she bucks and jolts with pleasure at my touch. I begin finger-fucking her. Massaging her clit. And she lifts her thigh, giving me full access to her sweet pussy. When she comes, I unbutton my jeans, drunk with arousal. And then I pick her up by her ass, pin her back to the wall next to an elliptical machine, and—

"Dax!"

It's Ryan.

Shit.

Violet and I scramble.

She leaps behind me to put herself back together while I stuff my hard dick back into my pants and scream bloody murder at my brother for his intrusion.

"There are surveillance cameras in every room of this house, Dax!" Ryan roars. "You're making a goddamned sex tape!"

"Oh my God," Violet says behind me.

Ryan's blue eyes are blazing. "If Z and I hadn't been in that security room, at exactly the right time, do you have any idea what a clusterfuck this could have been for you? That footage is set to upload to a server every hour on the hour while the house is on the market! God only knows who would have seen it from the security company, or if someone there would have recognized you and sold the footage to the highest bidder."

Violet whimpers behind me.

"I'm sorry, Violet," Ryan says. He's shaking with adrenaline. "I never would have barged in on you two, otherwise. Obviously. But I had to stop you."

"I understand," she squeaks out. "Thank you."

Ryan sighs. "Zander is making sure the footage is deleted and that it's not on the cloud somewhere. He's got Henn on the phone right now, making sure there's absolutely nothing he's missing."

"Thanks," I whisper. I look at Violet. She looks on the cusp of bursting into tears. "I'm sorry. It didn't even occur to me."

"I know," she says. She wipes her eyes. She's shaking.

"You've got to be extra careful, Daxy," Ryan says, his tone turning genuinely sympathetic. "There are plenty of people in the world who'd think nothing of making a buck off you. A sex tape featuring you... I'm sure that would be a goldmine in the wrong hands."

I exhale and rub my face. And then I flash Violet a wan smile. "Hey, on the upside, at least it would have taken care of our little Caleb-and-Reed problem, huh? No decision required. We'd be officially *out*."

I meant the comment as a joke. A little dark humor never hurt anyone, right? But, clearly, I've said something deeply offensive to her.

Violet looks at Ryan, her jaw set. "Thank you, Ryan. It would have been devastating to me to have that out there."

"I'm sorry I embarrassed you."

"Thanks. I'm grateful." Without looking at me, Violet marches toward the door of the home gym. "I need to find a bathroom for a minute. Excuse me."

When she's gone, Ryan whacks me across the shoulder. "Dumbshit."

"I gotta go after her."

Ryan grabs my arm. "Give her a minute. I'm sure she needs to be alone to cry. That had to be the most embarrassing thing that's ever happened to her."

I pace the room for a moment, adrenaline blasting through my veins. My chest is tight. My breathing shallow. I feel like I'm physically suffocating. I stop pacing and cover my face with my hands. "I'm crazy about her, Ryan," I choke out. "She's the most amazing girl I've ever met... and I think I'm royally fucking this up."

FORTY-ONE
VIOLET

The minute I stride into the hotel room, I burst into tears.

"Violet, talk to me!" Dax booms behind me, following me into the room. "I know you were embarrassed, but I was, too. That's no reason to give me the silent treatment the whole drive back."

I whirl around. "It wasn't the silent treatment. I didn't want to say anything until we were alone because I knew I'd burst into tears."

Dax tries to hug me, but I push him away. And that pisses him off.

He shouts, "You think I *knew* we were on camera? You think my diabolic plan was to unwittingly lure you into making a sex tape that would get leaked?"

"God, you're clueless!"

"Yeah, I guess I am, because you've been shooting daggers at me since we got into the car and I have no idea why!"

I begin darting around the room, gathering my clothes. "I can't do this anymore."

"Do *what*?"

"This! This fuck buddy situation. I'm not a fuck buddy kind of girl, Dax, and I refuse to be one, even for you."

"*Fuck buddy?* Violet, stop that." He grabs my arm to make me stop collecting my stuff. He makes me face him. "You're not my *fuck buddy*. I'm the one who said we should be exclusive, remember?'"

"Yeah, exclusive fuck buddies."

He throws up his hands, releasing me, so I march to the closet to gather my hanging clothes.

"When you found out about the video," I say, "your first thought was, 'Oh well, at least it would solve my Caleb and Reed problem.'"

"*That was a joke.* Oh my God. You thought I was serious?"

"A joke rooted in truth. You're looking for any excuse not to have to look Caleb in the eye and tell him you've banged me. Maybe it's subliminal, but, if you're being honest—"

"So, in your mind, I subconsciously *wanted* some video I didn't even know was being recorded to leak and—"

"No. I'm saying when you found out about the video, your first reaction was that it would at least make a decision for you—a decision you don't want to make. A decision that's tearing you up inside and tainting what we have."

Now it's Dax's turn to pace around the room. "This is nuts. It was a *joke.*"

I follow him around the room, shouting at him. "And what about at the hospital yesterday, when you kissed me in the hallway, right in front of all those nurses with their phones out? Was that a joke, too? Because we both know a little piece of you was hoping a photo of us would get posted somewhere, and do your dirty work for you."

He freezes like a guilty man. And, just that fast, I know my hunch is right. That kiss in the hospital wasn't merely the reckless act of a boy in love. It was the act of a coward. A flare gun set off by a man drowning in a sea of indecision. An invitation to fate to take the wheel. Well, fuck that shit. Fuck it!

I step forward and wag my finger in Dax's face. "I refuse to be your booby prize, Dax Morgan! I refuse to enter into a relationship with you by default, simply because you were too chicken shit to shout from the top of the highest mountain about your feelings for me. If you want me, for real—and not just to fuck me in secret—then you're going to need to make a decision. I want to be the woman you want. Not the woman who *happens* to you because someone else took it upon themselves to 'out' you. I'm not going to be your dirty little secret you hide from your friends. I understand intellectually why you're hiding me. But I can't be that girl anymore. It's making me feel ashamed of myself. Like a tramp. And I'm not a tramp!"

"Of course, you're not," he says, emotion ravaging his voice. "Violet, you know why I've been keeping us a secret. It's not that I'm ashamed of you, or because you're not amazing. It's killing me not being able to take you everywhere and—"

"No. That's bullshit. 'Not being able to...' That's not true. You're 'able to,' Dax. You just *choose* not to. For reasons that are logical and understandable? Yes. But you're conducting an analysis here, whether you realize it or not. Weighing the pros and cons. And by *not* making me your girlfriend, for real, by hiding me away and inviting Keane and Maddy wherever we go and looking like you want to barf rather than mention Caleb's name, you're telling me the answer to your analysis: *being with me isn't worth the damage I'll cause you.*"

Dax looks heartsick. And I'm right there with him. I feel like I'm going to keel over from the pain ravaging my heart.

"Violet. Please."

"Frankly, I think your analysis is correct. I think we're doomed, regardless. Even if you pick me, we can't last. If everything goes to shit on you, then you'll hold it against me. If you pick me, I'll feel like I have to be the world's most perfect girlfriend to deserve it, some kind of superhero. But the truth is, I'm not a superhero. I'm just a girl. How could I possibly be 'enough' for a guy like you, when you've got the entire world at your feet and you could have any woman you want? When there are a thousand women out there who are way sexier than me, who'll say, 'Oh, yes, Dax, keep me hidden!' Girls who wouldn't wreak any havoc on your life whatsoever?"

"I don't want anyone else, Violet," he says, his voice strained. "*I want you.*"

"Yeah, you want me. The same way my father wanted my mother. *Secretly.* The same way my mother wanted that dude she had an affair with—the one that blew her marriage to bits." My voice is trembling. "My entire life, the one thing I swore I'd never be is anybody's shameful secret. I feel dirty and used and guilty. *Ashamed.* You think I can't see the guilt that twists your face every time you think of Caleb? I understand why, Dax. And, frankly, I respect that about you—your sense of loyalty. But I'm done being the source of your guilt."

I stride to my suitcase in the corner, bring it to the bed, and throw it open, intending to pack the pile of clothes I've amassed on the bed and get the hell out of here.

"Wait, Violet," Dax says, rushing to my side. "I just need a little more time. I talked about you with the therapist during our appointment. I didn't tell you that part. He said, 'Be careful this girl isn't just another drug you're taking to numb the pain. Take it slow. Be sure she's not just another bottle of booze or a little white pill.' So I'm trying to be cautious. I'm trying to do this right. *I want to be sure.*"

I shove a pair of shoes into my suitcase. "It's good advice. Take all the time you need. But I'm not gonna sneak around with you while you take it." Tears streaming down my face, I march into the bathroom to collect my makeup and toiletries.

"Don't leave, Violet," he says, following me into the bathroom. His voice is sheer panic. "I love having you here with me."

Fuck. My heart skipped a beat when Dax started his sentence with the words "I love..." and then dropped into my toes when he didn't finish with the word "you." Wordlessly, I gather the last of my shit from the bathroom and march to my suitcase in the bedroom.

"Violet, stop. I need you."

"No. I'm done auditioning for the role of The Girl Who Fucked Up Your Life. And I'm certainly not going to stand here, tapping my toe, pushing you to do something you're not ready to do—something you'll eventually regret. You feel like you haven't had enough time to decide if I'm worth the damage? Cool. I get that." I've finished cramming everything into my suitcase and now I close it up and start zipping. "You're sane to feel that way, Dax. No sane person could possibly fall in love this fast. Especially when you're hiding away in a little fantasy together and nothing is real. What- ever you're feeling for me isn't worth gambling all your chips on. I totally get it."

My bag is packed and zipped. My eyes and nose are leaking. Holy hell, I'm a goddamned hot mess.

"Violet, you're just freaked out by what happened at that house today. If you calm down and—"

"I don't need to calm down!" I shriek. "I need to get out of here and save myself. That's what I need. I don't want to be your girlfriend by default, simply because you self-sabotaged. I want you to *choose* me."

Dax swallows hard. His eyes are glistening. He doesn't speak.

"We're in a no-win situation," I say. "Every bit as much as we were eight months ago. Only it's worse now. Back then, my worry was you'd get kicked off the tour if Caleb found out about us. Or if Reed thought you'd used me. But I stupidly thought, once the tour was over and your band was a huge success, you'd be bulletproof, and we could do whatever we wanted. But what I didn't anticipate was that you'd come back from the tour feeling genuine *love* for Caleb and Dean and the guys. You became brothers with those guys on tour. How can I possibly compete with that?"

Dax grimaces, revealing I've hit the nail on the head. His indeci- sion isn't about protecting his career. He doesn't care about money or fame, any more than he cared about it when I first met him. *He cares about betraying his friend.* He cares about love and loyalty and broth- erhood, and he can't reconcile choosing a relationship with me over those things.

I step forward, my anger supplanted by heartbreak. I touch his face. His gorgeous, tortured face. "I wish you all the happiness and success in the world. But I have to step out into the light now, without shame or secrets. My whole life has been secrets and betrayals and abandonments and loss. I'm done with all of it. You're too paralyzed to make a decision? I'm making it for you." I hug him and he clutches me fiercely.

His body heaves. He's shaking violently, like a junkie going through withdrawal. "Don't go, Violet," he whispers fiercely. "Please, baby. I don't think I can live without you."

I pull away and begin wheeling my suitcase toward the door, my jaw and mind set. Because, unlike Dax, I *know* for a *fact* I can't live without him. If Dax doesn't know that about me, with absolute certainty, then I'm most definitely doing the right thing. "Take all the time you need," I say, my voice steely as I roll my suitcase across the room. "This isn't an ultimatum, Dax." I wipe my eyes and open the door. "This is goodbye."

FORTY-TWO

DAX

In one hand, I hold the unopened bottle of Jack Daniels that came with the room. In the other, I press my phone to my ear. "I need a one-day hall pass on my promise to you, Colby."

"Ryan just told me what happened," Colby says. "I'm sure it was embarrassing, but that's no reason—"

"I don't want a drink because I almost made a sex tape!" I shout. "Violet left me, Bee. She's gone. And now, I'm gonna drink myself into oblivion."

"Go ahead. But if you do, I'm taking you to rehab."

"Fuck!" I slam the bottle down on the table. "This is so fucking stupid! I'm not an alcoholic. I just want a drink after a horrible, shitty day, the same way you wanted a drink at Henn and Hannah's wedding. The same way you wanted a margarita in my dressing room before my show. If you can do all that and *you're* not some kind of addict, then why can't I have a drink after Violet leaves me?"

"You can. But then I'm taking you to rehab."

"Fuck!"

"Talk to me, Dax. Why did Violet leave?"

I get up and pace around the room, eyeing the bottle on the table. "Fuck this shit! This is so stupid!"

"Dax, tell me why Violet left."

"She said she didn't want to be my fuck buddy anymore!"

"Your *fuck buddy*?"

"That's what she said!"

"But you've been obsessed with her for months. You wrote her that fireflies song."

I sit on the edge of the bed, practically panting. "Exactly! I wrote her that song and sang it to her in front of the entire world. And she was the one who came up with the 'secret fuck-spies on the run' thing, not me. And now she's gone because she says she doesn't want to be my guilty pleasure and I want a fucking drink."

"She obviously feels like you've been sending her mixed messages. She must feel strung along."

"I never strung her along! That's total and complete bullshit. I was up front with her, and we *both* agreed on the arrangement."

Colby audibly shrugs. "Something must have changed for her, then. Somewhere along the line. She obviously doesn't like the arrangement anymore."

My heart feels like it's physically breaking. I clutch my chest and mutter, "I gotta go."

"To drink?"

"No. A promise is a promise. It was a stupid promise—a totally unnecessary one—but I made it, and I'll keep it. Even though, to be clear, it's fucking stupid and you're an asshole for doing this to me and I hate you."

"Do you want me to send Ryan over there? He's taking the late flight back to Seattle tonight, but I'm sure—"

"No. I'll just play my guitar until I pass out. I'll get drunk on music, rather than Jack, even though Jack would have been a whole lot quicker."

"You promise?"

"Yes."

"Dax, don't lie to me."

"I'm not lying. Especially about the part where I said I hate you."

Colby exhales. "Call me again if you need me. Day or night. Anytime."

I end the call with Colby and immediately press the button to call Violet, but my call goes straight to voicemail. *Again.* I hang up without leaving a message, yet again, shouting obscenities to myself. If I knew what to say to her to change her mind, I'd leave a voicemail. But I don't know what the fuck to say to her that I haven't already said. And not only that, I'm so fucking pissed right now, I feel like I'm going to punch a hole in the wall if I don't have a drink.

I eye the bottle again. "Fuck!"

My heart racing, I pick up my guitar, sit on the bed, and start strumming. Cursing and strumming. Stuffing down tears and strumming. And, slowly, I begin to calm down a bit. I play whatever the fuck pours out of me, and soon, my angry, aimless strumming becomes a repeated riff. And then a specific chord progression on a running loop. My curses turn into humming. My humming turns into gibberish. And, finally, the gibberish turns into coherent lyrics. Until, soon, I'm writing a full-blown song. A fucking awesome one, at that. No, actually, I'm not writing it. I'm *channeling* it. Holding onto the song's tail as it hurtles, on its own, like a comet through outer space.

When my phone pings with a text, I glance down, praying it's from Violet—and when I see it's from Dean, I stop playing, my heart in my throat.

Dean: Looking forward to our songwriting sesh tomorrow after your meeting with Reed. Around what time do you think you'll be here? Can't wait to write something dope with you, Boy Wonder.

At the end of the text, Dean attaches his address in Malibu and a code for a gate.

"Shit," I mutter. I stare at the text for a long moment before calling Violet again. When my call goes to voicemail, I hang up and shoot her another text, begging her to call me. *Again.* What I'll say to her when and if she calls, I don't know, but I can't do *nothing.* I've at least got to *try* to convince that woman to come back to me.

When I'm done texting Violet, I feel frantic. I glance at the bottle of booze across the room on the table again, physically craving it. "Motherfucker," I whisper. I get up, grab the bottle, and set it outside the room in the hallway. And then I grab my phone with white knuckles and press the button to call my sister.

"Hey, honey," Kat says, answering my call.

"She left me," I say, my voice tight and steeped in pain.

"Violet?"

I sit on the edge of the bed. "I fucked up, Jizz. She's gone."

"Aw, shit, honey. What'd you do?"

I explain the situation, stuffing down tears.

"Sometimes, I forget you're not me in a male body," Kat says. "This is one time you've definitely proven you've got a dick and balls."

I rub my eyes. "What the hell does that mean?"

"It means you're a dumbass."

"Why? Violet and I both decided, *together,* to be secret fuck-spies while we got to know each other and figured out what to do."

"I'm guessing there was never a 'we' in that scenario, honey. Violet had no choice but to agree to whatever deal you were offering her. Surely, she figured getting *something* with you was better than nothing. I would have done the same thing in her shoes. But, clearly, skulking around on the down low didn't turn out to be enough for her. And do you want to know why, if I had to guess?"

"No, Kat, I have no desire to know why Violet left me," I snap. "I called to talk about the weather."

"*Because she loves you.*"

My heart squeezes.

"She loves you and she thinks you don't love her back so she ran away to protect herself. It's as simple as that."

My heart is clanging wildly in my chest. "I played her that song,

Kitty—in front of the entire world. I told her how I feel about her in that song."

"That song only gets you so far, honey," Kat says. "It's an amazing song, but telling a girl they're a flower who gives you fireflies isn't the same thing as 'I love you, Violet.' I'm sure she was blown away by the song at the time. But then, when her feelings grew well past fireflies, she needed to know your feelings had grown, too. She needed reassurance, and you didn't give it to her. Take it from me, when you love someone, anything short of love in return feels like a devastating rejection."

A little groan of torment escapes my throat. I feel wrecked. Demolished. Hopeless.

"Sweetie, she needed to hear the words from you. It's like in *Ghost*, when Demi Moore said 'I love you' to Patrick Swayze and he responded 'Ditto.'" Kat scoffs. "Demi didn't deserve a *ditto*. And neither does Violet."

I choke back emotion. "It's only been a week, Kat. How could anyone fall in love in a week?"

"I fell in love with Josh in a week. Ryan fell in love with Tessa in a week. Hell, to some people, a week is an eternity. Dad fell in love with Mom at first sight. He saw her in class, and later that night—"

"He told his buddy, 'I saw the girl I'm gonna marry today.' Yes, I know the story."

"Colby fell in love with Lydia at first sight, too. Like father, like son. Actually, come to think of it, Ryan didn't even need a week to know Tessa was The One. We all know he fell for her at first sight, too. We're Morgans, dude. When we know, we know. But, regardless, it hasn't been a week and you know it. You've been obsessed with Violet for months and months."

I nod, even though Kat's not here to see it.

"Daxy, she left because she thinks, if you loved her the way she loves you, then you wouldn't let anything or anyone stand in your way. And, frankly, I think she's right about that."

"I do love her," I whisper. And as the words come out, I know, with full clarity, they're true. I clear my throat and speak a bit more loudly, my heart racing. "I love Violet."

I can hear my sister's wide smile across the phone line. "Then prove it. Move mountains for her, baby. Because I'ma tell you right now, Violet Rhodes is the kind of girl who deserves the sun, the moon, and the stars—a spot on your arm. She deserves an 'I love you,' Dax Morgan. Not a freaking *ditto*."

Whent I walk into my apartment, Miranda is sitting on the couch with her laptop.

"You just missed Caleb," she says.

"He was here?"

"He left ten minutes ago. He's freaking out you haven't returned any of his calls or texts." Concern flickers across Miranda's face as I cross the room. "Have you been crying?"

"You didn't tell Caleb about Dax, did you?"

"Of course not. I told him you've been working a ton lately. Why have you been crying?"

I burst into tears and plop onto the couch, my hands over my face, and Miranda puts her arm around me.

"Dax?"

I nod.

"He broke up with you?"

"No, I broke up with him before he could do it to me."

I tell Miranda everything and she listens and says a whole bunch of sweet and sympathetic things. But the one thing she doesn't do is tell me I'm reading the situation wrong. Because, as we both know, I'm not. This thing with Dax is doomed.

As we're talking, my phone rings with an incoming call. I look down. *Caleb.*

"Please answer him," Miranda says. "Just so he knows you're alive. He's worried."

Exhaling, I press the button to take the call. Fuck it. Just because Dax is too chicken shit to talk to Caleb, doesn't mean I am. "Hey, Caleb."

"Hey, baby. I've been worried. You haven't answered any of my calls or texts."

"Yeah, I've been working. Sorry."

"Are you crying?"

"No. What's up?"

"I need to talk to you."

"About what?"

"I'd like to tell you in person. Where are you?"

"In my apartment."

"Can I come now? I'm close by. I can be there in ten."

I take a brief moment to consider. And then, "Yeah. Sure. Come now."

———

When I open the door to Caleb, he looks... stunning. Ripped and chiseled, and yet, uncharacteristically humble and sincere. *Tormented,* I'd even say. The minute he sees my tear-stained face, he lurches forward and embraces me. And, God help me, I crumple into him and nuzzle my nose into his broad chest and lose myself to sobbing.

"Sweetheart," he coos, his voice low and masculine. "Pretty baby."

As he leads me to the couch like a sack of potatoes, I hear the door to Miranda's bedroom close, signaling she's left us alone.

Caleb sits me down and pulls me to him and I crumple into him again, crying even harder.

"What happened?" he asks, holding me close. "Baby, tell me."

I shake my head and clutch him to me. Ah, yes, I remember this. The way Caleb smells. The way his arms feel wrapped around me when I'm sad. I remember what it felt like to be his. To love him with all my heart. He was so broken, but so was I, and I was positive we could fix each other, if only we loved each other hard enough. I thought love could conquer all, when it came to us, even if a part of me knew I loved him just a little bit more than he loved me.

Caleb wipes at my tears with his thumb. His green eyes are on fire. *"Did he hurt you?"*

My heart stops. "Who?"

"Your boyfriend. Whoever you've been seeing."

"I'm not seeing him anymore. It's over."

And that's all Caleb needs. His lips crush mine. His soft lips. The lips I ached for years to kiss again. I melt into his kiss like I'm reliving a beautiful dream. I open my mouth to receive his tongue and he claims me, the same way he did that very first time. This boy was my first kiss. The first boy to make love to me. And he did it so gently. So sweetly. Like I was a rare treasure. He was the boy who dazzled me with his talent and overwhelmed me with his passion. And pissed me off constantly with his short temper and stupid tantrums. He was the boy who threw punches at anyone who stared at my tits. Or so he thought. He was the boy I loved and would do anything for, and did. The boy who ultimately reached the stratosphere on a rocket, just like I dreamed he would one day... and then left me and my broken heart behind in the dust.

And now, out of nowhere, he's back, kissing me and begging for another chance. A new chapter. He could have anyone in the world, this magnificent, tempestuous boy. But, for some reason, he wants *me*. Or so he says. And now, with this kiss, this last kiss of ours, I know, without a doubt, I don't want him. And not because I want Dax. Which I do. But because, regardless of Dax, I simply don't want Caleb Baumgarten anymore. I'm sure of it.

I pull back from our kiss to find a forest fire blazing in Caleb's green eyes.

"I shouldn't have done that," I say, wiping my mouth.

"We've still got it, Vi," he says. "What we had—it's still there. Only better."

I shake my head and lean back. "No, honey. It's gone."

Caleb looks crestfallen for a moment. But then his face morphs into barely contained fury. It's a transformation I've seen many times in his eyes. Hurt turning into anger in the blink of an eye.

"Who is he?" he grits out.

"Forget him. I'm not with him anymore. But me being single again doesn't mean I want to be with you. Our time has passed, Caleb. We're done."

"No. Everything I said the other night was true. This has been building for a long time, Vi. This isn't a rash decision for me. I'm ready to commit to you now. I'm ready to do whatever it takes to win you back."

Oh, how I wish Dax had said those same words to me an hour ago in that hotel room.

"I know I hurt you," Caleb continues. "I was young and stupid and drunk on my new fame. But I'm done with all that now. I see what I lost and I'll do whatever it takes to get it back."

I take Caleb's hands. He looks so sincere. So beautiful and tragic. "The issue isn't me not believing you. I do. You say you've changed? I truly believe you. But I've changed, too. That's the thing you're not factoring in. When you loved me, I worshipped the ground you walked on, Caleb. I followed you around like a puppy. We both knew I was at your mercy. And that's not a healthy relationship."

"I want a healthy relationship. I'm ready."

I take a deep breath, suddenly feeling emotional. "Caleb, the girl you're remembering doesn't exist anymore. We didn't have a healthy love, Caleb. It sucked me dry."

"We can have one now. I'm sick of being worshipped. I swear. I want someone to push back. To keep me in check. Please, Violet. You get me like nobody else does. You always tell me the truth."

I close my eyes. "When we were together, I was broken. I thought clutching onto you for dear life, and having you hold me so tight I couldn't breathe, meant you were putting me back together. But the truth is you weren't giving me enough space to glue my broken pieces back together. You were clutching me so tight, my pieces were being ground into sand."

He looks distraught. "I don't understand. What does that mean?"

I touch his beard tenderly. "It means we're not good for each other. That's what I'm saying. You were my first love and I'll always love you. But our broken pieces don't fit together like a jigsaw puzzle, Caleb—they rub and grind in all the wrong ways. I've had a lot of therapy since I was with you, and I've figured out who I am. Who I want to be. You want the girl you remember, but she doesn't exist anymore. I don't *want* her to exist."

He touches my hair and the look of anguish on his face almost makes me want to kiss it away. *Almost.* "I want the girl you are now," he says, his voice awash in pain. "You're saying you've become a strong, independent woman? Well, that's what I want. I've had enough of groupies. Of girls saying only what I want to hear. I want someone to want me for *me*. Someone I can trust."

I smile. "And there's no doubt in my mind you'll find her one day, if that's truly what you want. But she won't be me. I'll always love you, Caleb, for all the firsts. For how it felt to watch you take off like a rocket. I'll always want the best for you. But I'm not in love with you, and I'm not going to be, ever again."

His nostrils flare. He grits his teeth. "Because you're in love with him."

"He has nothing to do with it. I'm not in love with *you*."

His jaw muscles pulse. "You love him."

I pause. Will it give him closure to know I'm in his exact shoes? That I love someone who doesn't want me, but I'm nonetheless forcing myself to move on, anyway, exactly the way he should? "Yes, I love him," I admit. "But it doesn't matter because he's not in love with me. And now, I'm moving on. And so should you."

If I thought my admission would inspire some sort of deep, philosophical epiphany for Caleb, I was dead wrong. He looks homicidal. "I'm not sure if I want to murder this asshole more for taking you away from me, or for not loving you the way you deserve. Either way, I want to fucking kill him."

My phone on the coffee table rings with an incoming call. I look down, freaking out "DJ" might appear on the screen, and that, somehow, those two letters might tip Caleb off about Dax's identity... but it's not Dax calling me this time. It's my mother.

"I've got to take this call," I say. Truthfully, I could probably let Mom go to voicemail, but I feel like I need a break from this intense conversation.

"Is that him?" Caleb says, his voice sharp.

"It's my mother." I show him the screen bearing my mom's name on it, to prove I'm telling the truth, and connect the call. "Hey, Mom."

"I just heard some bad news," she says. "I thought you'd want to know."

FORTY-FOUR

DAX

I shake hands with Reed and settle into a chair.

"The other goats aren't coming?" Reed asks, leaning back into a big leather chair behind his desk.

"Fish and Colin will come to our next meeting. Hope that's okay."

"Yeah, of course. Just didn't want you thinking I'm excluding them."

I pull my acoustic guitar out of its case and begin tuning it. "I spent the morning with them. They know I'm here and that I'm playing you all my new songs. I have their full support."

"Great. Can't wait to hear what you've got for me." He pulls a notepad from a drawer. "I think Owen's around here somewhere today. How about we call him in here to—"

"No, not today. I'd prefer to do this meeting with only you, if that's okay. We can let everyone else hear the new songs next time."

Reed holds up his phone. "Mind if I record you, then? We're gonna have some tight deadlines. I want to get the team going as quickly as possible."

"Sure."

Reed presses a button to begin recording and lays his phone on the edge of his desk. "Did you ever finish that song you were blocked on? The one you thought might be the lead-off single?"

"I did. But I wound up writing an even better one last night."

"Holy shit, Dax. You're on fire. Hang on. Let me write down the song titles real quick. We've got 'Fireflies'..." Reed writes it on his notepad. "What was that second one you played for me the other day?"

"'Ultra Violet Radiation.'"

"That's right. Great song." He writes the title onto his notepad. "What's this next one called?"

I inhale deeply. With my next words, I'll cross the point of no return. And I can't fucking wait. "'Caught Violet-Handed.'"

Reed looks up from his pad. His dark eyes register full understanding. His jaw pulses.

Quickly, without waiting for Reed to speak, I start playing the song. "You caught me violet-handed, baby, and now I'm drowning in blue. Not seeing red flags anymore, cuz all I see is you... You caught me Violet-handed, baby, and now I got them Violet blues..."

When I finish performing the full song, I immediately roll into playing the next one: "Hitwoman Elvis Disco Momma"—yet another song Reed will be able to attribute to Violet, assuming he remembers the "Elvis Reimagined" outfit Violet wore to his party.

After my disco song, I barrel into the next tune—"Ain't No Shrinking Violet"—and follow that one up with "Girl with the Dragonfly Tattoo," each song reinforcing, in no uncertain terms, the identity of the girl I'm singing about. And, more importantly, how I *feel* about her.

Finally, I play Reed the song I wrote last night, after Violet left me and Kat was done dropping truth bombs on me. After my fifth call to Violet went to voicemail and my tenth text went unanswered. After I'd paced ten miles in my room and called down to get someone to clear out my entire minibar. A song called "Lucky Number."

Not the dude wearing those

Stupid leather pants
Don't like leather
Unless it's on you
Skin tight, like glue
Show me every inch
Put 'em on so I can take 'em off

Never had blue hair
Or a child
Never loved a twin whose mother died
Not the sun or the moon
Just the fifth one who croons
Shuts himself away in his room
Feels all too human
All the time

Five
It's where I come from
Who I am
Who I've always been
Five
My lucky number
Till I found you
Now my lucky number is two
Two
It's where I'm goin'
But only with you
Only if I tell the truth
Two
Cuz I wanna be with you
My new lucky number
My lucky number is you

. . .

Not good at numbers
I leave that to Ry
Not the dude who dances
Or puts out the fires
Don't float through life
Like a blonde kitty on a wire
Not a fish head
Losing my mind
Playing punk thrashers
In my garage at night
Five
It's where I come from
Who I am
Who I've always been
Five
My lucky number
Till I found you
Now my lucky number is two
Two
It's where I'm goin'
But only with you
Only if I tell the truth
Two
Cuz I wanna be with you
My new lucky number
My lucky number is you
I write the songs
It's all I know how to do
Take away my guitar
I'd be sellin' shoes
Workin' in a cannery
In Juneau

Don't have much in my pockets

Those zeros aren't real
Same guy as before
Except a liar now
Wasn't brave enough
To deserve you

Stood on that balcony
Let him spill his guts
Let him down
Let me down,
Let you down...
But all that stops now
Gonna tell the truth
Wanna be with you
Wanna be two
Baby, baby,
The truth shall set you free
Gonna tell it now
So I can finally breathe
The truth, the truth
The only truth
That matters
Is baby, baby
I love you

I strum out my final chord and look up to find Reed's dark eyes boring into me like lasers. The air in the room is thick and heavy. My heart is thrumming in my chest.

After a long, tense moment of silence, Reed leans back in his leather chair. "Violet hasn't said a word to me."

"We didn't want to say anything to anyone—not to you or Caleb or anyone else—until we were sure we had something that would survive out in the light. We figured if it didn't work out between us, it would be best if nobody ever knew."

Reed says nothing. He looks tense. Homicidal?

"Violet doesn't know I'm doing this," I say quickly. "She dumped me yesterday because she felt ready to take things to the next level, and I was too big a coward to take a leap of faith."

"And now?"

"And now I'm ready. Right after I'm done here with you, I'm headed to Caleb to tell him about Violet and me. After that, I'm going straight to Violet to tell her I love her for the first time. That I'd move mountains to be with her. No more hiding. No more lies. I want her. I love her. And fuck anyone who doesn't like it."

Reed's eyes flicker. "How long has this been going on?"

I tell him the story, including the sequence of events that led me to find out, only recently, that Violet is Caleb's ex and Reed's sister. "By the time I knew the complications, it was way too late," I say. "I was already a goner."

Reed holds my gaze for a long, unnerving beat, and then he presses a button on his phone, reminding me for the first time since I started playing that he's been recording this whole time. His dark eyes hard, he pushes his notepad to the side, places he elbows onto his desk, and says, "None of this is news to me, Dax—although I didn't realize the extent of your feelings for her."

My breathing hitches. I say nothing.

Reed smirks. "Dax, I saw you talking to Violet at my party for Aloha—on the patio—and it was easy to see the sparks between you. A few days later, on the plane to London, Colin said he and you had met 'amazing girls' at the party you were both sorry to leave behind. Eight months later, you're playing me two songs you'd written during the tour. One of them was called 'Ultra *Violet* Radiation.' The other had lyrics about a girl being a 'flower' and a 'road.'"

I can barely breathe.

Reed continues, "At Henn and Hannah's wedding, your family was marveling about how you never dance, but, lo and behold, that night, for some reason, you danced the night away. And, huh, so did my sister. *Right next to you.* And, of course, when Violet got up to use the bathroom after dancing, Keane suddenly felt compelled to host a little weed party on my patio, right after receiving a text. I'm not complaining about that, mind you. I love a good doobie with friends and that was some damn good weed. Just saying I'm not a moron. Oh, and one more thing? Violet's on my cell phone plan. So, when she didn't answer my calls or texts for a couple days after the wedding, which is really unlike her, I hopped online to check her iPhone location. And guess what surprising thing I discovered? My sister's phone was sitting ten minutes away at a nearby five-star hotel. Now, why on earth would Violet be hunkered down at an expensive hotel for days, when she could be sleeping in her rent-free apartment, fifteen minutes away? And then I remembered you saying you were gonna be shacked up in a hotel for a while, not Caleb's place, until you figured out where to live..."

I can't decipher the smile on Reed's face. Does that shit-eating grin mean he wants to throttle me—or merely a sign he thinks he's so smart?

"But there was no reason to say anything to Violet," Reed says. "And I certainly wasn't going to say anything to you. There's no way in hell I was gonna say or do a damned thing to mess up your creative process. You're a genius, Dax. The songs you write... every artist on my roster, other than Dean and 2Real, would sell their soul to write the songs you do. Trust me, I've been dealing with 'sensitive artist' types long enough to know, when they're laying golden eggs, leave 'em the fuck alone. So, that's what I did."

Anger rises sharply inside me. "You're willing to pimp out Violet in exchange for some golden eggs? Violet told me you didn't want her messing around with anyone signed to your label. That doesn't apply if the dude is laying big enough golden eggs for you?"

Reed looks thoroughly amused. "No, Dax. That doesn't apply if the dude is *you*." He smiles at my surprised expression. "Yes, I asked Violet to please not to flirt with any of my artists. And, yes, I told every artist coming to my party—the ones I knew about, anyway—to stay the fuck away from my little sister. I even showed 'em her photo and said, 'Off-limits, boys.' But even if I'd known you and the goats were coming to my party for Aloha, I wouldn't have said any of that to you. And do you know why?" He leans forward, his eyes blazing. "Because if there's one guy on my roster—one guy on the *planet*—I consider worthy of my sister, that dude is *you*."

Goosebumps erupt on my skin.

"Do you have any idea how fucked up Josh was before he met Kat and got taken in like a stray dog by your family? That's why Josh and I became so close in college—because we were both hopelessly fucked up. All his life, Josh has been secretly drowning. And then Kat came along and became Josh's lifeline, and your entire family became his life raft. And now he's a new man. Honestly, sometimes, I don't even recognize that bastard, he's so fucking happy." Reed leans back in his leather chair. "Violet hasn't been drowning for quite some time now, I don't think, but only because she's worked so damned hard on herself. But she's definitely doing some kind of fucked up doggy paddle—maybe even treading water—a lot of the time. Though, of course, she always makes it look good, whatever she's doing. That's her superpower. Holding it all together. Doing the doggie paddle with panache. But if that girl can get a lifeline—and maybe even a life raft—the same way Josh did, then, shit, I'm all for it."

My nose is stinging. Same with my eyes. I'm feeling over-whelmed with emotion, but I swallow it down.

Reed's face hardens. He leans forward. "But if you hurt my sister, God help me, forget everything I just said. You fuck her over—cheat on her, lie to her—I won't give a shit what our contract says, or how big the golden eggs are that come out of your ass; you'll be a piece of shit to me and I'll deal with you accordingly."

My breathing hitches. "All I want to do is love her and take care of her. Everything I said in that song was the truth."

"Good. Amen." His dark eyes blaze for a beat. "Don't play with her, Dax. Don't fuck around on my sister."

"Never."

He nods, seemingly satisfied. "You're going to see Caleb next?"

"Straight from here."

A wicked smile spreads across Reed's face. "Man, I wish I could be a fly on the wall for that. After Caleb cheated on my sister and smashed her heart into a pile of rubble, I wanted to fuck him over so bad, but Violet swore up and down I had it all wrong, so I refrained." He rubs his palms together with brazen glee. "Not gonna lie, it gives me intense pleasure knowing that asshole is about to get exactly what he deserves—a nice, big knife, plunged straight into his cheating, lying back."

FORTY-FIVE

DAX

"Thanks for meeting me here, guys," I say to Fish and Colin. Colin gets out of his slick new sports car and slams his car door shut. "We're not gonna let you get your ass kicked alone."

"How about not letting me get my ass kicked at all?"

"Yeah, I think that's a tall order," Fish says, coming around from the passenger side of Colin's car.

"You look like the Unabomber," Colin says, looking me up and down. "What's with the hoodie? It's nice out."

"Just keeping a low profile." My therapist pointed out it's my hair that gives me away the most. And so, if I want to minimize being recognized, he suggested I make it a habit to cover it up in public. Which means, today, I'm wearing a dark beanie on my head with my hair tied back and stuffed into my sweatshirt, plus a hood over my entire head and dark sunglasses on my face. I explain all that to my friends and add, "My therapist also said, if I do happen to get recognized while dressed like this, I'll be giving off such big hermit energy, people will most likely respect that and leave me alone."

"Or maybe they won't recognize you at all," Colin says, "but they'll still leave you alone because you look like you're about to abduct their children."

"What else did the therapist say?" Fish asks.

"He encouraged me to get a new motorcycle to replace the one that crapped out right before the tour. But this time around, he said I should wear a full helmet with a face shield when I ride, not the half helmet I used to wear. He said lots of celebrities get around LA that way, totally unrecognized." I shrug. "I was gonna get a new bike, anyway. But he just lit a fire under my ass to do it right away."

Colin lights a cigarette, takes a drag, and speaks through his exhale. "What kind you gonna get?"

"Some sort of cruiser. I'll probably go shopping for it next week. You wanna come?"

Both guys say they do.

"We might have to bring a bodyguard with us. The therapist said I'm most recognizable when I'm with you two."

"Whatever, Daxy," Fish says. "We'll make it work."

I gesture to Colin's fancy new ride. "I like your wheels. Blatant dick metaphor."

"Yeah, pretty sick, huh?" Colin replies. "Now I just need a place to live. You find something yet?"

I shake my head. "I'll probably get a condo in one of those high-rises by the beach. There was this one cool place with a doorman and surveillance. That should be plenty of security. I don't need a lot of space. I just wanna see the ocean when I wake up."

Fish gestures up the street to Dean's gated beachfront house. "You mean you don't want a compound on the cliffs of Malibu?"

"I've got no interest in something like this. At least, not yet."

"I'm surprised Dean lives in a huge place like this," Fish says. "He seemed like such a simple guy on tour. He reminded me of you."

"I get it, actually," I say. "He got himself a place he never needs to leave. A place where everyone can come to him and hang out. I could see myself going that route one day, if the cash keeps rolling in. But I'm not there yet. I wanna save my dough in case the gravy train abruptly jumps the tracks."

Colin frowns, and I know he's thinking what I'm about to do inside Dean's house might very well derail our gravy train. But I also know, because Colin told me so this morning when I met him and Fish at Fish's new condo to hash things out, he's one hundred percent behind me. Every bit in my corner as Fish. Once I told Colin I'm in love with Violet, not just in lust with her, and that I think I might have lost her through indecision and cowardice and not wanting to hurt anyone or let anyone down, least of all Fish and Colin, Colin said, "You do you, Daxy. Life's short. Be happy."

"I'm honored you took a break from bonin' your dancer to meet me here, Casanova," I say to Colin.

"Kiera went to a couple auditions today," Colin says. "Aloha's not gonna be touring for quite a while, apparently, and Kiera doesn't want to tour with anyone else. So, she's looking for jobs that'll keep her in L.A. Music videos and stuff like that."

"Gosh, I wonder why she wants to stay in L.A.," Fish says, smiling.

Colin takes a drag off his cigarette. "Just to be clear, though, I would have come over here to Malibu to watch you get your ass kicked, regardless. That's just the kind of supportive friend I am."

"Yeah, you're a peach."

"Speaking of you getting your ass kicked, how'd it go with Reed?" Fish asks.

"Surprisingly well," I say. I give them the rundown. "I'm sure it made all the difference I love her. If Reed thought I was just banging her, I bet things wouldn't have gone so well."

"I knew he'd be cool with it," Fish says. "Reed's always had heart-eyes for you, ever since Maui. He was so damned sure you were going to become the next big thing, he was even willing to take me in the deal."

"Don't say that, Fish. Reed knows how valuable you are. Both you and Colin."

Colin and Fish chuckle like I'm a fool.

"Reed *literally* told me in Maui he didn't want me," Fish says.

"*What?*"

"He said he thought you were gonna top the charts, *despite* having to drag my sorry ass on your back the whole way."

"Please, tell me you're joking."

"Nope."

"That motherfucker actually said that to you?"

"Yep."

"Why didn't you tell me?"

"Because, one, he said it like he was joking around. To this day, I don't know if he was truly being a dick or just attempting to be funny. And, two, I knew if I told you, you wouldn't sign, just to give Reed the finger. And I didn't want that to happen."

"Shit. I'm so sorry, Fish. Reed was way out of line. God, he's such an asshole sometimes."

Fish shrugs. "Fuck Reed. I'm laughing all the way to the bank."

"Reed is such a complicated villain to me. A colossal dick sometimes, and yet, he's been so good to Violet."

"There's no such thing as villains," Colin says. "Just a whole bunch of people who are the heroes of their own fucked-up stories."

Fish says, "I don't think Reed meant to slam me. I think he was just calling it like he saw it. Like, calling his shot in pool. Turns out he was right. We're at the top of the charts, despite you dragging my sorry ass along for the ride. But guess what? I'm already ten times the bass player I was back in Maui. And I'm only gonna get better and better. In fact, I've got a couple basslines I've been working on. I thought maybe we could build on 'em to write a couple songs, if you're down to try writing with me. No pressure, though."

"Are you kidding me? I'd *love* to write with you, Fish. Hell yeah."

Fish is beaming. "Cool. I've got some lyrics, too. Some weird shit I wanna bounce off you."

"Awesome. And just so you know, you're a sick-ass bass player, Fish Head. Always have been. I wouldn't want anyone else standing there with me every night."

"Word," Colin says.

"Same with you, Colinoscopy. You're a sick-ass drummer beast, and I couldn't do what I do without you, either."

Colin and Fish are both clearly moved. And so am I. On impulse, we all step into a huddle and put our hands in. We make stupid goat noises, ever so briefly, but they don't make us laugh as usual. This time, they make our Adam's apples bob.

Colin clears his throat. "You were right to come at me at the wrap party. I crossed a line. I was speaking out of fear and greed. It was a master class in How to Be a Douchebag."

"No, it wasn't. You were just being honest. Always be honest with me—good, bad, or ugly. There's nothing wrong with wanting to keep this train going. I'm sorry I played a song with secret shout-outs to Violet without telling you what I was doing."

"Please, just tell me you got lucky after you did that, or it was all for naught," Colin says.

I chuckle. "Yeah, I got lucky. Very, very lucky. I'm the luckiest guy in the world, in fact."

"That's all I need to know." He shrugs. "If the situation had been reversed, and I'd had the chance to sing a song I'd written for Kiera in front of an entire arena, I might have done it, too. Talk about racking up points."

"It's going *that* well with your dancer?" Fish says to Colin. "Sing-her-a-song-in-an-arena well?"

"So far, so good. She seems like a four-leaf clover."

Fish rolls his eyes. "And then there's me. One day, you're gonna find me, a lone fish, flopping around on a riverbank, taking his last breath through his busted-ass gills, clutching a bottle of lube in his little fish-fin while Pornhub blares on his laptop."

"Interesting mix of metaphors," Colin says.

"Your premise is faulty," I say. "There won't be traditional laptops by the time you flop around on a riverbank, taking your last breath. You'll be gasping and fish-flopping while wearing *Google goggles*."

"Well, that'll be so much better."

There's a beat. We all look at Dean's gated house again.

"So... have you figured out how you're gonna tell Caleb the news you've been fucking his 'one that got away'?" Colin asks.

"I'm just gonna tell him the truth. Which, not coincidentally, is what I'm gonna do in my life, top to bottom, starting now. No more lies about anything. Hiding and lying just isn't my bag. If I've gotta sneak around to do something, then it's not something I should be doing." I pause for a long moment. "I think I'm gonna stay sober for a while, guys. At least through the next tour. After that, I'll reassess."

Colin nods. "Cool. You do you, Rock Star." He looks at Dean's house again. "You ready to go in there?"

I take a deep breath. "Yeah."

"The only thing I ask is when this is all done, I get to call her Yoko," Colin says. "That's all I ask."

"No. That would hurt Violet's feelings."

"Just behind her back, then."

"No way. Violet's *so* not Yoko, dude. She's the opposite of Yoko."

Colin sighs. "Fine. I won't call her Yoko. Goddammit. I ask for *one* fucking thing." He flicks his cigarette to the ground and stomps on it, and then gestures to Dean's house up the street. "Come on. I wanna get this over with. I've got a stomach ache."

"Me, too. Gimme a goat chant to pump me up, guys." I put my hand in the middle. We chant, "One, two, three, *goats!*" And then, off we go, an army of three, toward the iron gate enclosing Dean's sprawling estate.

FORTY-SIX

DAX

"Come in, come in," Dean says brightly. "I didn't realize all three of you goats were coming today. That's awesome." He bro-hugs each of us. "Caleb's shooting pool in the man cave. Come on."

I look at Colin and Fish like, *Here we go.*

As we walk through Dean's impressive house, we pass framed gold and platinum records on the wall, one after another. Framed music memorabilia. An elaborate fish tank. If we were here for a different reason—to actually write songs and hang out with our good friends—I'd be lighting Dean up with comments and questions about all of it. But now isn't the time.

We arrive in a gorgeous man cave with a sleek pool table, stocked bar, and massive TV on the wall—which, at the moment, is showing a baseball game. Plus, there's a shit-ton of sick musical instruments and gear littering the room and a state-of-the-art vocal booth in the corner. In other words, this place is heaven. Too bad I'll probably never be invited back.

When C-Bomb sees us, he puts down his pool stick and bounds over to us, clearly thrilled to see us. Shit. I really do love this guy. He's flawed, for sure. Temperamental as fuck. Kind of a caveman in some ways. But his heart is big and in the right place. From day one, he took my bandmates and me under his wing. Taught us what we needed to know about touring and the industry at large. He's had our backs in ways big and small. He's not the villain in this story. He's just the guy who doesn't get the girl. At least, not this time. *Because the girl in this story is mine.*

C-Bomb bro-hugs all of us, and we let him do it, even though I'm sure we're all feeling physically ill as we do. He asks us what we want to drink from the bar, but I immediately cut him off.

"There's something I need to talk to you about."

Caleb freezes on his way to the bar. Wariness flickers across his face. In a heartbeat, he looks like a guy used to getting really shitty news whenever someone begins a conversation with those words.

"Why don't we sit?" I say, motioning to a leather couch.

"Sure," he says, his tone tight.

"Me, too?" Dean says, shifting his weight.

"Yeah, this is gonna involve all of us at the end of the day. Might as well talk about it as a family."

We all sit. I'm on the end of the couch, right next to Caleb in an armchair, and everyone else is littered around us.

I clear my throat. "I don't know how to say this, so I'm just gonna come right out and say it." I take a deep breath. "I'm in love with Violet."

Caleb freezes. Color blasts into his cheeks. "*My* Violet?"

"Yes. I—"

Without warning, he lunges at me and throws a wicked punch that lands hard on my cheek. I cover my face with my forearms but otherwise don't fight back, because I know I deserve his wrath. Quickly, though, Dean or Colin, or maybe both, pull my attacker off me and drag him across the room. When I emerge from behind my forearms, they've got him pinned against the bar.

I hop up, adrenaline flooding me. I can already feel myself getting a shiner, but it feels good. I feel alive. I feel *free*. Emotion is expanding my chest and closing my throat. Panting, I blurt, "I didn't know she'd ever been yours when I hooked up with her. I met her at

Reed's party, right before the tour. I didn't tell her I was leaving on tour with you guys, and she didn't say a word about being Reed's sister to me."

Oh, the look on Caleb's face as Dean and Colin hold him back. He looks crushed. Raging. Homicidal. *Betrayed.*

"I'm sorry," I choke out. "I never meant to hurt you, and neither did Violet. I didn't find out she was your ex until she walked into the dressing room before the LA show and you introduced her. And I didn't find out she was Reed's sister until the next day, when I saw her, by chance, at a wedding."

"You were fucking around on her throughout the entire tour?" Caleb bellows.

"It wasn't like that. I was single during the tour. Violet figured out my connection to you at the last minute, right before I left—but she didn't tell me about it. All she said was she didn't want to get involved with me. Didn't want to keep in touch. But I never stopped thinking about her during the tour. Never stopped wanting her."

Caleb scoffs. "You sure had a fucked-up way of showing it."

I'm not the one who cheated on her, motherfucker, I think. But, of course, I don't say it. "Believe what you want," I say, breathing hard. "But I'm telling you, I didn't stop thinking about her. And then, eight months later, there she was, walking into that dressing room."

Caleb looks incensed. "You're telling me it's only been a *week* you've been with her? You don't even know her!"

"I *do* know her, and I'm in love with her."

Caleb's face flashes with unadulterated rage. "You let me stand on that balcony and tell you how much I want her. How much I *love* her! You stood there and let me pour my fucking heart out... *and you'd already fucked her?*"

Oh, fuck. This is torture. I nod, my body quaking. "I'm sorry."

Caleb's fury can't be contained. He breaks loose of Colin and Dean and charges me. But this time, I'm not just gonna take the hit. I gave him one free shot at me and that's all he gets. When he reaches me, I jerk out of the way of his oncoming fist and take a swing of my own, though I'm no match for him, and we scuffle furiously, with

Caleb getting the better of me, until Dean and Colin are there again, pulling Caleb back.

"You're dead to me, you fucking cocksucker!" Caleb shouts as the guys wrangle him, his green eyes bugging out and his neck veins bulging.

My heart is breaking. I'm breathing hard. Feeling dizzy. "Caleb, I'm sorry."

"I *love* her," he says, his voice breaking. He visibly crumples. "And I loved you. I loved you like a little brother and you lied to my face and stabbed me in the back."

I choke up. "I didn't know how to tell you. Or if I should."

"You were my *brother*."

"I was. I am. I'm so sorry."

"Fuck you." He literally spits at me.

"Okay, you guys gotta go now," Dean says. But when we three goats remain frozen like deer in headlights, Dean shouts, "*Go!*"

I look at Dean with pleading eyes. He's my idol. The musician and songwriter I respect the most. My *friend*. "Dean, I didn't know Violet was his ex when I hooked up with her and by the time I found out—"

Caleb screams at me to get the fuck out.

"Just go," Dean says firmly. "Please. Nothing you say is gonna make this any better, Dax. Only worse."

I look at Caleb again. "I'll always be grateful to you for everything you did. I'll always love you like a brother, even if you hate me."

"Fuck you, you piece of shit asshole. I'll always hate your fucking guts."

Fighting back tears, I turn to go.

"Hey!" Caleb shouts at my back.

I turn around, expecting a fist to my head. But he's still standing with Dean, being held back. He looks like a broken man.

"I don't understand any of this," he says, his voice dripping with emotion. "Violet said it was over with the guy she was dating. She said she broke it off with him."

"She did. The night of the concert. That's why she didn't come to the wrap party."

Now Caleb looks thoroughly confused. "The night of the...? *What?* When I saw her yesterday at her apartment, she was crying her eyes out, saying she'd just broken up with the guy because she loves him, but he doesn't love her."

My heart leaps and bounds in my chest, even though it shouldn't. "She said this to you yesterday—that she *loves* the guy?"

"Don't smile about it!" Dean shouts, suddenly livid.

Caleb's hurt is replaced by fury again. "What did you do to her to make her sob like that, motherfucker? If you're so in love with her after one goddamned week, then what did you do to her to make her cry and say you don't love her?"

It's too much to explain. And none of it will make any difference, anyway. And now that I know for sure Violet loves me, thanks to Caleb, I'm done here. I did what I came to do. I told the truth. With one last, "I'm sorry, Caleb," I turn and stride toward the doorway of the man cave, followed closely by Fish and Colin.

Just as I'm leaving the room, Caleb shouts at me, "Stay the fuck away from her, Dax! I'm warning you!" And when I don't respond, he adds. "If you hurt her, I'll kill you!"

I wind through the house, flanked by Fish and Colin, my heart racing, and finally burst through the front door like a burglar escaping a barking watchdog.

I feel a mix of emotions like nothing I've felt before. Heartbreak and elation. Pain and euphoria. Caleb literally wants me dead. *But Violet loves me.* In fact, she's so sure of it, she even felt the need to admit it to Caleb! Why Caleb saw Violet yesterday at her apartment, I have no idea. And I don't care. Whatever happened between them, she spent at least part of the time telling Caleb she loves me and not him.

When Dean's iron gate closes behind us three goats, Fish mutters, "Well, that went well."

"You okay, Rock Star?" Colin asks, as we stride down Dean's front walkway. "Your cheek is already swelling up like crazy."

"I'm fine. It feels good, actually, in a twisted sort of way."

"You think your face is broken?"

"No. He clocked me pretty good, but I don't think anything cracked."

We walk in silence toward Colin's car. I took an Uber here, so it's understood without us needing to say it Colin is going to be driving me to my next destination.

When we settle into Colin's car, I look at myself in the passenger side mirror. "Yeesh."

Colin says, "I think it's a good look for you, actually. Gives you some much-needed street cred."

"Makes you look like a rebel," Fish says. But then he pats my arm sympathetically. "Fuck it, shit happens, Daxy."

I let out a long, deep exhale. "Fuck it, shit happens," I whisper softly. "Ain't that the fucking truth."

Colin starts his fancy new car and it purrs like a kitten. "So, where to next, Rock Star? Violet's apartment, I presume?"

"Yep. It's time for me to get my girl. *Onward.*"

FORTY-SEVEN

DAX

Miranda opens the door to her apartment and gasps at the sight of me. "What happened to your face?"

"Is Violet here?"

"No. What happened to you?"

"I told Caleb about Violet and me."

"Oh, God. He's gonna be so pissed at me."

"At *you?*"

"For not telling him. I'm sure he's blowing up my phone right now, pissed as hell I kept it from him."

"Sorry. I didn't think about that."

"It's okay. Caleb knows when it comes to him and Vi, my loyalty is with her. I love my brother, but he broke her heart. Karma's a bitch."

"Do you think Caleb might get so pissed at you, he'd get physical with you?"

"Caleb? Oh, God, no. Never. Caleb yells and screams when he gets angry, and he'll punch any dude for the slightest offense—as you've obviously just found out—but he would never, ever touch me or any woman. He's one of the good ones."

I sigh with relief. "I told Reed about Violet and me, right before I told Caleb."

"Well, damn. You set off all kinds of atomic bombs today, didn't you? What'd Reed say?"

"He was cool with it. Not that he gets a vote. Nobody gets a vote but Violet and me. Do you know when she'll be back?"

"I'm not sure. Definitely not today. She dropped everything yesterday to fly to Seattle for a funeral."

My heart leaps into my mouth. "Who died?"

"Her stepfather. He had a massive heart attack. Dropped dead on the spot. She took off like a bat out of hell when she found out. The funeral is tomorrow morning."

"Oh, God. Jesus." I rub my forehead and exhale. "I called and called Violet yesterday and this morning. I thought she was ghosting me."

"She was probably on an airplane when you tried calling her yesterday. As far today goes, she's probably just grieving... but, yeah, also, ghosting you. When Violet gets really upset, she's notorious for taking a couple days to cool off before returning texts or calls. She was *really* upset when she left you yesterday."

My blood feels like it's physically heating with my need to see Violet. To set things right with her. To tell her those three little words. And, now, to comfort her, as well. "Do you know where the funeral is in Seattle?"

"No. Sorry. I didn't ask for details. Maybe I could call Vi's mom and find out if she has the information, but I doubt it. Apparently, the stepfather's new wife despises Violet's mom for cheating on him after his son died. I guess he had some sort of breakdown for a little while after losing his kid and marriage, all at once."

"Poor guy." I sigh. "I'm sure I can get the info from Reed or figure it out with a little internet sleuthing. I'm gonna head to the airport now."

"Do you need a ride?"

"No, thanks. Colin's sitting in his car out front, waiting for a text from me."

"Should I tell Violet you're coming to Seattle?"

"No. If she likes taking a few days to cool off when she's upset, let's give her that. I'd rather just show up tomorrow in Seattle and say what needs to be said, face to face. If it turns out she doesn't want me there, then I'm a big believer in asking for forgiveness, instead of permission."

FORTY-EIGHT

DAX

It's late morning in Seattle and pouring rain. I feel stupid to be sitting in the back of a limo right now, as opposed to a simple Uber, but Reed arranged the car for me, saying he wasn't going to let Violet get whisked off into the sunset in a fucking Uber. And so, here I am, a rock-star cliché behind tinted windows, directing my limo driver down the rain-soaked main drag of Lake View Cemetery.

I spot Violet. She's about forty yards away, wearing a long, black coat, but, even so, there's no doubt it's her. She's at the far back of a small cluster of mourners gathered around a gravesite, all of them taking cover underneath dark umbrellas.

"There," I say to the limo driver, and he parks the car at the curbside of the gravesite.

Violet's in profile to me, holding a dark blue umbrella to shield her from the driving rain. She's not merely at the back of that group of mourners. She's distinctly detached, her positioning clearly reinforcing her status as an outsider. Obviously, Violet doesn't think she's welcome at this funeral and nobody has bothered to disabuse her of that notion by inviting her to stand closer.

My baby looks impossibly small underneath that blue umbrella.

Her face in profile is somber. Heartbreaking. Elegant. She's visibly shivering in the cold. Because, of course, Seattle is always colder than visitors think it's going to be.

For a moment, I don't know what to do with myself. During the drive here, I resolved to catch Violet's attention *after* the funeral and guide her into the waiting limo. The last thing I want to do is insert myself into Violet's private grieving for the only father figure she's ever known. Her stepfather was the man who fathered her beloved baby brother, after all, and, ever so briefly, became a father to Violet, too... until her brother died and her mother betrayed her stepfather, and Violet's short-lived fairytale family came tumbling down.

I'm guessing Violet is thinking about a whole lot more than her stepfather as she's standing there in the rain. I'm sure she's remembering her baby brother's funeral. Maybe even the fact that she never went to her actual father's funeral because he'd never acknowledged her. Maybe she's wishing her stepfather had been willing to maintain a relationship with her after his marriage went down in flames. Knowing her, though, she's probably standing there forgiving him for turning his back on her. She's probably telling him, right at this moment, she understands and loves him, regardless.

Oh, my heart. I feel the urge to go to Violet now, but I waffle, feeling unsure. Clearly, this is a deeply private and poignant moment for her, and I don't want to make it about me and what I want. But when I notice Violet's slender shoulders shuddering violently underneath that blue umbrella—when I realize my baby is standing there, bawling her eyes out—there's suddenly no question what I should do. I stuff my hair into my beanie, zip up my jacket, and throw on my hood. And then I bound out of the limo and sprint to Violet through the driving rain... until, finally, sliding underneath her blue umbrella and wrapping her in a warm hug.

When Violet sees me, her face registers shock... and then, massive relief. Wordlessly, without asking how or why, she crumples into my chest and loses herself to wracking sobs. I take the umbrella from her and use it to protect her from the storm as I hug her to me with my free arm... and then, when I'm sure she's safe and protected, I let my own tears fall and mingle with the rainwater soaking my cheeks.

When the funeral concludes, I guide Violet's sobbing frame to the waiting limo. The moment we settle into the backseat, both of us wet and trembling, I tell the driver to put up the barrier between us, take Violet's beautiful face in my palms, and kiss her tenderly. And, thank God, she kisses me back.

After our brief kiss, I put my forehead on Violet's and stroke her wet cheek. "I'm sorry about your stepfather."

"They don't want me here, but I felt like I had to come. I needed to say goodbye."

I kiss her cheek. "Violet, I'm so sorry I made you feel like a mistress. You're not the mistress, baby. You're the stone-cold *wife*."

She chuckles through her tears.

"I love you, Violet. With all my heart and soul. Those fireflies are a blazing sun inside me now. A thousand blazing suns. They're an entire sky full of twinkling stars and a bright, full moon."

She chokes on her tears. "I love you, too. So much. I've got a thousand blazing suns and infinite stars and the brightest moon inside me, too. All for you." She wipes her face. "Reed sent me a recording. I heard you singing song after song about me." She bites her lip. "I heard you say you love me."

I touch her face gently. Every cell in my body feels alive and free. I feel euphoric, even as my heart aches for my baby's tears. "I should have told you I love you in the hotel room when you needed to hear it," I say. "I just needed time to figure myself out. To gather enough courage to leap off the cliff. But I'm ready to do it now. To leap with you. In fact, I already have. After that conversation with Reed, I went straight to Caleb and told him everything."

She touches my shiner gently. "He didn't take it well, huh?"

I shake my head.

"Are you okay?"

"Fuck it, shit happens." I smile. "Fish always says that. He also said the shiner makes me look like a rebel."

She smiles through tears. "It does."

I notice cars around us beginning to depart the gravesite. "Is there a reception or wake you need to go to now?"

Violet shakes her head. "Nobody wants me there. I've said what I needed to say to him. I got my closure."

She's shivering violently, so I press the button on the intercom to talk to the driver. "Can you please blast the heat back here? Full throttle, man."

"Yes, sir."

I smile at Violet. "Can I give you a tour of my hometown?"

"Now?"

"Just a little driving tour."

She smiles. "I'd love it."

"You've never been to Seattle, right?"

"Never."

"Cool. I'll show you the basics and then we'll head to my parents' for dinner. Sound good? Everyone's expecting us."

"Everyone?"

"The Seattle Branch of the Morgan Clan. My mom is cooking a big pot of spaghetti and meatballs. One of her specialties. Everyone is coming for dinner."

"Who, exactly?"

"Colby and Lydia, Ryan and Tessa, Josh and Kat, and all their respective kids. They're all coming, in full force, to welcome you to our city. Our home." I grin. "Our family."

Violet's face contorts with emotion. And, I must admit, I'm feeling pretty overwhelmed with emotion myself.

"Oh, and Colby's dog, Ralph, too. You like dogs?"

"I love dogs."

"Good. Or else, we'd be done."

She laughs.

"Where's your suitcase? At your hotel?"

"No, in a closet in the mortuary office." She gestures up the road. "I was going to head to the airport right after the funeral."

"Change of plans. We're staying the night at my parents' tonight."

She nods, clearly fighting back tears.

"You know how to play Hearts?"

"Is that a card game?"

"Yeah."

"No idea."

"Then we'll teach you. In my family, it's a must. How about backgammon?"

"I know how to play that one."

"Good. Play it with my dad, please. Nobody else will."

She laughs.

"Foosball? Are you any good at that?"

"Is that the one with the little soccer players on poles?"

"Oh, for the love of fuck. You say this to me *after* I confess my undying love to you?" I sigh like I'm deeply annoyed. "Yes, it's the one with the little soccer players, trying to kick a ball into a goal."

"I've seen it from afar."

"It's okay. I'll teach you to become a pro, because that's how much I love you."

"Thank you. Wow."

"And don't worry, if you suck, there's still no way you'll be worse than Kat. That's all that matters."

Violet is lit up. Absolutely gorgeous. "I'll do my best."

I squeeze her hand. "But, first, let me give you a driving tour of my beautiful hometown. Appropriately, in the driving rain." I push the button for the intercom again and tell the driver to drive us past all the usual tourist spots. "You know the drill," I say. "The Space Needle, the Fish Market, the wharf."

"Yes, sir."

"Are you hungry?" I ask Violet.

"A little."

Back to the intercom. "First off, take us somewhere to get some really good Seattle coffee and a cupcake."

"I know just the place," the driver says. He tells me the name of the place he's thinking and I tell him that's exactly where I had in mind.

As the limo pulls away from the curb, I pull Violet close to me, kiss the side of her head, and whisper to her. I tell her she's gonna be okay. That I'm here now and I'm not going anywhere. I tell her I love her again and again. And as I talk and cuddle her and kiss her, I know I'm exactly where I'm meant to be. I know I've found my tribe of two. My lucky number two.

FORTY-NINE

VIOLET

As we get out of the limo to walk into the coffee place, I'm fully expecting Dax to stuff his signature hair into his black beanie and cover his head with his hood, the same way he did on our way in and out of the children's hospital in L.A. The same way he did when we were out and about during our house-hunting excursion. The same way he did when we were sitting in the backseat of Ubers, heading to and from Aloha's house. But he doesn't do it this time. He leaves his beanie on the backseat and doesn't flip his hood over his head. Shockingly, he doesn't even put on sunglasses.

And so, predictably, as we walk into the coffee place, a whole lot of eyes around the room immediately lock onto him and then bug out. Dax was born and raised in Seattle, after all. This is his town. Surely, this city, more than any other, has been watching the meteoric rise of 22 Goats with pride. And, surely, they're especially aware—and proud—of the band's most recognizable member.

Cell phones come out. Some people brazenly start snapping photos. Others pretend to be looking casually at their phones while they covertly do the deed. But it doesn't take a rocket scientist to realize they're secretly capturing Dax, in all his golden glory, all in the name of posting and bragging and memorializing their unexpected brush with greatness for posterity.

"This place has the best cupcakes," Dax says brightly, ignoring the obvious electricity zinging around the room, all of it directed squarely at him. "I swear, you've never had a better cupcake in your life."

"I can't wait. But I think I'm going to need a little bite of real food before I indulge in dessert."

"Well, lucky for you they also have the sickest salads and croissant sandwiches known to man. Will that work?"

"Fabulous."

Without warning, he pulls me to him and kisses me—in full view of everyone. And it's not a peck, either. It's a kiss that's every bit as sexy and passionate as any of the ones he gave that model in his now-iconic music video. Actually, no. This kiss is far more passionate than any of the ones on display in that video. Because this one is undeniably *sincere*.

When he pulls away from kissing me, Dax nuzzles my nose and whispers how happy he is to be here with me in his hometown.

I'm shook to my core. Elated. *Swooning.* I'm physically clutching Dax's arm so I won't tip over from light-headed glee.

When we reach the counter, arm in arm, Dax looks up at the menu on the wall above the cashier's head and says, "What looks good to you, Vi?"

The cashier, a young woman who looks to be in her late teens, is visibly freaking out. Like, legit about to pass out. But, somehow, she holds it together enough to take our order.

"Is this for here or to go?" the cashier asks, her face bursting with color.

"For here," Dax says, at the same time I say, "To go."

"Oh," Dax says, turning to me. "I was thinking we'd relax and eat here, if that's okay with you. We're not in any rush, are we?"

"Oh, I'd love that," I say. "I just figured you'd want to take it on the road."

"Nah. Let's take our time. I love this place. I love the art on the walls." He smiles at me. "And I love you."

Holy shit.

I look at the woman behind the counter and she looks like she's a hair's breadth away from emitting a hysterical scream.

But Dax is unfazed. He calmly pays the flush-faced woman, giving her a mammoth tip, and guides my still-shocked body toward a corner table.

"I'm sorry to ask," the cashier blurts as we walk away. "But would you mind taking a selfie with me? 22 Goats is my favorite band. Every song on your album is amazing."

"Thank you," Dax says. "Yeah, sure." He returns to the counter and leans over it while she does the same thing from her side, but the angle for the selfie is weird. "Hey, maybe we should have my girl-friend take the shot?" Dax offers, making my knees wobble at his easy use of the word "girlfriend." He calls to me. "Baby, would you mind?"

"Not at all," I manage to croak out.

"Can I come around and give you a hug, Dax?" the cashier asks. She looks at me. "If your girlfriend doesn't mind?"

My heart is soaring. "No, I don't mind at all. Get your shot, girl."

She squeals, thanks me, apologizes to the people at the front of the line, and sprints around the counter like a bat out of hell. When she reaches Dax, she hugs him like he's her beloved boyfriend who's been lost at sea for eighteen months and finally, just now, returned safely to her.

Laughing, I snap the shot and the young woman thanks Dax and me profusely. It's clear Dax is making a lifelong memory for this adorable girl. And it's also clear he's happy to do it. Watching Dax enjoy this interaction, seeing this girl's excitement, I feel overcome with a sense of joy. Relief, too. Like everything's truly going to be all right.

The woman says she'll bring our food to our table, so we make our way to the corner of the room and take a seat next to a large window that's being assaulted by pounding rain. We huddle together and talk softly. I tell Dax how happy it made me to see that cashier looking so thrilled, and he laughs and says it was actually fun for him.

Our conversation is cut off when a couple comes by and asks for a selfie. They tell Dax he's made Seattle proud. That 22 Goats has picked up Nirvana's torch—a compliment that obviously enthralls Dax.

Another group approaches. And then another. Everyone heaping love and genuine affection on Dax, their hometown hero. And I can plainly see he's deeply appreciative of their kind words—that these interactions are giving him more than pleasure, they're giving him some sort of healing.

Finally, three young dudes approach. They say they used to go to 22 Goats shows "back in the day" in local clubs, and Dax laughs and says his band used to play at such and such club for nothing but tacos and beer as their payment. The guys tell Dax they caught his show here in Seattle when 22 Goats came through with Red Card Riot, and they couldn't believe how amazing they were—how much the guys' showmanship and musicianship had skyrocketed since those early days. They tell Dax that his band, their success, and especially Dax's artistry, have been the biggest inspirations for their own band.

"Honestly, if I had to pick one person who's inspired me the most, it would be you," one of the guys says. "You, followed closely behind by Dean Masterson."

Oh, Dax. By the look on his face, it's clear the mention of Dean's name has pained his heart. But it's also clear hearing his name, mentioned in the same breath as his idol's, is deeply meaningful to him—confirmation that, no matter what craziness has attended the *selling* of Dax's music, it's nonetheless still the music itself, Dax's art, that's touched people the most. Not his gorgeous face or golden hair or bare ass.

Dax gives the guys his publicist's number and tells them to contact her for backstage passes to his next show in Seattle and they flip out. When the cashier comes with our food, the guys politely leave us to eat, thanking Dax profusely as they go.

Dax and I scarf down our food and coffee and cupcakes, smiling like goofs at each other the whole time. And when we're done, Dax takes my face in his hands and kisses me again.

"Man, I love Seattle," he says against my lips, his forehead on mine. "The city that knew me when..."

"I can see why you love it."

"I also love you."

"Good, because I love you."

"I can't wait to show you my hometown."

"I can't wait to see it."

Dax stands, puts out his hand, and says, "Let's paint this gray, soggy Seattle day all kinds of *violet*, baby. *Onward*."

FIFTY

VIOLET

I t was built for the 1962 World's Fair," Dax says. And, of course, he's pointing to the Space Needle as we drive past in the limo. "There's a restaurant at the top that rotates around and around that's pretty dope. My family went there for Kat's eighteenth birthday. And there's this sick museum of glass right over there. Sounds like an old-fart thing to do, I know—go to a glass museum. But my mom dragged me there once as a kid, and I've been hooked ever since."

"I'd love to see it some time."

"And that's the Museum of Pop Culture right there. So sick. We had passes when I was a kid. They have a Jimi Hendrix exhibit and a Nirvana exhibit I've seen at least ten times each. I'm gonna have to bring you back here some time to show you."

"I'd love it. Any time."

His face lights up. "How about now? Are you in any rush to head back to L.A. tomorrow?"

"No. I'm self-employed. And just barely, at that."

"Then let's stay three or four days in Seattle. My parents will be stoked to have us. Unless you'd rather I book a hotel?"

"I think I'd rather take a break from hotels for a little while," I say, chuckling.

"Oh, God, same."

We share a huge smile.

"Do you think it will be okay for me to do some laundry at your parents' house? I've only got one change of clothes."

"People doing laundry at my house isn't a unique phenomenon."

"Yeah, I guess not. Not with five kids."

"So, are you down to check out the Jimi and Nirvana exhibits now? We're right here and they're my all-time favorite things."

"Awesome."

He pushes the intercom button and tells the driver the plan, and twenty minutes later, we're wandering around the museum together. And, yet again, Dax doesn't cover up in public. And not only that, he packs on the PDA as we wander from exhibit to exhibit.

"Oh, this is new," he says as we come to a stop in front of an exhibit for Pearl Jam—another legendary Seattle band. "God, Pearl Jam is so fucking dope." He leans in to closely examine a photo of Eddie Vedder and then whispers reverently, "*Eddie*. My man."

After Dax has paid appropriate respects to Eddie, Nirvana, and Jimi, we check out a few other random things, all of it while holding hands. And, through it all, as we talk and walk and kiss and cuddle, I can't help noticing people constantly taking covert snapshots of us... but leaving us alone.

An hour later, just as we settle into the back of the limo again, my phone pings with an incoming text.

"Oh my God!" I shriek, looking at my screen. "Aloha Carmichael wants to hire me! I sent her a sketch last night—an idea for this music video she told me about—and she just texted she loves, loves, loves the sketch and wants me to run with it. Oh my God, Dax, this is a dream come true!"

He high-fives me. "What's the idea?"

"She wants me to make her a superhero costume!"

I swipe into my photos and show Dax the design I sent to Aloha and he gushes about it. With shaking hands, I reply to Aloha's text and express my elation and gratitude, and she immediately replies to say she and Zander are with "Kaddy" right now—Keane and Maddy —and that everyone says, "Woohoo!"

Of course, I reply to say I'm with Dax in Seattle—no "group date" required this time!—and Aloha sends me a gif of two people jumping on a bed and opening a spritzing bottle of champagne. Two seconds later, I get a text from Maddy, attaching a gif of a baby doing a happy dance.

I'm about to shove my phone into my bag when I get a text from Miranda.

Miranda: Look at the "Dax in the Wild" Instagram account. OMFG.

Dax points at something through the limo window—some tourist sight he wants me to check out—but I cut him off. "Miranda just told me to look at 'Dax in the Wild,'" I say. "I'm guessing today's escapades have made it on there."

"Yeah, my PR person already texted me. We're everywhere. Not just there."

"*Everywhere?*"

"You're being called a 'mystery girl.'"

My heart in my mouth, I swipe into Instagram and check the account. And I'll be damned. There's a photo of Dax and me kissing at the coffee place. And another one in the museum. And then I google and find our photos on several gossip sites.

"Well, that was quick," I say.

"Welcome to the internet," Dax says. But he's smiling. Indeed, if I were a betting woman, I'd guess all the PDA he just showered on me in public places was designed to get the word out, far and wide, in exactly this way.

I scroll through the comments underneath the photos on the "Dax in the Wild" account and cringe. "Holy hell. People *hate* me.

Apparently, everyone thinks they've got a shot at actually marrying you one day, and I'm standing in their way."

Dax rolls his eyes.

I keep scrolling. "They're all wondering who the hell I am. They're shocked I'm not some famous supermodel."

"I'm sure they'll figure it out soon enough," Dax says. "Some people live for internet sleuthing."

My phone pings with another text from Miranda. It's a screenshot from Caleb's Twitter account. Without explanation or context, he's just now tweeted out a meme of Jesus, flipping off the viewer, captioned boldly, in all caps, "FUCK YOU, JUDAS."

"Oh, God," I mutter.

"What?"

I show him the screenshot from Caleb's Twitter, my stomach twisting into knots.

Dax says, "Looks like Caleb's been alerted to our coming-out party."

My stomach feels like it's turning inside-out. I take no pleasure in knowing Caleb is hurting. And it kills me to see the anguish on Dax's face right now. "I'm so sorry, Dax."

"It's fine. He's right to feel that way about me. I *was* a Judas to him. At the wrap party, I followed him out to a balcony because he said he needed someone to talk to, and I let him go on and on about his feelings for you. I was an asshole for doing that. If I could rewind the clock, that's the only thing I'd do differently. I'd tell him I had to go to see my family and I'd walk out the door. It's my only regret." He squeezes my hand. "My only one. No matter what happens, Violet, this was worth it. I'm the happiest I've ever been, right here, with you. I'll never regret getting to feel this with you, as long as I live."

I rub Dax's forearm, gathering my thoughts. I'm thrilled at everything he just said, but I can't help feeling horrible I'm the reason Caleb hates him. It's so unwarranted. I don't want Caleb, and not because of Dax. Can't Caleb grasp that and find a way to be friends with Dax, regardless? "I just want Caleb to be happy, the same way I want happiness for you and me," I say.

Dax nods.

"I'm sorry being with me has messed up your friendship with him. I never wanted that."

"It's not your fault. Like I said, Caleb's got reason to feel betrayed. I screwed up." He squeezes my hand again. "I think we should both strap in for a bumpy ride. With Caleb vague-tweeting the same day those photos of us are flying around—and with me having a shiner—people are gonna put two and two together any minute now, if they haven't already. We're probably gonna become paparazzi bait for a little while."

I sigh. "Twenty bucks says the internet is going to think this is some sort of illicit love triangle. That's the juiciest version of the story, isn't it? You *stole* me away from Caleb?"

"Yeah, I'm sure you're right. The rags are gonna juice this for all it's worth, the truth be damned." He pulls out his phone. "I'm gonna ask Reed to arrange a bodyguard for our sightseeing over the next few days, just to keep things extra mellow for us. Cool?"

"Whatever you want to do."

As Dax begins tapping out a message, I start tapping out a text to my mother. She already knows about Dax. I called and told her everything last night. So now, I tell her the good news that Dax followed me to Seattle and told me he loves me. I tell her I'm safe and happy with the man I love and not to worry about anything she might see online.

"Reed says Barry's already on it," Dax says. "A couple of his best guys will be hopping a flight today."

"Who's Barry?"

"Reed's head of security. Zander's boss."

"Hey, maybe Barry can send Zander as one of the guys," I say. "And maybe Kaddy and Aloha will want to tag along with Zander on his assignment?"

"Brilliant." He begins tapping out another text. "Let's get the L.A. Branch of the Morgan Clan to join the Seattle Branch for a few days."

"Hey, what's *our* couple name?" I ask. "Keane and Maddy are *Kaddy*. Who are we?"

Dax shrugs. "Diolet? Violax?"

"Violax sounds like a violent laxative."

Dax laughs. "Diolet it is, then. Dial... It. Because we're so damned dialed in, baby, we *flow*."

"That's right, baby. Hell yeah. We're all about the *flow*."

He pauses. "Hey, let's promise each other something, baby. The internet might get pretty rough for us for a while. So, let's agree to ignore it. Haters gonna hate. All that matters is what we feel. What we think. We're a tribe of two. Okay?"

I nod enthusiastically. "I think I'm going to delete my Instagram account and completely ignore the internet for a while."

"Great idea. I'll do the same. Fuck 'em all."

"You're not going to reply to Caleb?"

"Nope. I'm not going to reply to anyone. This relationship is nobody's business but ours."

I beam a huge smile at him. "Sounds good."

"There," he says, tapping on his phone. "Instagram officially gone."

"Don't you need your account for PR?"

"The band's got an account. That's plenty. I don't need to know what anybody 'out there' thinks and I don't need to give them oxygen. All I need to know is what you think."

"Well, I think I love you."

Smiling, he leans in for a kiss. When he pulls away, he says, "I love you and you love me and that's all that matters. Anyone who doesn't like it—whether that's Caleb or some troll on Instagram or Twitter—can go to fucking hell."

FIFTY-ONE

VIOLET

"And that's my high school," Dax says, pointing out the limo window at a large brick building with lots of windows.

"Were you a big man on campus?" I ask.

"Not really. I didn't play football or baseball. I wasn't class president or prom king. Didn't even go to prom. Because... *why?*"

I laugh. "I'm sure you were the shit, without realizing it."

"No, I was Keane Morgan's weird little musician skater-boy brother who didn't go to any of the dances. Keane was prom king. All-American in baseball. He slayed it with the ladies. Everyone— and I mean *everyone*—knew him and wanted to be his friend. Of course, he only had room on his dance card for Zander. But they didn't know that. They all wanted a piece."

"Sounds like you and Keane have more in common than you realize."

Dax considers that. "Yeah, maybe."

The car turns another corner, onto a quiet suburban street, and a moment later, Dax says, "Casa Morgan."

We're parked in front of a two-story, Cape Cod-style house—a lovely home that couldn't be more perfect for the Morgans, or more different than the tiny condo I shared with my mother growing up.

"I'm so excited you're here," Dax says, a beaming smile on his face. "I've never brought a girl home before."

"*Never?*"

"Never."

My heart leaps.

Dax tips the driver and then, holding my hand firmly in one hand, and my overnight bag in the other, leads me through sheeting rain to the front door of his childhood home. He's tucked his hair into his beanie for the walk, I notice. Apparently, he's done letting his long hair flap in the stormy wind and give him away. Most likely, he made his point about me around town, and now he's determined to go back to anonymity.

Dax opens the front door with a loud, "Helloooooooo!" and leads me inside—and, instantly, I'm blasted with warmth, both figuratively and literally.

There's a chorus of cheers and greetings. We're swarmed as we enter the living room. Encircled and hugged. Mr. Morgan takes our wet coats and Mrs. Morgan tells us to sit near the fireplace. Everyone freaks out about Dax's shiner and he tells them the gist. The smell of spaghetti sauce fills the air. A boxer comes over and sniffs me. I meet kids and babies, all of whom are freaking adorable. Everyone offers condolences about my stepfather. They say they're elated to see us. Not just Dax, but me, too. They're making sure I feel included in their warm welcome. And I do.

"Would you like some wine, sweetie?" Mrs. Morgan asks me.

"No, thank you," I say. "Dax and I aren't drinking for a while."

Mrs. Morgan looks pleased. "Sparkling water, then."

Dax pops up. "Hey, how about a quick tour of the mansion, Vi?"

"I'd love it."

"We'll be back soon, fam," Dax says, grabbing my hand. "If we don't come back in ten, it's because I'm doing lines of blow off Vi's stomach."

He pulls me around his house. I see the kitchen and various rooms on the first floor. The family photos on the piano, all of which make my heart ache and swoon and pang. He brings me into a garage where, he says, many a legendary foosball tournament has gone down. Not to mention countless 22 Goats practices. He says, "My mom used to come out here to get clothes out of the dryer and Fish would mess up his chords whenever she bent over. For years, I'm positive that boy popped a boner every time he came near my mother."

I can't stop laughing.

"You know that song, 'Stacy's Mom'?" he says. "Just to annoy me, Fish used to sing it at the top of his lungs, only he'd change it to '*Daxy's* Mom.'"

I giggle. "Well, in Fish's defense, your mom *is* hot."

"Fish told you to say that, didn't he?"

I laugh. "No, I swear. Your mom is gorgeous."

"Fish *always* says, 'Your mom is hot.' Motherfucker."

Chuckling, he leads me back inside and up the stairs. He shows me a pink bathroom where he says Kat used to give him regular pedicures and facials as a young boy. He shows me a doorjamb where his height was faithfully marked throughout the years, alongside his siblings'. A banister against which he "cracked his head like a walnut" while wrestling with Keane one night. "Oh, man, my mom was so pissed about that one," he says. "She explicitly told us not to wrestle there. I needed twenty-two stiches that time."

"Holy hell, Dax."

Finally, he brings me into his childhood bedroom, closes the door, presses me against it, and kisses me. And, quickly, I feel his boner pressing against me. In short order, we're both passionate and aroused and barreling toward a quickie... until we hear a voice in the hallway —his nephew, Theo, walking past with Colby—and we spring apart.

"To be continued tonight," he says, buttoning his pants.

"Are you sure your parents won't mind me sleeping in here with you? I don't want them to think I'm a floosy."

"Well, first off, my family doesn't subscribe to the 'floosy' theory of female sexuality. Kat was raised the same as us boys to believe sex isn't shameful. I mean, they wanted us to have respect for our partners and be safe. They always said it's best if you're in love. But they've never expected us to wear chastity rings or chastity belts or some other hypocritical bullshit like that. Second off, my parents know I flew up here, spur of the moment, for no other reason than I wanted to profess my undying love to you, Violet Rhodes. So if they expect you to sleep alone tonight after that fairytale ending, they can go fuck themselves. And, third off, they know you went to a funeral today. Do you really think they're the kind of monsters who'd make a girl sleep alone after the kind of day you've had? You need TLC, baby. And I'm gonna give it to you. We all are. Although, to be clear, I'm the only one who's going to have sex with you."

I laugh. "I should hope so."

He shows me around the room. I riffle through his yearbooks and he blushes and rolls his eyes at his teenage photos. He shows me his first-ever guitar and rhapsodizes about the first time he played it and just *knew* it was his destiny. My attention drifts to a crystal vase on a shelf and I gasp.

"Is this the vase you Super-glued back together? The one that was supposedly your mother's prized possession?"

"That's the one." He chuckles. "My mom and I have a running gag with it. She puts it in here. And whenever I see it, I sneak it back downstairs to the exact spot in the dining room it sat for five years, without her noticing all the cracks. And then, like clockwork, whenever I come back home, it's in here again."

Giggling, I slide my arms around his neck. "I love your family."

"And they love you. Having you here feels so right, Violet. It's crazy. It doesn't feel like I'm bringing you home for the first time. It feels like you're simply coming home."

"I feel that way, too."

We kiss again. And my heart leaps and bounds. If I'd thought, even for a minute, Dax and I had possibly rushed things with our "I love yous" earlier—which I didn't, actually—then I'd surely be convinced at this point we're right on time.

"We'd better go," he says. "Make sure you touch your nose a lot when we get downstairs, like we just did three lines of blow together."

"I'll do no such thing."

The minute we get downstairs, we're dragged into the garage for an all-hands-on-deck round-robin foosball tournament. Thanks to me, we're the worst team, by far. But we have fun.

"Don't worry, I'll teach you all the tricks," Dax says. "By the time Kaddy and Zaloha get here tomorrow, you'll be ready for battle."

"Oh, they're all coming, for sure?"

"First thing in the morning."

After foosball, we wander into the living room, where we're treated to a performance by Dax's three oldest nieces, Isabella, Beatrice, and Gracie, who dance around the room to "Pretty Girl" by Aloha Carmichael, all of them with varying levels of skill and coordination, commensurate with their ages. After that, we listen to Dax's nephew, Theo, perform a new song he just finished—a tune that includes a key modulation suggested by Dax. And we all cheer and hoot and applaud enthusiastically.

After Theo's performance, I play a game of backgammon with Mr. Morgan. And I can honestly say it's one of the loveliest experiences of my life. The dude barely talks to me throughout our game, other than to show me a couple moves I should have made but missed —just because he wants to be sure I won't miss them the next time we play together, if the same rolls come up. But, even though he doesn't talk my ear off, he sure smiles at me a whole lot. And with each smile he shoots me, I feel his unreserved acceptance of me. His desire to get to know me. And I know, in my heart, I'm going to fall deeply in love with this kind man, if I haven't already.

After backgammon, I find myself in the kitchen with the women while the boys set the table and fill glasses of water for each place setting. As I cut garlic bread with Kat, and Lydia and Tessa chop veggies for a massive salad, the ladies tell me they've never seen Dax looking so happy. I tell them I've never seen *myself* looking this happy, either.

I also tell them the great news that I'm designing a superhero costume for Aloha and a wedding dress for Maddy and they lose their minds like it's happening to them. And then, somewhere along the line in talking to all of these lovely, nurturing women, I find myself tearing up. I don't know why I do it. Nobody said anything specific to make me cry. I just suddenly feel like my heart is so full, it's forcing water out of my eyes. Or maybe I've just had an emotional day.

When Mrs. Morgan sees my tears, she ditches whatever she's doing at the stove, takes me into her arms, and holds me until my tears stop.

When I'm sniffling but no longer crying, Mrs. Morgan pulls back from me and smiles kindly. "Are you ready to sit and eat, or do you need a minute?"

"No, I'm ready. Thank you, Mrs. Morgan."

"Call me Louise," she says. "Or Lou."

"Or, if you really want to get on her good side, Momma Lou," Kat says.

"Momma Lou," I repeat reverently.

"Whatever is comfortable for you," Louise says, her blue eyes twinkling. "You're sure you're okay? You've had quite a day. A roller-coaster ride of emotions, I'm sure."

I nod. "I'm only feeling happiness right now, though. Gratitude."

She pats my cheek. "And so are we. Our home is yours, little flower. You're not a guest here. You're family."

My heart squeezes. "Thank you so much."

Dinner is served. As we sit around the table eating Louise's wonderful meal, conversation flows easily. I realize I've never been part of a big family dinner like this. Not even once. And that, holy shit, this is what I've been craving my whole life, without realizing it. What I've desperately *needed*. And the best part of all? Throughout dinner, Dax keeps grabbing my hand and kissing it in plain view of his family, clearly signaling to all of them that he's all-in. And each time he does it, I catch yet another contingency of his family noticing the gesture and smiling about it. Or, on occasion, winking at me. Indeed, Dax's father winked at me a moment ago, and damn near made me tear up again.

As dessert is served, Ryan says, "All right, let's get down to business, fam. I think we can all agree: Violet deserves to be christened with a nickname."

Everyone agrees wholeheartedly.

Dax leans into me and whispers, "Welcome to the family."

Ryan continues, "Obviously, all manner of violet puns and idioms are a given. Ultra Violet Radiation. No Shrinking Violet. Violet Underground."

Dax's niece, Isabella, pipes in, "Roses Are Red, *Violets Are Blue?*"

Everyone laughs and agrees that's a great one.

"Thanks for the idea, Izzy," I say. "But the only problem with that one is that, when I'm around this family, I don't feel the least bit blue. Take today, for instance. I went to a funeral this morning, and now, look at me: I can't stop smiling."

"Aw, Violet," Kat says.

"To be honest, I think it's a copout to use any play on Violet," Colby says. "Dax has already cornered the market on all things 'Violet' in his songs. We should come up with something original."

"You've written more songs about Violet than that fireflies one you sang at the concert?" Louise asks.

"I've written a whole album about Violet," Dax says. "In fact, we're calling our next album *The Violet Album.* You know, like how The Beatles had *The White Album?*"

"Well, my goodness, you really are smitten, aren't you, Daxy?" Louise says, a massive smile on her lovely face.

Dax returns his mother's wide smile and doesn't deny it.

"Who died at the funeral today?" Isabella asks.

My smile fades slightly.

"Honey, maybe Violet doesn't want to talk about that," Lydia, the girl's mother, says.

"It's okay." I look at the little girl, Isabella. "My stepfather died. I hadn't seen him in years, so I went to say goodbye to him today. I didn't grow up with a father and my stepfather meant a lot to me, even if he didn't realize it. For a short time, when he was married to my mother, he was like a father to me. The only one I'd ever had—and I really liked having a father." I steal a look at Mr. Morgan and, yep, he's looking at me with kind eyes. I glance away, feeling my cheeks rise with heat.

"Why didn't you have a father?" Beatrice, Isabella's younger sister, pipes in to say. "Did he die like mine? Our first daddy died, but now we've got our second daddy." She points at Colby.

"Bea," Lydia says. "Violet, I'm sorry."

"Nothing to apologize for. If it's okay with you all, I'd actually like to answer Bea's question. I'd like to tell all of you a bit about my life, just so you can get to know me better."

"We'd love that," Louise says.

I take a deep breath, and proceed to tell the table my life story. I keep it fairly brief, of course. These poor, captive people don't need to know every detail. I also keep my language coded when I talk about my father's crimes and suicide, due to the kids at the table. But I'm sure the adults at the table can read between the lines, based on the way I've phrased things. I tell them about my stepfather and the divorce. And, of course, I tell them about my beloved baby brother, Jackson. "I really found myself in college," I say. "I got some therapy there, which helped me a lot. I found my calling. My art. My life's purpose. Two months ago, I graduated and moved to L.A." I smile at Dax. "And now, in a shocking twist I never saw coming, I'm sitting here with Dax and all of you, feeling so happy, I could burst. I honestly can't wait to see what comes next."

"Amen to that," Mr. Morgan says. He raises his beer. "To whatever comes next. You're an inspiring, beautiful young woman and we're happy to welcome you into our lives."

Oh, my heart. It's pounding like a steel drum. I swallow hard, trying to catch my breath. "Thank you, Mr. Morgan."

"Thomas."

"Thank you, Thomas."

"Is your last name Rivers?" Ryan says.

"Rhodes. It's my mother's name."

"What if we call you Yellow Brick Rhodes?" he says. "Because you're like Dorothy, on a journey home."

Everyone around me scoffs and rolls their eyes saying that's stupid.

"Actually, Keane already beat you to the punch on that one," Dax says. "When Violet and I were hanging out with him a couple times this past week, Keane called Violet that one, in addition to all the obvious 'violet' references. Plus, he threw out Fork in the Rhodes, Rhodes Scholar, Rhode to Terabithia, Violet Rain. Oh, and *Viagra.*"

Everyone laughs at that last one.

"I exercised my veto power on most of them," Dax says. "Nobody's calling my girlfriend Brick or Fork on my watch. And certainly not a medication for erectile dysfunction."

"What's erectile—?" Dax's niece, Isabella, begins, but her mother, Lydia, quickly cuts her off.

"It's something you don't need to know about, honey," Lydia says, eliciting laughter from the entire table.

"Sorry, Lydi-bug," Dax says, but Lydia merely chuckles and shakes her head.

Ryan says, "By the way, there's no such thing as veto power in this family, Rock Star."

"Of course, there is."

Kat says, "Ha! If there were such a thing as veto power on nicknames, I would have vetoed every single one of mine throughout my entire life, except for Kitty Kat."

Dax says, "That's not true and you know it. You secretly love each and every one of your nicknames, no matter how disgusting. In fact, the grosser the better, as far as you're concerned."

Kat makes a face that concedes Dax is right.

"There's no veto power with respect to people *born* into our family," Dax says. "I'll grant you that. But we have to be gentler and kinder with the latecomers, because they have a choice, unlike us, whether they want to be a part of this crazy family or not. They can *choose* to run away, screaming, if we scare them too much."

I've got no choice, I think. *No matter what you guys call me, I'm staying put.*

Lydia swats Colby's broad shoulder. "You mean to tell me you've had veto power all along, and yet, I've been letting Keane call me Flip Yer Lyd all this time?"

Everyone laughs.

Ryan says, "Only Keane calls you that one, Lydia. You're nothing but Lydi-Bug to the rest of us."

Mr. Morgan says, "I'd say we could call Violet 'Take the High Rhodes,' but since she's decided to stay clean and sober along with Dax, I don't think that one will work."

Everyone groans and chuckles at the stupid dad joke. But I wink at Mr. Morgan to tell him I loved it.

"How about 'Let's Get This Show on the Rhodes'?" Kat says. "We can shorten it to 'Showtime'?"

Everyone agrees that's a fairly good one. And I'm feeling pretty confident that's going to be it, until, out of nowhere, Louise says, "No. If you guys insist on giving Violet one of your silly nicknames, then at least give her one that pays tribute to what a strong and powerful flower she truly is. She's Rocky Rhodes. Her road in life, no doubt, has been a rocky one, at times. But like Rocky, the legendary fighter, she just keeps on getting up, and dreaming big, no matter how much life tries to knock her down."

There's a momentary pause as everyone processes.

And then Kat raises her wine glass. "To Rocky!"

Everyone lifts their glasses and echoes Kat. And, stupidly, tears well in my eyes.

"Cheers, sweet little flower," Louise says. "I won't be calling you Rocky. I never partake in the kids' ridiculous nicknames. But whatever they call you, please know we all thank you for sharing yourself with us tonight. You're always welcome here."

Dax leans into me. "Don't get too attached to Rocky, baby. They're never gonna call you that, just so you know. I can already tell you're gonna be Viagra till the end of time."

FIFTY-TWO

DAX

A guttural sound escapes my throat as I eat Violet. I'm so turned on, I'm dripping. All I want to do is get inside her, feel the way the pieces of our jigsaw puzzle fit together. But I keep going, swirling her tip in my mouth while stroking her wetness firmly with my fingers. Because if there's one thing I crave more than my own release, it's hearing the glorious sound Violet Rhodes makes when she comes.

Finally, when Violet arches her back and grits out my name, when the muscles gripping my fingers begin clenching and releasing rhythmically, I crawl up to her face and kiss her passionately and sink my cock deep inside her. And the moment I'm nestled all the way in, I feel like I'm home.

A jolt of electricity flashes through my body that sends goose bumps erupting on my arms and neck and back. As I move inside her, I kiss her and whisper to her. I say the words I've never said to a woman before, not since I was fourteen and didn't know what the words meant. Or, if I've said them before and I'm simply not remembering, then I'm positive I've never said them to a woman while making love to her, the way I'm doing to Violet now.

I need to go deeper. I need more of her. I grab her thighs and yank them up around my torso, and she moans at the depth of my strokes. With each thrust of my body, I'm telling her what words can't say. Something even my songs can't tell her. *I'm all yours. No turning back.*

But she's not gonna come like this. Not in this position. So, I rearrange us, seating myself onto the edge of the bed and positioning her on top of my cock. She wraps her legs around my waist and her arms around my neck. And, with her lips locked with mine, she begins fucking me hard.

I grip her hips and guide the grinding movement of her pelvis and feel myself spiraling into full-blown ecstasy. I reach down and touch her clit and she hurtles into an intense climax in my arms.

A couple more thrusts and I come like a rocket inside her, so hard I'm seeing little yellow stars.

After we've both stopped shuddering, I kiss and nip at her neck and jawline. I lay her down on the bed and suck on her nipples, not wanting whatever that was—that supernatural energy between us—to be over just yet. When my lips meet Violet's again, we kiss so passionately, it feels like my heart is physically banging against hers. Knocking for permission to *please* be let in.

I've never had sex like that before. All the same parts were involved. The same motions. But I've never in my life *felt* like that while doing it. I wasn't just fucking Violet, I was fusing my soul with hers. Giving her my heart. I was telling her, with my body, the whole truth: she's got me completely. My heart is in her hands now, with nothing to shield or protect it. I'm laid bare.

She kisses my shiner gently. "Does it hurt?"

"No. When I'm with you, I'm invincible."

She sighs happily. "I feel invincible, too. No matter what happens, it won't matter, because I've got you."

I take her face in my hands, feeling my love for her coursing in my bloodstream. "You do have me. Every inch of me. I was yours the minute I saw you at that party. You're a flower, a road, my destiny."

She's bites her lip. "You've got me, too." But something flashes across her face. Something she's not saying. She twists her mouth. Her brow furrows.

"What?"

She pauses. "There's just so much at stake now. Now that I've fallen in love with not just you, but your whole family..."

I stroke her face. "Just trust me, okay? Let down that last little bit of your guard and trust me completely. I don't have a crystal ball, but I can promise you this: I'll never betray you. I'll always be honest and true. Violet, I swear, I'm ready to love you with everything I've got."

PART THREE
THE HAPPILY EVER AFTER

FIFTY-THREE

VIOLET

"**M**addy and I want to thank everyone for traveling here to celebrate with us this week!" Keane says into his microphone, his free arm wrapped around his soon-to-be-wife. "Huge thanks to Josh and Kat for the gift of this amazing week for all of us!"

Keane raises his glass to Josh and Kat, who are seated at a table with their daughter, Gracie, across the balmy restaurant, and everyone joins him in raising their glasses.

It's the first night of Keane and Maddy's destination wedding in the Bahamas, a weeklong shindig that will, of course, culminate in Kaddy's exchange of vows. Before that blessed event, however, all sixty of Keane and Maddy's wedding guests will spend this coming week relaxing on white sand beaches, partaking in every watersport known to man, and eating and drinking ourselves into oblivion... and all of it with the people we love the most.

It's been nine months since I exchanged "I love yous" with Dax in Seattle. Three months ago, *The Violet Album* was released to staggering success. Indeed, as successful as 22 Goats' debut album was, the success of their second album has dwarfed the first by every standard of measurement—from downloads to streams to charting to tour revenue. There's simply no denying *The Violet Album* has propelled 22 Goats to rock royalty status. They're the hottest band on the planet at the moment. In their genre, at least, nobody else has even come close to their success this year.

And thank God that's the way everything landed for Dax and the goats. Because for a minute there, I was anxious things weren't going to end up quite so well. When Caleb had his little tantrum on Twitter and the internet quickly figured things out, the entire world decided, predictably, I must have cheated on Caleb with Dax. Obviously, that wasn't even close to true, but the internet liked that version of the story a whole lot, and so it was. And since Dax and I didn't say a word, the false story hardened into fact. Overnight, The Love Triangle of Dax, Violet, and Caleb became a pop culture juggernaut. The most talked about love triangle since *Twilight.* Of course, a vocal faction of the Twitterverse went ballistic in defense of Caleb. Another faction ferociously defended Dax. The only thing everyone could agree on unanimously was that I was trash. Disloyal and disgusting. Certainly not worthy of the golden god, Dax Morgan. For God's sake, I wasn't even famous! Not even a model! And certainly not pretty enough. Kind of fat, actually. And, oh, yes, a gold digger, seeing as how I'd also slithered my way into Reed River's life, too.

It was lovely. Or so I hear. I've tried very hard to tune it all out. Indeed, Dax and I both ignored the haters, just like we'd agreed to do from the start. But I must admit, I worried about the goats' forthcoming album and what all the bad publicity would do to its chances for success.

And then the album released at number freaking one—it *released* as the number one album in the country!—and I learned first-hand there's no such thing as bad publicity. At least, not in the music industry. After all the gossip and innuendo and paparazzi shots of Dax and me, and the horrendous memes, and all the horrible things said about me, the world was ravenous to hear every song on *The Violet Album* by the time it came out. And if curiosity initially drew them in to listen, the amazing music kept them glued to the songs on a running loop.

This time around, Reed dispensed with meting out singles and, instead, opted to push the entire album out for radio play, all at once. And, I'll be damned, seven songs off the album hit Top 100, all at once. And in the months that followed, several songs—four in total, so far—have climbed all the way to that coveted number one spot, and the album isn't even close to being done racking up accomplishments yet.

One of the biggest hits off the album so far has been a song called "Judas"—a tune Dax slipped onto the album at the very last minute. Holy fuck, did people love parsing the hell out of those lyrics! In the song, Dax basically admits he was a Judas, a horrible friend who deserves every lashing he took, every punch to his cheek... but, at the end of the song, he basically says the girl was worth it and he'd do it all again, no regrets... except for one—the only thing he'd undo if he could: *the balcony*. But then, in his next breath, he says, if changing a single thing would mean he wouldn't be "the guy sniffing that sweet bouquet of violets every night," then he wouldn't change a thing and he'd choose to be a Judas again.

So, yeah, in the end, "Judas" was very much a "sorry, not sorry" sort of "flip off the haters" song. And the world ate it up. My theory on the staggering success of "Judas" is as follows. One, it's an amazing song. A catchy-as-hell, head-banging anthem people can sing along with at top volume while mentally flipping off their ex or boss or anyone who's ever done them wrong. Two, music fans really love it when their favorite rock stars have a bad-boy streak. They like their rock stars to be bad boys with hearts of gold. And "Judas" solidified Dax's reputation as one of rock's best examples of the trope, even though anyone who knows Dax Morgan knows he's not the least bit bad. Only golden. A momma's boy who loves his family and friends and only wants to do right by everyone he loves the most. And, three, people are willing to forgive just about any sin, as long as it's committed in the name of love, which anyone can plainly see is the case here. Nine months after "the love triangle" hit the internet, Dax and I are still going strong. Better than ever. And everyone can see it.

We're deeply, totally, thoroughly in love and won't ever apologize for that. Fuck the haters.

It's not all good news, of course. Nine months in, and Caleb still hates Dax's guts. But like I told Daxy, we just have to let it go. We can't change what happened, or Caleb's feelings about it. In the beginning, Caleb texted and left me voicemails several times, but I ignored him. My loyalty is with Dax now. If Caleb hates Dax, that's the same thing as hating me, as far as I'm concerned. And the last thing I'm going to do is try to convince Caleb of anything. He's a big boy. He's on his own to figure this out.

Dax, being Dax, reached out to apologize to Caleb about a month ago, thinking maybe time had healed the wound. But Caleb said, "You're dead to me, you piece of shit" and hung up the phone. So, all righty, then. That was that. *Onward.*

A few days after Caleb hung up on Dax, Dean and the other RCR guys unexpectedly called Dax. They said they weren't personally pissed at Dax. That, as far as they were concerned, Caleb had treated me like shit during our relationship and this was karma. They assured Dax they'd never badmouth him or 22 Goats—and especially not me, because, they said, they'll never forget it was me who hooked them up with Reed in the first place and changed their lives forever.

Dean, in particular, said, "If Violet's happy with you, and we can easily see she is, then we're happy for her. For you both. We love you both." But he further told Dax that, in the interest of keeping his band intact, the guys wouldn't cross the picket line publicly, meaning RCR wouldn't ever play a festival or awards show if 22 Goats was playing there, too. Dean admitted it pained him not to get to write a song with Dax, but he just didn't see how it would be possible. At least not for the foreseeable future.

Dax told Dean he understood the guys' position and wished him and the other guys and the band well. He told Dean he'll always love and admire him, and hoped that one day, the pair would be able to create music together because, Dax admitted, that remains his biggest musical dream. To get to create music with his idol, Dean Masterson. In reply, Dean said, "Yeah, hopefully, someday, man. I'd love that."

When Dax hung up from his heart-wrenching phone call with Dean, he looked like he wanted to cry. And in that moment, I knew losing Dean as a friend and potential collaborator was a much bigger loss to him than losing Caleb. But Dax hasn't dwelled on that, as far as I know. Or, at least, if he has, he hasn't admitted it to me. All he's ever said on the topic, when I've prodded him, is, "Even the shitty stuff has led me to this moment. And, I swear to God, baby, there's no place I'd rather be than in this moment with you."

I turn to look at Dax sitting next to me. He's listening as Zander tells the rapt crowd in this beachside restaurant his "Keane and Maddy story." It's what everyone's been doing at this dinner to kick off the wedding week—telling a cute Keane and Maddy story. And Zander's story is one of the cutest so far: the story of Keane and Maddy's very first, highly combative, interaction via text exchange.

As Zander continues talking, my phone buzzes with a text.

Miranda: All ready

My heart leaping, I show the text to Dax, and he smiles and nods.

"...And I told Peenie Weenie," Zander says, "'I like that Maddy Milliken. She's *adorbsicles*.'"

Everyone laughs.

"And, man, was I right about that," Zander continues. "This girl is as adorbsicles as they come. These two are perfect together." He raises his drink. "To Keane and Maddy. *Kaddy*. I knew you were made for each other, even before you met. I love you both."

Raucous applause erupts and Zander sits back down. Dax signals he wants the microphone—and the minute Dax stands with it, everyone goes ballistic. Because, come on, he's Dax fucking Morgan. Even in his own family, he's a rockstar.

"Hey, everyone," Dax says smoothly. "I'm super stoked to be here." He smiles at me and my entire body electrifies with excitement. "What I'm about to tell you will end up as a *Kaddy* story, I promise, but bear with me because it *begins* as a *Diolet* story. As most of you already know, Vi's been on tour with me and the goats for the past three months. We've been having a blast, but we're also super pumped to take this week off before the final three months to relax with all of you." He smiles at me again. "Recently, Vi and I did something kinda cool, which we immediately told Keane and Maddy about. And they said we should tell all of you about it here tonight. We were worried about stealing their thunder, but Keane and Maddy insisted. So here we go." Dax grins. "About a month ago, I got down on bended knee, right after our show in Barcelona, and I asked the love of my life to be my wife. *And she said yes.*"

Pandemonium. That's what's exploding around me. Dax's parents and siblings beeline to us from their seats. They hug and kiss us and welcome me into the family. I catch Colin's and Fish's eyes, sitting next to each other at the next table, and they smile and wink at me. Of course, those sweet boys have known about our happy news since the night Dax popped the question, and they were both instantly as happy for Dax and me as we were for ourselves.

A beaming smile on his face, Dax says, "Violet hasn't worn her ring since the big day because she wanted to put it on after we'd told all of you." Dax fishes the ring out of his pocket, kneels, and looks up at me, a massive smile on his gorgeous face. "Violet Rhodes, you're the love of my life. You make me feel like the luckiest guy in the world, every day. Will you please say yes and agree to become my *wife?*"

When I nod profusely and say yes, Dax slides the ring onto my finger and leaps up to hug me. Of course, everyone cheers and swoons.

There's another round of hugs with Dax's parents and siblings and best friends until, finally, everyone heads back to their seats.

When everyone settles down, Dax brings the mic to his lips again. "Thank you, Keane and Maddy, for letting us share our good news like this. That's you guys in a nutshell—always willing to share the love and the spotlight. That's why we love you the most."

Everyone cheers and claps and clinks glasses, clearly thinking that's the end of Dax's speech.

But they're wrong. Instead of passing the microphone to the next person, Dax brings it to his mouth again. "There's one more thing I want to mention. Something else Keane and Maddy insisted we tell you tonight." He grins, a boy with a juicy secret. "Three days after I proposed to Violet... we found out she's preggers."

Dax's parents look floored. Same with his siblings. But I'm laughing along with Dax, feeling hugely relieved to finally have our huge, exciting secret out in the open.

"Looks like we've reached a *bump* in the Rhodes, folks," Keane shouts, holding up his rum punch, and everyone laughs.

Chuckling, Dax says, "I want to say a quick word of thanks to my sister for getting knocked up accidentally long before I had to stand up here and make this announcement. Thanks for breaking in the parentals, Kitty Kat. Look at 'em. They don't even look upset. Just surprised. And that's good because, guys, Violet and I are stoked about our baby news. It wasn't planned. But we both feel like it's the best news, ever. I'd already proposed *before* we found out, and we've both always wanted a kid. So all it means is our timeline is a bit faster than originally envisioned. It's all good."

Dax's closest loved ones come at us again. Another round of hugs are administered. Tears are shed. Finally, Dax brings the microphone to his lips again. "So, one more thing. We told Kaddy about the proposal and pregnancy, and they were like, 'You know, every single person you'd invite to *your* wedding will already be at *our* wedding...'"

The crowd loses it at Dax's obvious implication.

Dax raises his voice to be heard above the growing din. "So, we figured, why make everyone travel *again*, especially when Violet is knocked up?'" He chuckles. "Surprise, everyone! You're invited to *two* weddings this week!"

I text Miranda: *Now!* And, two seconds later, the double doors leading into the restaurant fly open and my paltry little contribution to our guest list files in, all of them waving like contestants at a beauty pageant: my mother, Reed, Miranda, my three roommates from college, and Ashley—Puppy Girl—plus her parents and two siblings.

Dax lifts his water glass and shouts, "Violet and I are getting married on that beach right over there tomorrow at five! We hope you'll all come! No shoes required!"

FIFTY-FOUR

DAX

The sand feels soft and warm underneath my bare feet.

Violet, staring up at me with those blue-gray eyes of hers, is beautiful in her simple white dress. The girl who's been obsessed with sketching wedding gowns her whole life designed the simplest one imaginable for herself. A backless white sheath with zero frills or flourishes, that fits her curves like a second skin.

Right before we left for the Bahamas, Violet chopped her long dark hair into a sharp bob again, just for me, turning herself into a hitwoman, yet again. This time, my hitwoman bride. Lights and darks, all swirled together, ever so beautifully. She's a work of art, my Violet, from every angle. Music in motion. Intriguing to me, endlessly.

Holding my hands, Violet says her vows. "Dax, you've made this Violet anything but blue. I can't wait to be your wife and make a family with you." She looks out at our audience. "And to be a part of your entire, incredible family, forever." She returns to me, tears in her eyes. "I promise I'll always be your faithful and loving wife, right by your side, through richer and poorer, and sickness and health, through anything that comes our way, no matter what it is, good or bad, forever and ever. I love you."

I swallow my tears and squeeze Violet's hands, overwhelmed with joy and hope and love.

The Bahamian dude with the sick accent turns to me. "Dax, please tell Violet your vows."

I take a moment to gather myself, and then say, "Violet, the minute I saw you across that crowded room, I felt like I'd known you in a past life. It was like some part of my subconscious thought, '*Of course*, you look like a mash-up of Elvis and ABBA and Uma Thurman—that's so *you.*'"

Violet laughs, along with everyone in our audience.

"And in return, I recognized in your gaze a woman who instantly understood exactly what she was seeing in me. The fact that I'm two guys at once—a guy who's just as likely to be brooding in a corner as performing at center stage. And with each and every glance and smile and conversation and touch since our first meeting, that initial feeling of deep-seated mutual understanding and respect, that incredible feeling of destiny across a thousand lifetimes with you, has only grown and blossomed. And now, my love, my flower, my destiny, you're in my blood. Under my skin. Fused with the very tissues of my every organ and tethered to my every thought and idea. You're a part of me now, Violet. You're the air I breathe. You're my heart and soul. My dreams. My everything. And I promise to take care of you, to love you—and our beautiful baby—forever and ever, with every breath I take and every beat of my heart, until the day I die. I love you."

Violet is crying. There's sniffling in the audience. And I'm barely keeping it together.

Somewhere in the line of groomsmen behind me in the sand, I hear Fish's voice mutter, "*Whoa.*"

I chuckle, because I know Fish is stoned out of his mind back there, and everything I just said was probably quite a trip for the dude.

Other than Fish, my groomsmen include the usual suspects: Colin, Colby, Ryan, Keane, and Zander. Not sure exactly how many of them are stoned back there, but I've got to think Fish isn't the only one. Which is fine with me. I'm not partaking these days, but I don't care if they do. Especially not here, in paradise, at the chillest wedding ceremony that ever was. A wedding where the bride and groom are both barefoot, and half the wedding guests are barefoot and sloshed on rum punch, and the endless aquamarine ocean is our serene backdrop.

I would have asked my brother-in-law, Josh, to stand up for me, too, since he's become another big brother to me. Plus, he's indirectly paid for my wedding, just by paying for Keane and Maddy's. But I figured if I asked Josh to stand up here, then I'd have to ask Reed, seeing as how he's Violet's brother. And while I'm super friendly with Reed, and grateful to him for being there for Violet, and also for what he's done for my band, he's not my brother, not like the dudes standing here with me. I mean, he's technically my brother now. And Ryan's, too, actually. Which amuses me to no end. But he'll never be a part of my inner circle the way these other guys are. It's just the way it is.

The Bahamian dude—who, actually, might also be stoned out of his mind, now that I'm looking at his bloodshot eyes—smiles broadly at Violet. "Do you, Violet, take Dax to be your lawfully wedded husband?"

Violet squeezes both of my hands. "I do."

The Bahamian dude turns to me. "Do you, Dax, take Violet to be your lawfully wedded wife?"

I've never felt so sure of anything in my life. I know guys my age are supposed to be on the warpath, in constant search of their next conquest. But that's just not me. I did that for a stretch, and it just wore me down. Made me feel like I was following the instructions to a board game I didn't even want to play. I'm so sure of Violet and me, in fact, we've got no prenup. If my billionaire brother-in-law could take the leap with my sister, no holding back or Plan B, then that's good enough for me. This way, I'm putting it all on the line, in every way, come what may. And it feels amazing. I want this woman to be my wife and the mother of my baby, more than I've ever wanted anything in the world. And so, without the slightest doubt or reservation and my heart soaring, I look into

Violet's kind eyes and say the easiest two words I've ever said in my life: "I do."

"*Whoa*," a voice says behind me. And this time, I'm pretty sure that was Keane. Which means, yeah, my big brother is stoned out of his mind, right along with Fish. I'm not surprised.

The Bahamian dude instructs us to exchange rings, which we do, both of us beaming and blushing. And then the dude starts giving us marriage advice. Telling us colorful stuff like, "Don't let your mouth carry you where your foot can't carry you back from."

As he talks, I glance over Violet's shoulder at her bridesmaids, or maids of honor, or whatever the heck they are: Miranda, Maddy, Aloha, Kat, Tessa, and Lydia. They're all smiling from ear to ear. They've got tropical flowers in their hair, just like Violet. Everyone's hair is blowing in the warm breeze. Just like Violet's and mine.

I feel at peace.

In love.

Serene.

Truly happy.

I'm exactly where I want to be. Where I'm meant to be. With the woman I love. And a baby on the way. I've got it all and I know it. And I'll never, ever fuck it up.

I glance out at our audience and meet my mother's twinkling eyes. She's wearing a sundress and a straw hat. She looks a little sauced. She blows me a kiss and I smile. When I meet my dad's eyes, he nods and wipes away a tear. And that makes me well up with the tears I've been stuffing down this entire ceremony, because, damn, Thomas Morgan never cries.

My eyes blurred with emotion, I return to Violet, just as the Bahamian dude pronounces us husband and wife and tells me it's time to kiss my bride. And so, I do. I lean in and press my lips against Violet's, the woman I'm going to love and cherish and take care of forever. The woman who's never had a family, and now has one with me. The woman I know was sent down from heaven to save me from the wrong path. A path of darkness and misery and pointlessness that was beckoning to me—but which I dodged like a bullet, thanks to Violet and the ones I love the most.

When I release Violet's lips from mine, I lean into her ear. "I love you, *wife*," I whisper. And as I say that last word, electricity, euphoria... *love* sweep over me and bathe me in a warm, peaceful golden light.

"I love you, *husband*," she whispers back, tears floating down her pretty face.

I wipe a tear from her cheek and smile. "It's us against the world, my love. Forever."

EPILOGUE

VIOLET

Holding Jackson in my arms, I clap and cheer for Aloha as she finishes singing one of my favorite songs off her new album—a song called "Boy Toy." During this tour—22 Goats' third, but their second as a headliner—Aloha's been the opener. But, really, a co-headliner, if you ask Dax.

Of course, where there's Aloha, there's Zander. He's been taking care of Aloha's personal security on this tour, as usual, while Dax's security has been handled by his usual team, led by Brett—the ex-Navy SEAL who's been handling Dax's personal security ever since Dax texted Reed and asked for reinforcements during our first sightseeing trip in Seattle.

Keane and Maddy have also been hanging out on this tour quite a bit, as much as Keane's busy shooting schedule on his TV show and Maddy's busy life as a documentarian allow. When Maddy's documentary about Aloha came out earlier this year, it catapulted Maddy into the big leagues of the documentary filmmaking world. There's even talk about Maddy being nominated for an Academy Award. And even though I had absolutely nothing to do with my sister-in-law's amazing documentary about Aloha, it gives me infinite pleasure to feel like I've played a tiny part in it whenever I see Aloha wearing the superhero costume I designed for her on the movie's poster.

In addition to Keane and Maddy joining us almost every other weekend during this tour, Dax's other family members have dropped by quite a bit, too, on a rotating basis. Since Dax makes sure there's always plenty of relaxation time built into the touring schedule, we've had a blast hanging out with everyone in different cities and doting on each other's kids and babies.

Speaking of babies, I double-check the protective headphones nestled against Jackson's wispy blonde hair. They're designed to protect my baby's little eardrums in the midst of blaring live music. And, yep, they're still firmly in place.

"All good, Action Jackson," I say to my son's smiling little face. And he coos at me happily, melting my heart. Oh my freaking God, I love this boy! I didn't know I could love someone as much as I love our little donut.

The crowd in the arena applauds raucously, signaling Aloha's set is over, and I lift Jackson's little hand and puppeteer him into giving Aloha a little "Action Jackson" cheer.

"Oh, my, is someone cheering for Aloha?" my mother-in-law coos.

I turn to find her standing next to me in the skybox, smiling at her newest grandson. She offers to take Jackson from me, to feed him a bottle and change his diaper, while I run to the bathroom and relax with our family in the skybox for a bit. Gratefully, I hand my baby over to Gramma Lou and sprint for the bathrooms.

"Take your time!" Louise calls after me. "I've got him!"

I don't normally hang out in luxury skyboxes during Dax's shows. I typically sit front-row center, which is unusual for wives and girl-friends and VIPs. Everyone else tends to prefer watching shows from the wings. But Dax loves seeing me in the audience when he performs, holding his mini-me with his protective earphones on. Dax says he never gets tired of that sight, especially because he knows it won't last forever. At some point, we're not going to be able to lug our little donut around everywhere we go. One day in the future, when Jackson is older, Jackson and I might have to hop private planes to visit Daxy during his tours, rather than traveling full-time with him. Which is why, for now, I try to sit where my husband can see his wife and baby as he performs, so we can all savor these early days of our little family.

There have been some shows where I haven't made it to my front-row seat, simply because I've been breastfeeding Jackson in a dressing room, or rocking him to sleep, and couldn't tear myself away. On occasion, though rarely, I've handed Jackson to our traveling nanny during a show, and then watched and danced in the wings. But, mostly, I sit in the front row with Jackson, and Dax and I use the nanny only when we need alone time together. Which, I must admit, we enjoy on a daily basis.

When I come back from using the bathroom, I quickly scarf down tacos from the buffet like a starving hyena, until my mother-in-law approaches and tells me to relax and slow down.

"Sweetie, it's fine," she says. "I'm having my grandma time. *Relax.*"

My shoulders soften. "I'm not used to relaxing. We're always on the go."

Louise looks down at Jackson. "Well, Gramma Lou is here now so Jackson's mommy can take all the time she needs." Louise kisses Jackson's little forehead and looks up at me again. "*Go, honey.*"

After saying a quick hello to several of Fish's and Colin's family members who've joined the party tonight, and hugging my brothers-in-law, I gravitate to my sisters-in-law around the skybox. With Kat, I touch her incredibly swollen belly and listen to her moan about how ready she is to pop any day now. With Tessa, I touch her swollen belly and listen to her moan about how ready she is to pop in two months. And then, to finish off the pregnant-sister-in-law trifecta, I find Maddy and touch her teeny-tiny itty bitty baby bump and listen to her rhapsodize about how magical pregnancy is and how excited Keane is and how she can't wait to hold her baby in five months.

Lydia comes along and takes my boy from our mother-in-law,

saying, "Gimme gimme." She gives me an update on her four kids—the older three and toddler Mia—and then leans into my ear and whispers, "Colby and I have been officially trying for baby number five."

"Holy crap, Lydi-Bug," I say. "That's exciting. Pretty soon, there's going to be a whole tribe of second-wave cousins for Action Jackson to lord over."

"Jackson will have the best of all worlds," Lydia says. "He'll be an Only, a Little, *and* a Big."

She's absolutely right about that. Jackson is an only child, obviously. And he'll likely stay that way, because that's the life Dax and I envision for ourselves. As Dax likes to say, "It's you and me, and our baby makes three." But by keeping Jackson a singleton, we don't feel like we're depriving him of the kind of upbringing Dax had and loved, because, with so many cousins, Jackson will always feel like he has siblings. And not only that, thanks to the spacing of his cousins, Jackson will get the unique experience of feeling like the youngest sibling with one "wave" of cousins, and the oldest with respect to another.

As I continue chatting with Lydia and my mother-in-law, Tessa comes over and demands to hold my sleeping baby, saying "Gimme gimme." So, of course, Lydia hands Jackson over.

My mother-in-law asks me the latest on The Superhero Project and I'm proud to tell her, and my sisters-in-law, that my charity now has programs serving children's hospitals and families in fifteen cities throughout the country. "And next year," I say, "we hope to double that number."

The ladies express admiration and awe.

"I couldn't have done it without everyone's support."

It's an understatement. Dax and the various members of our inner circle have used their significant star power, social media platforms, and/or wealth to help raise awareness and support for my charity. So much so, we've not only brightened a whole lot of sick kids' lives with costumes, we've also raised a crapton of money and support for families going through the worst time of their lives.

Kat approaches and slides into the conversation. She compliments me on the costumes I designed for Aloha for the tour, and I thank her.

"Aloha's kept me busy," I say. "She's always got some new project or idea. A music video or photo shoot she's excited about."

"Are you still designing wedding gowns?" Kat asks, her hands cradling her huge baby bump.

"Here and there, but not very often. I'm just too busy. I go to children's hospitals in almost every city of the tour and send my designs for the kids' costumes off to the seamstresses. That keeps me busy enough, in addition to taking care of Jackson and spending time with Daxy. I think I'll focus on designing wedding gowns when we get back to L.A. and stay a while. And if not, then when Jackson is a bit older. One day, I want to start my own line. But all that can wait. I'm in no rush."

"Just make sure you always keep the embers of your own dreams burning," Louise says. "In addition to being a wife and mother, a woman needs her own personal passions, separate from her role as wife and mother. Keeping your own dreams alive will ultimately be the thing that allows you to give the best of yourself to the people you love the most."

Oh, how I love my mother-in-law. She rarely gives me, or any of us, advice. But when she does, it's always a gem.

"Thank you. I'll always remember that, Momma Lou."

"That's exactly why I've been writing my book," Kat says. "Because I feel, gah, lit up when I write it. Sometimes, I completely lose track of time when I write. I forget to eat or sleep or pee. Who knew I was born to tell stories like this?"

"*Who knew?*" Louise says, chuckling. "Kitty, you're the extroverted version of Dax and the second-biggest BS artist in our family. Of course, you're a storyteller like Dax. Just in a different way. Keane's also a storyteller, in yet another way."

My sisters-in-law and I agree with that assessment—and don't even bother to ask who the "*first*-biggest BS artist" in the family is, according to Louise. We all know it's Keane, by a long mile.

We ask Kat for an update on the book she's been writing—a spicy romantic comedy she's been working on diligently for the past few months—and she lights up like a Christmas tree as she tells us about it.

Finally, when I can't take it anymore, I ask for my sleeping baby back, and Tessa begrudgingly complies.

"He looks exactly like Dax at that age," Louise says as Tessa hands Jackson to me. "And so much like Kitty Kat, too."

"And Gracie," Kat adds, referring to her own daughter.

"And all four of them look exactly like you," Tessa says to our mother-in-law.

"Yes, well, the Russian doll doesn't stop with us five," Louise says, looking at my son in my arms. "My grandmother and mother both looked just like Kat, Dax, Gracie, and me—and now, our beloved Action Jackson. We're the ones who, for whatever reason, keep springing like arm buds out of the same cosmic starfish—no added DNA required, apparently."

We all chuckle, including me. But, secretly, I know my mother-in-law is wrong about Jackson being an arm bud like the rest of them, despite appearances. Although my baby does, in fact, look exactly like Dax and the others, at first glance, I happen to know my son has my late baby brother's ears, to a tee. *Not* Dax's ears. Which means, whether it's apparent to anyone else or not, my son, Jackson, has my baby brother, Jackson, floating around inside him somewhere. And that makes me so damned happy, I could fly around this skybox, just thinking about it.

Recorded music begins blaring in the arena—the cue that we're fifteen minutes from 22 Goats hitting the stage.

"I'd better get to my seat," I say. "I like being in the front row for Dax to see us."

"Have fun," Louise says. "FYI, I changed Jacky's diaper and he's had a full bottle."

"Thank you so much. That's why I love you the most."

I kiss everyone and tell them I'll see them tomorrow morning at Casa Morgan. Because, of course, Dax made sure the tour is staying a few extra days in Seattle. Not just for him and me and Jackson to get to hang out with our family, but because Colin and Fish and Zander all love taking a few extra days in their hometown, as well.

But before I've made it to the door of the skybox, my new dad, Thomas, strides up to me. "Hello, Flower Girl," he says. Because, yeah, nobody in this family calls me Rocky. As it's turned out, they call me Flower. Sometimes, Flower Girl and Flower Child. Also, Dax's siblings call me Viagra quite a bit, as Dax predicted. And, of course, the entire family calls me every variation of Violet anyone can think up, Ultra Violet Radiation and No Shrinking Violet originally being the most popular selections—that second one leading to them sometimes calling me "Shrinky Dink." Which then led to "Dink" and "Dinky." Yeah, that's the Morgans for you. Oh, how they love their nicknames.

I give my father-in-law a semi-hug, as much as I can manage while holding Jackson, and he kisses my cheek.

"Hey, Daddy-o," I say, using the nickname I've christened him with. It felt too obvious to call Thomas straight-up "Dad." Too needy. But "Daddy-o" seemed lighthearted and fun, right in line with the Morgan "brand," while still allowing me to sneak that magic word in there. "What's shaking, Daddy-o?" I ask, shamelessly using his nickname a second time.

"Just living the dream, Flower Girl," he says. "Actually, that's true. I'm living the dream, same as you."

A huge smile splits my face. *Truer words were never spoken.* "Yep, we're lucky sons-of-guns, aren't we?"

"We sure are." While talking to me, Thomas absently offers his finger to his grandson, who grips it and coos. "Are we on for backgammon tomorrow, Dinky?" he asks. "Me and you—to the death?"

"You know it, Gramps," I say. "And this time, I swear, I'm gonna kick your butt."

"I'd like to see you try." He kisses my forehead, and then does the same thing to Jackson. "See you back at the ranch, love."

Emotion threatens, the same way it always does when my father-in-law addresses me as "love." But I swallow it down. "See you there. You might want to strap a cushion to your butt, because it's gonna get beat."

"Oh, please. I've been beating kids in backgammon since before you were born."

I hug him. And kiss his cheek. And then, my heart full, head outside the skybox where my personal bodyguard stands at the ready to lead me to my front-row seat.

Dax is sweaty up onstage. Glistening. Glowing. As usual, he's giving every note, every stroke of his guitar, every word, his all. He's light as a feather up there tonight. Unburdening himself of all the deep thoughts and anxieties that come with the territory of being an artist. And I'm so proud. Especially because, through it all, Dax keeps finding Jackson, his mini-me, along with his wife, and flashing us secret, adoring smiles. Smiles that say, *You and me, and our baby makes three.*

As Dax moves his arm, I get a glimpse of the new tattoo inked onto the inside of his forearm, an extension of his ever-expanding "family tattoo." It's a second solar system, this new tattoo, adjacent to his original family one—a solar system featuring a giant, blazing sun emitting ethereal yellow, orange, and violet rays. Next to this violet-infused sun, there's a bright, beautiful, boyish moon. And next to those two heavenly bodies, a small, twinkling star—our beloved Rock Star husband and daddy—basks in their light and glow, just as much as they bask in the star's breathtaking, shimmering sparkle. As usual, my heart swells at the sight of Dax's new tattoo—my husband's visual declaration of undying love for our little family—the same way it always does whenever my gaze happens to fall on it.

The audience in the arena cheers the last chords of "Hitwoman Elvis Disco Momma." Out of nowhere, a roadie appears, bringing with him a stool and Dax's acoustic guitar. Quickly, the guy helps Dax swap out his electric for his acoustic, and Dax takes a seat on the stool. All of which means my husband is about to sing the sole acoustic hit from 22 Goats' catalog: "Three," the monster hit off their third album of the same name.

"Three" was a revelation when it came out two months ago. Totally off-brand, in terms of instrumentation, and yet so raw and vulnerable and honest, so Dax Morgan, it still came off as quintessential 22 Goats... which is probably why it unexpectedly became one of the band's biggest hits.

"You having a good time, Seattle?" Dax says.

The crowd cheers like crazy.

"So am I. Time of my life, in fact. It's good to be home." He looks down at me and Jackson and, once again, beams a wide smile at us that makes my heart melt. He begins playing the iconic riff of "Three," and pandemonium strikes. Dax chuckles at the exuberant reaction, like he always does, plays the riff again, leans forward, and sings:

They say two's company
Three's a crowd
Phony as a three-dollar bill
Three strikes, yer out
Three-ring circus
Three moves bad as fire

You and me, our baby makes three
You and me, it's what makes me happy
A new lucky number
The number is three
Saved me, healed me, gave me a family

Used to get three sheets to the wind
Not no more

Three, my lucky number now

Three, right where I wanna be
Three, my lucky number now
Three, you gave me a family

People lied about our bed
About our love story
They were wrong about that
Wrong about me
Three little words
Made me complete

They were all talkin' trash
Not no more

Three, my lucky number now
Three, right where I wanna be
Three, my lucky number now
Three, you gave me a family

Wasn't in-fat-u-at-ed
Wasn't stealing ya
Fulfilling des-tin-y
Turning myself to three

Three, my lucky number now
Three, right where I wanna be
Three, my lucky number now
Three, you gave me a family

The arena applauds uproariously. Dax thanks everyone, like he always does. But then, he does something he's never done before...

Maybe it's because we're in Seattle and he always feels extra loose in this city. Like he can do whatever the hell he wants and everyone will always have his back. Maybe it's because he knows his entire family is here to cheer him on tonight. Or maybe he's just feeling particularly good after the enthusiastic blowjob I gave him earlier in the dressing room. I don't know what's got my rock star hubsters under this crazy spell tonight, but whatever it is, he goes to the edge of the stage and instructs the security personnel to lead his wife and baby to the stage. And so, they do.

It takes a while, since I've got Jackson with me and I need to do this slowly and carefully, but, as the arena cheers and chants, I'm escorted with my bodyguard through several barriers and up a staircase... and finally across the expansive stage to meet Dax.

When I get to my husband, the crowd goes insane. But I'm wary. What the hell is Dax doing? I steal a quick look at Fish and he shrugs, telling me he has no idea what's up. A quick glance at Colin yields the same result.

Dax raises his mic stand and slides his microphone into the holder. He takes Jackson from me, who's now awake and elated to see his beloved daddy, and, of course, the crowd goes nuts at the sight of Dax with his son. After a moment of cooing at Jackson, Dax takes my hand with his free one and says into the microphone in the stand, "Some of you may know I'm a pretty private person. Not big on posting on Instagram."

Everyone cheers. Yes, they know this about him.

"But there's been a lot of shit said about my wife. A lot of bullshit that was just plain wrong and mean. And I've never addressed it because I felt it was beneath us. I felt like acknowledging the haters only gave them oxygen. But as long as I've got you all here, could you do me a favor and take out your phones and post this for me?" He pauses as every person in the arena, pretty much, holds up their phones. "Thanks. Now hear this. My wife is the most incredible person I've ever met. Hot as fuck with a heart of gold."

The crowd cheers wildly.

Fish leans into his microphone, the one he uses to sing backups, and says, "Word."

"So, if anyone's got something negative to say about her, I just want you to know you're saying something negative about the person

I love the most. The mother of my baby. You're saying something negative about *me* and my *family*. My wife has never done anything disloyal to *anyone* in her life. If you've heard otherwise, it's not true. If anyone was disloyal, it was me. But for a very, very good reason. Because I'd reached a fork in the road, and I took the path to a lifetime of love and happiness. And I don't apologize for that." He looks at me. "I love my wife and baby more than life itself. I'll love her and protect her with my last breath. And I'll never apologize for that." He looks to the farthest rafters of the arena. "Everybody out there got all that on video for me?"

The place explodes.

"Good. Good talk. Now, be sure to post what I said every-fucking-where for me, okay?"

The arena cheers to let Dax know they've got his back.

As the crowd goes crazy, Dax kisses me, rather passionately, eliciting a raucous reaction from the arena. When our kiss is done, he kisses Jackson's forehead and hands him back to me. And then he leans into my ear. "Watch from the wings, baby. Where I can give you a kiss any time I wanna."

My heart is racing. Until this moment, I had no idea how much I craved having my honor defended. I thought I was perfectly fine with our strategy of ignoring the trolls. But that speech just now meant more to me than I could ever express to Dax. And the fact that he felt the desire to make it, unprompted by me, means even more.

Dax leans into my ear again, "Fuck 'em all, baby. It's us against the world."

"I love you so much, Dax."

"I love you, too, my beautiful wife. Forever and always." He kisses me again, and then our baby, for good measure. And then I float off to the wings, feeling like three is a very lucky number, indeed.

Visit http://www.laurenrowebooks.com/22-goats-three to listen to 22 Goats perform Three.

To listen to **even more ORIGINAL MUSIC** by 22 Goats, visit
https://www.laurenrowebooks.com/music-from-rockstar and check
out original music and music videos, created by Lauren, just for you!

Also, be sure to check out 22 Goats' website page: http://www.
laurenrowebooks.com/22-goats
to read tons of bonus material, including an interview of 22 Goats,
while you're there.

Also, as a thank you for reading ROCKSTAR, keep reading for the
bonus epilogue regarding Keane and Maddy, the adorbsicles
couple from BALL PEEN HAMMER!
To find out how to get the audiobook version of the bonus epilogue,
narrated by John Lane and Lauren Rowe, visit: http://www.
laurenrowebooks.com/ball-peen-hammer

Do you want to read about Reed Rivers? THE REED RIVERS
TRILOGY is complete, start reading now with *Bad Liar*.

Want to read the swoony romance between Fish & Ally? Start
reading *Smitten* today!

Perhaps, you want to read about the rest of the Morgan brothers—
Colby, Ryan, Keane, and their best friend, Zander? The recom-
mended reading order is
Hero (Colby)
Captain (Ryan),

Ball Peen Hammer (Keane),
Mister Bodyguard (Zander)
These are all **standalones** that can be read in any order.

Maybe you want to read about feisty Kat Morgan's love story with Josh Faraday? Head to *Infatuation*.

BONUS EPILOGUE: KEANE AND MADDY

From *Ball Peen Hammer*
By Lauren Rowe

Keane

I look at myself in the full-length mirror of the bathroom. Damn. I'm lookin' fresh 'n' fine in my tropical-print collared shirt and white linen pants. Of course, I'm always a handsome and happy lad, all the livelong day. But today, on this once-in-a-lifetime special day, I'm something way better than handsome and happy: I'm *groomalicious*. Shrink me down, hollow me out, cover me in plastic, and put me on top of a wedding cake, son! Because Keane Elijah Morgan is getting hitched today—to the best girl in the world!

Ho-lee shit, I'm a lucky bastard. Madelyn "Mad Dog" Milliken is the holy trifecta of perfection. First off, she's one of only two women in the world who makes me want to be a better man. The second being my momma, of course. Second off, she's one of only two people in the world who consistently makes me laugh so hard, I almost piss myself. The second being my best friend and Wifey, Zander. But, see, the great thing about Maddy is that she's got a third thing on the menu, too. A third thing, when added to the first two, that makes her the holy grail of women: she's my all-time favorite person to fuck. So, of course, I'm marrying the girl. I mean, come on. A dude finds a woman who checks those three boxes, he's gotta lock that shit down.

A knock on the bathroom door slices into my thoughts, followed by the low-baritone voice of Zander, my best man. "Peenie? Did you fall into the toilet, sweet meat?"

I open the bathroom door, a grin on my face. "I was just admiring my groomalicious self in the mirror—thinking about how this is the last time in my life I'll look into a mirror and see an unmarried dude smiling back at me."

Zander chuckles. "Deep thoughts."

"Indeed."

"The wedding coordinator just poked her head through the door and said she'll be back in fifteen to lead us to the beach for the ceremony. The guys and I want to do a shot of whiskey with you before we head out."

My stomach leaps with excitement. "Let's do it."

Practically skipping with glee, I follow Zander into the main area of my hotel suite to find my three brothers—Colby, Ryan, and Dax—plus, my brother-in-law, Josh, hanging out, all of them dressed pretty much like me: like male models in a vacation catalog.

Josh holds up a fancy bottle of booze. "I thought we'd toast you with the good stuff. It's a Faraday family tradition."

I barrel over to the group. "And by 'tradition' I'm guessing you mean you and your brother?"

Josh chuckles. "In my family, we don't have enough family members to wait around for 'traditions' to happen more than twice. Good thing I've got you Morgans to keep my Faraday 'traditions' going." He hands me a glass, filled with a finger of whiskey, and then proceeds to pass out glasses around the group. Josh raises his glass. "To you and Maddy. I don't know how you convinced that woman to say yes, but you did. And we're all glad about it. Don't fuck it up."

Everyone says some version of "Amen" or "Hear, hear." And then we all clink and drink.

"Wow," I say after the amber liquid has slid down my throat. "That's smooth, brother."

"It'd better be," Josh says. "It ain't cheap."

"Ballpark?"

"You don't want to know," Josh says.

"I really do."

Josh motions to my empty glass. "Based on the price of the bottle, what you just drank was worth about three hundred bucks."

I hoot and shove my empty glass under my brother-in-law's nose. "Hit me again, brah. A man only gets married once in his life. Let's send me off right."

Chuckling, Josh refills my glass, and others. But before we drink again, Ryan raises his palm, signaling he's going to make a toast.

"Peenie," Ryan begins, his glass raised. "I never thought this day would come—the day I'd watch you get married, *on purpose.*"

Everyone laughs, including me. I'm not sure how Ryan imagined I might one day get married *accidentally.* And yet, it makes a vague kind of sense, actually—the idea that I could wake up one day, married, and not know how it came to pass.

Ryan continues, "And I definitely never expected you to be marrying a girl of Maddy's caliber. How'd you do that?"

I wink. "Apparently, a girl can forgive a shit-ton of idiocy when she gets catapulted to The Promised Land on a daily basis."

"Apparently."

Ryan's chiseled face softens with sincerity. "All kidding aside, Peenie. We all love you. We razz you mercilessly, but the truth is the world is a far better place for having you in it. Thank you for always making us laugh. Sometimes, at you. Sometimes, with you. And thank you most of all for bringing Maddy into our family. I like her more than I like you, to be honest."

Everyone expresses agreement with that statement.

"My turn," Dax says, halting everyone from drinking. "Keaney, more than anyone else, you've taught me to live in the moment. To laugh. Thank you for that. I love you the most, brother."

I press my lips together and nod, suddenly feeling a bit emotional.

Colby raises his glass. "Peenie, I'm fond of saying you're not our family's black sheep. You're our *neon* sheep. It's the truth. Our family wouldn't be the same without your 'ebullient charm.' You're irreplaceable. I give you a hard time, sometimes, I know. But I want you to know you mean the world to me. I'm so grateful you're in my life, and I couldn't be happier for you." He winks. "I love you the most, weirdo."

A tsunami of emotion rises inside me. Colby never says he loves me the most. Because, let's face it. He doesn't. He loves Daxy the most. Also, Ryan. And Kat, too. But right now, the way he's looking at me... the way he said *weirdo* with so much love and warmth, I honestly feel like he means every word. "I love you the most, too, Superman," I manage to say through my emotion, even though, as we all know, Daxy is the one who's at the top of my list. Ryan, too.

Everyone begins to drink, but Zander holds up his big palm, halting them. He takes a deep breath and shifts his weight. Throughout my brothers' speeches, Zander's silence has been thick. Clearly, he hasn't been mute due to disinterest. He's been quiet because, predictably, my Wifey is feeling emotional.

Zander swallows hard, his dark eyes glistening. "Keaney . . ." He swallows hard again. He opens his mouth to continue, but his face contorts sharply. Tears prick his eyes. He clamps his lips together and shakes his head, incapable of saying more.

My heart squeezes. I chuckle. "I love you, too, Z," I say, putting my hand on my best friend's broad shoulder. "We don't need words, brother. I know."

Zander nods, looking like he's a hair's breadth shy of losing it. But finally, he whispers, "Let's drink."

Gratefully, we all down our drinks. And when our glasses are empty, Zander puts his big, brawny arm around my shoulder and asks, "You got your vows ready, sweet meat?"

"*Vows?*" I blurt. "I was supposed to come up with *vows?*"

Zander's face drops. "Peenie—"

"That was a joke, Z. Yes, of course, I've got my vows ready. I've been working on 'em for a full month. You got the rings?"

Zander pats his pocket.

"Kewl. So, let's do this thing. I'm dying to get going."

Three seconds later, as if on cue, the wedding coordinator pops her head into the suite. "You ready, Keane?"

"Ready," I say. And it's the truth. I'm ready to marry Maddy Milliken and make her my wife. I crack my knuckles like a prize fighter about to enter the ring and hop from one foot to the next, jiggling my arms. "Time to lock my woman down."

The sun is setting over the ocean, creating a starburst of colors in the sky. Purples, oranges, reds. It's magnificent. Stunning. Breathtaking. But none of it compares to the sight of my bride walking toward me in her white dress.

The future mother of my sixteen babies, give or take thirteen babies, is a modern princess today. Her dress is clean lines on top and "princess" on the bottom. She's sexy and pretty walking toward me in that dress. But she could be in a paper sack and knock me out, thanks to that glowing smile.

When Maddy reaches me, I shake her stepfather's hand and he takes his seat. I grab Maddy's hands and smile like a dope, and she beams a huge smile back at me.

"You look like a cloud," I whisper.

She smiles. "Thank you."

Now, see? This is why we work. Any other woman would be like, "Huh?" But Maddy knows what I mean. She always knows. I place my palm on Maddy's cheek, suddenly overcome by the enormity of this moment. "I love you," I whisper, even though the Bahamian officiant is saying something. "I never thought I could love like this, Maddy."

Maddy's face softens. She leans forward and kisses me gently, even though it's not the scheduled moment for that, strictly speaking. And so, fuck it, I wrap my arms around her and return her kiss.

I'm vaguely aware the officiant has stopped talking, and that our audience is applauding and laughing and hooting. I bring my lips to Maddy's ear. "I'm already married to you, in my heart."

Her chest rises sharply. "Same here. But let's do this, anyway, seeing as how I'm wearing this pretty white dress and all."

My smile widens. "That dress is definitely too pretty to waste." We break apart, our hands clasped. "Proceed," I say to the Bahamian dude.

And away he goes. As he talks, I look down the line of Maddy's bridesmaids behind her: her sister, Hannah, her best friend, Aloha, plus all Maddy's new sisters-in-law. They're all beaming at me. Nonverbally thanking me for bringing Maddy into their lives. Into our family. They're thanking me for making our family complete.

"... vows, Keane?" the officiant says, drawing my attention. And, suddenly, I realize it's time for me to say the big speech I've been practicing for a month.

I squeeze Maddy's hands. "Maddy," I begin. But, suddenly, realize the speech I've prepared is all wrong. Too irreverent. Too silly. Now isn't the time for jokes. Now is the moment to lay myself bare. I pause. And then whisper, "My love. I love you. I admire you. I respect you. I'd *die* for you, without a moment's hesitation."

Maddy's eyes prick with tears.

I clear my throat. "You're an angel. A gift from God. I don't know who I'd be without you. I don't know how I could ever be happy if you weren't mine." I swallow hard. "You're perfect. The complete package. The whole enchilada. The total falafel. The entire *soufflé*. I never thought I could love someone the way I love you. So completely. So honestly. You make me feel like I can leap over tall buildings. With you by my side through life, I know I can handle anything life throws at me, good or bad."

Maddy bites her lip and nods.

"I know everyone is probably expecting me to be witty today. To make 'em laugh. And I was all set to do that. But, suddenly, standing here with you, looking into your beautiful face, I don't want to make a joke. I just want you to know I'm yours. Forever and always. I'm gonna be an awesome husband to you, Maddy. Faithful and true. Supportive and loving. I'll make you laugh and hold you when you cry. I'll support you and cheer you on. I'll tell you the truth, unless you give me that special wink that tells me you want nothing but a little white lie."

Everyone laughs.

"Maddy, I'm gonna be the best husband, ever. Forever and ever. Amen."

Maddy's mouth contorts, like she's trying not to cry.

There's a beat, during which my mother sniffles.

"That's it," I finally say, because it feels like people are waiting on me to say more, but I've definitely shot my wad.

"Beautiful," Maddy whispers, just as a tear rolls down her lovely cheek.

As I wipe her tear with the tip of my finger, the officiant says, "Madelyn? Your vows?"

Maddy takes a deep breath. "Well, damn," she says, much to my surprise. "I had an entire roast prepared for this moment, because I assumed your vows would be a stand-up routine. And now, I've got to scrap the whole, hilarious thing I prepared and say something sweet and sincere. Way to screw me over, Keane."

Everyone bursts out laughing, nobody harder than me. Now see? Perfect girl.

When the laughter dies down, Maddy's face turns earnest. She squeezes my hands and takes a deep breath. "All kidding aside... Keane, you're the sweetest person I've ever known. You're loyal and goofy and silly and kind. You're gentle and honest. You make me laugh like nobody else. You make me feel *special*. I can't wait to be your wife. To build a family with you. I promise to be your faithful and loving wife, through good times and bad, sickness and health, richer and poorer. Forever and ever."

Without waiting for whatever comes next, I take Maddy's face in my palms and kiss her, and she surrenders to me completely.

I'm vaguely aware the crowd is tittering and the officiant is waiting. But fuck 'em all. This is my wedding and I wanna kiss my soon-to-be wife. And so I do.

The officiant says, "Okay, well, you can now kiss your bride, Keane. Whenever you're done, please exchange rings and I'll pronounce you husband and wife."

Laughing, Maddy and I disengage. Zander hands the rings to me. The officiant says the ring-related stuff, and we slide them on.

"Ladies and gentlemen," the dude says, "I now present to you Mr. and Mrs. Keane and Maddy Morgan."

Everyone cheers. Maddy and I hoot and high-five.

"Hop aboard, milady," I say. And without hesitation, Maddy hikes up her flowing dress and leaps onto my back, and I gallop down the center aisle to our married life with my new wife riding me.

Maddy

One year later

"Lana?" I say, when the song "Blue Jeans" by Lana Del Rey comes on Keane's laptop.

My husband and I are lying in bed, naked. Keane is caressing my tiny baby bump. And I feel like I'm floating six inches above the mattress—and not just because Keane just finished licking me to heaven. But because, today, we found out we're having a girl.

To accompany our first discussion about possible names, we've got a Spotify station playing—a station filled with nothing but songs by female artists—women we're hoping might prove inspirational to our search.

Keane twists his gorgeous lips. "Lana sounds too much like Llama. People are gonna call her Lana the Llama."

"And by 'people,' you mean *you*?"

"Correct. Which will then lead to me calling her Tina."

I don't need to ask. It's a reference to one of Keane's favorite movies: *Napoleon Dynamite*.

Keane continues, "So, really, if we name our daughter Lana, we'd be naming her Tina. Is that your intention?"

"No."

"Then, no."

"Okay, then," I say. "Rey?" I'm not serious, actually. But I'm curious where Keane's mind will go from here.

Keane shakes his head. "If we name her Rey, everyone will call her Raymond. And that will lead everyone to saying 'Everybody Loves Raymond' to her, all the time, for her entire life. At least, until everyone alive when that show was on the air is dead. Unless, of course, the show gets picked up for syndication on one of those stations showing old timey hit sitcoms. But if not, then it'll be the year 2069 or whatever, and our daughter be, like, 'Dude, I don't understand why all the old farts always used to say 'Everybody Loves Raymond' to me all the time. It was so fucking weird.'"

I giggle. "Every name we come up with is going to come with an instant nickname, isn't it?"

"Of course. The key is coming up with a name that will lead to a series of *dope* nicknames. We're her parents, Mad Dog. We gotta look out for her."

The song ends and a new one begins. But it's a song by Tori Amos. And, for whatever reason, neither of us feels inspired to name our baby girl after her.

"Zanderina?" Keane says in the middle of the song.

I roll my eyes and don't bother to respond.

"I'm not kidding," Keane says. And, by God, his face tells me he's being sincere. "Let's name her Zanderina."

I pull a face. "I'm not going to name my daughter Zanderina."

"*Our* daughter."

"Not anymore. You just forfeited parental rights by suggesting we name her Zanderina."

"Aw, come on. It'd be cool. *Kewl*."

"It'd be weird and wrong."

"Please?"

"No."

"Pretty please with extra sauce and these?" He smiles and points to his dimples.

"No."

Keane grimaces. "Okay, the thing is, I already promised Zander we'd name the baby after him, boy or girl.

"Well, un-promise him."

"A promise is a promise."

"Wasn't my promise."

"Come on."

"You'd honestly want to saddle this poor child with the name *Zanderina*?"

"Why not? It doesn't matter what's on a person's birth certificate. All that matters is what we call her in real life. Look at Dax. He's got David on his birth certificate, but all anyone ever calls him is Dax."

"'David' isn't *Zanderina*."

"Okay, then. We could call her Z. Oh my God. Yes! For real, babe. Let's name our baby Z! We'd spell it Z-e-e!"

I pause. It's not the worst idea I've ever heard. *Zee Morgan*. Yeah, it's a little bit weird. I admit that. But Keane is a little bit weird, and so am I. And I like that about us.

"Ha!" Keane says. Because, apparently, he's interpreting my silence as assent. He sits up, his eyes on fire, and grips my forearm. "So it's settled? Our daughter will be Zee?"

I open and close my mouth.

Keane hoots. "This is gonna be epic! Zee Morgan! Ho-lee shit! That sounds like a French accent, doesn't it? Like Pepe Le Peu! Bonjour, mademoiselle! Thees ees *Zee Morgan*. And thees ees zee Louvre." He makes a series of guttural ho-ho-hoo sounds I'm interpreting as a mimicry of a French waiter in a cartoon. And, suddenly, I realize this is a complete nonstarter.

I palm my forehead. "I can't believe I was momentarily tempted to agree to this ridiculousness. I was seriously about to say yes to Zee, but, thank God, you've quickly made me realize it would be the worst, most catastrophically cruel idea in the history of mankind."

"Aw, come on. It'll be awesome."

"No."

"It'll be amazing, baby. Think about the fun we could have with our little French baby. *Zee Morgan*. We could nickname her Frenchie. French Fry. French Toast. French Manicure. French Kiss."

"Keane!"

"Okay, scratch French Kiss. I was just riffing. That would be weird. And gross. Sorry. I'm new to this father thing. I'm still learning." He sits up, excited. "But, still. The possibilities are endless. Oh! We could call her Zebra! We could decorate her nursery in black and white zebra stripes! We could—"

"Stop. No. Enough. I'm sorry, honey. I can see you're genuinely excited about this. But we can't name our daughter Zee. Now that I know you're going to do a cartoon French accent every time you say it, I know for a fact our marriage would end in divorce. And I love you too much to leave you."

He laughs. "Come on."

"No."

"Please?"

"No. Seriously. Over my dead body."

Keane sighs. "Damn. Thought I had you for a minute."

"You did. But I came to my senses."

He looks highly disappointed. "Well, can Zee be her middle name, then?"

I pause for a long beat. "Sure. If it's that important to you, then, yes, Zee can be her middle name."

Keane fist pumps the air and settles back into bed next to me, smiling from ear to ear, just as "Ocean Eyes" by Billie Eilish starts playing on his laptop.

Keane and I gasp simultaneously.

"Billie!" we both shout at the same time.

Suddenly, we're both nodding profusely and laughing.

"Billie," I say, touching my belly. My head is spinning. My heart is racing. "*Billie.*"

Keane looks like he's going to cry. He leans into my belly and kisses it. "Billie," he whispers softly, his blue eyes blazing. "My little Billie goat." He kisses my tiny bump again. "I love you, Billie goat. *Maaaah.*"

I giggle and touch my bump. "Your daddy is so silly, Billie."

"That's okay, though," Keane says, "because you're my Silly Billie, right? My silly Billie goat. Wait until you meet your Uncle Daxy. He's a really famous goat. You're gonna love him."

I feel euphoric. "Well, that was easy. *Billie.* You're sure?"

"Positive."

"Me, too. I don't have a single doubt."

"Same." He kisses my belly again. "I can't wait to meet you, Billie Zee. I can't wait to be your daddy."

I melt. "Come here, my love."

Keane crawls up to my face and kisses me deeply. And when he places his palm on my cheek, I feel the metal of his wedding ring brush against my cheek. It's one of my favorite sensations.

"I love you, Keaney," I whisper into his lips.

"I love you, Mad Dog," he whispers back. He kisses me again. And then abruptly breaks free of me. "She should have *two* middle names on her birth certificate! Zee *and* Goat. She'll be Billie Zee Goat!"

I giggle. "I'm not going to name my daughter Goat."

"Not like a farm animal. Like 'Greatest of All Time.'"

"And what will we tell our children who come after Billie? They're the second and third 'greatest of all time?'"

Keane shrugs. "My siblings have had to live with that reality, and they've all survived it."

We both laugh.

"Sorry, I'm not going to name my child Goat."

Keane scowls. "It's against the law to name a child Billie and not give her the middle name Goat."

"Wouldn't Dax think you're naming the baby after him?"

"So what if he does?"

I sigh. "No, Keaney."

Keane strokes my cheek and flashes me what I'm sure he assumes is an irresistible smile. "What if we give all sixteen of our babies the middle name of GOAT, in all caps—'Greatest of All Time'? It'll even the playing field."

"So, now you're going to saddle some kid named... I don't know, Austin, with the middle name GOAT?"

"Yeah, okay, you've convinced me. You can have your way. Only Billie, then. She'll be Billie Zee Goat Morgan."

I giggle. "No, Keane."

"Okay, okay. You can have your way. We'll switch it to Billie Goat Zee Morgan."

I'm not sure if he's kidding or not, but I'm laughing all the same. "Stop. My answer is no. She's Billie Zee. No Goat. If you keep pushing, I'm taking Zee away."

"You can't take Zee away. She already overheard us and got excited about it." Smiling, he stretches his body onto the bed next to mine and nuzzles his nose into my cheek. "Fine. But I'm gonna call her Billie Goat, whether you like it or not, and that's non-negotiable."

"Well, of course."

"Like, literally, all the time. I doubt I'll even call her Billie. She's just gonna be Goat to me."

"I'm sure you won't be the only one."

"As long as we understand each other."

"We do."

He kisses me, and presses his steely erection into my thigh, telling me my horny husband is ready to go again. And that's a mighty good thing, because I'm ready, too. I reach down and grip Keane's naked hard-on as he kisses me, and he slides his fingers inside me. And, soon, I'm coming and he's dripping against my hand and my eyes are rolling back into my head.

Maddy

"One more big push," the doctor says. "Come on, Maddy. Take a deep breath and push as I count."

I'm exhausted, but I do as I'm told. And the next thing I know, my body feels strangely voided and there's a high-pitched wail filling the small room. I burst into tears. I'm shaking. Gasping. "Is she okay?"

"She's perfect," the doctor says calmly. "Beautiful." She holds Billie up and I whimper with joy. I look at Keane standing right next to me and my heart bursts with joy and love. He looks exactly like I feel. Euphoric. Overwhelmed. *Scared shitless*. And, God, I love him for it.

Tears are streaming down Keane's gorgeous face. He's visibly trembling. "You did so good, baby," he says, grasping my hand. "So, so good."

The doctor calls to Keane to cut the umbilical cord, which he does with a terrified expression on his face. And the next thing I know, I've got a tiny little creature on my chest—a little girl with big eyes and rosebud lips and a tiny cleft in her chin that tells the world she's a Morgan, through and through.

"Hi, Billie Zee," I whisper to my daughter, choking on a sob. "Welcome to the world, sweetheart."

Keane kisses my sweaty forehead. "You did so, so good, Maddy." He strokes our daughter's tiny head and swallows down his tears. "Welcome to our family, Billie Zee Morgan," he chokes out, his voice breaking. "We already love you the most."

ACKNOWLEDGMENTS

Thank you, dear reader. If you're a longtime reader of mine who couldn't wait to get your hands on Dax's story, I send you hugs and gratitude. I hope Dax was everything you hoped he'd be. If you're a brand new reader, then I also send hugs and gratitude for giving my writing a whirl.

Thank you to the all the bloggers and readers who tirelessly read and post and spread the word and post reviews.

Thank you to all the musicians in my life who made writing Dax second-nature to me.

Thank you to my cover model, Dylan, for answering my questions about long hair so thoughtfully.

Thank you, Becca Hensley Mysoor, for your insights. You're amazing.

Thank you to my team, including my beloved Sophie Broughton, Andrea, Jill, Melissa, and Abby. Letitia Hasser, your cover artistry is amazing. Amy Jackson, my dear friend, thank you for being the first reader of this book. You're so dear to me.

Thank you for reading my stories! If you loved the book, please consider writing a review. I'd be grateful!

BOOKS BY LAUREN ROWE

Standalone Novels

Smitten

When aspiring singer-songwriter, Alessandra, meets Fish, the funny, adorable bass player of 22 Goats, sparks fly between the awkward pair. Fish tells Alessandra he's a "Goat called Fish who's hung like a bull. But not really. I'm actually really average." And Alessandra tells Fish, "There's nothing like a girl's first love." Alessandra thinks she's talking about a song when she makes her comment to Fish—the first song she'd ever heard by 22 Goats, in fact. As she'll later find out, though, her "first love" was

actually Fish. The Goat called Fish who, after that night, vowed to do anything to win her heart.

SMITTEN is a **true standalone** romance that will make you swoon.

Hate Love Duet

An addicting enemies to lovers romance with humor, heat, angst, and banter. Music artists Savage of Fugitive Summer and Laila Fitzgerald are stuck together on tour. And convinced they can't stand each other. What they don't know is that they're absolutely made for each other, whether they realize it or not. The books of this duet are to be read in order:

Falling Out Of Hate With You

Falling Into Love With You

The Reed Rivers Trilogy

Reed Rivers has met his match in the most unlikely of women—aspiring journalist and spitfire, Georgina Ricci. She's much younger than the women Reed normally pursues, but he can't resist her fiery personality and drop-dead gorgeous looks. But in this game of cat and mouse, who's chasing whom? With each passing day of this wild ride, Reed's not so sure. The books of this trilogy are to be read in order:

Bad Liar

Beautiful Liar

Beloved Liar

The Club Trilogy

Romantic. Scorching hot. Suspenseful. Witty. The Club is your new addiction—a sexy and suspenseful thriller about two wealthy brothers and the sassy women who bring them to their knees . . . all while the foursome bands together to protect one of their own. *The Club Trilogy* is to be read in order, as follows:

The Club: Obsession

The Club: Reclamation

The Club: Redemption

The Club: Culmination

The fourth book for Jonas and Sarah is a full-length epilogue with incredible heart-stopping twists and turns and feels. Read *The Club: Culmination (A Full-Length Epilogue Novel)* after finishing *The Club Trilogy* or, if you prefer, after reading *The Josh and Kat Trilogy.*

The Josh and Kat Trilogy

It's a war of wills between stubborn and sexy Josh Faraday and Kat Morgan. A fight to the bed. Arrogant, wealthy playboy Josh is used to getting what he wants. *And what he wants is Kat Morgan.* The books are to be read in order:

Infatuation

Revelation

Consummation

The Morgan Brothers

Read these **standalones** in any order about the brothers of Kat Morgan. Chronological reading order is below, but they are all complete stories. Note: you do *not* need to read any other books or series before jumping straight into reading about the Morgan boys.

Hero.

The story of heroic firefighter, **Colby Morgan**. When catastrophe strikes Colby Morgan, will physical therapist Lydia save him . . . or will he save her?

Captain.

The insta-love-to-enemies-to-lovers story of tattooed sex god, **Ryan Morgan**, and the woman he'd move heaven and earth to claim.

Ball Peen Hammer.

A steamy, hilarious, friends-to-lovers romantic comedy about cocky-as-hell male stripper, **Keane Morgan**, and the sassy, smart young woman who brings him to his knees during a road trip.

Mister Bodyguard.

The Morgans' beloved honorary brother, **Zander Shaw**, meets his match in the feisty pop star he's assigned to protect on tour.

ROCKSTAR.

When the youngest Morgan brother, **Dax Morgan,** meets a mysterious woman who rocks his world, he must decide if pursuing her is worth risking it all. Be sure to check out four of Dax's original songs from *ROCKSTAR*, written and produced by Lauren, along with full music videos for the songs, on her website (www.laurenrowebooks.com) under the tab MUSIC FROM ROCKSTAR.

Misadventures

Lauren's *Misadventures* titles are page-turning, steamy, swoony standalones, to be read in any order.

- *Misadventures on the Night Shift* –A hotel night shift clerk encounters her teenage fantasy: rock star Lucas Ford. And combustion ensues.

- *Misadventures of a College Girl*—A spunky, virginal theater major meets a cocky football player at her first college party . . . and absolutely nothing goes according to plan for either of them.

- *Misadventures on the Rebound*—A spunky woman on the rebound meets a hot, mysterious stranger in a bar on her way to her five-year high school reunion in Las Vegas and what follows is a misadventure neither of them ever imagined.

Standalone Psychological Thriller/Dark Comedy

Countdown to Killing Kurtis

A young woman with big dreams and skeletons in her closet decides her porno-king husband must die in exactly a year. This is *not* a traditional romance, but it *will* most definitely keep you turning the pages and saying "WTF?"

Short Stories

The Secret Note

Looking for a quickie? Try this scorching-hot short story from Lauren Rowe in ebook FOR FREE or in audiobook: He's a hot Aussie. I'm a girl who isn't shy about getting what she wants. The problem? Ben is my little brother's best friend. An exchange student who's heading back Down Under any day now. But I can't help myself. He's too hot to resist.

All books by Lauren Rowe are available in ebook, paperback, and audiobook formats.

Be sure to sign up for Lauren's newsletter to find out about upcoming releases!

AUTHOR BIOGRAPHY

Lauren Rowe is the USA Today and international #1 best-selling author of newly released Reed Rivers Trilogy, as well as The Club Trilogy, The Josh & Kat Trilogy, The Morgan Brothers Series, Countdown to Killing Kurtis, and select standalone Misadventures. Lauren's books are full of feels, humor, heat, and heart. Besides writing novels, Lauren is the singer in a party/wedding band in her hometown of San Diego, an audio book narrator, and award-winning songwriter. She is thrilled to connect with readers all over the world. To find out about Lauren's upcoming releases and giveaways, sign up for Lauren's emails here!

Lauren loves to hear from readers! Send Lauren an email from her website, say hi on Twitter, Instagram, or Facebook.

Find out more and check out lots of free bonus material at www. LaurenRoweBooks.com.

Made in the USA
Middletown, DE
04 May 2021

38405016R00243